Late Bloomer

Also by Fern Michaels in Large Print:

Annie's Rainbow
Captive Embraces
Captive Passions
Captive Splendors
Celebration
Charming Lily
The Guest List
Plain Jane
Sara's Song
Sins of the Flesh
Whitefire
Wish List
Kentucky Heat
Cinders to Satin

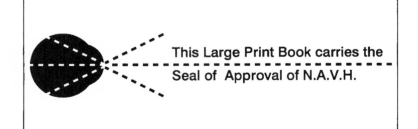

This Large Print Book carries the Seal of Approval of N.A.V.H.

FERN MICHAELS

Late Bloomer

WHEELER
PUBLISHING

Published in 2003 by arrangement with Atria Books, an imprint of Simon & Schuster, Inc.

Wheeler Large Print Hardcover Series.

The text of this Large Print edition is unabridged.
Other aspects of the book may vary from the original edition.

Set in 16 pt. Plantin by Ramona A. Watson.

Printed in the United States on permanent paper.

Library of Congress Cataloging-in-Publication Data

Michaels, Fern.
 Late bloomer / Fern Michaels.
  p. cm.
  ISBN 1-58724-461-6 (lg. print : hc : alk. paper)
  1. Grandparent and adult child — Fiction. 2. Recovered memory — Fiction. 3. Pennsylvania — Fiction.
 4. Grandmothers — Fiction. 5. Young women — Fiction.
 6. Large type books. I. Title.
 PS3563.I27L37 2003
 813'.54—dc21   2003049662

To Sara and Bob Schwager,
without whom
this book could not have been written.

National Association for Visually Handicapped
------------------------ *serving the partially seeing*

As the Founder/CEO of NAVH, the only national health agency solely devoted to those who, although not totally blind, have an eye disease which could lead to serious visual impairment, I am pleased to recognize Thorndike Press★ as one of the leading publishers in the large print field.

Founded in 1954 in San Francisco to prepare large print textbooks for partially seeing children, NAVH became the pioneer and standard setting agency in the preparation of large type.

Today, those publishers who meet our standards carry the prestigious "Seal of Approval" indicating high quality large print. We are delighted that Thorndike Press is one of the publishers whose titles meet these standards. We are also pleased to recognize the significant contribution Thorndike Press is making in this important and growing field.

Lorraine H. Marchi, L.H.D.
Founder/CEO
NAVH

★ Wheeler Publishing is an imprint of Thorndike Press.

Prologue

Indigo Valley, Pennsylvania: 1981

Ten-year-old Cady Jordan sat on the front porch swing and hugged her knees as she watched the family's belongings being loaded into a big yellow truck with the words MAY-FLOWER MOVING AND STORAGE printed on the side. She turned slightly on the swing to see if her pink bike was still behind the holly bush at the side of the house, where she'd hidden it earlier.

It was.

Her heart kicked up a beat as she tried to figure a way to cajole her mother into letting her make one last trip down to the Judas Grove to say good-bye to her friends. She ran her mother's possible objections over in her mind. She would get dirty and need a bath. The cleaning supplies and the towels were packed already; therefore, she had to stay clean until the church supper and the final round of good-byes. The Judas Grove was a dangerous place to play was the second objection. The third objection would be that her mother didn't care for the Hollister twins. The truth was, her mother didn't like Mrs. Hollister because she wore skimpy clothes and lots of makeup, *and* one time she'd seen Mr. Hollister pinch Mrs. Hollister's bottom in full view of everyone at the church picnic. The fourth objection, and possibly the worst, was her father. For some reason he hated the Judas Grove, as the kids called it. His face always turned red, and his eyes got mean and hard when it was mentioned.

She heard her name being called. She looked down at the Mickey Mouse watch on her wrist, a gift from her grandmother, and winced. If she was going, she had to go soon or the others would leave. She had to show up, she just had to. Even if she pedaled as fast as she could, she knew time was running short. "I'm on the swing, Mom."

Agnes Jordan came out to the porch. "You look like you're up to something your father wouldn't approve of. Are you, Cady?"

Cady shook her head. "Mom, what does sanct-ta-moneus mean?"

"Good Lord, Cady, where did you hear such a big word?" her mother demanded. Cady wished there was a smile on her face. Her mother hardly ever smiled even when she tucked her into bed at night. She had never, ever, seen a smile on her father's face. Her grandmother, on the other hand, smiled all the time.

8

"Mr. and Mrs. Hollister said you were sanct-ta-moneus. Mrs. Hollister said the raisin cake you made for the bazaar last week was heavy enough to be used as a doorstop."

"Well I never . . ." her mother sputtered as she went back inside.

"Don't worry, Mom, I like your raisin cake. I even told Mrs. Hollister I liked it." Cady jumped off the swing and ran down the steps. "I'm going to take a ride on my bike. I'll be back in time to change my clothes for the church supper."

Cady pedaled her bike as fast as she could, careening around corners and coasting down the hill, then pedaling again on a straight road that led to the Judas Grove on the outskirts of Indigo Valley. Her favorite place in the whole, wide world.

The little group waiting for Cady acted like the ten-year-olds they were, jumping up and down, whistling, and clapping their hands.

"Gee whiz, we thought you weren't coming," Andy Hollister said, linking his arm with Cady's. "Don't be afraid. I did it, and all your heart does is beat real fast until you land. It was Pete's turn to bring the Kool-Aid and cookies. Do you want to eat first and then *do it* or the other way around?"

Cady could feel her insides start to shake as she looked at her friends. It was probably better just to do it and get it over with. She took a moment to ponder her immediate problem.

She was moving away, and she would probably never, ever, see her friends again so why did she have to climb the hill and ride down the zip line? The zip line was a homemade contraption of old telephone cable wire, one end of which was attached to the mighty oak at the top of the hill and the other end to a smaller oak at the base of the hill on the other side of the pond. The object was to slide down the taut line, over the thirty-foot drop, out over the pond, then skid to a stop at the edge of the pond without getting wet. Because if she didn't, she'd be leaving with her tail between her legs, and the kids would call her a sissy chicken. She wasn't even going to think about what her parents would say if they ever found out she was at the Judas Grove and she rode the zip line. Knowing her father, she wouldn't see the bright light of day until she was thirty-five, maybe longer. Her mother wouldn't intervene either.

"You ready, Cady?" Pete asked.

Pete Danson was a nice kid, nicer than the Hollister twins. They'd been her friends from the time they met at Bible school at the age of four. Pete knew she was afraid. They all knew she was afraid. Afraid or not, she still had to do it. At least their tormentors weren't around to heckle her. She voiced her thought as she wondered what was in the paper sack Pete was holding in his hands. It looked heavy.

"They were here about an hour ago. We pretended to leave so they would. Then we came

10

back to wait for you," Andy said. "Remember now, don't close your eyes. You have to keep them open so you don't smack into one of the trees. You can do it, Cady. We'll be waiting for you on the other side of the pond. Amy has her camera. We'll send you the picture at your new address, okay? You can't show your mom or dad. If you do, she'll call our moms and tell them we hang out here. Promise, Cady."

"Okay, I promise." She solemnly crossed her heart. She'd seen the pictures of the others taken just as they hit the middle of the zip line. They were all so proud of those pictures because Amy managed to capture their looks of horror, elation, and devil-may-care attitude when they were dead center over the pond, thirty feet above the water. You had to be brave and fearless to ride the zip line. She wanted her own photo, too, so she could show it to her new friends in Vermont.

Cady climbed the hill, slipping and sliding until she made it to the top, where the grove of trees, including the Judas tree, peppered the little bluff. Her heart pounded in her chest when she looked down at the homemade zip line the boys had first hooked up over a year ago. They'd gotten the cable from the junkyard, the wooden handles from Pete's mother's shopping bags. They checked the cable every day, and every day they proclaimed it to be safe even though the biggest of all the trees, the Judas tree that stood sentinel over the others, now had deep wounds in the trunk. It was Amy's idea to move the cable from the Judas tree to the oak tree because it was higher and gave a more thrilling ride. Pete had agreed but not because he wanted a more thrilling ride. He had been concerned that the cable was harming the Judas tree.

"Anytime you're ready," freckle-faced Andy shouted. "Go on the count of five. We'll count together. You can hear us, can't you?"

"I can hear you. Just hold your horses, Andy Hollister. I'm gonna do it. Give me time to climb the tree and get out to the branch."

They knew she was afraid. She knew she could just go home and let them think what they wanted to think. In just a few hours, she would be on her way to Vermont, and she would never see them again.

Her insides started to shake. She looked down at the pond. Not a ripple showed on the water's surface. Her gaze went to the zip line attached to the biggest tree in the grove. She wasn't afraid to make the jump. Making the jump meant she had to leave the safety of the branch, jump off into thin air, and grab the wooden handle that would enable her to sail down the line. If she didn't jump the right way, she'd drop thirty feet into the pond. But heights didn't bother her. It was falling into the water that scared her because she couldn't swim.

Five minutes later, Cady was up the tree and belly-crawling along a thick branch. She turned when she heard a hissing noise. Her arms froze on the limb when she heard Pete Danson shout, "It's *them!*" She half turned to see Jeff King and Boomer Ward in the tree next to hers. Her stomach started to heave as she tried to slide backward. Who cared if they called her a sissy chicken. All she wanted to do was to go home and sit on the swing.

"Get down! Back off, Cady," the three on the ground shouted.

"I can't. My overalls are caught on something!" she shouted. She risked a glance over her shoulder in time to see Jeff King do a Tarzan leap to the tree she was in.

"Hurry up, Cady, do it now before he pushes you," the three on the ground shouted in unison. "Hurry up! He's almost up to you."

In her panic, Cady closed her eyes. Maybe she was having a bad dream and would wake up any second. She heard her friends shouting to one another to throw rocks at the bully climbing out on the branch behind her. She risked opening her eyes to see rocks of all sizes sailing through the air. One hit her ankle, but she barely felt the pain. Amy Hollister had the best pitching arm in Indigo Valley. She was even better than the boys.

They were all screaming now at the top of their lungs, "Go! Hurry up! He's right behind you! Boomer's out of the tree. Go, Cady, go!" Pete yelled.

Cady wiggled and squirmed just enough to

see that Jeff King was almost up to her. "Don't you dare come out on this branch, you big creep."

"Oh yeah, what are you going to do about it?" the bully blustered. Out of the corner of her eye, Cady could see movement. That had to mean Boomer Ward was doing something to the zip line. Fear, unlike anything she'd ever felt before, consumed her, but she reached for the wooden handle. Then she did exactly what her friends told her not to do: she squeezed her eyes shut. She felt Jeff behind her, felt his hands on her shirt, heard him saying stuff in her ear she didn't want to hear. His hold was secure, she couldn't shake him off. She saw the rock whizzing through the air, felt the pain.

"No! No!" the kids on the opposite side of the pond shouted.

"Don't do it, Jeff! The cable won't hold you both!" Boomer shouted.

His warning came too late as the wooden handle slid down the zip line, Jeff King hanging on to her skimpy yellow tee shirt. She felt it rip, felt his grappling hands. She heard the screams, heard the splash, then she was in the water herself. Pain ricocheted up and down her body. She wanted to cry out, but she couldn't move.

"They're dead! Look at all the blood on Jeff's head. One of our rocks got him good. Cady isn't moving either. We have to get help! Pete, run to town and get help!" Andy shouted, his face registering horror and terror.

14

"They'll blame us. If we tell, they'll blame us. They'll send us to one of those places where they lock you up. If we don't tell, they won't know. We can't do anything now because they're dead. Dead means you never wake up. Let's go to the park and pretend we were there all afternoon," Amy said.

"Where's Boomer? He was monkeying around with the zip line. I bet he loosened it. He's *thirteen*. He could do that," Andy said.

"I saw him running away," Amy said. "He doesn't want to get blamed either. C'mon, c'mon, we have to get out of here. If her dad finds out we made her do the zip, he'll make us burn in hell. He's a preacher, he can do that!"

"Are we going to promise not to tell?" Pete Danson asked. The twins nodded. "Then, run," Pete said as he sprinted off, the paper sack still in his hands, the twins right on his heels.

The moment the three were out of sight, Boomer Ward crept out of the undergrowth and crossed the pond. He knew Jeff King was dead because he could see his brains. He wasn't sure about Cady Jordan. He pulled and tugged until she was completely out of the water. He put his hand on her chest to see if her heart was beating. He'd seen actors do that on television. He almost fainted with relief when he felt her heart beating. "I'm going for help, Cady. I didn't do anything to the cable. I was just trying to make sure it was tight enough to hold you both. I'll get someone to help you. Don't cry, Cady."

Boomer ran up the embankment. He looked back at the Judas tree and felt sick to his stomach. He didn't stop to think. In a flash, he undid the zip line from the smaller oak, yanked the other end from the larger oak, and tossed it down to the pond. He backtracked, shouting to Cady to hold on. Then he climbed on his bike and rode home. He was so dizzy with anxiety he almost fainted when he realized his mother wasn't home. Finding the telephone number of the police station on the list of emergency numbers taped to the refrigerator, he dialed it. He spoke deep in his throat, trying to disguise his voice.

Then he ran out to the toolshed, where he crouched down and hid behind the lawn mower. He prayed, saying all the prayers he'd learned since starting catechism classes.

Chapter 1

Brentwood, California
Twenty Years Later

Cady Jordan felt sick to her stomach and wasn't sure why. She looked down at the pizza she was eating as if it were the culprit. She'd already consumed four slices. Two would have been enough. She couldn't ever remember eating four slices, much less five. She dropped the wedge in her hand into the box. It wasn't just a sick feeling in the pit of her stomach she was experiencing. She was jittery, too, her right eye twitching, something that only happened when she was under a great deal of stress. She sighed as she swigged from a can of Coca-Cola. Just what she needed, caffeine for her already jangled nerves.

Cady tucked her yellow tee shirt into her worn, faded jeans. Her favorite jeans. They had to be ten years old at least. Holes in both knees, the back pockets long since gone. She would never give them up because they were like an old friend. Like Pete, Andy, and Amy. She de-

17

cided to make a fashion statement and tied a yellow ribbon she plucked from the doorknob around her ponytail. Now, she was ready.

The sounds of the movers seemed exceptionally loud to her ears. Maybe that's why she was jittery. No one liked to pack up and move. She thought of all the hours she'd spent packing her belongings, being extra careful to wrap the dishes and glassware securely. Her books, mostly hardcover novels and reference books, had taken up an unbelievable twenty-five boxes. Brentwood, California, was a long way from Indigo Valley, Pennsylvania, where her grandmother had grown up and returned to live after being away for so long.

The grunts and groans of the movers in the living room reminded her that she still had some miscellaneous packing to do before the movers left. She got up and took the last of the small appliances out of the pantry.

Her grandmother needed her, at least that's what her mother had implied. Not that she really paid much attention to what her mother said these days. Then she thought about her grandmother's age, and the fact that she'd been in the hospital. That alone couldn't be good. It was time to pay her grandmother back a little for all the wonderful things she had done for her. Her grandmother had always been there for her, even putting her own life on hold to take care of her after her accident. Now it was her turn to put her life, such as it was, on hold.

How could she not head back to Pennsylvania to help in whatever way she could?

If it wasn't that her grandmother needed her, she probably would have stayed right where she was for the rest of her life. New places, meeting new people intimidated her. When she bought the house in Brentwood five years ago, she'd thought she was putting down roots. What she was really doing was picking a nice safe haven where she could work at her own pace and not have to get involved too much with people. Writing technical manuals for Integrated Circuits, Inc. part-time allowed her the freedom to choose her own hours as well as her own workplace, thus enabling her to work on her dissertation and still remain independent of her parents and grandmother. She might have thought she was putting down roots, but what could she possibly know about that process? She had never been rooted anywhere when she was growing up because her mother and father had always lived like gypsies, moving from town to town, preaching the gospel according to Asa Jordan.

On her eighteenth birthday, when her parents had announced they would be moving again, right after her high school graduation, Cady had made the decision to stay where she was, get a job, and work her way through college. She had graduated from UCLA with a master's in English and was just months away from getting her doctorate. Now she would have to put that goal on hold.

At least she wouldn't have to give up her job. Although writing technical manuals for a Los Angeles-based electronics firm wasn't the writing career she had dreamed of, it paid the bills.

One of the movers popped his head into the kitchen. "That's the last of what's in the front, miss. Do you have any last-minute items you want to go into the truck?"

"Just this stool and a few boxes there by the pantry. I guess I'll see you in Indigo Valley in seven days. You have my grandmother's phone number, right? And the name and address of the storage company where you'll be delivering my things?" The man nodded and she handed over a check and waited while the driver scribbled his name and logged in the check number and recorded the amount. He ripped off a yellow copy that said Recipient on it and handed it to her. She shoved it into her purse.

She could feel tears burn her eyes when the door closed behind the mover. How empty everything looked. She knew if she shouted, the words would echo around the entire house. Moving was such a sad business. She swiped at her eyes with the sleeve of her shirt before dumping the empty soda can into the pizza box that she would deposit into the trash when she closed the door behind her for the last time.

The house, a 1930s California bungalow, was ready for its new owner, a young professor and his wife. She'd lucked out when she posted a notice on the university bulletin board and was able to sell the house without going through a Realtor. She'd also made a handsome profit in the bargain.

Now it was time to go. Time to get into the car and drive cross-country. She wished she had a dog. She'd always promised herself that she would get a dog when the time was right. A lot of things could happen to a young woman traveling alone across the country. A shudder rippled up and down her body. Fear was a terrible thing. She should know, she'd lived with it almost her entire life.

The fear hadn't entered her life gradually. It had grabbed hold of her when she'd woken up in the hospital to the agonizing pain, with no memory of what had happened to her. The fear had stayed with her for the next three years as she'd fought and struggled to learn how to walk all over again. She might have had a chance of conquering the fear had she been allowed to stay with her beloved grandmother but that hadn't happened. The day the doctors told her she could leave, her parents had whisked her away.

And now she was returning to the town where she'd had the accident she couldn't remember. Just the thought made her jittery and nervous. Or was it her fear returning all over again?

Cady stood in the open doorway staring at the empty rooms. She hadn't entertained much while she'd lived there. That was her own fault since she didn't have any real, true friends. She had a friend she jogged with. A friend she played tennis with and a friend she went out to dinner with on occasion. The plain and simple truth was, she preferred her own company to making small talk and pretending to be interested in people's lives that were just as boring as her own. As for men friends, there had been a few. None of them made her want to walk down the aisle.

Was it because she really wasn't interested in pursuing relationships or was it because she was afraid? She'd had friendships with guys when she was younger, and look what it had gotten her. When she got this far along in her thoughts, she backtracked, and convinced herself she was content being by herself. Why did she need to fight off guys on the prowl and listen to her female friends plot and seek ways to snatch a guy from some unsuspecting friend only to lose both in the end? She liked her life just the way it was, thank you very much.

She looked down at her watch. If she wanted to, she could go to the SPCA and rescue a dog. She tried to talk herself out of doing it, unsure if her timing was right or wrong. What if the dog got sick in the car? What if the motels she stopped in wouldn't allow a dog? What if . . . a lot of things. An animal lover friend of hers had once lectured about how many dogs and cats were destroyed every year because their owners had either lost them or just didn't want them anymore.

She had never been one to spout ideals or get involved with causes. She had more or less skated through life after the accident, keeping to herself and doing her own thing. But the idea of *saving* a dog was suddenly very appealing.

Cadwell Sophia Jordan, named after her maternal and fraternal grandmothers, never made a decision until she talked it to death, made a blueprint, then ran it up an invisible flagpole to see if it was a decision worth saluting. It was always better to err on the side of caution. Predictability was her philosophy. It all came down to that one word again, *fear.*

Cadwell Sophia Jordan, a.k.a. Cady Jordan, ignored her own credo for the first time in her life and climbed into her four-by-four. Her destination, the SPCA.

Thirty-five minutes later she was staring into the dark eyes of a mangy, filthy, scrawny German shepherd named Atlas. "I'll take him."

"Good choice. He's about three years old. He was picked up on the street. He was wearing a collar that was little more than a string, and his name tag was matted into his coat. That's how we know his name is Atlas. He's a good dog," the young boy said. "Once he's cleaned up and a vet checks him over, I'd say you got yourself a great dog. Give him a good life, and he'll love you forever. That's fifteen dollars for the leash and five dollars for the dog."

Cady handed over a twenty-dollar bill. The

23

dog cowered when she reached out to him. She dropped to her knees and whispered softly. "I know how you feel. If you trust me, we'll be okay. I'm just going to put this leash on you, and we're going to a vet I know. It's okay, Atlas. I'll never hurt you."

"He has some scars on his back, miss. My thinking would be, somebody mistreated him along the way. Good food, some vitamins, and a lot of love will make him right as rain."

"Okay." Physical abuse, mental abuse, what was the difference? she thought. Abuse was abuse.

"I'm sorry he doesn't have any gear. I can't even give you any food. We're short on rations here. I guess you know we depend on donations." His voice sounded as hopeful as he looked.

"I see. I guess I'm not thinking clearly. I'd like to make a donation. How does two hundred dollars sound?"

"Two hundred dollars sounds great. We can buy a lot of dog food and a lot of Clorox with that much money."

Cady wrote out the check and handed it over. She felt better than she'd felt in a long time. "Okay, Atlas, it's time to start your new life. Maybe we can do it together. We're going to Indigo Valley by way of Burger King, the vet, and a pet store."

Atlas settled his bony frame in the passenger side of Cady's Mercury Mountaineer. He looked tired and wary as he dropped his head onto his paws. He didn't perk up until she swerved the four-by-four into the drive-through lane at Burger King. The smell of grilling hamburgers permeated the air. She ordered five double cheeseburgers, a large Coke, a bottle of water, and an empty cup.

"Okay, I'm going to pull into one of these parking spaces, and we'll eat here." For some reason she expected the dog to wolf down the food, but he didn't. He ate slowly and methodically. He drank almost the entire bottle of water, then he whimpered. "I get it. I get it. You gotta go. Listen, Atlas, I've never had a dog before, so you're going to have to help me here. You know, bark, whine, whatever. I know you're going to have accidents, but we'll work on that. Careful, careful, it's a drop to the ground. Do your thing," she said, letting go of the retractable leash to give him room to roam, which he did. When he was finished he walked to the door of the truck and waited until Cady opened it. He hopped in, settled down, and went to sleep.

Two hours later a disgruntled Atlas climbed back into the truck. This time he was exhausted from being bathed and groomed and his trip to the pet store, where Cady bought everything the salesgirl said she would need. She even bought a seat belt harness that Atlas did not like at all. He settled down when she scratched his belly and spoke soothingly to him. At one point, he licked her hand in appreciation. Tears blurred her vision as she slipped the Mountaineer into gear.

Getting Atlas was the first unorthodox, serendipitous thing she'd done since she was a little kid back in Indigo Valley. She decided she liked what she was feeling. Maybe it was time for her to do more unorthodox, serendipitous things.

"I think we can drive for about five hours, then we'll stop. I'll turn on the radio for company since you're going to sleep." The dog opened one sleepy eye, then closed it, knowing he was in safe hands.

Six days later, Cady stopped the car along the side of the road and pulled out her map. She should know the area. After all, she had lived there for *ten* years when she was growing up, but it all looked so different, with little clusters of housing developments, fast-food outlets, and new roads. She'd looked for familiar landmarks on the drive in, but the only thing she'd recognized was the town square and St. Paul's Church. She looked up from the map to see Atlas slapping at the car window with his paws. "Twenty years ago this was my hometown. I don't know if I love this place or hate it. I should be feeling something, but I'm not," she muttered to herself.

Where was her grandmother's house? Her mother had told her it was the only house on a street called Indigo Place. A street that her grandmother had named when she had had her house built. She wondered how that could be. She saw it then, a curlicue of a street that appeared to be tucked behind what looked like some high-end real estate. The sign said it was a gated community. She slipped the Mountaineer into gear and drove slowly, paying careful attention to the street signs.

Cady sucked in her breath. It wasn't a house. It was probably called an estate. Or, maybe, a creation would be a better word. Whatever it was, it was certainly befitting of Lola Jor Dan.

"This is it, Atlas. Our new home. I told you all about Lola on the long drive here. She used to be a famous movie star. She was wild and wicked during her heyday. They called her a sex symbol even back then. She had six husbands and buried them all. My father was so ashamed of her, he would never tell anyone she was his mother. Mom pretended she didn't exist, but that was because of my dad. I think she secretly admired Lola. Dad said she was a disgrace to the name Jordan, and that's why she changed it to Jor Dan. I loved her. Still do." Atlas barked to show he understood.

Cady reached across the console to tickle the shepherd behind the ears. She'd only had the big dog a little more than six days, but they had bonded that first night when they'd slept together in the cargo hold. He'd put on a few pounds, and his eyes were now bright and alert.

27

She loved him as much as he loved her.

She stopped the car in front of a pair of huge, green, wrought-iron gates. "I guess we're supposed to press this buzzer, and maybe someone will open those huge gates. Boy, if this place is as big as it looks, you are going to have some playground to romp around in."

"Yes?" a woman's hollow voice sounded through a grille in the stone wall next to the gate.

"I'm Cady Jordan. I'm here to see my grandmother."

Inside the house, Mandy Ebersole, retired stuntwoman and lifelong companion to Lola Jor Dan, looked at Anthony Borellie, another lifelong friend of Lola's, and grinned. "She's here! That should perk Herself up a bit, don't you think?"

The retired film director grinned and nodded. "Some young blood around here is just what we need. Let's see what she's made of."

"Do you have an appointment?" the faceless voice asked.

"No. Do I need one?"

"Yes, you need an appointment. Miss Jor Dan does not receive callers. She's retired and likes her privacy." Cady thought she could hear the woman sniff.

"She'll see me. Tell her if you don't open these gates, I'll plow them down. Now, hop to it. My dog is getting antsy," Cady said with more bravado than she felt. It was the second most unorthodox, serendipitous thing she'd ever done.

"Dog?" Inside the house the two conspirators looked at one another. "She's got some spit to her. Lola's going to love this. She is, isn't she, Anthony?" The director nodded uneasily.

"D-o-g! Dog. It rhymes with log or bog or hog. Take your pick. Please tell my grand-mother I'm here. I'll give you five minutes, or these gates are going to go down."

Atlas woofed his agreement. "I sounded tough, didn't I? I didn't mean it, though," Cady whispered. Atlas woofed again just as the gates swung open.

Cady drove a mile up a long winding road that was lined with poplar trees. The grounds were lush and well tended with what looked like acres of flowers and carefully pruned to-piary. Her jaw dropped. Outside of a movie set, she'd never seen anything so beautiful. Off to her right she could see a tennis court and a grottolike swimming pool. Did her eighty-two-year-old grandmother play tennis and swim? Maybe in her younger years. So, who availed themselves of these sumptuous surroundings? Why did her grandmother need a six-car ga-rage? Who lived in the two Hansel-and-Gretel-looking cottages in the back? So many ques-tions.

The car came to a grinding halt in front of the house. She craned her neck to stare at the imposing white columns and was reminded of pictures of Tara. Lola had a soft spot in her heart for anything concerning *Gone With the Wind.* She remembered her grandmother telling her how she'd missed out on playing Scarlett because her studio wouldn't let her out of her contract. Lola had a story for everything.

Cady's heartbeat quickened as she got out of the car. Surely her mother had notified Lola that she was on her way. On the other hand, Agnes Jordan might have felt it was her husband's place to tell his mother she was on her way. If it had been left up to Asa Jordan, then this visit was going to come as a total surprise to her grandmother.

Lola did love surprises. Cady hoped she was going to like this one. She'd played with the idea of calling her grandmother and always ended up saying, no, she'll try to talk me out of making the trip. Cady figured that if she sold her house, packed her stuff, and just came, Lola would have to let her stay and take care of her. If there was one thing she knew about her grandmother, it was that she liked being independent. Thus, the element of surprise. Lola would never turn her away. Never.

She wished she knew more about her grandmother's health. All she had to go on was her mother's phone call. That in itself was reason enough for alarm because her mother *never* called her. When she'd asked what was wrong with Lola, her mother had said, she's old, things go wrong when you get old. Her voice had been so controlled, so ominous-sounding, Cady had felt fear race up her arms. She knew in that one split second that she had to go to her grandmother. If it turned out to be a hangnail, so be it.

Cady opened the door for Atlas. She attached the leash to his collar and walked up the four steps that led to the wide verandah. The huge double doors opened just as she reached the fourth step. She stopped and pulled Atlas to her side. "I'm Cady Jordan, Lola's granddaughter."

"Yes, you did say that back at the gate. Come in. You should have called ahead, Cady. Miss Lola doesn't like surprises."

"I thought my mother or father called. I guess they forgot," Cady said lamely. "Is my grandmother all right?"

"Now that depends on what you mean by all right. Well, don't stand there, come into the house. That's a sorry-looking excuse for a dog. Don't let him mess in the house."

"Just a minute, whoever you are. You can say what you want about me, but leave my dog out of it. He was beaten and starved before I got him. He's doing fine now, thanks to me. My grandmother likes dogs. Who are you?"

"I'm Mandy. I'm the housekeeper, the companion, and the secretary, plus a lot of other things. You're just a visitor, so you shouldn't be asking questions. Do you have a problem with

31

all of this?" A round butterball of a man stood behind the housekeeper, his eyes sparkling as he listened to the verbal exchange.

The housekeeper had to be as old or almost as old as her grandmother. She had a mouth on her just like her grandmother's. "I remember now. You were Lola's double. She used to tell me about you. She said you were the greatest stuntwoman to come out of Hollywood, and she would never have been the actress she was without your help." Cady's hand shot out. "I'm very pleased to see you again. And you must be Anthony, Lola's director. She said no one but you were fit to direct her. It's a pleasure meeting you, too." Not to be outdone, Atlas barked and held up his paw.

"*Herself* said that now, did she?" The woman and man seemed evidently pleased with Cady's compliment. Mandy seemed to be debating something with herself before she finally spoke. "You haven't seen Lola in over a year. She's not doing all that well. She lies and says she's fit as a fiddle. She can walk, but mostly she stays in her wheelchair. Part of it is pure stubbornness and to some extent laziness. She has osteoporosis. I saw her X rays. And she has a heart condition. Neither is life-threatening at this time. She claims to be ready to die, but that's a lie, too. What's the dog's name?"

"Atlas. They have medicine for osteoporosis. The wife of one of my professors had it, and I remember him mentioning it to me."

"You'll have to talk to *Herself* about that. She's in the sunroom. I told her you were here, and she's excited. I haven't seen her this excited since we moved here ten years ago. Please try to be cheerful, and don't be shocked by her appearance."

A feeling of dread settled over Cady as she led Atlas forward.

She knew the sunroom was beautiful because Lola liked beautiful things. Later, when she wasn't in such shock, she would peruse the entire house. Right now, all she could see was her once-beautiful grandmother huddled in her wheelchair, an outlandish Dolly Parton wig on her small head. She was made-up, but then she was always made-up, and often boasted that none of her six husbands had ever seen her without her makeup. Now, though, the expensive, theatrical makeup only made her look more gaunt and haggard. Her green eyes were bright and alert when she smiled at her granddaughter. "What a lovely surprise! How are you, precious? If you had called to tell me you were coming, I would have rolled out the red carpet for you. It's wonderful to see you, Cady."

"I'm fine, Lola," Cady said, hugging her grandmother. "Are you saying you didn't know I was coming? Mom told me someone from the hospital called her and said you needed your family. Dad's not well, and Mom has her hands full with him. I decided to come instead. I up

33

and sold my house, got myself this dog, then drove cross-country. I still can't believe I did that. But I'm here, and that's all that matters."

"What you're saying is Asa couldn't be bothered to come or even call me, is that it?"

Cady shrugged. The bad blood between her father and her grandmother was legendary.

"I cut him out of my will. He doesn't deserve to have me as a mother. That poor excuse of a mother of yours isn't much better. I still can't figure out how you turned out so well. If you discount that little episode when you were a child. I'm delighted that you're here, child. I truly am, but to answer your question, no, I did not know you were coming. Hospitals call family because they feel . . . well, whatever it is they feel. I told them not to call, but obviously they didn't listen to me."

"I can get an apartment in town. I have Atlas now."

"Nonsense. This house has seventeen rooms, and the two cottages in the rear have five rooms each. We have plenty of room. If I seem less than enthusiastic, it's because I'm shocked to see you. I missed my trips to Los Angeles last year because I opted to go to Europe to see if they could help me. Aside from an entire bone transplant, there was nothing they could do for me."

"I should have come here. I didn't know there was anything wrong, Lola. I thought you were just too busy to visit. Why didn't you say something? I would have come sooner."

"You're a young woman, Cady. You don't need to be saddled with an old woman. I don't want to be a burden on anyone. You have your own life to live. You are living it, aren't you? Oh, don't tell me you're still hibernating and living in that little community because it's safe and oh-so-boring. Is there a young man in your life?"

"Absolutely." Cady grinned as she pointed to Atlas.

"So you aren't over it. Cady, Cady, when are you going to start to live? Ever since that accident, you haven't been the same. I think you might have had a chance if your parents had allowed me to keep you. But no, they came and got you and took you to all those different towns — in how many different states? — before they settled in that backwoods place in Vermont. I was good enough for them for the three years it took for your rehabilitation, but after that, I was just a glitzy movie star who'd had one face-lift too many and shamed them. Don't get me wrong, I don't begrudge one minute of those three years. I thought I was going to die when they took you away. You cried so hard my heart broke."

"Let's not talk about Mom and Dad or . . . *that time*. Let's talk about you. I want to know how this all happened, and I want to know what I can do for you."

Lola grimaced. "Years of decadent living, I

guess. The condition is irreversible, so let's not waste our time talking about it. I had a great life, and if I had it to do all over again, I'd do it all the same way. I *lived* every single minute of my life. As to what you can do, well, you can help me with my memoirs. Mandy said she has many capabilities, but writing isn't one of them. I had previously thought about talking into a recorder and sending you the tapes. That was on my good days. On my bad days I decided no one would be interested enough in an old film star to buy the book. I've outlived all the people I would include in the book, so there isn't anyone left to sue me if I go ahead and decide to write it. What do you think, Cady?"

"I think it's a wonderful idea if you tell *everything*. Are you prepared to do that?" Cady grinned.

"Your father will dig a hole and crawl into it if I do that. How did you survive living in that household with all that sanctimonious crap the two of them spout? What's wrong? You're white as a ghost."

"What . . . what did you just say?"

"Mandy, get the child some brandy. I just said your father would dig a hole and crawl into it. He would, you know. He's my son and he hates me. I don't much care for him either. The truth is, he doesn't like anyone, not even your mother."

"No, no, you said something else. You said . . . you said sanctimonious. I . . . know that word.

It means something to me."

"I guess you would *know* it having lived with *them*." Lola leaned forward in her chair, her green gaze locking on Cady. "Or, do you mean the word has something to do with that episode in your life that you can't remember?"

Cady shivered, her eyes miserable. Atlas moved closer to her leg. She fondled his ears. "You know what I think, Lola. I think I'm just tired from the cross-country trip. I got all wired up when the movers came. All of a sudden I felt like something was hanging over my head, and it's stayed with me. I can't seem to shake it loose."

"Never try to force anything. Maybe coming back here after all these years, you'll finally get your memory back. They say you can't go home again, but that isn't true. I came back to Indigo Valley. And now you've come back. When I left, there were four stores and sixteen houses. I think the population was around three hundred. Now the little town is a city of forty thousand people. I imagine it's changed even more in the twenty years since you've been here.

"Cady, dear, I know that we've talked about this in the past and I know how you feel about Indigo Valley. I know why you never wanted to come back here, and it's all right. That's why I always visited you in California. I knew it would be a trauma for you to come here. And now you're here. I think I always knew you'd come, I just didn't know when. I told Mandy and Anthony the day would finally come when you would want to explore your past. I think that time is finally here. I'm just so very glad to see you.

"Mandy, show Cady to her room. It's time for my nap, too. Give her the Ginger Rogers suite. Dinner is at seven-thirty. Would you like Mandy to make something special for your dog? He looks like he could use some good food."

"He pretty much eats what I do. I tried dog food, but he won't eat it." Cady dropped to her knees in front of her grandmother's wheelchair. "I wish you had told me you weren't feeling well. There was nothing keeping me in California. I can study and do my job anywhere. Just because Mom and Dad . . ."

"Shhh," Lola said, putting her finger to her lips. "It's all right. In all fairness to your father, I wasn't a perfect mother. Hell, I wasn't even a *good* mother. Oh, well, that's all in the past. I'm so glad you're here, Cady."

"Me too, Grandma."

"None of that Grandma stuff. You always called me Lola from the time you were able to talk. Don't stop now. I don't need to feel any older than I am. Go along and take a nice shower and a little nap. We can talk all night long if you want."

Cady kissed her grandmother's wrinkled cheek. She was appalled at how thin and bony her shoulders were. She could feel tears start to burn her eyes. She should have come sooner. A lot sooner.

"This is the Ginger Rogers suite," Mandy said, opening the door and standing aside for Cady to enter. "I'll have your bags brought up shortly. If you want or need anything, just press the buzzer on the phone console. It's clearly marked."

"Thank you. We'll be fine."

While Atlas meandered around the suite of rooms sniffing and growling, Cady checked out her surroundings. Aside from a pair of silver, sequined dancing shoes in a glass case, there were no other indications that Ginger Rogers had ever slept there or even visited. She felt disappointed.

It was a showy room straight out of a decorator's portfolio. She sniffed, trying to identify the strange smell. Wallpaper paste, she thought. Everything looked new, unused, and incredibly expensive. The carpeting was thick and hugged her ankles. The drapes were raw silk and brocade to match the custom bedcoverings on the huge four-poster complete with lace canopy. She couldn't help but wonder if Ginger would have been comfortable in a bed you needed a ladder to get into.

Ginger must have liked the color of champagne since the whole room was done in delicate tones of white and gold. A champagne-

colored chair with burgundy cushions beck-
oned her. She just knew Fred Astaire would
have loved the chair. She sank down gratefully
and swung her legs over the arm. From her position in the chair she could see the sitting
room and what was probably a dressing room.
Same carpet, same drapes, same chairs.

She hopped off the chair to check out the
bathroom. It was blinding in its whiteness.
Every single thing was white. She blinked,
wishing for sunglasses. She picked up a towel
and was surprised at how heavy and thick it
was. Not to mention expensive.

Lola had always liked fine things, costly
things. She smiled when she remembered some
of the presents her grandmother had sent her
over the years. Things that were for looking at,
not playing with. Things like rare porcelain
dolls, fancy jeweled fans from the Orient, a ki-
mono with a fire-eating dragon on the back
stitched in gold thread, silver jewelry from Af-
rica, jeweled combs, a sable hat and mittens
from Russia. Then there were the wonderful
storybooks, her first makeup kit, the pretty
cashmere sweaters, the designer handbags, real
leather gloves, fine jewelry and perfume. And
then there was the time a big truck had pulled
up in front of the house with a pony named
Edgar. Everything, even Edgar, had been
snatched away by her father. She'd never told
Lola, though, because she didn't want to hurt
her feelings. She'd always sent long thank you

notes. She wondered where those wonderful things were now. If she could only regain her memory of that long-ago accident. Atlas whimpered at her feet when he heard her sigh. She reached down to pet him. "I think I need to call my mother and let her know I arrived safely."

Cady fished in her purse for her cell phone and dialed her parents' number. Her mother picked up on the third ring, sounding breathless. "Mom, it's me, Cady. I just wanted you to know I got here safely."

"I knew you would. You're a cautious driver. I was wondering if you would call."

"I said I would, Mom. I got a dog before I left. He was a great car buddy on the trip. Mom, where are all the presents Lola gave me when I was a kid?"

Her mother's voice turned chilly. "We gave some of them away to less fortunate children, and the rest were sold. They were decadent, not appropriate for a child like you."

"Did you ask me if it was okay to do that?"

"No, I don't believe I did. Is it important? Don't tell me Lola wants them back."

"No, Mom, she doesn't want them back. I just wanted to know where they were. For some reason I thought you might have saved them. Did you save anything of mine?"

"No, not really. We moved so often, we had to travel light."

"Aren't you going to ask how Lola is? You said Dad was going to call her to tell her I was coming. He didn't call, Mom. I felt like a fool barging in here. Couldn't he have called her, Mom?"

Cady didn't think her mother's voice could get any colder, but it did. "Obviously Lola is well, or you would have said something straight off. I'm no hypocrite. I don't like her, and she doesn't like me. Your father said he was going to call. I want to say he did try and there was no answer. I can't be sure, though. If he was having a bad day, he probably didn't try a second time. I have a cake in the oven, Cady, and I hear your dad calling me, so I have to hang up now."

Cady ignored her and kept talking. "How is Dad?"

"He's the same. Parkinson's disease doesn't get better, only worse. He has good days and bad days. He prays a lot. For some reason God doesn't seem to be responding to his prayers."

"Maybe that's because God knows he's a sinner. He is, you know. Look at how he treats his own mother. Let's not forget the way he treated me when I returned home after the accident. I wish you had left me with Lola."

"That will be enough of *that*, young woman. I have to hang up now, Cady."

Cady switched off the cell phone before she threw it at the bed. She slid off the chair and sat down next to Atlas. "They're my parents, and I don't even like them. I don't think they like me either. You know what, Atlas, I don't care. Someday I'm going to remember all about that time, and then I'll have the answers to a lot of things. At least I hope I will. C'mon, let's check out the grounds and see if there are any places where you can dig a hole."

Chapter 2

The smell told her it was a sickroom, so much so that Cady flinched when she saw her grandmother nestled in the mounds of pillows and comforters, her night table laden with pill bottles and a portable oxygen tank next to the little table. "You lied to me, Lola," she said, fear ringing in her voice. "Why didn't you let me know sooner how serious your condition is? I would have dropped everything and been here in a heartbeat. Why? Why did you keep sending me those upbeat, cheerful letters, telling me everything was all right? These last ten days you've knocked yourself out trying to convince me you're just under the weather. I can see now what a toll that effort has taken on you. Damn it, Lola, I need to know. I hate secrets, I really do. I've had enough of them to last me a lifetime."

"Dying is a dreadful business, sweetie. I didn't want to put you through that the moment you got here. I did, however, want to put my son through it. For some crazy reason I thought your parents would come here if for nothing else, to wait for the death rattle so they could collect. My little scheme backfired. What's a has-been movie star to do? I have good and bad days. Today is a bad day. Tomorrow I might be able to jump rope. We take it one day at a time around here."

"Whatever it is I can do to help, I'll do it. I'm here now, and I'm staying."

"I take great comfort in that, Cady. All I really want is for you to get some guts and stiffen that backbone of yours. Get your memory back and start to live, child. Stop hiding. The world is a magical place, and life is wonderful. I've been fearful a time or two in my life, but out of necessity I had to learn how to harness that fear. You let it consume you, and Asa and Agnes allowed you to do that. For their own reasons, I'm sure. I'm sorry I couldn't have done more for you. God knows I tried."

Cady sat down on the edge of the bed. "I have lived without the memory of that accident for a lot of years. All I know is what other people told me. It doesn't matter at this stage of the game. The truth now, Lola, how bad is your condition?"

"It's iffy. The doctors say I could live another twenty years if I take care of myself. Or, it might not be twenty years. It isn't just this bone thing, my heart is . . . well, let's just say it loved one time too many. The old fool suggested I develop some interesting hobbies. Let's not talk about any of this. I want to talk about the im-

45

portant things in life. Mandy will help you, but for now, I want you to hear all this from me. I have a will that probably needs to be updated. Mandy's on top of that. Where's your dog?"

"He's waiting outside the door. I didn't think you'd want him in here."

"Baloney! At this stage of the game, do you think it matters? Call him in here. Let him sit here on the bed with us while we talk. I miss having an animal. When my last dog died it was so heartbreaking, I swore I would never get another one. I swear, I grieved more over the loss of that animal than I did for any of my six husbands."

Cady whistled. Atlas got up, looked around, then walked into the room, where he stood by Cady's side. "C'mon, boy, Lola said you could get up on the bed. Easy now."

The shepherd moved backward and leaped forward, to land gracefully at the foot of the bed. He eyed the frail-looking woman before he bellied up to her chest. Lola stretched out a bony hand and patted his head. The dog whimpered and laid his head on her shoulder. "He knows. It's uncanny the way dogs know when someone is ill and not long for this world. I've watched him in the ten days that you've been here. I don't think I've ever seen a dog as protective and devoted as this one. I've had many dogs over the years, you know, so I know what I'm talking about." She continued to stroke the dog's big head. "He comes in here in the middle of the night. You didn't know that, did you?"

Cady shook her head.

"Oh, yes, we talk for hours. I never sleep. I doze from time to time. Well, I talked, and he listened. He's a real good listener. I think he understood everything I told him. If he didn't, it doesn't matter. Now, let's get to it. In the top drawer of my secretary is a yellow folder. I so love the color yellow. When I'm buried, I want my casket covered with sunflowers. Bring the folder here, Cady."

Cady was so choked up she didn't trust herself to speak. She brought the folder over to the bed and handed it to her grandmother. Lola stopped petting Atlas long enough to shake out a single sheet of paper. While she made a pretense of scanning the contents Cady knew she had memorized, Cady looked around the haremlike suite of rooms.

World-traveled as she was, Lola obviously liked all things with a Middle Eastern flavor. There were Persian rugs, silk wall hangings, sheets that were more lace than material, and a coverlet with brilliant peacocks in the center. The ornate tables and bric-a-brac, along with huge brass containers that contained lush green plants, were the only concession to Western decor. Lengths of delicate silk fell from golden rods over the windows. A huge round ottoman in a zebra print filled one whole corner, and a waist-high brass horse filled another. The smell of incense permeated the air. The scent was not unpleasant.

"It's all fairly cut-and-dried," Lola said. "Everything goes to you. There are brokerage accounts, all manner of trusts so you don't get socked with inheritance taxes, insurance, property, and, of course, my jewelry. Everything is in the vault. When I moved back here ten years ago, I made a new will. Mitchell, my attorney, passed away while I was in Europe hoping to find a cure for my bone problem, but his son, who was his partner, took over. I've never met him, but that doesn't matter. Everything is in order. I'm not sure, and you'll have to check with Mandy on this, but I think a new firm has taken over the Agulera firm. Something about the son not wanting to practice any longer. I don't foresee you having any problems with a new firm. A lawyer is a lawyer if you know what I mean. If you do, you'll just have to deal with it at that time. I left my son, your father, ten dollars. I didn't want to leave him anything, but Mitchell said I should, so ten dollars seemed like a good amount. I imagine he'll try to break the will, but he won't be successful. If he ever got his hands on my money, he'd start up one of those cults, and I won't stand for that, dead or alive.

"Well, aren't you going to ask how much?" Lola asked.

"No. I don't care, Lola. I don't want your money. I just want you. I came here thinking we could be close again the way we were when I was little. Mom just said you had some health problems and had been hospitalized. She led me to believe it was arthritis, nothing more. Oh, I know you came to see me four or five times a year, but those visits were just for fun. We never seemed to have the time to talk or just hang out. I guess the reason we went full tilt twenty-four-seven was so that we wouldn't have to go down Memory Lane. I didn't want to relive the accident, and you knew it. I don't like thinking about that time, and I hate having to talk about it. You told me once I would know when I was ready. Maybe I'm ready now. Then again, maybe not. It would be nice to get my memory back, but if it doesn't happen, I'm okay with that, too." Cady sighed.

"Those visits are memories I will treasure forever," she continued, her expression brightening. "Remember the day we went rollerblading and some photographer couldn't believe it was really you? I laughed my head off when you sent me the cover of *Variety*, and there you were with your knee pads and helmet! I framed it, Lola. The best, though, was when we went hiking and I had to piggyback you the last mile because you were wearing those cockamamie designer boots and sprained your ankle. Everyone should have a grandmother like you. I just love you to pieces in case you don't know it already."

Lola smiled at the memories before she said, "Well, for God's sake, Cady, I'm not exactly eager to go either, but that's not my decision to make. Are you going to write my memoirs for me? It's around sixty-five million."

"Dollars?" Cady gasped, her jaw dropping.

"So, are you going to write my memoirs or not?"

Cady nodded. "If you want me to." She tried to absorb the news that she'd inherit sixty-five million.

"You'll have to quit that safe, boring job of yours and devote all your time to me. Well, not *all* your time. I want you to continue working on your dissertation. Are you willing to do that? It also means you'll have to get out and about, and it damn well means you're going to have to start to live."

A gamut of emotions swirled through Cady's head. Was she willing to do all that? Could she do as Lola asked? "Yes. Yes, I'll do that. I'll fax my resignation today. But I really don't know much about writing memoirs. Writing memoirs and writing a dissertation are two different things. In case you're interested, mine is about fear in the works of Joseph Conrad and I'm having a hard time with it. We can talk about that some other time, Lola.

"When would you like to get started?" Cady asked with a smile.

"You learned to be a technical writer, so I don't think you'll have a bit of trouble. To-morrow if you're up to it. I think I'm going to take a little nap now. Ask Mandy to show you where all my scrapbooks are. I know they're someplace in the library. I haven't looked at them in years. You might want to familiarize yourself with the contents before we start tomorrow. Have you gone to the pond yet, Cady?"

"No. I have to work up to that, Lola."

"Have you gone by your old house?"

"No. I have to work up to that, too."

"How about the cemetery where the boy is buried?"

"I don't know if I can ever go there, Lola. I wish you'd let me call you Grandmother. Calling you Lola sounds so disrespectful. Maybe I'll . . . go *there* one of these days. Then again, maybe I won't."

"Are you going to call your old friends?" Lola yawned elaborately.

"I thought about it but . . . maybe later on. There's no hurry. I'll go down to the library and let you take your nap now. Do you want Atlas to stay with you?"

"That would be nice," Lola said, closing her eyes.

"Stay with Lola, Atlas. I'm going down to the library. Come and get me if she wakes up."

The big dog squirmed closer to the frail woman. Cady swore the shepherd nodded in agreement.

The library had the look of Winston Churchill's personal library. She had seen a picture of it in a book when she was in college. Cady pulled out the leather chair behind the desk and sat down. The rich scent of leather permeated the air. Her gaze swept the room. A frown built between her brows as she stared at the wall-to-wall shelves of books. Lola couldn't sit still long enough to read a book. She just knew the spines had never been broken on any of the books. To test her judgment, she got up and walked over to what appeared to be a shelf of recent best-sellers. She pulled out books at random. All of them looked like they had just come from a bookstore. Even the leather-bound classics looked new and unread. So, who were the books for? She decided they were just for looks.

Lola's third husband loved to read. She remembered Lola telling her he had developed macular degeneration several years before he died. Lola read to him constantly.

Mandy appeared in the doorway. "I guess you could say this room is a memorial to Lola's third husband. She never comes in here now, though. Actually, she never goes into any of the rooms. She looked them all over when the decorator was finished, but that's about it. There's a room on the second floor that's called the game room. Lola's fourth husband was a big-game hunter. He died wrestling a crocodile in the Amazon. Lola saw it all. She had a set of luggage made from croc skins, but she threw it away after the accident," Mandy said through tight lips.

"Oh," was all Cady could think of to say.

"Mandy, do you know anything about my grandfather? Over the years I asked Lola a dozen times, and all she would ever say was that he was just an ordinary man. All I know about him was that he was a lot older than Lola and that he died in his sleep. It seems to me there should be more to say about a man other than that he was ordinary."

"If that's all there is to say, what else can a person say? He looked ordinary. He dressed like everyone else, so that made him ordinary-looking. He sold furniture, and from time to time, decorated a client's house, but he wasn't really a decorator. Now, if you want *Herself* to make up something that will suit your fancy, I'm sure she can do that. To tell you the truth, I don't even think she remembers him because . . ."

Cady grinned. "Because he was so ordinary. Okay, I have the picture."

"All the scrapbooks are in these cabinets. I labeled them by the year, so you shouldn't have any problem following Lola's life and career."

"Who was the real love of Lola's life? Do you know?"

Mandy yanked at her apron. "Of course I know, but it isn't my place to tell you. If she wants you to know, she'll tell you."

"Why didn't you call me, Mandy?"

"Because *Herself* said not to. She would have booted my fanny out of here if I had done that. I know my place, and so does Anthony. That's why we've lasted this long. Your grandmother can be stubborn as a mule. Are you sure you can't get your father to come here? It doesn't seem right that his mother is . . . and he can't be bothered. As much as Lola says she doesn't care, I know it's a heavy weight on her heart."

"He's not well. My mother said Dad was diagnosed with Parkinson's disease, but she never mentions a doctor. Personally, I think Dad thinks that's what he has. He's in a wheelchair and takes tons of over-the-counter medicine. At least that's what my mother told me. The wheelchair is an attention-getter. Again, that's my opinion."

Mandy snorted again as she started pulling out scrapbooks from the cabinets. "There's one whole scrapbook devoted entirely to your father, but only until his sixteenth year. There's one concerning that day when your . . . accident happened. I'm the one who kept it up. Lola didn't want to. It was too painful. I offered it to your parents, and they said no thank you. Are you going to . . . stay on . . . *after?* Whenever after . . . happens. I don't know what Anthony and I are going to do," she said, wringing her hands.

"You're both going to stay right here is what you're going to do. This is your home. I'm sure Lola provided for you."

"It's not the money. She's paid both of us ten times what we're worth over the years. It's all been invested. Both of us have always taken care of Lola. We won't know what to do without her."

"You can take care of me and Atlas. But that's a long way down the road. It looks like I'll be staying on here."

Mandy wiped her eyes with the hem of her apron. "She loves you so much. I thought she would have a breakdown when your parents took you away. She was never the same after you left. I'll never forget that day. You didn't want to go either. You were wailing and carrying on just the way Lola was. She thought you would come back here after you finished college. That's why she built this big place. The tennis court, the pool, this fancy house, all those books in the library, it was all for you. She wanted you to come on your own. She said she would never ask or beg you. She said if you came, it would be because you wanted to come."

"I wasn't ready to come back. Lola knew that," Cady said. "Mandy, fear does terrible things to people. I'm still not comfortable being here. I love Lola more than anything in the whole world, you know that. I probably wouldn't have come now if I didn't feel she needed me. I don't think she needed me before. I could be wrong about that, but I don't think so."

Mandy nodded. "I'm cooking up a pot of gizzards, chicken, and some rice and vegetables for Atlas. Lola always fed that to her dogs, and they all lived long, healthy lives. I've been giving him cod liver oil, and his coat is getting nice and shiny. He's put on some weight, too, since he's been here. He does like his cheese treats."

"Yes, he does, and he loves to play with that sock you made him with the bell inside. I don't think he ever had any toys. He's a good dog."

"Yes, he is. Would you like some coffee, Cady?"

"I would, Mandy. How long will Lola sleep?"

"She's not sleeping. She's just lying there talking to your dog. She's afraid to sleep for fear she'll die, and she isn't ready to do that yet. It's almost like she's waiting for something. Whatever it is, she isn't sharing it with me."

"Do you think she's waiting for my father?"

"No. In her heart, she's given up on him. I think she's waiting for you to remember. Now that you're here, I think, and this is just my opinion, she thinks you're going to wake up one morning and magically remember that day."

"That day is gone from my life, Mandy. I've tried to remember, and I can't. The last thing I remember is sitting on the porch watching the movers put our stuff into the van. I remember everything afterward, waking up in the hospital and all the rest, but I don't remember that day."

"If you stay locked up here in this house, your memory will never come back. I'm thinking you're going to have to search for it. That's just my opinion. I'm an old lady, what do I know? I'll get you your coffee."

Cady crossed her arms over her chest as though warding off a chill. She leaned back in the leather swivel chair. She burst out laughing a minute later when she let her gaze rake the walls. Winston Churchill stared down at her. There was probably a story behind that picture, but at the moment she didn't want to know what it was. She looked down at the pile of scrapbooks on the floor. She had the rest of the day and evening to look through them.

She was rummaging in the desk drawers for a phone book when Mandy returned with a silver tray holding an elaborate silver service. A fragile cup and saucer along with a linen napkin were on the tray.

"My goodness, Mandy, a mug with a paper napkin would have been fine. I'm a Crate and Barrel kind of girl. I'm not used to . . . this," she said, pointing to the elegant tray and its contents. "I usually drink my coffee out of a heavy-duty mug."

"Lola likes fine things. Actually, she insists upon them. Here, this is what you're looking for," she said, holding out a sheet of paper with telephone numbers next to a column of names. The phone book is in the kitchen. Enjoy the coffee. I grind the beans myself. *Herself* is hell on wheels when it comes to her coffee. She has it shipped here from Hawaii."

Cady nodded as she looked at the slip of

paper. So many names.

Andy Hollister, Amy Hollister Chambers. Amy must have gotten married. Fred and Alma Hollister. The twins' parents. Peter Danson. Susan and Peter Danson Senior. Maxwell (Boomer) Ward. Albert and Victoria Ward. Cyrus and Maxine King, Jeff's parents.

Cady sipped at the coffee in the fragile cup. Right now, right this minute, she could call any of the numbers on the list. If she wanted to.

While she couldn't remember the accident, she did remember her friends. She wondered what they were like now and what they had done with their lives. Would they be happy to see her? More to the point, would they even *want* to see her?

Maybe she needed to look at the scrapbook about the accident. She'd never seen any of the newspaper articles. Even when she'd gotten older and asked her mother if she would get them for her, both her parents had been adamant that there weren't any articles. Even Lola had said when the time was right for her to see them, she would know. The time seemed right *now*.

Cady sucked in her breath as she reached for the scrapbook that chronicled the accident that had left her partially paralyzed for almost three years. She reared back at the bold, black headline of the *Indigo Sentinel*. *INDIGO VALLEY TEEN DIES.* Cady flipped the pages as the headlines got uglier and uglier. Perspiration beaded her forehead.

MYSTERY SURROUNDS TEEN'S DEATH.
PARENTS BLAME TEN-YEAR-OLD
IN SON'S DEATH.
NO WITNESSES IN MYSTERY DEATH.
TEN-YEAR-OLD PARTIALLY PARALYZED
WITH MEMORY LOSS.

Cady gulped at the remaining coffee in the fragile Dresden cup. She felt clammy and dizzy. She was the ten-year-old Jeff King's parents were blaming. She squeezed her eyes shut as she tried to visualize what Jeff King had looked like back then. He and Boomer Ward were three years older than she and her friends. Both boys had been big for their ages. Jeff had a mean streak and terrorized her and her friends. For some reason he'd always home in on her. Back then she had never been able to figure out why he hated her more than the others. Once he'd cornered her, his eyes full of hate as he spewed out something despicable, but she couldn't remember now what it was.

The four of them had spent hours and hours trying to figure out ways to outwit Jeff and Boomer. Boomer had always been nice to her when Jeff wasn't around. She didn't know why that was.

She should read the articles. She really should.

A cold, wet nose touched her ankle. Atlas had come into the room. That had to mean Lola had awakened. "These papers say I killed Jeff King. Even though I can't remember the accident, I would remember something that awful, wouldn't I? I'm not a murderer. I could never kill anyone."

She was so light-headed, she jumped up and ran out of the room, down the hall to the French doors leading to the garden. She sat down on a bench and put her head between her legs as she struggled to take great gulps of air into her tight lungs. "I wouldn't do something like that. It's a sin to take a life. I didn't like Jeff King, but I didn't hate him enough to kill him. They said I fell off the zip line. I never rode the zip because I was afraid. If no one was there, how can they say I did it?"

Cady pushed up and off the bench. She started to run, Atlas at her side. She ran until she collapsed against a giant lilac bush in full bloom. The scent from the clusters of flowers was so heady she almost passed out.

"I'm not a murderer. I'm not!" she screamed at the top of her lungs. Atlas reared back, his hair standing on end. Seeing that she had frightened the shepherd, Cady drew him to her and sobbed into his neck. He whimpered, unable to help his mistress.

"I should have stayed in California. I should have done a lot of things, but I didn't. Why didn't I? Why?" Cady cried brokenly.

"I think she's starting to get that backbone you're always harping on, Lola," Mandy said from her position by the window. "She's bawling her eyes out, and if she isn't careful, she's going to squeeze that dog to death. I hate to say this, but that young woman is nothing like she was as a child. I remember her being a little daredevil, a bright, sassy little thing with that long pigtail swinging down her back. She zipped around on that bike you bought her like she was born on it. She could do those pop-wheelies or whatever you call them better than the boys. She's so withdrawn, so inside herself, I'm having a hard time with it."

Lola shook her head. "I will never understand her parents. They said she, a little slip of a girl, killed that bully, Jeff King. I know that Asa was parroting the Kings. He derived great pleasure out of doing that. Since he and Agnes never had an original idea of their own, I think they just accepted the Kings' version of what they *think* happened. I say it was just the other way around, that bully probably tried to hurt Cady but no one would listen to me. Just because Asa and Agnes said it was better for her not to remember doesn't make it so. The only thing the authorities had to go on was the Kings' insistence that somehow, some way, Cady killed their son."

"We need to do something. Knowing that people are blaming her for that boy's death must be tearing her apart," Mandy said.

Anthony placed both hands on Lola's shoulders to calm her. He gently massaged her neck. Lola all but purred.

"Yes, Mandy," Anthony said, "but she'll weather it. She's got Lola's spunk."

"We are doing something. We're waiting. We planted the seeds. They'll sprout. She's got the dog now, so that's giving her some confidence. As much as we want this to happen overnight, it isn't going to happen. Did you spread the word in town that she's back?" Lola asked.

"I went to the post office to pick up her mail and to tell them from now on to deliver it all here. Miriam Terwilliger is the worst gossip in town. She'll tell everyone. I stopped by the pet store and purchased a heavy-duty dog leash for Atlas. I said your granddaughter was back with her *big* dog. I think I might have said, big *killer* dog. Big killer dogs aren't something we have a lot of around here. I was trying to get my point across. Then I went to the bakery and picked up a dozen cream puffs for your granddaughter. Betty Donovan is almost as big a gossip as Miriam Terwilliger. I think it's safe to say the town knows she's back."

"It bothers me, Lola, that none of her so-called friends have called. I think we might need to worry about that a little bit," the roly-poly Anthony said.

"I don't have time to worry, Anthony. I just have time for action. Now, let's put our heads together and see how we can shake things up. Maybe it's time for me to do that interview the *Indigo Sentinel* is always pestering me about. I could introduce Cady to the reporter, have them take her picture, that kind of thing. We'll say she's helping me with my memoirs, and there is a possible movie deal in the works. I still have that defunct production company, don't I?"

"Yes. You pay the taxes every year."

"Good, then it won't be a lie. We'll say the memoirs will be right up to the present and encompass Cady's accident and how we're going to investigate it vigorously. We're going to have to fix me up so I don't look so . . . *deadly*. We can do that, can't we, Mandy?"

"Of course we can do that. We know all of Hollywood's makeup tricks. When do you want me to schedule the interview?"

"The day after tomorrow. Let's not tell Cady until the last minute. Lord, I have to think about what I'm going to wear. What do you think, Mandy?"

Mandy smiled. She hadn't seen Lola so excited in years. "Depends if you want to look like a grandmother, a recluse gone to seed, or a movie star. Why don't we schedule it for late in the afternoon and have an English tea? Well?"

"A movie star, of course. English tea will be wonderful. We haven't had scones in ages. Why is that, Anthony?" Anthony and Mandy took turns cooking, but Anthony's culinary expertise far outshone Mandy's. Consequently, Anthony did most of the cooking.

"Because you don't like scones, Lola. You like English muffins with grape jelly along with your *decaffeinated* tea."

Lola squirmed in her nest of quilts. "I had no idea getting old was going to be so painful. I'm afraid, Mandy. I'm getting like Cady. I understand her fear. There are so many things I haven't done, things I still want to do. Why did this happen to me? I'm not ready yet. I thought I would be able to handle all of this, but I'm not. If I tell you a secret, will you promise never, ever, to tell anyone?"

"Of course, Lola," Mandy said, sitting down on the bed. She reached for Lola's hand and squeezed it.

"You can hear, too, Anthony. I thought when it was my time to go, my son would come and be at my side, and he would pray with me. That isn't going to happen because he's a damn quack. I don't want him spewing some lingo he picked up out of some trashy book. I thought he would know all the words that would make it right. It always happens that way in the movies. Then at the end you see a bright light, and those left behind know you're in a better place. There isn't anyone to tell me the words."

"I can call the minister from St. Paul's for you. I know a lot of those words, Lola. I can get out the Bible, and we can read it together," Mandy said, her voice sounding desperate. Anthony wrung his hands as he looked everywhere but at the two women.

"No, no, it wouldn't be the same. It should be my son saying those words to me. It isn't going to happen, so we need to move on here," Lola said as she dabbed at her eyes.

"Do you want to get up now? It's a beautiful day out. You could sit out on the terrace for a while. We could have a gin and tonic and pretend like it's the old days."

"Yes, let's do that. What's she doing now?"

Mandy walked over to the window. "She's gone. I guess she's somewhere on the grounds, or else she's in the house.

"What would you like to wear today, Lola? Let's go with something cheerful. I'll help you to the bathroom and pick something out."

"What would I do without you, Mandy?"

"You'd do just fine, Lola. Let's not go down that road today. You don't really want scones, do you?"

"Good Lord, no. I'll take the muffin with jelly. Perhaps Cady and Atlas will join us. You're right, it is a beautiful day." Lola craned her neck to see out onto the third-floor terrace, where colorful summer chairs and brilliant pots of flowers bordered the railing. She loved sitting on the terrace on warm summer evenings, with her memories and the fireflies. She wondered if she would make it through the summer. *Just let me do it one more time,* she pleaded silently. *Just one more time.*

Amy Hollister Chambers opened the door of the bakery, a tiny bell tinkling overhead. She loved the quaint little shop, with the green-checkered curtains on the windows and the little soda-fountain tables with the matching table-cloths. The smell of freshly made bread had no equal as far as she was concerned. Some days, especially when she was dieting, she stopped by just to sniff or to chat with Julie Ambrose, an old school chum who was co-owner of the bakery with Betty Donovan.

"Hey, girl, you're late today. All the goodies are gone. We just have bread left," a smiling Julie said, wiping her hands on her flour-specked apron. "How about a cup of coffee?"

"Sounds fine to me. Are you sure you don't have any eclairs left? I got behind today and didn't have time to make dessert. My kids will freak out if they don't have something sweet after dinner. Especially tonight since we're having liver and onions. Arnie loves liver, and I have to make it once in a while to keep him happy. All I need is three," she cajoled.

"Sorry, Amy. Guess you're going to have to make some instant pudding. Stick some vanilla wafers in it, and they'll be happy. Pete Danson bought the last six about thirty minutes ago. He said he was going to eat them all. I thought that was rather strange since he said he just came in for a loaf of bread."

Amy Chambers stared at her reflection in the

bakery case. She needed to lose some weight. She needed to do something with her flyaway hair, too. Maybe she needed to get a job, even if it was just part-time. Something to occupy her time when the kids were in school. Then again, if she got a job, her friends would think Arnie didn't make enough money. Maybe it would be better to do more volunteer work. That way if she didn't feel like it, she wouldn't have to do it.

"Did you hear the latest news?"

"Did something exciting happen?" Amy asked as she twirled a lock of hair behind her ear, hoping it would stay in place.

"I guess it depends on what you call exciting. Cady Jordan is back in town. Wasn't she your best friend back when we were kids?"

"Cady's back! When? Did you see her? No, I didn't know. We . . . used to play together. I don't know if you would call her my best friend, though."

Julie Ambrose laughed. "You look just the way Pete Danson looked when I told him the same thing a little while ago. After I told him, he bought the six eclairs. I never believed for one minute that she killed Jeff King. Not for one minute. Did you believe it, Amy?"

"That was so long ago, I can barely remember. What I do remember is her father was one of those funky preachers. He was into fire and brimstone and stuff like that. I think he talked in tongues. Andy said it was just gibberish."

"This is *so* weird. Pete Danson said almost exactly the same thing you just said, right down to the fire and brimstone stuff. Where is my head today? I do have other news. Boomer Ward is back in town, too. Seems they snared him away from the Pittsburgh Police Department. My mother said they voted to pay him twice what he was getting there. Homer Logan is retiring as police chief, and Boomer is taking over. He was here in town last week, but I don't know if he's moved back officially yet. Donna Little said he was one hunky-looking dude, and he's not married. Imagine that! I might take a crack at him myself if he's available."

"I didn't see anything about that in the *Indigo Sentinel*, and I read it cover to cover," Amy said, perspiration beading on her forehead.

"It's going to be in the paper tomorrow. Right on the front page. Betty told me they took a picture of him with his police dog. She said Erwin Potter is the one who took the picture. Police chief at the age of thirty-three. That's pretty amazing. Donna Little said he majored in criminal justice in college, and he's up on all the latest policing techniques. He even worked at the FBI for a couple of years. I guess our crime will go down real quick. So, do you want that loaf of bread or not? You didn't drink your coffee, Amy Chambers!"

"Yes, I need the bread. I think I had one cup too many today. My nerves are twanging. Will you look at the time! I have to pick up the kids at Joellen's house." She counted out a dollar and a half and laid it on the counter. "See ya, Julie."

Her stomach in knots, her head pounding, Amy climbed into her Windstar. Instead of driving to her friend's house, though, she turned the corner, drove down Central Avenue, crossed over Exeter, and parked in front of the Hollister Insurance Company. She tapped the horn lightly when she saw her twin brother walk out the door. He smiled and loped over to the car. Amy rolled down the window. "Get in, Andy."

"You look awful, Amy. Are the kids okay? What's wrong?"

"Cady Jordan is back in town, that's what's wrong. I stopped at the bakery, and Julie told me. She also told me our new police chief is going to be Boomer Ward. For God's sake, Andy, say something."

"What do you want me to say, Amy? We always knew this was going to happen someday. I wonder if Pete knows."

"Oh, he knows all right. Julie said he was in the bakery thirty minutes before I got there. She told him what she told me. Boomer knows we were there," Amy hissed.

"He was there, too. I still say he's the one who called the police that day. Pete said he didn't do it. You and I didn't do it, so that just leaves Boomer. For Christ's sake, he's a police lieutenant in Pittsburgh. Now he's coming here. This damn well can't be good."

"What if she calls one of us? My God, Andy, she's back!"

"Listen, I have to run. I was on my way to the judge's office. He's unhappy with his group insurance and wants me to come up with something better. I'll call you at home tonight. I'll call Pete, too. Relax, Amy. You look like you're guilty of something."

"That's because I am guilty, just like you are, as well as Pete and Boomer. You're wrong about my thinking Cady would come back here. I never thought she would. Never, ever."

"Go home, Amy, and have a drink. I'll either stop by or call you tonight."

Go home and have a drink, she thought. Like that was really going to make things better.

Chapter 3

The sweet scent of lilacs permeated the evening air on Ribbonmaker Lane. Overhead the night was clear, with stars sprinkling the heavens. Porch lights glowed warmly, and off in the distance a dog barked from time to time.

Ribbonmaker Lane was in a quiet neighborhood, with two-story Tudor houses and well-manicured evergreens. Spring flowers in tended beds couldn't be seen in the darkness, but they were there, a testament to the wives and mothers who planted their tulip bulbs in the fall so their walkways would look like rainbows when spring finally arrived.

The development, known as Indigo Grove, was divided into three parts: the expensive, high-end Tudors with swimming pools on full acres; the medium-size Colonials on half-acre lots; and the smaller Cape Cods on quarter-acre lots. Amy Chambers lived in the high-end section of Indigo Grove, as did her brother Andy and his wife. Pete Danson lived in one of the Colonials with a live-in housekeeper. His legal office was a separate structure behind the main house, with its own driveway.

The three old friends looked at one another as they settled themselves on the wicker chairs on Amy's small side porch. A tray with three bottles of beer along with a bowl of pretzels sat in the middle of a little table. No one made a move to help themselves. It had been a long time since they had all been together. The fun times they had shared as children were all but forgotten.

"I didn't think the kids would ever fall asleep. I'm glad Arnie had to go back to the office. We need to talk and get this over with before he gets back," Amy said. "What are we going to do? She should have called one of us by now. Why hasn't she called?"

Pete Danson stood up and jammed his hands into his pockets. He looked down at his two friends, and said, "If you were her, would you call us? I don't think so. So, what is it you want to talk about?"

Amy stretched her neck to look up at Pete's six-foot-two height. She particularly loved his curly blond hair. She'd had a crush on Pete her whole life, but he'd only been interested in Cady. Pete Danson was the one she'd wanted to marry back then, but Pete hadn't been interested in her other than as a friend. So, she'd married Arnold Chambers. Still, every time she was in Pete's company, her heart beat a little faster. How good he looked tonight in his khaki slacks and Izod tee shirt. He looked loose, ready for anything. One hundred and eighty pounds of manhood. He worked out religiously in the gym and was known as the best catch in town. Who wouldn't be attracted to the good-looking, successful lawyer? She swallowed hard. Arnie had a beer belly that was starting to hang over his belt. The closest he ever got to a gym was to walk past one on the way to his parked car. But, he was an excellent provider, and that meant a lot.

"I heard you bought out Ken Agulera's practice, Pete. How'd that happen?" Andy asked. For some reason his voice sounded belligerent, even to his own ears.

Pete raised his eyebrows but decided to ignore his friend's tone. "I guess you could say I more or less fell into it. Ken came up to me on the tennis court a while back and said he was selling his father's practice. He hung on a year after his father died, but his heart was never in the law. He took his inheritance and the money from the sale of the practice and is now a bona fide NASCAR driver. I hope to hell he doesn't kill himself. This may or may not blow your socks off. I bet you can't guess who my star client is? No other than Lola Jor Dan. I inherited her from Ken. I got a call yesterday asking me to come by her house to discuss some legal matters. That was before I knew Cady was back in town. The appointment is Saturday afternoon. It would be nice if one of you would say something," Pete drawled, enjoying the look of amazement on the twins' faces.

Amy bit down on her lower lip as she watched a swarm of fireflies in her line of vision. Pete was single. Cady was single. At least she thought she was. Pete was going to see her on Saturday. "Do you want us to genuflect?" she sniped.

"I was making conversation, Amy. Look, you were the one who called me to come over here. I'm here. Let's get to it, whatever *it* is." He turned to Andy. "I don't think I've ever seen you at a loss for words. Say something, for God's sake."

"How's this for starters. Cady Jordan is back in town. Twenty years after the fact. What if she dredges up all that old crap? How are we supposed to respond? What do you think the people in this town who patronize our businesses will have to say about us then? Don't you think it's more than a little strange that she hasn't contacted any of us? We were a tight little group if I remember correctly. That's my contribution to this conversation," Andy snarled.

"You're a lawyer, Pete. What can happen to us?" Amy demanded as she jumped up and started to pace the small porch. "I should have called Boomer. If I knew how to reach him, I would have called him. He's in this as deep as we are. Well?"

"There's no statute of limitations on murder, Amy. One of us killed Jeff with those rocks we were pitching. We let everyone believe Cady did it. We were gutless and let them pin it on her. The truth is, we deserve whatever happens to us. I don't know if you thought about this or not, but maybe Cady never got her memory back. If that's the case, it would explain why she hasn't called any of us. Think about it; at this stage, we would be like strangers to her."

"Jesus Christ, Pete!" Andy exclaimed. "We left her there to die! She could have died, too, so don't try to tell me differently. It doesn't matter if we *thought* she was dead or not. She was alive when we left, and we were too damn stupid to know it. It's a miracle she didn't die. Think about those three years they said she was partially paralyzed. She's got to hate us for that. I sure as hell would." Andy was sputtering so badly, spittle flew in all directions.

Pete's tone was patient-sounding. "The law would call what happened to Jeff death by mis-adventure. There are no criminal charges attached to that. Now, if it will make you both feel any better, we could go down to the police station and confess. If you two agree, I'll go along with it. The big question is, before or after Boomer takes office? Or, we can wait it out and see what Cady does." Pete looked at them and waited, knowing exactly what they would say. He wasn't disappointed.

"Are you crazy?" Andy asked. "I'm not confessing to anything. It was an accident. We were throwing those rocks to get Jeff away from her.

In case you forgot, we were trying to *help* Cady." He stared off into the night, refusing to look at either Amy or Pete.

"I remember everything about that day, Andy. What's more, I think about it every single day of my life. We took a life. It doesn't matter if it was an accident or not, and we kept quiet about it," Pete said.

"That's a brilliant summation coming from a lawyer if I ever heard one. Do you think you're the only one who thinks about it? Jesus, I can't drive by that place without getting physically sick. I drive ten miles out of my way just to avoid it," Andy said.

"I don't want to talk about this. We need to decide what we're going to say if and when Cady gets in touch with us. How are we going to act?" Amy fretted.

Pete reached out to let a firefly settle on his finger. "Isn't that going to depend on whether or not Cady has her memory back? Remember how we used to catch these and put them in a jar? At the time it didn't seem cruel, but it does now. Think about how awful it must be to be locked up in a small place. Even if it's in your mind. I think I'll say good night. I have an early court date. If you come up with anything, give me a call," Pete said.

Andy reached for one of the beer bottles on the tray. He took a long swig, looked at the bottle, and drained it. "He was pretty blasé about all of this, don't you think?"

"That probably means he thinks either you or I threw the rock that killed Jeff, which could only mean he's certain he didn't do it. I thought he was really going to be upset. It bothers me that he *wasn't* upset. All I have to do is look at you to know you're as upset as I am." Amy reached for one of the beer bottles and gulped at the contents.

"Maybe he's thinking he has an inside track now that he has Lola Jor Dan's business. It's getting late, Amy. I need to go home. Jill bitches for hours when I go out at night even if it's on a business call."

Amy sat down and stretched out her legs. "Pete was right. We never should have put those fireflies in the jars. Why would we do such a stupid thing? I'm never going to let my kids do stuff like that."

"Was that any more stupid than killing Jeff King and letting everyone think Cady did it? Good night, Amy."

Amy waved her brother off, not bothering to say anything as she moved over to the swing, the beer bottle still in her hand. She curled into the corner to wait for her husband. Arnie would make her feel better when he got home.

Pete Danson waved an airy hand when Andy Hollister tapped his horn before turning the corner. He'd walked to Amy's house. Sitting behind a desk all day made him want to stretch his legs. He'd missed out on the gym that day because he'd been in court until four-thirty and had to play catch-up when he got back to the office.

He tried to think about what had transpired in court, but his mind was blank. All he could think about was Cady Jordan and what her return might mean to all of them. He'd played the cool lawyer to the hilt in front of the twins. But the truth was, he was scared. Damn scared. Were the twins right? He rather suspected they were. Who would want to hire any of them for anything if the past came out? No one, that's who.

He'd busted his ass all these years to make something of himself. How in the hell could a tragic accident that happened twenty years ago take it all away? They were just kids trying to do the right thing, trying to save Cady, and it had all backfired. They weren't *bad* kids back then. Adventuresome, yes. A little on the wild and daring side, but they were never mean or malicious like Jeff and Boomer.

He wished there was someone to blame for the past. Hell, why not lay it on his drunken father or his weird mother, who thought she was a direct descendant of some alien life force. His father had died of cirrhosis of the liver the year Pete had graduated from law school. His mother was busy and happy directing traffic to Mars via Venus and Jupiter at the mental health facility where she lived now. He'd pretty much raised himself.

Maybe that was why he'd had a soft spot for

Cady in his heart. She'd told him about her own parents and how she hated what she called the preaching circuit where her parents used God to beg for money.

Andy and Amy's parents were so far over the top, even back then, that the twins avoided talking about them and their antics. As far as he knew they hadn't improved with age.

Maybe that's why the four of them had gravitated toward each other. A messy family life wasn't easy for a kid to live with, but it was easier if you didn't suffer alone. Back then, they'd shared everything — their secrets, their young desires, and even their hates.

Misfits.

Jeff King, now, he was something else entirely. Jeff's father owned the local glove factory, and his mother had blood so blue she could have posed for the Blue's Clues. His sisters and brothers excelled in sports and life. The Kings were one of Indigo Valley's finest families. If they had had their way, Cady Jordan would have been locked up in an asylum never to see the bright light of day. It might have happened, too, if Lola Jor Dan hadn't stepped in with the best criminal lawyer in the state of Pennsylvania to defend her granddaughter's reputation. The movie star's celebrity hadn't hurt their case either. With no concrete evidence to support the Kings' theory, the case had been dismissed, at which point, Lola Jor Dan had whisked her granddaughter to California to a private hospital and, from what he'd heard, years of painful therapy.

Pete stopped in midstride, realizing how selfish his thinking was. Yes, he had suffered through a lousy childhood and adolescence. And yes, he had suffered feelings of guilt for twenty years. But his suffering was nothing compared to what Cady had been through. From the little he'd heard, her life after the accident had been pure hell. The blow from the rocks, along with the fall, had done serious damage to her spine, and it had taken her more than three years to regain the ability to walk again.

The loss of her childhood, all that pain, all that suffering — physical and mental — because he and the twins had accused her of being a sissy chicken and dared her to ride the zip line. If only she *had* been a sissy chicken, none of it would have happened.

Pete turned the corner to his house, the streetlamp lighting the way down the block. At his house, he walked up the driveway, but instead of going into the house, he continued around back to his office.

Inside, he turned on the light and smiled. He always smiled when he entered the office, just as he always smiled when he walked into his house. Everything was warm, cozy, and comfortable-looking to the eye. Something he'd never had when he was a kid. He'd lived in a stripped-down house with a stripped-down bedroom. Clothes, food, and comfort were wherever he could find them. Andy, Cady, and Amy never knew how many nights he'd spent in the tree house at the Judas Grove during the warm summer months just because the tree house was cozy and warm, with its posters and strips of carpeting. Boomer knew, though, and he'd never given it away. He'd always wondered why, but he had never asked.

Boomer. aka Maxwell Ward. An enigma.

Pete flopped down on his ergonomic chair. His smile was gone, replaced with a frown. He swiveled around to open the minibar behind his desk and popped a bottle of Miller Lite. He positioned his feet on the corner of his desk and closed his eyes, his thoughts going in all directions.

It was *pissifying* that Boomer was about to take up residence in Indigo Valley as the chief of police at this point in time. Beyond *pissifying*. How would it play out over time? He had to admit he didn't have a clue.

He hadn't seen Boomer since Boomer graduated from high school. When Pete and the twins graduated, Boomer was already a senior at Penn State. They'd all gone their separate ways to different colleges. Andy had gone to Villanova. Amy to West Chester University, while he had gone to Princeton.

Boomer hadn't attended his ten-year high school class reunion. If he had ever come back to town, he sure hadn't seen him. Why would

81

he give up an exciting job in Pittsburgh to come back to Indigo Valley? Maybe big-city life had gotten to him. Maybe his parents needed him. Hell, maybe he loved Indigo Valley.

Pete drained his beer and opened a second bottle. Fear was a terrible thing. He knew a thing or two about fear. He'd seen fear and guilt tonight in Andy's and Amy's eyes. That fear could translate to any number of things, none of them good.

He would give up everything he held dear if he could turn the clock back to that day at the Judas Grove.

His feet hit the floor with a hard thud. The middle desk drawer held a key to the bottom desk drawer. He used it to open the drawer. The small box in the back was covered with some of his more important papers, which he didn't want his secretary to see. He knew what it was. How could he forget? He'd worked like a dog collecting bottles and cans to buy the going-away gift for Cady. He opened it and wondered what she would have written in the little diary with the silver key? He tried to remember how many times he'd opened the drawer to look at it. Every single time he'd wondered why he hadn't just thrown it away. It had gone with him and his meager belongings all through high school, college, and law school. He'd never told Andy or Amy about the diary for fear they would laugh at him. They'd never said if they had bought her a going-away present. They didn't have anything with them that day. He'd had the diary in the paper sack because it was his turn to bring Kool-Aid and cookies. No, he was almost certain the twins didn't have a going-away gift. They had no money. It wouldn't have occurred to either one of them to do what he'd done because that was work. Amy would never pick through garbage, and Andy would have thought it humiliating to scrounge up bottles and cans.

He decided he didn't really like Andy and Amy very much these days. In retrospect, he wasn't even sure he'd liked the twins back then either. He also knew both of them would sell him out without the slightest regret if it ever came down to him versus them. Hadn't Judas done the same thing for thirty pieces of silver?

The diary went back into the drawer. Pete locked it and tossed the key into the middle drawer of his desk before throwing the two empty beer bottles into the trash. Time to head up to the house for the dinner he hoped was warming in the oven. Annie, his housekeeper, always made sure she prepared something that wouldn't dry out on his late nights. He'd part with his right foot before he would part with Annie because she fussed over him and nursed him when he came down with the flu in the winter. She worried about him the way a mother worried about a son. She also probably made the best coffee and blackberry pie in the state of Pennsylvania.

Pete turned off the lights. It really was a beautiful night, he thought as he locked the door to the office. The dew was heavy on the grass as he walked across the yard to the terrace in the back of his house. The sliding glass door was open, the screen drawn across the opening. He let himself in. He smiled because the family room was so warm and inviting. Annie had helped him find just the right furniture to accommodate his 180-pound frame. *You don't want it too manly in case you entertain ladies from time to time* was the deciding vote on the wheat-colored sofa and chairs.

Pete meandered out to the kitchen. He sighed with happiness when he smelled his favorite dinner warming in the oven — stuffed peppers, mashed potatoes, Mexicali corn. And there would be sour cream cucumbers with lots and lots of onions in a covered dish in the refrigerator. He knew there were fresh, warm rolls someplace, just the way he knew there was a strawberry rhubarb pie. It didn't get any better than this.

No one was going to take this away from him.

No one.

Andy Hollister stared at his wife, wondering what in the hell had ever possessed him to marry her. She was clingy, insecure, demanding, and could turn ugly in a heartbeat. She was turning ugly now, screaming that he spent more time with his sister than he did with her. Amy called her *Gimmee,* an apt name, since the only thing that made her happy was a charge card and a full tank of gas.

He was so wired up he didn't give a damn what he said. "You know what, Jill, I don't care anymore. I'm leaving. Do whatever the hell you want. Take the house, take your car, and you can have the furniture, too. I'll go stay with Amy. You're going to have to get a job, though, because the minute I walk out of this house, the bills you run up from here on in are yours. Tell your lawyer to see my lawyer, who, by the way, is Pete Danson. It's time you got off that skinny ass of yours and did something worthwhile with your life. Staying in bed till noon, watching soap operas and talking to your mother for hours on the phone every day is not a healthy lifestyle. Don't tell me it isn't true. Amy told me she's stopped by during the day and that's what she's seen you do. That means I will no longer be supporting that lazy mother of yours, too." This last was called over his shoulder as he made his way to the second floor, where he started throwing things into suitcases.

"You're leaving!" Jill cried, following him. "You can't leave me. My mother doesn't believe in divorce. I don't believe in divorce. Unpack those bags right now, Andrew Hollister. This is all your sister's fault. Damn it, Andy, why can't you see how she's ruining our marriage."

"What part of, 'I'm leaving and will stay with Amy,' didn't you understand? I've had it. Let me make it even plainer to you. I no longer want to be married to you *and* your mother. Three's a crowd."

"Make that four, Andy Hollister. Your sister is more involved in this marriage than I am." She clawed at him, her silver jewelry, which wasn't paid for yet, clanging on her arms. He shook her off and stormed out of the house. He could hear her sobbing and screaming as she threw things against the windows. One of them shattered. He shrugged. Light-headed with relief, he headed for his sister's house.

Ten minutes later, Amy got off the porch swing and walked over to the steps. "Did you forget something, Andy?"

"Nope. I just got back my life. I left *Gimmee*. Can I stay here with you till I find an apartment?"

"Sure. The guest room is more or less yours anyway. What happened?"

"Same old thing. She lit into me the minute I walked in the door. Said I spent more time with you than her. It was the last straw. I blew up, she got ugly, and I left. Told her Pete was my lawyer and to have her lawyer call him. She can have the house, it's mortgaged to the hilt. I won't have to support that shiftless mother of hers anymore. That's a plus no matter how you look at it. I feel like a thousand pounds just came off my shoulders."

"Do you think you did it because you're upset about Cady? Or do you think I finally got it through that thick head of yours that Jill isn't the one for you?" His sister's voice was so speculative, yet happy-sounding, Andy stared at her.

"I'm not sure. I knew on our honeymoon I'd made a mistake. What new bride talks to her mother five times a day on her honeymoon? I stuck it out for four years. Why are you looking at me like that, Amy? You hate Jill. You said all she does is breathe air other people need to live. You said she was a noncontributor in life."

"I don't hate her. I just don't like her. She doesn't do anything, Andy. I just want to make sure you left for the right reasons. This Cady thing has us all jittery."

"Do you have any cigarettes?"

"Arnie might have some in the kitchen drawer. Let me check. Do you want a beer?"

"A triple shot of Old Grand-dad would taste good right now."

"Okay. Sit down and relax. I'll be right back."

Amy was as good as her word and was back within minutes.

"It isn't Cady coming back here that has me jittery. At least I don't think it is. I'm jittery because Boomer's coming back. Shit, Amy, he was there. If this thing gets stirred up, he might decide to open up. We were the ones who threw the rocks, not Boomer. Hell, he's going to be the new chief of police. Who are they going to believe, us or him?"

"Listen, Andy, Boomer was fiddling with the zip line. We all saw him. He could have loosened it. We don't know that he *didn't*, now do we? He's just as guilty as we are. Furthermore, they never recovered the zip line. We've talked about this a thousand times. Where is it? Who took it? I am not owning up to anything, and neither are you."

"Amy, I honest to God don't know. It all happened twenty years ago. We were just snotnosed kids back then. If we had a brain among the four of us, we would have been dangerous. Yeah, we should have told, but we didn't. We didn't mean to kill anyone. All three of us thought Cady and Jeff were dead.

"On second thought, I don't think I'm going to use Pete for my divorce. Do you ever get the feeling he doesn't like us? Like tonight. It was so obvious, I wanted to punch him out. Does he think he's better than us? What is it with him?"

"It's the guilt, Andy. We all react differently. He does what he has to do to live with it, just the way you and I do. But, to answer your question, no, Pete doesn't like either one of us."

"What do you think Jeff's parents will do when they find out Cady is back in town?"

"There isn't anything they can do legally. I'm sure they'll talk it to death. A lot of the people who lived around here back then have died off or moved away. I'm sure they'll go at it tooth and nail with their own circle of friends. Those of us who graduated together and stayed on in Indigo Valley might be interested." She sighed. "I think I would sleep a lot better if I knew one way or the other if Cady has regained her memory. How about you, Andy?"

"There's Arnie. I think I'm going to go to bed. I don't want to talk about this anymore to-night. All I want to do is sleep. I had a hell of a night. I'll get my bags. Are you sure Arnie won't mind me staying here?"

"Of course not. I'll explain things to Arnie."

"You never told him, did you?"

"My God, no. Why would I do a thing like that?"

"Because you're married, and you're sup-posed to share things with your spouse. I told Jill."

"Oh, my God, Andy! Tell me you're lying. How could you have been so stupid to do a thing like that? I swear, if I don't map out your days, you'll screw it up."

"Yeah," Andy said, going down the steps to head for his car. "Oh, my God, pretty much sums it up," he muttered.

When the screen door squeaked shut behind Andy, Arnie Chambers sat down on the swing next to his wife. "Did Andy have another fight with Jill?" he asked, putting his arms around his wife's shoulder. Amy snuggled closer.

"He walked out. He said tonight was the last straw, and he was getting a divorce. You don't mind, do you, honey?"

"Not one little bit. Family is family. Was it the same old stuff, or did something new happen?"

She should tell him. How many times she wanted to, but she just couldn't bring herself to utter the awful words. Arnie loved her with all his heart, more than she loved him. Every day of her life she tried to make up for the uneven love between the two of them. She looked at him in the yellow light from the porch lamp. At thirty-five, he was packing on weight and losing his hair. He wasn't a hunk like Pete Danson. Arnie was like a big, lovable, squishy teddy bear. She did love him in her own way. It just wasn't the bells and whistles kind of love she longed for.

She hugged him then, hoping she could somehow make up for what she was feeling. "I think you work too hard, honey. Why can't people do their taxes on time? All those extensions you have to file! I don't know how you do it. You don't charge nearly enough, Arnie."

"I charge what's fair, honey. I don't want to get rich at the expense of other people. We're doing just fine. The kids have college funds, we have everything we need and then some. We take three vacations a year. I don't think it gets any better than that."

Amy snuggled closer. "I don't deserve you."

"Let's not go there again, Amy. I love you. You love me. We both love our family. We all deserve each other."

"What would you do if you found out or someone told you I did something really terrible? Would you still love me?"

"Amy, what's wrong? Is it Andy and Jill? First of all, you aren't the type to do anything wrong. I would still love you no matter what. Does that make you feel better? Besides, we told each other everything. There are no secrets between us. We talked it all to death before we got married so that no surprises would ever pop up along the way. Our lives were open books. Now, if I ever found out you lied to me, that would be something different. You know how I feel about liars and people who try to cheat the government.

"You know what I would really like right now? A pizza with everything on it. Everything. And a nice cold beer. What do you say, Mrs. Chambers?"

Amy's heart thumped in her chest. "I think that's a sterling idea, Mr. Chambers. We'll worry about our diets tomorrow."

"Sounds like a plan to me," Arnie said, patting his protruding belly.

"I'll call in the order. You stay here and unwind. I'll bring the beer after I make the call."

"What would I do without you?"

What indeed?

Chapter 4

Cady yawned when she looked at the small digital clock on the desk. She'd slept through the night on the library floor. How could it possibly be five o'clock in the morning? She yawned again before she started to roll her shoulders, then stretched out her legs.

"It's still dark out, Atlas, but if you want to go out, I'm game. Let's do it," she said, scrambling up off the floor. "I think this is probably going to be one of those delicious spring mornings where the world and everything in it is beautiful." She opened the door for the shepherd. He turned around to make sure she was following him.

Atlas lifted his leg on two trees and four bushes before he nosed her leg to let her know he was ready to go inside. "Good boy," she said, patting him on the head. "Now, let's see about getting some breakfast before we go upstairs. I'll bet you'd like some sausage and eggs."

The kitchen was beautiful, a picture right out of *Veranda* magazine. Cady found herself smiling. It was a happy kitchen in spite of its elegance. It was also a highly functional kitchen, with every conceivable convenience, including her favorite, a built-in cappuccino machine. Back home, before going to school, she'd gotten into the habit of stopping by Starbucks for a large latte. But here, all she had to do was push a couple of buttons and she had a latte, a cappuccino, or a mocha. What a delicious luxury.

Lola didn't even know how to boil water. She must have had Mandy or a kitchen designer put it all together. Anthony might have had some input.

The focal point of the large kitchen was a huge bow window and a beat-up round table that screamed antique and character. A table that was always set with colorful place mats and matching dishes. A round yellow vase held fresh flowers, something else that Lola loved. Today the flowers were daffodils with feathery fern mixed between the long stems.

The floor was a combination of old-looking brick and heart of pine. It, too, screamed of times past. The appliances were modern, all Sub Zero, and monstrous in size. Double everything. Why? The huge butler's pantry held two freezers besides the one in the kitchen, and she knew there was a fourth one in one of the garages.

Mandy was seated at the table. Lola's major-domo, Anthony, was already at the massive Sub

Zero range cooking; tantalizing aromas wafted through the room. "We have everything this morning, Cady. *Herself* is up. She likes to test me this early in the morning. I'll ask her what she wants, and she thinks she's throwing me a curve by saying some outlandish thing. I have her number. I make *everything* in the hope she'll eat more than a bite or two. Lola has this thing about food. I guess when she was younger there wasn't enough to go around, so she went hungry a lot of the time. Right now all four freezers are full. I donate it all to the homeless shelter at least once a month, then buy a new supply and start all over again. Let's just keep this our little secret, okay?

"Lola has always been a nester of sorts. You'd never know that, with her being such a famous star and all. Frugal, too. She saw early on how unkind Hollywood could be to aging actors and actresses. She didn't want that to happen to her, so she made sure to save for her old age from the start."

Cady nodded to show she understood. "Do you have blueberry waffles this morning?"

"I do. And I have sausage and bacon for Atlas and some beautiful scrambled eggs warming here in the oven. Sit down, and I'll get it all ready. Help yourself to the coffee. There's fresh melon in the fridge, all cut up."

"It's such a waste of money. I didn't mean that the way it sounded," Cady said hastily.

"I know what you meant. All of Lola's husbands left her handsome sums of money that she invested wisely. I think she saved every penny *she* ever earned. Like I said, she was always frugal, and yet she lived extremely well. Like Lola said, a woman's worst fear is that someday she might be homeless and hungry. Now she never said this, and it's just my opinion, but I think she always had the fear in the back of her mind that somehow, some way, her son would snatch everything away and say she was incompetent or something like that. Don't take offense at that, Cady. But those are controllable fears, and on top of that she has Mandy and me. Now, she has you. I think it's all working out the way she wants it to. At least I hope so. You never went to bed, did you?" Anthony said, switching the subject.

"No, I didn't. Time got away from me. I had no idea there were so many scrapbooks. I only got through the early ones, which took Lola up to her third marriage. I read the one Mandy kept on my father, and I just finished going through my own. It's all pretty mind-boggling. It didn't jar any memories, though. Maybe I need to commit the contents to memory or something like that. Ohhh, these waffles look delicious. I always get the frozen ones in a box."

Mandy rolled her eyes. "The morning paper is on the table. I'm going upstairs to see what *Herself* is going to want for breakfast. There are more sausages and eggs in the warmer if Atlas is still hungry. Turn to the front page of the Lifestyle section. Tell me what you think." She winked at Anthony before she left the kitchen.

Cady picked up the morning paper and leafed through the pages until she came to the Lifestyle section. She stared down at a picture on the front page. The man was tall, with dark curly hair. He looked pressed and creased. A meticulous dresser. He could have posed for *Town and Country*. Cady peered closer at the picture. He looked to be self-assured, comfortable in his own skin. She just knew he hated his curly hair. Men always hated curly hair and women would kill for it. "Whoever he is, he's certainly good-looking. Is he a friend of yours?"

"No. He was a friend of yours. Don't you recognize him?" Anthony said, peering over her shoulder.

"No. Should I?" Cady squinted to see the fine print under the picture. "Who's Maxwell Ward?"

"You knew him as Boomer Ward. He's going to be Indigo Valley's new police chief. They've been running his picture in the paper every day for a week now. I guess they're doing it to acquaint the people with the new chief. I expect you to eat every bit of that fine breakfast I made for you."

Cady didn't start to shake until she heard the kitchen door close behind Mandy. She picked up her fork, but her hand was trembling so badly she had to put it down on the table.

Boomer Ward. Jeff King's best friend. What a coincidence that he was returning to Indigo Valley at the same time she was. Her fire-and-brimstone-spouting father would probably call it divine intervention or something equally silly.

She struggled with her memory. Did she ever know that Boomer's name was Maxwell? She didn't think so. She wondered what they called him now that he was an adult? Probably Max or perhaps Mac. Did it even matter?

Cady looked down at her plate. The waffles had gone cold. She scraped them onto Atlas's dish. The shepherd ignored them.

Had Boomer been at the pond that awful day? The newspaper articles she'd read last night hadn't mentioned him. That was strange because Jeff and Boomer had always been together. How awful he must have felt when Jeff died. Boomer had never been as mean-spirited as Jeff. And now he was going to be the town's new police chief. Was it an omen of some kind?

She reached for her coffee cup, relieved to see that her hand was now steady. Would she undergo these same strange, fearful feelings when she met up with Pete Danson and the Hollister twins for the first time?

Time for a shower and maybe an hour or two of sleep. She needed to be fresh and alert when Lola did her interview with the local paper. She hated the idea of being put on display.

But, if Lola wanted her to do it, she would.

"Let's go, Atlas," she said, heading upstairs.

The shepherd uncurled himself and was on his feet the moment Cady spoke. He walked ahead of her and up the back staircase to the second floor.

At the top of the stairs, Atlas turned to look at his mistress as though unsure where he should go. "It's okay. Go see Lola. I'm going to take a shower and lie down." The shepherd obediently trotted down the hall to Lola's room.

When she closed her eyes, she promised herself not to fall asleep. All she needed was ten minutes of quiet to give the aspirin time to work. She snuggled her head into the pillow and found the most comfortable spot. There was nothing like the feel of a silk pillowcase next to your cheek. The scent of freshly mowed grass wafted in through the French doors. Her last thought before she slipped away was that this was what heaven must be like.

The dream when it came was more frightening than ever before. The fear was choking off her air supply as she struggled to find a hiding place and still not make a sound. How was that going to be possible, she wondered as she gasped to take in air?

She saw them creeping up like brush rats to spy on her friends. She hugged the ground, her hand clamped over her mouth as she prayed she wouldn't have to sneeze or cough. "Don't let them see me, please don't let them see me," she prayed, making no sound as she mouthed the words.

They were belly-whopping through the tall grass waiting for Andy to run around the side of the pond, then up to the hill. She needed to warn Andy, but if she did that, they would know where she was hiding. Jeff King was meaner than a junkyard dog. She risked raising her head to peek out through the brush. Andy was almost to the top of the hill, almost to the Judas tree.

She knew what she had to do, and she did it. She was up on her feet, shrieking Andy's name, telling him to run. She whirled around and lost her footing, sliding down the embankment just as Andy slid down to flat ground. He reached for her arm, and together they ran around the pond to where Pete and Amy were waiting.

Her heart pounding in her chest, Cady turned around and shouted at the top of her lungs. "You're just a big fat jerk, Jeff King! You're so fat your pants fall down when you run!" She continued to taunt the meaner of the two older boys.

"Yeah," Andy flung back.

Rocks and chunks of wood sailed through the air.

"C'mon, c'mon, we have to get out of here," Pete Danson shouted. "Run, run! Boomer's on the zip line! Can't you go any faster, Cady?"

"I can hardly breathe," Cady panted. "Go to the cave. Hurry!"

They were silent as they huddled together until they were sure their tormentors were gone.

"Let's fix the zip line so the next time they go down it they get a good dunking in the pond. If we come here early tomorrow morning, we can do it, then come back later and let them pretend to catch us. Amy, bring your camera and take their pictures when they drop into the pond. All we have to do is loosen the twist tie on the trunk of the tree at the bottom. We'll do it the minute one or the other starts down the line," Pete whispered, excitement ringing in his voice.

"He's so fat he'll go straight to the bottom," Andy said.

"Does Jeff know how to swim?" Amy asked.

"Who cares. Boomer will save him," Pete said.

"Are you with us, Cady?"

"Yeah. I'd like to see him flopping around in the water."

"Good. Let's meet back here at nine o'clock tomorrow morning. We need to split up now in case they're lying in wait somewhere. I had to walk here. Jeff busted up my bike the last time we were here."

"I'll ride you on my handlebars, Pete. We got all kinds of junk in our garage. Bring your bike over, and maybe we can fix it up. We can always go to the junkyard for parts if we don't have what you need. Hey, here's an idea. If you can sneak out tonight, we can go over to Jeff's house, and snatch his bike and hide it," Andy said.

"Wait! Wait! I just had a better idea. Let's snatch his bike and send it halfway down the zip line. He'll have to go down the line to get it, and that's when we let it go, and he and the bike both go in the water. The bike will go straight to the bottom." The same excitement that was in Pete's voice now rang in Andy's. His face turned red with the imagined outcome. "You guys with me on this one?"

"Yeah," Amy, Cady, and Pete chorused.

"His parents are rich. They'll just buy him another one," Cady said.

"Yeah, but it won't be *that* one. He loves that bike. He'll know we're smarter than he is. He knows we'll tell everyone. Amy will have the pictures to prove it."

Cady and Amy watched as Andy pedaled off. "I have thirty cents. Want to get a cherry Popsicle at Dementos?"

"Where'd you get thirty cents?" Cady asked, banging at her kickstand.

"I snitched it out of Mom's purse." At Cady's stunned expression, Amy said, "I just took half of my allowance early, that's all. It's not the same as stealing, Cady."

"Oh, okay. Sure, a cherry Popsicle will be great."

They were halfway home, their mouths cherry red, their hands a sticky mess, when Jeff

King and Boomer Ward popped out of the bushes and blocked the sidewalk. Both girls skidded to a stop, their feet firmly planted on the ground.

Cady could feel the fear building up in her stomach. What would the two bullies do to them? Knock them off their bikes? Bust up their bikes? Her father would strangle her if her bike got ruined. She looked at Jeff King, then at Boomer Ward. "Don't you two have anything else to do but pick on girls?" she shouted.

"Shut up, Cady Jordan. I'm gonna cut that pigtail right off your head, then I'm gonna hang it on my bike. There ain't nothing you can do about it either, so shut up!"

"Knock it off, Jeff. You said we were just going to scare them. You didn't say anything about cutting off her hair. Her father will put a spell or something on you. I'm going home," Boomer shouted.

"Scaredy cat!" Amy yelled.

"Who you calling a scaredy cat, Amy Hollister?" Jeff blustered as he hitched up his pants.

Cady put her feet on the pedals of her bike and moved backward and then forward, straight into Jeff King's fat stomach. He toppled over as Amy barreled ahead. Cady could hear Boomer Ward laughing his head off.

Jeff caught up with her a block away, yanking her off her bike. He reached down for her and jerked her to her feet. Her heart pumping in her chest, Cady tried to kick out, but Jeff held her in a viselike grip. "You think you're smart, don't you? Well, you're dumber than dog shit. So there."

She saw the pocketknife at the same time she saw Boomer Ward.

"Don't do it, Jeff," he said, trying to knock the pocketknife out of Jeff's hand. "Stop being so mean. She's just a little kid, leave her alone." Jeff elbowed Boomer's arm out of the way and sliced at the pigtail that hung down Cady's back. He laughed so hard he almost choked.

Cady, her eyes full of tears, lashed out, knocking Jeff off-balance. He fell to the ground, still laughing. She kicked him again and again, but he wouldn't stop laughing. Winded, she got on her bike and pedaled off, tears streaming down her cheeks until she caught up with Amy.

"Why didn't you help me?" she cried. "My mother is going to kill me. Now I won't be able to go to the grove tomorrow. I would have helped you. I hate you, Amy Hollister! I hate you!"

Cady sat up in bed, her body drenched with sweat. She swung her legs over the side of the bed. The dream was so real, so vivid. Maybe that was because the pigtail incident was just the way it had happened a long time ago.

Cady dropped her head into her hands. Why was it she remembered something like that and didn't remember the day Jeff King had died?

Pictures.

Something flashed in her head, but she

couldn't catch the thought.

Her father had whipped her rear end good that day over her mother's protests, but she hadn't been grounded the way she'd feared. She'd gone back to the grove the next day and watched as Pete and Andy sent Jeff's bike halfway down the zip line. Jeff had been as good as his word and tied her pigtail to his handlebars. Pete had given it back to her.

She'd stood on the sidelines that day, next to Amy, while the boys rigged the line. She watched as Amy snapped her pictures, pictures she showed to all the kids in the neighborhood.

Pictures! Amy would have taken pictures that day. But the papers said they weren't there when the accident happened. That had to mean there were no pictures. She would never have gone to the grove alone. Never.

Unless something happened to *make* her go alone.

After the splashdown with Jeff's bike she still went back to the grove, but she was no longer Amy's best friend. She'd paired off with Pete, and the Hollister twins had hung together.

Maybe Lola was right, and it was time to visit with her old friends.

Pictures didn't lie.

People lied.

Mandy poked her head in the door. "Hurry, Cady, the reporter from the *Sentinel* is due to arrive. What's wrong?"

"Nothing's wrong, Mandy. I took a nap and had a bad dream. I'm fine. I just need ten minutes. Is Lola ready?"

"She's been ready. The interview is going to be in the music room. Lola thinks it will be a perfect backdrop. Her fifth husband was a musician. She really liked him and his hippie ways. She wants me to serve cucumber sandwiches and green tea. Don't ask." She smiled as Cady raised an eyebrow.

"Atlas is with her. By the way, he's sporting a jeweled collar. The fifth husband gave Lola a tiara that she traded in for a jeweled choker, but she said it didn't do anything for her so now it belongs to Atlas. He seems to like it."

"Oh," was all Cady could think of to say.

Cady looked in her closet and groaned. Her clothes were so *schoolmarmish*. There wasn't a bright color anywhere to be seen. There was nothing befitting this beautiful spring day, nor were there any summery clothes hanging in the closet. Clothes had never been a priority with her until she arrived at her grandmother's and Lola had chastised her for looking and dressing like a drab, brown mouse. Obviously, she needed to go on a shopping trip soon. She ended up choosing a beige safari skirt with matching blouse.

Instead of pulling her honey-colored hair back into a ponytail, she swirled and twirled it until she had a style she knew Lola would approve of. A glance in the mirror told her she looked downright dowdy. She made a promise to herself to go shopping in the morning.

Mandy poked her head in the door a second time. She shook her head. "No, no, no! Wait right here." She was back within minutes, holding an emerald-colored silk scarf that she tied around Cady's waist as a belt. "The fringe is just the right touch. Now, put on these emerald earrings and fasten this emerald comb in your hair. Now you look carelessly elegant. Lola will approve." Cady sighed with relief.

Cady walked into the music room to see Lola sitting in a thronelike chair, her rainbow-colored caftan spread out around her. *To cover her thinness,* Cady thought. A matching turban covered her thin hair and was so tight she knew it was a Hollywood trick to pull her skin tighter. She wondered if Lola would be able to move her jaw to talk. "You look beautiful, Lola."

"That's exactly what you were supposed to say, sweetie. I forgive you for the lie. My husband would have loved this room." Lola pointed to the Steinway. "He could bring me to tears with the way he played. He could have been a concert pianist, but he liked jazz and rock and roll. He didn't like the classics, said they were boring. I think Elvis stole his moves. Lord, how I lusted after that man. I made him a peach pie once. I had never made a pie in my life, but I had a cookbook. It was rather chewy as I recall. He thought me making that pie was the most wonderful thing in the world. The next day he bought me a jeweled tiara. It made all the newspapers because it was outrageously expensive. There aren't too many places where you can wear a diamond tiara, so I took it to a jeweler and had him make me a choker. After he died, of course. I wore the tiara to his funeral. He would have liked that. It looks good on Atlas, don't you think? It's insured, sweetie, so don't fret."

"I like this room," Cady said as she struggled to absorb Lola's monologue.

Lola twinkled. "Sweetie, if these walls could only talk! Desmond could play every single instrument in those glass cases. And, he had a voice like a bird. How that man could sing. He would sing sometimes when we made love, which was almost all the time. He made a deal with the studio for these two thrones. His and her thrones, he called them. When we sat in them, we were the king and queen. I don't know anyone else who has two thrones, do you? We often sat here far into the night and listened to his recordings. The man had such passion."

She's nervous, that's why she's babbling, Cady thought. "I wish I had known him."

"I wish you could have known him, too. I've been thinking a lot about when I . . . you know, go to wherever it is you go when you die, and I was wondering if all my husbands will line up and expect me to pick one of them. The line will be *really* long if all my other . . . *paramours* are there, too. What would you do, Cady?"

She was serious. "How many paramours were there, Lola?"

"Several dozen. Each one was more wonderful than the other. I'll never be able to decide."

"In that case, you might have to flip a coin," Cady said with a straight face. "Or you could put all the names into a hat and pick one . . . before . . . so when you get there . . ." *God, did I just say that?*

"Now why didn't I think of that. I have just the right coin, too. Tyler gave it to me on our first anniversary. Maybe it wouldn't be right to take that one with me," Lola fretted. "My second husband was a gambler and owned several casinos. That man was so lucky. Everything he touched literally turned to gold. He could buy a swamp, and the next day they'd discover oil on the property. That darling man left me so much property I couldn't keep it straight. What a love he was. He taught me how to play poker. Tyler would have loved the Casino Room I had decorated for him. It has everything — gaming tables, slot machines, the wheels, pictures of all his properties, jukeboxes. I went into the room once after it was done, but I cried so hard, I never went back in. I want all this to go in my memoirs, Cady. I think I'll do the names in the hat thing."

"You know I'll do whatever you want. I think the reporter is here. The bell just rang. Are you sure you want me and Atlas to stay?"

"I'm sure. Remember our game plan now. Just sit there and smile. I want you to smile a lot, and I want you to look confident, like you don't have a care in the world. I know you can do it, Cady."

"Yes, I can do it. Touch your turban when you've had enough, and I'll intervene."

"Child, you are just full of grand ideas today."

Cady settled in a chair off to the right so that she had a view of the doorway, where she knew Mandy was stationed. She could see her shadow in the hallway from the sun streaming through the stained-glass windows in the foyer. Mandy wouldn't let things get out of hand.

The reporter, a chubby young man who looked familiar to her, shook Lola's hand and sat down beside her. He started asking Lola questions right away. He didn't take notes but relied on a tape recorder instead. Listening to both voices drone on and on, Cady let her mind wander back to the dream she'd had earlier.

Over the years she'd asked herself hundreds of times why she'd gone to the grove alone the day of the accident and had never come up with an answer. Why weren't the twins there, and where was Pete Danson that day? Maybe she was late getting there, and they got tired of waiting for her and left. The paper said they hadn't been there at all that day, though. According to the papers, Boomer wasn't there either. Jeff King never went anywhere without Boomer at his side. He didn't have the guts to be a bully when he was alone. The funny thing was, Boomer never did anything. He was just there.

Cady jerked to attention when she heard her name mentioned. She sat up straighter in the chair when she heard Lola say, "Yes, my granddaughter is the one who is going to write my memoirs. Her name is Cadwell Jordan. Her parents named her after me. We call her Cady. It was the studio who changed my name from Jordan to Jor Dan. They thought it was more glamorous-sounding. I don't know who it was who picked the name Lola. One minute I was Cadwell Jordan, just like Cady here, and the next minute I was Lola Jor Dan.

"There is so much interest in my memoirs, there's talk of a movie. It's really very exciting to know a movie is going to be made of your life.

"Of course my memoirs will name names, and of course it will give explicit details; and let me tell you, they are delicious. It will be my life right up to the present. It will even take in that nasty, ugly episode at the Judas Grove that involved my granddaughter. I really don't want to go into all the details of that tragic event. You can research it when you get back to your paper. Cady and I are going to get to the bottom of it all. Of course you can print that. In fact, I insist you print it. It will be in the movie, too, because as I said, it will go right up to the present.

"Cady, sweetie, come here and meet this nice young man."

Cady fixed a smile on her face as she offered her hand to the chubby reporter. He looked familiar. She said so.

"I was a year ahead of you in school. Larry Denville. I work out with Pete Danson at the gym every day. It doesn't look like it right now, but I'm working on it," he said, patting his stomach. "Mac Ward is coming back to Indigo Valley, too. I've been reporting on it all week now. I imagine you'll want to be renewing old friendships if you haven't already."

"Why would you think that, Larry?" Cady said.

Lola smirked.

The reporter looked uncomfortable. "No reason. I just remember how it was when we were kids. Everyone had a little clique. I was a nerd back then, so I didn't belong to any of those little groups. So, does that mean you won't be looking up your old friends?"

"What that means, Mr. Denville, is this, my granddaughter is going to be kept very busy helping me with my memoirs and trying to solve that nasty business that left her partially paralyzed for three years. Plus she's working on her dissertation. The mind is a wonderful thing, isn't it? Now, if you'll excuse me, I have another pressing engagement. My secretary will give you a promotional kit we keep on hand. It's current. Feel free to use any of the material that's in it."

He was dismissed, and he knew it. Mandy swooped in with a folder in her hand. Within seconds the reporter was out the door and out of the house.

"How'd I do, ladies?" Lola cackled.

"You didn't miss a beat, Lola. It was perfect. No pun intended, but I do think you set the stage for future events. How about a good stiff drink? I'll dump these cucumber sandwiches and bring us some homemade pizza."

"Put lots of pepperoni on mine," Lola said.

"Garlic and onions on mine," Cady said.

"What about Atlas?" Mandy asked.

"Tomato sauce isn't good for dogs. Just bring him some dog biscuits."

"I'm thinking that young man, who by the way looks like a pumpkin, is going to print his interview verbatim. Mark my words. I think it's safe to say we're on a roll now, sweetie. The paper is giving me the entire front page of the Lifestyle section on Sunday. *Everyone* reads the Sunday paper. Monday morning should prove interesting."

Cady laughed.

Mandy demanded to know what was so funny as she set down the heavy tray she was holding. She dropped to the floor, where Cady was sitting next to Atlas. "You're supposed to drink beer with pizza," she grumbled.

Cady handed Atlas a dog biscuit. He looked at it, then at Cady and Lola. He walked away, his tail swishing indignantly.

"That dog of yours has turned into a gourmet, Cady."

Cady chomped down on her slice of pizza, wondering if Lola was going to eat anything. Cady watched as Lola devoured a slice that had ten circles of pepperoni on it.

"I think that's the best pizza I ever ate," Lola proclaimed. "When I finish this drink, I'm going to take a nap. What are you going to do, Cady?"

"I'm going to work on the scrapbooks. Then again, I might go into town to do some shopping. You keep telling me my wardrobe needs to be updated."

Lola looked horrified. "You're going to buy *off the rack?* I already have a call in to my designer, Danielle. She arrives on Monday with her seamstresses. By the end of the week, my dear, you will have a wardrobe like no other. What do you think, Mandy, should we put in a call to Mona to come, too? Cady needs a fashionable hairdo. Yes, yes, let's do that. I want you looking like a force to be reckoned with when this town sees you for the first time."

In spite of herself, Cady felt excited at the prospect.

Chapter 5

Pete Danson hung up the phone, a frown on his face. His Saturday meeting with Lola Jor Dan had just been canceled and rescheduled for Monday afternoon. He continued to frown as he recalled the curt words of the secretary named Amanda. He told himself the rescheduled appointment didn't mean the movie star wanted to cancel his legal services. Damn, he would hate to lose the robust yearly retainer Ken said came with representing Lola Jor Dan.

He told himself that a rescheduled appointment wasn't anything to worry about. People hated seeing a lawyer almost as much as they hated going to the dentist. He hoped he wasn't kidding himself.

The day loomed ahead of him. Several weeks ago he'd made a date to spend the day with a luscious beauty who said she would drive up from Pittsburgh, spend the night, and return early Sunday morning. He'd canceled the date when the request came in to meet with the famous Lola Jor Dan. He wondered if it was too late to call the long-legged Mariah. Yeah, it was too late.

It wasn't that he had nothing to do. He had a brief to write, his gutters needed to be cleaned out, and he had plans to blacktop his driveway. Then there was the gym and his Saturday afternoon visit to see his mother.

Nothing held his interest, though.

He wondered what would happen if he called the Jor Dan estate and asked to speak to Cady. Maybe he could invite her to lunch or dinner. Old friends, that kind of thing. He knew in his gut Amy and Andy hadn't called her. If they had, they would have let him know immediately.

Pete stared out the window. It was raining, and he couldn't see across the yard because of the low-lying fog. That took care of his driveway and the gutters. If the fog continued, there would be no point to visiting his mother because she would refuse to leave her room, saying opposing alien forces created the fog in order to vaporize anyone who left the security of their room. Hopefully the weather would be better, and he would be able to go tomorrow and take her a new supply of pellets for the air gun that she was never without. He wished there was something he could do for his mother, but he'd exhausted every medical option open to him. The last doctor had patted him on his shoulder, and said, "Son, there are some things medical science can't cure or help. Your mother is happy in her own little world. Accept it."

That left the brief, the gym, and the call to Cady. He had two weeks to work on the brief. That narrowed his options to the gym and Cady. "I don't think I'm ready for Cady Jordan today," he muttered.

"I'm going to the gym, Annie." He shouted to be heard over the roar of the vacuum cleaner. "Don't worry about lunch. I'll pick something up or eat with some of the guys. Take messages."

The first person he saw when he entered the gym was Larry Denville, sweating, huffing, and puffing as he chugged along at 3.5 on the treadmill. He waved. Larry took his deathlike grip off the bar and waved. Pete winced when he saw the chunky young man almost fall off. There was out of shape and then there was *out of shape*. He felt proud of himself, though, for getting Larry to give up his jelly donuts and all the other fast-food junk he consumed on a daily basis and join the gym. The only problem was, the reporter wanted instant gratification.

Pete went straight to the weights, adjusted them, and positioned himself on the bench.

"Hey, Pete, I saw a friend of yours yesterday. She's turned into a real looker," the pudgy newsman gurgled as he tried to wipe the sweat dripping down his face onto his sleeve without taking his hands off the bars.

"Oh, yeah, who's that?"

Pete almost dropped the barbell when he heard Larry say, "Cady Jordan." He struggled to take a deep breath. He was supposed to say something. "A looker, huh?"

"Yeah. I finally snagged an interview with Lola Jor Dan that I've been wanting to get for years. We're giving it the whole front page of the Lifestyle section tomorrow. She *never* gives interviews. This one just dropped into my lap. She called me. Do you believe that? Good interview if I do say so," Larry continued, hopping off the treadmill and collapsing on the floor. He fanned his beet-red face. "Get this," he gasped. "Lola said they're going to get to the bottom of that tragic, ugly business that happened years ago in the Judas Grove. Those are her exact words. Cady doesn't look anything like her grandmother, but she's a knockout. Have you seen her yet?"

"Nope."

"Uh-oh, look who's here," Larry said, rolling over and sitting up. "It's Boomer, and he looks like he's set to work out. Jesussss, he looks like Arnold Schwarzenegger."

His body slick with sweat, Pete settled the barbell in its rack and looked around. The gym was filling up. There could have been a hundred people in the room, and he would have been able to pick out Boomer Ward at a glance. The picture in the paper hadn't done him justice. With a gun strapped to his waist and his dog at his side, the Indigo Valley native would be a force to be reckoned with.

"Take it easy, sport. It took you a long time

to get that gut, so don't expect twenty minutes on a treadmill to make it go away. Watch your diet and take it slow. You should think about hiring a personal trainer."

"Sounds like a good idea. Hey, let me know how you like my story in tomorrow's paper."

"Will do."

Pete took a deep breath as he approached Boomer Ward, who was grinding away on a stair-stepper.

"Pete Danson," he said, holding out his hand. "What do I call you? Boomer, Chief, what?"

"Mac will do it. How are you, Pete? If you're more comfortable with Boomer, that's okay, too. It's been, what, twenty years?" he said, crushing Pete's hand.

"About that. Saw the article about you in the *Sentinel*. Congratulations. It's turning into Old Home Week around here. I just heard Cady Jordan has moved back here, too."

Mac hopped off the stair-stepper. "No kidding."

"No kidding," Pete said. "Larry Denville, the same guy that did your write-up, interviewed Lola Jor Dan, and the article is going to be in the paper tomorrow. Pick up a copy. She said they're going to get to the bottom of that nasty, ugly business that happened in the Judas Grove a long time ago."

"Did she now? How are they planning on doing that? I'll be sure to pick it up tomorrow."

"I don't have a clue. Guess it's one of those stay tuned kind of things. You here for good now?" Pete asked.

"Got in last night. I found an apartment the last time I was here. My stuff will arrive tomorrow. What are you doing these days, Pete?"

"I'm a lawyer. Andy has his own insurance business. Amy is a wife and mother. She married Arnie Chambers. He crunches numbers."

"I'll look forward to seeing everyone again," Mac said.

"What made you come back to Indigo Valley, Boomer?" He would always be Boomer to him.

Mac laughed. "They made me an offer I couldn't refuse. I only agreed to a year. I know how small-town politics work. I figure I'll know in a year if I want to stay here permanently. Nice seeing you again, Pete."

"Yeah, you too."

Pete waved him off. "Yeah, sure," he said, anything but. He licked at his dry lips as he moved forward, knowing his workout was over. Now what the hell was he supposed to do with the rest of the day? Call Cady Jordan. Instead of heading home, he drove to a drive-through fast-food joint and ordered two chili dogs and a giant root beer, which he wolfed down.

Memories, depending on the circumstances, could be either wonderful or terrible. Sometimes tragic.

He drove aimlessly once he left the Super Dog Haven stand, the windshield wipers slapping back and forth. He passed the Super Wal-Mart where Annie loved to browse, a Japanese hibachi-style restaurant, and a new business called Ragtag Outfitters.

This end of town had undergone a transformation during the past several years, with new stores, new medium-priced housing developments, three banks, two churches, and numerous restaurants. He rarely came here and wasn't sure why. No, that was a lie. He knew why. This part of town was where the Judas tree stood high above Indigo Pond.

It wasn't a grove of Judas trees, it never had been. It was more like a grove of oaks and maples. He struggled with his memory to remember why it was called the Judas Grove, but couldn't come up with anything. Maybe it was the young saplings that never seemed to grow. He shrugged because, in the scheme of things, it really didn't matter. His mother always called it the way station for those waiting to go to Pluto. Everyone else just called it the Judas Grove. One tree a grove does not make.

He could see it now through the rain, high on the hill, its pinky-purple buds standing out like beacons. The Judas tree was a late bloomer, and the only thing that looked familiar. Now, bright orange plastic fencing circled the whole grove. Glaring red-and-white signs with huge letters said trespassers would be prosecuted. He wondered when the town fathers had the area cordoned off like this?

Pete climbed out of his car and was drenched within minutes. Once this place had been like a magic fairyland to four lonely little kids. They'd kept the wild grass cropped to make it easy to run through. Where was the beautiful green moss that had felt so wonderful on their bare feet?

He pulled at the orange mesh fencing and stepped over it. The level of water in the pond was down and looked muddy and dirty. They'd skipped stones in the pond and waded in around the edges, always mindful that they didn't know how deep it was. Slipping and sliding, his sneakers squishing in the wet mud, Pete made his way to the far side of the pond.

Damn, where was it? His gaze raked the old trees as he searched for some sign of the club-house they'd built with stolen boards and nails. It was all gone. He cursed loudly and ripely. No, no, there was a board. One board remained. They must have had some really big nails back then for one lonely board to survive twenty years of the elements. One lone board hanging drunkenly from one of the thick oak branches. He looked around to see if there were any of the other boards lying around. He squished his way around the base of the tree but couldn't find even a splinter from the old clubhouse.

Something drew his gaze up to the Judas tree. Twenty years ago the four of them had carved their initials in the trunk. Were they still there, or had they faded with time?

God, how he'd loved this place. Secretly, he'd always called it Paradise. At least for him. He thought Cady felt the same way. For Amy and Andy it was just a place to play and have fun. He didn't think, even now, all these years later, that Jeff King and Boomer felt anything in particular about this grassy, green grove with the beautiful, old trees.

His eyes burned with his memories. He jammed his hands into the pockets of his sweats and made his way up the hill, to where the Judas tree stood solitary and watchful. There had always been something special about the Judas tree. It was protective and spooky at the same time. One lone tree, not particularly big, standing off by itself, its reflection glaring up at him from the pond. How was that possible? It was raining. He could feel himself start to shiver.

The tree was older, fuller. He wished he could remember the legend that went with the tree. Maybe Annie would know.

"Maybe it's time I found out," he said, picking a bud that was about to bloom. It smelled so sweet he regretted taking it. Holding the flower bud, he walked to the edge of the cliff and let it go. It was only a thirty-foot drop to the pond below, but the blossom seemed to take forever before touching the water.

Pete stared into the water as if mesmerized. He saw the flower and he saw . . . something else . . . his reflection. He wiped at his eyes, thinking he was imagining things. When he looked again, it was still there. Impossible, he told himself, backing up a step. It was raining; the pond's surface wasn't still.

He turned away, a shiver chasing down his spine.

He looked for the initials on the tree trunk. He smiled when he saw them. P.D. Then underneath his initials were A.H. and A.H. The twins. Red-hot anger roared through his veins when he saw that someone had X'd out Cady's initials. Who would do that? He hadn't done it, so who did that leave? Jeff? No, Jeff was dead. Well, maybe Jeff had done it before the accident, and he'd just never seen it. Boomer then. Amy or Andy? Was it done before or after the tragedy?

He tried to remember what they'd done that summer after the accident. He'd drifted away from the twins and stayed close to home. Boomer had gone away somewhere and hadn't come back until school started in September. What did Amy and Andy do that summer? To his knowledge, nothing. Together, they would have had the guts to sneak back to the grove. Did they hate Cady? Did Boomer hate her? He knew Jeff King had hated her but didn't know why.

Pete closed his eyes as the rain beat down on him. He was ten years old again, his heart thumping in his chest as he watched Cady inch out to the zip line, Jeff King behind her. Andy was the first one to throw a rock. Amy laid her camera down on the mossy bank and joined her brother by picking up a rock. He'd done the same thing. His eyes snapped open. He didn't want to relive the last part of that particular vision.

Did Amy take pictures that day or not? He'd asked her at the Fourth of July town picnic that summer, but she'd whispered that she didn't want to take them to the drugstore because then everyone would know they'd been there that day. She'd said when she saved up enough money from her allowance she would send them away because if you did that, the company sent you a free roll of film. He'd never asked her again.

Pete ran his fingers along the grooves of his initials, wishing the sun was shining and that he was a kid again. He climbed into his car, staring up at the Judas tree. His heart felt heavy in his chest as he realized, one way or another, they were all Judases. The only difference between them and Judas Iscariot was they didn't have thirty pieces of silver to show for what they had done.

Pete swung out onto the highway to head for home. He did a double take as he sailed through the yellow light at the Super Wal-Mart. He saw Boomer Ward seated behind the wheel of a dark green Range Rover headed in the opposite direction. Where was he going? At the gym, he'd looked like he was prepared to work out for a few hours. Maybe he rented a house or an apartment close by. He shivered in his wet clothes, wondering if Boomer was going to the Judas Grove.

Mac Ward climbed out of the Range Rover, his face set in grim lines. He waited for his dog Ozzie to leap to the ground.

He alternated between hating this place and loving it. Today he hated it. Yet, each time he came back to Indigo Valley to see his parents, he came here. Hell, this place and the events that took place here twenty years ago were the reason he was a cop today.

He looked around. If he closed his eyes, he could see Amy, Andy, and Jeff whooping and hollering. It was all so long ago, and yet it seemed like yesterday. The police dog inched closer, sensing his master's distress. Mac reached down to scratch the animal behind his ears before he trudged through the mud over to the Judas tree. He clenched his teeth when he remembered how badly he'd wanted to carve his initials into the tree next to the others. Jeff had sensed it and yanked him away, calling him a *retard* for wanting to associate with ten-year-olds. Jesus, how he had hated Jeff King.

Mac sucked in his breath when he saw how Cady Jordan's initials had been gouged out of the bark. Jeff must have gone back alone to do that. The others probably thought *he* had something to do with it. Hell, why wouldn't they? Back then he'd been Jeff's shadow.

He looked up at the Judas tree's delicate buds being pelted with the rain. He thought it the prettiest tree he'd ever seen.

He smiled when he thought about that last year. The four of them had been a gutsy bunch of little kids. He'd envied them their simple fun and the tree house, and had hungered to be part of it but didn't know how. Maybe it had something to do with Jeff and how big he'd been back then. How many times he'd gone to the grove *without* Jeff to lie in the brush and watch them play Robin Hood or cops and robbers. They'd picnic by the pond, climb into the tree house, and laugh and laugh. They played checkers and Old Maid. He knew this because after they left, he'd climb up to their clubhouse and play by himself. Once Jeff King had almost caught him.

Jeff King. He was a spoiled brat and a bully. He didn't have a single friend back then. He knew it, too. He'd hated him. Jeff knew that, too, and had just laughed. So, he'd been tarred with the same brush as Jeff.

It all happened the year he and Jeff turned eleven. Until that winter he'd had a wonderful childhood. New hockey skates had been under the Christmas tree that year, and he couldn't wait to try them out. Every day he prayed for freezing temperatures, so the pond would freeze. His mother warned him that the ice wasn't solid enough to skate on because while it was cold, it wasn't cold enough to freeze the ice. Of course he hadn't listened. He'd gone ice-skating on the pond at the Judas Grove with his new skates. Jeff had been on the pond that day, too. He'd whirled and twirled around twice before the ice cracked and his right leg went through. He'd panicked, but it was Jeff who calmed him down, told him not to move and that he'd get him out. The other kids had run home, scared out of their wits. Jeff had seemed so knowledgeable, so matter-of-fact, he lost his fear and did what he said.

Jeff had gotten a broken limb and inched it toward him, telling him to lie down flat and slide toward him. He'd done everything Jeff had told him to do and managed to reach the edge before the ice cracked all across the pond.

He'd gone home with Jeff that day. His savior had dried his clothes in the dryer and made him a cheese sandwich and a cup of hot chocolate. When he was leaving, Jeff had looked at him, and said, "You owe me now, Boomer. Bigtime. You do what I say when I say it. I saved your life, so that means I control you now."

And that was the story of Jeff King.

Maybe it was a mistake to come back to Indigo Valley. Maybe he should have stayed in Pittsburgh.

The dog at his side whined softly. "Yeah, this isn't the best place in town, Ozzie. We're both drenched. Something draws me to this place every time I come home. C'mon, boy, let's get in the car."

Ozzie climbed into the backseat and stretched out on his blanket, nestling his big head between his paws. Mac smiled as he looked into the rearview mirror. Man and his dog.

He fumbled in the console for a cigarette that he fired up. He hardly ever smoked these days, but refused to give it up entirely. There were times, like now, when he needed *something*. He leaned back and puffed away, his mind going in all directions.

He'd lied to Pete Danson. He had jumped at the offer to come back. The money had been incidental. His life, as he saw it, was in a holding pattern. How he regretted his decision that day to say nothing about the accident. He wondered if the others felt the same way.

With Cady back in town maybe things would come to a head. The article in tomorrow's paper would probably start the ball rolling. He could, if he wanted to, reopen the case and follow through. He would have to suck up the consequences. Was he prepared to do that?

The worst-case scenario was everyone's reputation would be ruined, including his own. Maybe that's what he needed in order to sleep at night. He was still young . . . thirty-three. He could start over.

Then he thought about Cady Jordan because Cady was what this was all about.

That first year after the accident had been pure hell. All anyone at school had talked about was Jeff King and little Cady Jordan, who had lost her memory and was partially paralyzed.

He'd cried the night he heard his mother tell his father that Cady was being transferred to some famous hospital in California. Then she'd said, "I never liked Jeff King, and there's more to this story than anyone knows. I'm just glad our son isn't involved in all of this."

But he had been involved in *all of this,* right up to his eyeballs.

Mac looked down at the street map of Indigo Valley lying on the passenger seat. His finger traced the route he would have to take to drive past Lola Jor Dan's palatial estate. He was, after all, the new police chief, and as such he needed to acquaint himself with where the citizens of the town lived.

BullSHIT! What he wanted was a glimpse of Cady Jordan.

It was after eleven o'clock when Mac headed for Tony's Pizza Parlor. He'd called ahead to order a large pepperoni and sausage pie and a double meatball sub for Ozzie. He'd purposely waited till then, knowing the *Sentinel* filled the newspaper containers all along Main Street at eleven o'clock. He picked up his pie, depositing it on the front seat of the Rover, before he walked over to the corner of Pepperdam and Madison. He smiled to himself when he saw Pete Danson, a pizza box in his hand and a paper in the other, head toward his car. Farther down the street he saw a woman with an identical pizza box in one hand while she dropped two quarters into the blue-and-white newspaper box. Amy Hollister Chambers?

Two down and one to go. Where was Andy Hollister?

He laughed out loud when he turned the corner onto Old Trolley Road and saw Andy Hollister heading to his car, the newspaper under his arm.

All present and accounted for. Obviously they could no more wait until Sunday to get the paper than he could.

The smile stayed on his face all the way back to his new, empty apartment.

Inside, he ripped at the cardboard box to make a plate for Ozzie while he chomped down on the delectable pizza. He read through the article, not once, not twice, but three times before his closed fist shot into the air. Little Cady Jordan was just a hair away from getting her doctorate. "Good for you, Cady," he exulted. "Good for you."

Chapter 6

Lola sat on a comfortable lounge chair on her second-floor terrace, admiring the clay pots full of tulips and daffodils Mandy had just watered. Even though it was a warm day, she was bundled into soft, fleece blankets, only her face exposed to the warm spring sunshine.

"For God's sake, Mandy, I feel like a mummy," she grumbled.

"It's better for you to feel like a mummy than it is for you to catch a chill and pneumonia. My goodness, will you look at all those bolts of cloth. How is Cady going to choose one over the other?"

"We're just here to nod approval, Mandy. Danielle has an eye, as you know, for fabrics, textures, and the person as a whole. She'll make the right choices. I want our girl to look like a million dollars. Looking good and knowing you look good gives you confidence, something she is sorely lacking. I'm having a hard time with her being so shy and withdrawn. I should have done all this ten years ago. Why did I wait so long, Mandy?"

"You waited because Cady wasn't ready. You had other more personal problems to deal with. Don't start second-guessing yourself. When you set out to fix an old wrong it's never too late. I think the new haircut is going to do wonders for Cady. I don't know if you realize this or not, Lola, but she let her hair grow as long as it is for a reason. Remember how she told us that awful boy cut off her pigtail?I know in my heart that left some kind of lasting impression on her. She had to have been traumatized by that. I think she let her hair grow because she's been trying to go back to that time to understand it all. Cutting it off now, I'm hoping, is the right thing. Her hair has a bit of a natural wave to it, so she won't have to fuss too much with it. Mona will cut and shape it, and she will be beautiful. Trust me."

Lola's eyes widened in alarm. "Maybe her hair has become her security blanket, so to speak. Perhaps we shouldn't ask her to cut it."

Mandy waved her hands in front of Lola's face. "She's too old to still have a security blanket. You said yourself, she needs to get with the program."

"I do trust you. She still can't remember a thing. I'm thinking hypnosis. What do you think, Mandy?"

"I'm thinking you need to mind your own business, Lola. Let it be Cady's decision. I have a feeling once she sees her old friends, the grove, and maybe goes to the cemetery, it is all going to trigger something and play out the way it's supposed to. I don't know anything about stuff like that, and neither do you. That means we shouldn't meddle. She wants her memory back as much as you and I want her to get it back. Trust me on that, too. Just for the record, Anthony agrees with me."

Lola knew she was outnumbered. The truth was, she knew that Anthony and Mandy were probably right. "All right. All right, I surrender. What time is that lawyer coming?"

"Two o'clock. I have everything laid out in the library. All you have to do is sit there and listen. Did you tell Cady who the lawyer is?"

"No. I was going to, but then I changed my mind. I thought for sure one of the four would have called her by now. The paper did come out Saturday night. Maybe we should arrange a little luncheon or maybe a dinner party."

"We need to mind our own business. Besides, it's a little soon for something like that. I'm glad now you didn't let that reporter take Cady's picture for the article. No sense in giving any of them the edge. I hear the elevator."

"Ta da!" Cady said, running out to the terrace and whirling around for her grandmother's benefit. "What do you think? Mona said this is the real me! This stuff in my hair is something called sun glitz. Do you like it? What do you think of the makeup? I look different, don't I? I had no idea I could look like this. My head feels so light."

Lola's face lit up with a smile. "Sweetie, you look gorgeous," Lola said, sincerity ringing in her voice. "You look ten times better than I did on my best day. Now, aren't you sorry you didn't do this sooner?"

"I'm still me on the inside, Lola. Doesn't the inside have to match the outside?"

"It will when you dress yourself in some fashionable clothes. You don't have to hide out, and you don't have to be afraid any longer. We're going to get to the bottom of everything. Take a look at all those wonderful fabrics Danielle brought. Look through them and tell me what you would like. Her French seams are flawless."

Danielle Laroux was an elfin woman with dark, brooding eyes, incredible red lips, and a hawkish nose. One ear seemed to be bigger than the other. Her smile was toothy, with gaps in between her teeth.

"Yoo-hoo," a voice trilled from the hallway.

"We're on the terrace, Danielle. Come in."

"Lola, I hope that blanket is *cashmere*. This granddaughter of yours is a beautiful young lady. I approve of the hairstyle. Now, let's see what we can do for her. Strip down to your undies, young lady, so I can take your measurements. Oh, my God!" she squawked. "JCPenney cotton underwear! White, no less. No, no, no, this will never do. You need silk, lace, gossamer-thin material. The idea is to give the illusion of nakedness and still be covered. Not to worry, I brought everything. The child is wearing *bloomers,* Lola!" Her outrage was so intense, Cady laughed.

"Women wore underwear like this in the 1800s back on the prairie. This is the twenty-first century, and we are far away from the prairie. You smell like Ivory soap. Lola, the child smells like Ivory soap! Mandy, find it and throw it out. I had no idea this job was so monumental. We need to start from scratch. Scratch, ladies." The little designer waved her arms to indicate she was prepared to take on the world if necessary where Cady was concerned.

"I think I'll leave you two for a while," Lola said. "It's past the luncheon hour, and I have an appointment soon. Mandy will bring you both some lunch. Take your time. Cady, cooperate with Danielle. I want your promise."

Cady winked at her grandmother. "I promise, *Granny.*"

"And she's wicked, too."

"Like someone else I know," Danielle said as she whipped out a tape measure.

Pete Danson winced when the heavy gates behind him closed with a loud clanging sound. He drove slowly up the winding road to the main house. His heart was beating faster than normal, and he could feel a fine beading of perspiration over his upper lip as he got out of the car. He swiped at it with the back of his hand.

He looked around while he waited for the

door to open. His new client must pay a fortune to her gardener to keep the place looking so manicured. There didn't seem to be a leaf or a blade of grass that was out of place.

The door opened. "Peter Danson to see Miss Jor Dan."

"I'm Mandy, Mr. Danson. Miss Jor Dan is waiting for you in the library. Follow me, please."

The introductions made, Pete tried not to stare. He had no idea Lola Jor Dan was so old. The pictures in yesterday's paper had been more than kind to the actress. He stretched out a long arm to grasp her hand. He shook it gently. "It's a pleasure to meet you, ma'am."

"Likewise, Mr. Danson. Would you care for some coffee or a drink?"

"No thanks."

"Have you gone over my affairs? Is everything in order? Do I need to make any changes?"

"Everything is in good shape, ma'am. I wouldn't change a thing. You can, of course, update your will if you want to. Other than that, I don't think you have anything to worry about. The market's down right now, but it will rebound, and your brokerage accounts will flourish again."

"That's good to know. Are you sure you wouldn't like some coffee or a soft drink?"

"No, ma'am, I'm fine. I would like to say I think the article the *Sentinel* did on you yesterday was very interesting. I'm intrigued with the idea of a movie. I understand Cady is back. We used to be friends a long time ago. Is she here? I'd like to say hello. I didn't know until I read the article that Cady never regained her memory of the accident. That must be horrible for her."

"Cady is here, but she's busy right now and can't join us. You should call her. I'm sure she'd love to hear from you. We're working on her memory with some very interesting doctors who are promising us a full recovery. It's all going to be in the movie. Cady is so excited about that. I am, too. That was a very tragic time in our lives, but we've moved forward. Cady is so resilient. How she was able to put those three years of agony behind her is something I will never be able to understand. It was all so . . . tragic," Lola said for the second time.

"Yes, it was a terrible thing and something I'm sure you don't want to dwell on. I guess that wraps up our business then, Miss Jor Dan. If you need me for anything, I'm just a phone call away. Tell Cady I said hello, and I'll give her a call. Perhaps she would like to have dinner with me one night. It's always nice to meet up with old friends. Mac Ward, we used to call him Boomer, is back in town, too. I ran into him over the weekend. I'm sure he'll be calling Cady, too."

"That will be nice. Cady needs to be around young people, not stuck here in the house with us old codgers. She's helping me with my memoirs and trying to finish up her dissertation, and you know how that goes. She's just a very busy young lady these days." Lola looked toward the ceiling, her expression right out of her third scene in *To the End of Time*, her first Oscar-winning role.

"I understand. There are many days when I wish for a few more hours myself. I'll see myself out. By the way, this is a lovely house. Remember now, call me any time of the day or night if you need me."

"I'll do that, Mr. Danson."

"Call me Pete."

"All right, Pete. It was nice to meet you."

After Pete left, Mandy stuck her head in the door. "Well?" she asked.

"Well nothing. He said my affairs are in good order. Asked to talk to Cady, and he let me know Boomer is in town again. It might be my imagination, but I think he was a little nervous. Maybe we should pretend we have a prowler tonight. Perhaps our new chief, who started his job today, will come by himself to check it out. Of course, we won't mention it to Cady. It might be worthwhile to send a *generous* check to the police department. Let's wait until the first of next week, after he has settled in. Address the envelope to him. Tell them it's for the K-9 division and those new cameras other police departments have in their patrol cars. The ones we were reading about last week. Tell them to allocate some to the PBA. *Generous,* Mandy. If we decide not to go with the prowler thing, this will work just as well. I would think a personal visit by way of a thank-you would be in order."

"Does your mind *ever* stop, Lola?"

"No. What did you think of him, Mandy?"

"Nice-looking young man. Good body build. It's obvious he works out. And, he's a bachelor. He's got a thriving practice, so he must be a good lawyer. I asked around in town, and nobody had a bad word to say about him. He does a lot of pro bono work, so that's in his favor. If you're asking me if Cady will like him, my answer would be, I don't know.

"When I went to the market this morning I heard that Andy Hollister and his wife have split up. He's Amy's twin. That makes for three eligible bachelors. That's if we're counting, Lola."

"It does, doesn't it?" Lola smiled. "Of course we're counting."

The weekend after the newspaper article was the talk of Indigo Valley, Cady stared into her empty closet, a look of dismay on her face. Atlas whimpered at her feet. She stepped into the closet to be sure she wasn't seeing things. No, it was empty. There wasn't even a stray sneaker or sock to be seen. She ran to the built-in dressers and yanked at the drawers. Scented drawer liners were the only thing to be seen.

Mandy stepped into the room. "Danielle's ladies will be bringing up all your new clothes in a few minutes. Lola had me pack up all your old things. She said they belong to your past, and you don't need them anymore. I didn't throw them out, Cady. I packed them all up and put them in the storage area of the attic. You can have them anytime you want. When you see all those gorgeous clothes, I don't think you'll want them, but you never know."

"Maybe just my old bathrobe. It's like an old friend."

Mandy nodded. "I left it hanging on the back of the bathroom door. I have an old robe like that myself. Lola looked everything over and gave her nod of approval. The things those ladies made for you are breathtaking. I haven't seen *Herself* this excited in a long time. Well, actually, I saw her just as excited the morning the newspaper with her interview arrived. She was so tickled with that article. Now everyone knows you're back."

"What do you think I should do? Should I call my old friends or wait to see if they call me? I know Lola wants me to hit the ground running. I think I'm ready now to beard my old ghosts."

"You can look at this two ways, dear heart. If you initiate the calls or the meetings, that puts you in control. That's always a good place to be. If you wait for them to get to you, they could, conceivably, catch you off guard, get you at a bad time, and they have the control. That means the results invariably won't be what you wanted them to be. If I were you, I'd hit the ground running. Lola is rarely wrong, Cady."

"I know. Who do you think I should call first?"

"Who do you *want* to call first? I look at it this way. You have all their addresses. You don't have to call unless you want to be socially correct. You can just pop in to say hello and wait to see what develops. For starters, first thing tomorrow morning, Lola has something she wants hand-delivered to the new police chief. You could do that for me, saving me a trip into town. That will then become your first contact. From there, I'd stop by Mr. Danson's office. Hell, girl, I'd hit them all, one after the other. Surprise them! From that point on, the next move will be up to them. That's when you sit back and wait to see what develops."

"Okay, I think I can handle all that."

"I don't *think* you can, I *know* you can," Mandy said.

"Do you think I should go out to the grove before I meet my old friends? Just thinking about that place gives me the jitters. I know I have to do it, and the sooner the better."

Mandy patted Cady's shoulders. "There's no time like the present."

Cady bit down on her lip. Her heart started to pound as soon as Mandy left the room. Atlas looked up at her as he nudged her leg. "I guess

141

she's right. There's no time like the present. Let's go, boy."

The drive through town was uneventful until she came to the street where she'd lived as a child. She turned the corner at the last second and drove down the street until she came to the small Cape Cod house. She pulled to the side of the road and stared up at the house. The swing was still on the porch. The shrubbery looked the same, just bigger and thicker. She wasn't sure, but she thought there was a new roof on the house. The cement driveway still had the crack up the middle, and the curb was still painted yellow.

Did children live in the house? She wished she knew. What did it look like inside? When she'd lived there it had had a temporary feeling to it. Everything in her and her parents' lives had been temporary back then. She wished there were fond memories of this house for her to draw on, but there weren't any. It was just a house. There was nothing special about it except maybe the swing and the old wooden screen door on the back porch. Maybe there were memories, and she just couldn't remember them. Except mealtime. Those hellish hours when she had to sit with her hands folded in her lap while her father droned on and on about starving people, homeless people, sinful, wicked people like Lola. She always hated the part where, just as the food got cold, he'd stand up, wave his arms, stomp his feet, and shout to the heavens as he blessed everything and everyone, even his sinful mother. The words were always the same, his actions the same. Even her mother was the same. She'd stare at the calendar over the kitchen counter. She never blinked either. Cady wished now that she hadn't come here, wished she hadn't remembered those ugly mealtimes.

Atlas whined, as though to say, Move on.

Cady turned the Mountaineer around in the middle of the road and headed out to the Judas Grove, surprised at how little traffic there was at this hour of the day.

She was so deep in thought she almost missed the dirt road that led back into the grove. Years ago there had been no Taco Bell or Pizza Hut on the corner. The Hess gas station and the eight-floor office building on the opposite side of the street were new to her, too.

The dirt road was a series of deep ruts filled with the heavy rain that had fallen the night before. There had never been any ruts when she skimmed down the road on her bike back then. It had been gravel and hard-packed dirt.

The huge NO TRESPASSING signs and the six-foot-high orange mesh fencing brought her up short. This was the grove, wasn't it? She looked up to see the Judas tree standing sentinel. It was thicker than she remembered, taller, not yet in bloom. She'd always thought it beautiful. Now for some reason, it looked scary and spooky. She felt unnerved as she risked a glance in the rearview mirror. How old the other trees looked. Twenty years of growth had thickened the branches and trunks. They were in full leaf and shaded both ends of the pond.

"This is as far as we can go, Atlas. We have to walk the rest of the way. Stay close, boy."

Time and the elements had changed the terrain drastically since the last time she'd been there. Waist-high weeds and pampas grass covered the hill and what was once a well-worn path. It looked to Cady's untrained eye like someone had been there recently. The brush and weeds were broken down, the rocks disturbed. Everywhere she looked she could see the bright red letters of the NO TRESPASSING signs. Where was the mossy carpet they'd played on as children? Now all she could see were the ugly reeds and spiky grass. The clubhouse was gone, one lone board hanging from one of the limbs. She'd always thought of the clubhouse as Pete's special place. She knew he often slept there, but she'd never told anyone.

Atlas didn't like the tall weeds, and whimpered at her side. "Easy boy, easy. It's okay. I used to come here a long time ago. See that limb up there? That's where Pete, Andy, and Amy used to climb to get to the zip line. I never did. You had to go all the way out on the limb, grab the handle on the zip line, and slide down it. I was afraid to do it because I thought the zip would break and I'd land in the middle of the pond. None of us knew how deep it was. I guess I was afraid I would drown because I really didn't know how to swim. None of us could swim. Oh, we could dog-paddle on the edge, but that was it."

The late-afternoon sun shone down on the pond, which was almost full now since the heavy rain. She could see the reflection of the Judas tree in the center. A shudder rippled up and down her arms.

"I can't believe I ever climbed that tree. I wasn't afraid of much back then, but I was afraid of the zip line. I was afraid of that tree, too. I don't know why, because it's so beautiful. We put our initials in it that last week. Come on, Atlas, I want to see if they're still there."

The shepherd was so close to her leg she could feel his body heat. It was comforting. She was winded when she climbed to the top of the embankment. She stopped, remembering her dream. Where had she hidden that day? Where was the spot she'd cowered in before she'd yelled out to Andy? Maybe she could find it another day when she wasn't so jittery. The tall grass made everything look different. She felt saddened that this lovely spot was no longer the Robin Hood playground of her youth. It looked ugly and frightening. Anyone or anything could hide in the tall weeds.

How strange that nothing grew beneath the Judas tree. Not even moss. The ground was squishy soft after the rain. Weeds grew everywhere, even between slabs of concrete. Why didn't weeds grow under the Judas tree? Was it important for her to know the answer?

She saw the initials then and smiled. Until she saw her own, or what was left of them. Pete had carved them. Andy had carved Amy's. Pete had said they would last forever and ever or until the tree died. Forever and ever was a long time.

She felt sick to her stomach when her fingers reached her gouged-out initials. Someone must have hated her a lot to do something like that. Jeff King.

It had been such a happy day. They'd picnicked under the tree, danced and played, singing and laughing. Pete held her hand that day when they ran around and around the tree until they got dizzy.

She saw the hair on Atlas's neck stand on end before she heard his deep growl. She swung around to see a patrol car parked next to her own. Staring at her was a police officer dressed in gunmetal gray, his hand on the holster at his side. "Can't you read?" he bellowed.

Cady nodded as she made her way to her car. "Easy boy, easy."

"Yes, I'm sorry. I didn't touch anything. I just came here to see the tree because it's so beautiful."

"You're going to get a ticket for that. I could see if you didn't see *one* sign, but there are eleven signs. You had to have seen one of them."

"All right. I'll take the ticket," Cady said as she opened the door for the shepherd. "Just as a matter of curiosity, where were you when the others were tromping around here?" she asked, boldly pointing to the trampled-down grass. "I didn't do that, so it has to mean someone else was out here."

The officer stared at the grass, then at her. He didn't respond to her question. "Let's see your driver's license." Cady whipped her wallet out of her hip pocket and handed over her license. She watched the officer carefully to see if her name registered with him. If it did, he gave no sign. "It's a forty-five-dollar ticket. You have ten days to pay it."

"Where should I pay it?"

"The courthouse. Don't let me catch you back here again."

"Who owns this property?" Cady asked.

"I don't know. Get in your car now and don't come back. A second offense is thirty days in jail. We take our laws seriously around here."

Cady nodded as she climbed behind the wheel. She turned the Mountaineer around to head for home. It could have been worse. It could have been Boomer Ward who had found her there.

Chapter 7

Cady opened one eye and then the other. It wasn't quite light out yet, which meant it had to be around five-thirty. Her heart kicked up a beat when she thought about the busy day she had planned. She closed her eyes so she could conjure up the image of the Judas Grove. Her happiest childhood memories, and there weren't many, had to do with the gang and the grove. *Nothing lasts forever,* she told herself. If she could just remember what had happened that day. If she could just remember *one* little thing, maybe the rest would fall into place.

She snuggled into the fluffy comforter, her head nestled in the downy pillow as she let her mind soar. In the first newspaper article dealing with the tragedy her mother had said she was sitting on the swing. That's where her memory began and ended. She'd been watching the movers load the truck. Her bike was the last thing to go into the truck. She'd hidden it in the bushes. The article didn't say anything about her bike. Was it pink or lavender? She couldn't remember, pink maybe. The bike had been a special gift from Lola.

She wasn't supposed to get dirty that day because of the supper and all the stuff was packed away. Her mother had come out to the porch and she'd said . . . something. She'd said something that upset her mother. That wasn't in the article either. Her mother went back into the house. *What did I do then? I got my bike out of the bushes.* That wasn't in the article either.

Cady swung her legs over the side of the bed and headed for the first floor. She let Atlas out while she waited at the door. He was back within minutes.

Barefoot, she padded to the library, where she dug out the scrapbook that had her name embossed in gold on the front cover. She trembled with excitement as she let her index finger trace down the words. There was no mention of her taking her bike out of the bushes. That had to mean it was part of her lost memory. Maybe the conversation with her mother was another part of that same memory.

Cady didn't stop to think about what time it was when she dialed her parents' phone number. "Mom, it's Cady. I need you to answer a few questions for me. What did I say to you that day on the porch? It doesn't say in the paper. I said something that upset you because you went back into the house. What did I say?"

"For heaven's sake, child, that was twenty years ago. Do you really expect me to remember what you said? I can barely remember things that happened yesterday."

"Yes, Mom, I do. What did I say? I think I'm starting to remember. I remember taking my bike out of the bushes where I hid it so the movers wouldn't pack it till last. I didn't remember that before."

Her mother's voice sounded so bitter and angry, Cady held the phone away from her ear. "Why are you doing this? You can't change anything. Lola put you up to this, didn't she? Why can't you just let well enough alone? No good can possibly come of this. You'd be better off if you'd get on your knees and pray."

Something snapped in Cady. Her back stiffened, and her eyes narrowed. "Is Dad standing next to you? Did he tell you to say that? Pray? You want me to pray?" She hissed. "I prayed every day, hour after hour, for three long years. I spouted that bullshit you and Dad used to preach to me until I learned the real way to pray. Oh, my God, I remember the word now. *Sanctimonious.* I said you were sanctimonious. I said that because . . . because . . . Well, right now, I can't remember why I said it, but I will. I told you my memory was coming back. You're hiding something from me. I'm asking you now to tell me what it is. I'm going to remember, Mom. If I have to, I'll get hypnotized."

Cady yanked the phone away from her ear when she heard the dial tone buzzing in her ear. Overcome with emotion, she curled into the corner of the chair as she hugged her knees.

Mandy scurried away from the doorway and up the back steps to Lola's room. Winded from the long climb, she could barely get the words out. Lola jerked upright. "I knew it! I knew if she went to the grove, it would trigger something. I think we're on a roll, Mandy. Is she all right? Why didn't you take the elevator? You're too old to climb three flights of stairs."

"I forgot. I was in a hurry to get up here. I don't know if she's all right or not. She is pissed off, though. Her mother hung up on her. What kind of mother is that?"

"You know what kind, Mandy. Let's not go there. Not right now anyway. I have an idea. Do you want to hear it?"

"No!"

"Yes, you do. I think you and I need to go to the Judas Grove."

Mandy looked properly horrified. "Oh, no! No! No! No! Do I have to remind you how old we are? You're eighty-two, Lola! I'm seventy-eight! Anthony is seventy-nine! No!"

Lola ignored her housekeeper. "Cady is going to be out all day. We can go as soon as she leaves. I went there once after the accident, but there were police all over the place. I had to turn around and leave. I'm an actress. I *was* an actress," Lola clarified. "I know make-believe from reality. You were a stuntwoman. Anthony was one of the best film directors Hollywood turned out. Among the three of us, we might

151

gain some insight into what really happened there if we try to see it through children's eyes. I'll go myself if you won't go with me. Are you in or out?" Lola cackled gleefully.

"What if the police show up and give us a ticket like they did to Cady yesterday?"

"You'll have to create a diversion, then, while I make my getaway. I'll bail you out." She cackled again.

Create a diversion. She was serious. "Why don't you just buy the damn place?"

Lola reared back in her nest of pillows. "Buy? As in purchase it? What a splendid idea? Who owns it? I am so excited. Yes, yes, let's do that. A quitclaim deed. I know how things like that work. At nine o'clock, I want you to call the courthouse. Maybe we can get this taken care of today. Now, wouldn't that be nice?"

Mandy sat down on the edge of the bed and struggled to regain her composure. Sometimes Lola was like a runaway train on a downhill grade. You never knew when she was going to jump the track.

"It belongs to the town. I remember reading that in the paper a while back. There's going to be red tape, and the council will have to vote. I'm thinking a month here, Lola."

"Money talks, Mandy. You tell them we're putting the offer on the table for ninety minutes. That will give them enough time to call all the council members. If the offer is outrageous enough, they'll vote for it. That's Plan B. If they don't accept our offer, we go back to Plan A and just go there and take the chance we'll be arrested. It's perfect. What's for breakfast?"

They're up to something was Cady's first thought when she took her place at the dining room table. "What's for breakfast?" she asked cheerfully.

"Cornflakes," Mandy said, plopping a bowl in front of her. "It's Anthony's day off."

"Cornflakes are good. I used to eat them a lot," Cady said, her gaze going from her grandmother to her housekeeper. Something was *definitely* going on. Something they didn't see fit to include her in. They reminded her of two precocious squirrels watching their pile of nuts.

Cady had a pile of nuts, too, but she wanted to share them. "I have good news. I've started to remember a few things, nothing big, just little things, but it's better than nothing."

"That's what I said," Lola chirped. "I knew it was just a matter of time and concentration. I was right about you going to the pond. I think that's what triggered it. Don't try to force it, though. Let it happen naturally."

Mandy brandished the coffeepot. "Are you all set for your big day? Don't be nervous now. By the way, I left the envelope for the chief on the hall table."

"I'm a little nervous. I didn't sleep much wondering what kind of reaction I'll get from my old friends. I don't know why, but I don't think any of them are going to be happy to see me. I hate it when I get feelings like this because there's no explanation for what I'm thinking. I hope I'm wrong."

The old ladies stared at her intently, so intently, she felt like a bug under a microscope. Absolutely, the two of them were up to something.

"I think they're going to be *shocked* to see you. Shouldn't you be getting ready? It's almost nine o'clock," Lola said.

I'll be damned. They're trying to get rid of me.

"You're absolutely right, ladies. It won't hurt me to do a little primping. Enjoy your . . . cornflakes."

"I don't think she likes cornflakes, no matter what she said," Mandy fretted.

"Give me these damn cornflakes again, and you're fired," Lola said. "When you call the courthouse, ask for the mayor. He's the only one with any brains in this town. The offer is only on the table for ninety minutes. Be sure to say that."

"Since you're so good at this, why don't you do it yourself," Mandy sniffed.

"Because you have to pay for this breakfast, that's why. It's nine o'clock, start dialing."

Lola listened to Mandy's end of the conversation, her head bobbing up and down in agreement with everything she was saying. When she hung up the phone, she glared at her. "Well, what did the old fool say?"

"He said he would call the council members personally and get back to us in the allotted time. That means we have until ten-thirty to get ready."

The phone rang. Mandy picked it up and mouthed the words, "It's the mayor. He wants to know what you're going to do with the property."

"Tell him it's none of his damn business and the clock is ticking."

"Miz Jor Dan said it's none of your damn business and the clock is ticking," Mandy said, repeating Lola's response verbatim.

Lola held out her cup for a refill when Mandy hung up the phone. "I'm excited, Mandy. This is what's been missing in our lives, *excitement*. Cady coming here was the best thing that could happen for us. Maybe I won't die after all. Not just yet is what I mean."

With tears in her eyes, Mandy wrapped her arms around Lola's neck. "I'm blubbering because I'm finally seeing that old spark in you. I wish you could see yourself. You have color in your cheeks, and your eyes have a gleam. You're in a fighting mode, old girl. I like that." Lola reached up to pat her old friend's hand.

An hour later, the phone rang.

The two women looked at one another. Lola nodded. Mandy picked up the phone after the third ring. She nodded for Lola's benefit to let her know it was the mayor. She listened intently. "I'm terribly sorry, Mr. Mayor, but the

155

price is carved in stone. Who is the board member holding out for more money? Cyrus King. Oh well. Tell Mr. King he just cost your town a million dollars. Good-bye, Mr. Mayor."

"You play hardball real good, Mandy. He's the boy's father, isn't he? The one who died. Am I right?" Mandy nodded. "He still has some time. Doesn't the majority rule in something like this?"

"I don't know, Lola. I guess it's back to Plan A."

Lola's eyebrows shot upward when the phone rang again. She knew immediately that it wasn't the mayor on the other end of the phone. "Answer it, Mandy. I'm thinking it's Mr. Cyrus King on the other end."

"Jor Dan residence," Mandy said. A smile tugged at the corner of Lola's mouth as she watched Mandy listening to the caller. "I'll see if Miss Jor Dan is taking calls this morning, Mr. King." Her eyes questioned Lola. She held out the phone.

"This is Lola Jor Dan, Mr. King. What can I do for you?" She listened, her eyes starting to spark. "There's no place for verbal abuse in my life, Mr. King. I simply won't tolerate it. Let me remind you of something in case you may have forgotten. I know all about your dirty little secret. You know us Hollywood types. We can't keep anything to ourselves. We thrive on media attention, unlike you phony churchgoing types. You will apologize to me now, or you will be reading about that dirty little secret in tomorrow's paper. Yes, yes, I accept your apology even though I know you don't mean it. I'm sorry, I'm no longer interested in buying the grove. The offer was on the table for ninety minutes. The time has expired, thanks to you. Don't ever call me again, you son of a bitch!" Lola dusted her hands dramatically after she handed the phone over to Mandy.

"Whoa," Mandy said.

"Don't say it, Mandy. I hate that man. I mean I *really* hate that man. We can talk about this later. We're back to Plan A. We'll get dressed and go to the grove as soon as Cady leaves the house. When we get back, we're writing one of those letters to the editor. We'll fax it to the paper. They might even put it on the front page."

Herself was really into it, and Mandy was ecstatic. She clapped her hands in glee. "Encore! Encore!"

"Thank you." Lola bowed over the table. "Unfortunately, my performance didn't get me what I wanted."

Upstairs, Cady stood inside her closet, her eyes wide and speculative as she tried to choose an outfit for the day. Whom did she want to impress? The guys or Amy? None of the above, she decided. *I'm going to dress for myself in one of these gorgeous outfits, but which one to choose and what color?* Yellow had always been her favorite color, but she'd never bought yellow clothing. She'd been a beige, brown, gray, or black kind of person. A dull, boring introvert who had no distinction. Now there wasn't a beige, brown, gray, or black anything in her closet. Not even a scarf or a pair of sweat socks. What she had now was every color of the rainbow. She had business suits, pantsuits, dresses, dresses with jackets, skirts with blouses and sweaters that matched. She had party dresses, cocktail dresses, evening wear, shawls, and rows and rows of shoes. She even had three full drawers of delectable underwear and sleepwear.

In the massive dresser, there were loads of shorts, sun tops, tees, cropped pants, and slacks. In her wildest dreams she never, ever, imagined she would have a wardrobe like the one she had now. And this was just the summer stuff. The fall and winter clothing had to be made and would be sent in the next couple of months. She almost swooned with happiness.

"I don't know what to wear, Atlas. Each outfit is nicer than the one hanging next to it." The shepherd sniffed his way around the walk-in closet before he sat down patiently to watch his mistress as she picked through the hangers. She finally chose a powder blue dress that had a matching jacket. According to Danielle, it did wonderful things for her blue eyes. It fit her like a glove, showing off her bosom, her narrow waist, and knees. Mandy said she had good knees. Lola had agreed. The outfit came with a matching clutch bag a shade darker. The shoes were sinful strappy heels the same shade as the bag. Danielle called them slut shoes. "It's what Hollywood is wearing, dear. They show off your beautiful legs."

She knew she smelled good because she'd taken a bubble bath, used the same scented lotion and powder, then sprayed her entire body with *eau de* something or other that Danielle said would drive men to the brink of madness. So far it hadn't affected Atlas at all.

One piece of jewelry is all you wear, Lola had said as she handed over a pair of three-carat diamond earrings. Diamonds, Lola said, didn't belong in a velvet box, they belonged *on* a woman. That's why they wrote that song, "Diamonds Are a Girl's Best Friend," she'd added as an afterthought.

She smelled wonderful, she sparkled, and she looked damn good, she thought as she stood in front of the pier glass. The vision staring back at her stunned her. *It's me. I'm her.* She laughed, a joyous sound. Cady shook her head, side to side, then up and down. Sure enough, her new hairdo, a layered cut, bounced right back into place, making it look like her hair had volume. Wash and wear, hit and run, get out of bed, run your hands through it and you were good to go. And, it looked good. Even she, dumb as she was when it came to fashion, knew she had a marvelous hairdo, and it complemented her facial features perfectly.

"Good God Almighty, would you look at our girl," Lola said from the doorway. "Cady, my dear, you are ravishing. What do you think, Mandy?"

"Honey, you look beautiful. You smell as good as you look, too. That's important. You want to leave a trail behind you when you walk past someone."

Cady laughed again. "I think I'm ready to meet my old friends. What are you two going to do?"

"I think I'm going to watch the flowers on my terrace grow," Lola said.

"I'm going to bake some bread," Mandy said.

They're both lying.

"I guess I'll see you later then."

"Cady," Lola called after her, "remember that silence is golden. Let them talk. You can learn more by listening than talking. Play it by ear!"

Cady's heart slammed back and forth against her rib cage when she parked the Mountaineer in the police guest parking lot. It looked like any other police station in the country, with its brick walls and stout, wooden door. Perhaps it was a tad more picturesque with the bright, new spring ivy climbing up the walls. Nestled between City Hall and the United Commerce Bank, it blended into the town square.

She was jittery. Atlas knew it, too. He whined, wondering if he was going to get to go with her or not. She handed him a rawhide chew from the pocket on the driver's side door. Resigned, he put his head between his paws and watched his mistress. "I don't think I'll be long. Wait for me and watch the car. Good boy," she said, tickling him behind the ears.

Lola's envelope in her hand, she climbed out of the Mountaineer and walked across the parking lot to the front door. She passed two police officers and grinned when one of them whistled approvingly. She attributed the whistle to the slut shoes. She fought the urge to laugh out loud as she received two more whistles and four approving looks as she went up the steps to the main door.

Inside, she walked up to the desk and asked for the police chief. "Miss Lola Jor Dan asked me to drop this off personally to Chief Ward."

"Go on back, second door on the right. I'll buzz him to tell him you're on your way."

Cady smiled. The desk sergeant smiled back.

Cady licked at her lips when she brought up her hand to knock on the plate glass door that said, CHIEF OF POLICE, MAXWELL WARD, in gold leaf. A deep voice said she was to come in.

The picture in the paper didn't do him justice, she thought. Twenty years ago he'd been tall for his age. Then again, she'd been little, shorter than the others, so maybe he'd just looked tall back then. Boomer looked like he had stepped right out of *GQ* magazine. She knew all about *GQ* magazine these days because Anthony had copies all over the house.

She blinked and changed her mind. Boomer looked *better* than the guys in *GQ*. Much better. He got up, walked around his desk, and introduced himself.

"Hello, Boomer! It's me, Cady Jordan. I guess maybe I shouldn't call you that. What do they call you these days?"

"Cady! My God, you grew up! Boomer's fine. Most people call me Mac these days. Or Chief. I guess they still call you Cady. I heard you were back in town. I think we got here around the same time."

Cady's mouth broke into a wide-open smile. "I think so. I saw your picture in the paper. In a million years I never thought you'd be Indigo Valley's police chief. I don't know why, but I thought you'd be an architect or an engineer."

"I majored in criminal justice. How about you? I have no manners. Sit down, please. Would you like some coffee or a soft drink?"

"No thanks. I'm fine." Cady sat down in a comfortable leather chair and crossed her legs, the skirt of her dress hiking up. She swished her ankle back and forth. "I'm working on my dissertation. My grandmother is in frail health, so I came back to help her. That's why I'm here today. She asked me to drop this off to you. She said it might make your new job a little easier. Actually, I think she said she hoped it would ease your way into your new job. It's really nice to see you again after all these years, Boomer."

"Yeah, yeah, you, too. I can't get over the fact

that you just walked in here after all these years. It really is good to see you. I said that, didn't I? I saw Pete Danson at the gym the other day. He's a lawyer. I don't know why, but that blew me away. Andy is into insurance, and Amy is a stay-at-home mom. Do you ever think about the old days? Hey, before I forget, I saw that article on your grandmother. She sounds like quite a character. I watch her old movies late at night. It was really a good article, though. I never knew what happened to you after she took you away. It must have been tough on you."

Cady sucked in her breath. "It was hard. I remember the pain, the therapy. For a while there they thought I might not walk again. Sometimes when I'm really tired, I limp."

"I'm really sorry, Cady. Listen, I have to go to a meeting with some of the town fathers in a few minutes. Since this is only my second week on the job, I don't think I should be late. How about dinner this evening? We can talk all night long."

"Dinner would be nice. What time?"

"How does seven-thirty sound?"

Cady nodded.

"Ozzie, come out here and meet a friend of mine. Ozzie, shake hands."

Cady blinked. Staring at her and offering his paw was the biggest dog she'd ever seen in her life. "I have a shepherd, too," she blurted. "His name is Atlas."

"Somebody said you had a killer dog. Maybe it was in the article. All women should have a dog as a protector."

"Oh, he protects me all right. I never go any-where without him. He's waiting in my car for me. I have to go next door now to pay a ticket. I went to the Judas Grove yesterday, and one of your officers gave me a ticket for trespassing. Forty-five big ones." She laughed.

Mac Ward stared at the laughing young woman standing in front of him. She was so beautiful, she took his breath away. He felt like he was thirteen again, when he was trying to protect her. "Give it to me. I'll take care of it."

Cady shook her head. "The law is the law. As the officer pointed out, there were eleven signs. I ignored them, so I have to pay the ticket. I'll see you tonight. Did you ever go back there, Boomer?"

"Just the other day. It doesn't look the same."

"No, it doesn't. I don't want to hold you up. I'll see you tonight."

"Uh-huh. You bet. Let's do casual, okay? I don't feel like decking out in a suit unless you want me to impress you."

"Casual it is. You might want to peruse the contents of that letter before your meeting."

Mac walked around the room sniffing. *Damn, she smelled good. Little Cady Jordan all grown-up.*

The smile on his face stayed with him all day long.

Next stop, the offices of Peter Danson, Es-quire.

It was a nice setup, Cady thought as she walked up the driveway to the law offices of Pete Danson. No overhead, since the building was on his own property. No cars on the streets because he provided ample parking in the back. Pete must be doing well for himself.

If anything surprised her, it was that neither Boomer nor Pete was married.

She opened the door and walked in. The reception area was small, with just a desk and four burgundy leather chairs for clients. A table with a plant and law periodicals sat in the corner.

"Stacy, will you bring me the Lassiter file. I want to go over it before Mr. Lassiter and his wife get here."

Cady looked around for the elusive Stacy. She shrugged as she followed the voice, and knocked tentatively on the side of the door. "Stacy isn't out there."

"Oh, I'm sorry. And you are . . . ?"

He looked delicious, good enough to eat in his dark suit, white shirt, and red tie. Damn if he didn't actually *look* like a lawyer. He was as tall as Boomer, perhaps a tad leaner, and his hair was just as blond as it had been when he was ten. He did look . . . scrumptious. Oh yeah. She felt herself blushing.

"Cady Jordan, Pete." She held out her hand and quickly withdrew it when he made no move to reach for her hand. He stared at her, his eyes blinking rapidly.

"Cady! I can't believe it's you. I've been thinking about you all week. I was going to call you."

"Was going to doesn't count. You have to pick up the phone and dial the number. I think that's the way it works." She smiled. "It's nice to see you again, Pete."

"God, yeah. You look great. We all grew up."

"Now that's an observation if I ever heard one."

"Sit down, Cady. Can I get you some coffee? It's fresh."

"I'm coffeed out this morning. I just took a chance you wouldn't be in court. I just wanted to touch base and say hello. I wasn't even sure you would remember me. We had some good times back then, didn't we?"

"We sure did. What brings you back here, Cady? Are you here to stay, or is this just a visit?"

"I'm here to stay. My grandmother is in frail health. I'm working on my dissertation and helping Lola with her memoirs. The town has certainly grown and changed. Nothing looks the same anymore. I'm sure people aren't the same either. You're a lawyer, Boomer Ward is the police chief. I find it amazing. What is it Andy and Amy do?" she asked guilelessly.

"Andy is in insurance. Amy doesn't work. She could teach if she wanted to. You know Amy, she's lazy."

"Are you all still friends?"

"No. No, we aren't. After the accident we drifted apart. Maybe that was our parents' fault, maybe it was our own. We went our separate ways. Oh, we still speak when we run into each other, but we don't socialize together. I saw Boomer over the weekend at the gym. In a lot of ways, he's the same old Boomer. Andy just separated from his wife. I ran into him at the Rotary Club last week. Amy is Amy. She has two little girls, so she's involved in stuff that concerns them. She married Arnie Chambers."

"I always thought you and Amy would get together since she had such a crush on you back then."

Pete stared at her, his jaw dropping. "Me and Amy?" His voice was so incredulous, Cady laughed.

"I had a crush on *you*. I was heartbroken when you left here. I always wondered what happened to you. The papers said you were partially paralyzed and that you lost your memory. Every year on the anniversary, the papers rehash the story. I'm sure the Kings have something to do with it." He looked at her expectantly, his eyes full of questions.

"It was a miserable, long, agonizing three years. They thought I would never walk again, but my grandmother kept after them with new doctors, new methods. She wouldn't give up. I have a bit of a limp that's pretty noticeable when I get tired, but other than that, I'm doing okay. My memory is starting to come back."

"Really. That's . . . that's wonderful."

"I think so. Look, I don't want to hold you up. I just stopped in to say hello."

"I'm glad you did. Are you busy this evening? I have an early day. How does dinner sound?"

Cady grimaced. "You're too late, Pete. Boomer asked me to dinner a half hour ago. I'm free tomorrow, though."

"Good. Let's do it then. How does seven sound?"

"It sounds fine. I'll be ready. It was real nice seeing you again, Pete." She offered up her hand again. This time he took it.

She knew he was watching her from the window. What was he thinking?

Next stop, Amy Hollister Chambers's house.

Cady drove around the development, marveling at the high-end houses and the manicured lawns. There must be a lot of well-to-do people in Indigo Valley these days. Ribbonmaker Lane was just one street over from Pete's place. She turned on her blinker and drove slowly down the street looking for number 119. She pulled to the curb and cut off the engine.

She'd looked forward to seeing Boomer and Pete. She dreaded seeing Amy. *Why am I even here?* She shrugged as she walked up the flagstone path. She rang the doorbell and waited. She could hear a melodious chime echoing in the house. When there was no response, she rang the bell a second time. She jumped back when the door suddenly burst open. "Yes?"

The two women stared at one another. "Amy, it's me, Cady Jordan."

"Cady?"

Cady wondered if Amy always sounded and looked as ridiculous as she did right now.

"It's me, Amy. Aren't you going to invite me in?"

"Of course. Come in. The house is a mess. I'm a mess. Everything is a mess. What in the world are you doing here?"

"I'm visiting you, Amy," Cady said cheerfully. She was right, the house was a mess. A mess was one thing, but a dirty house was something else. This house was both messy and dirty. Amy wasn't exactly spit and polish either. She wore baggy sweatpants and a sweatshirt full of stains and white spots from too much Clorox.

"Would you like some coffee? I can make it fresh. I was just going to clean up the kitchen. I just can't seem to get it in gear in the morning. Getting the girls off to school, packing lunches. Arnie likes me to pack him a lunch, too. Cooking breakfast, it all takes time. Andy is staying with us until he finds an apartment. He and his wife split up about ten days ago. He comes home for lunch. I guess you'll get to see him if you're still here," she babbled breathlessly.

"No thanks. I'll only stay a minute. I just wanted to stop and say hello. I went by the police station and met Boomer, then I stopped to see Pete. It was so nice to see them again."

"Why? Why would you do that?"

Cady tried not to look at the messy kitchen she was standing in, tried to see some sign of the ten-year-old Amy that she had played with. "Because I wanted to see them the way I wanted to see you and Andy. Obviously, this wasn't a good time to stop by. Perhaps we can get together another day when you aren't so . . . overwhelmed."

"What makes you think I'm overwhelmed?" Amy asked, obviously annoyed. "I'm not. This is my life. I live like this. When you're married with kids, you can't dress up in fancy clothes and high heels and go visiting in the middle of the morning. Why did you *really* come here?"

"This *is* a bad time." Damn, Lola and Mandy both would have had a snappy comeback on the tips of their tongues. What was it Lola said? Throw out some bait. She whirled around, and said, "I came by to ask you why you lied. I can see myself out."

Cady was halfway down the flagstone walkway when Andy Hollister pulled into the driveway. She waved. "Hi, Andy!"

"Hi yourself, whoever you are."

"Cady Jordan," she said, climbing into the Mountaineer. "See you around." She fastened her seat belt, gunned the engine, and tore off down the street.

"I don't know if I blew that or not, Atlas. Time will tell."

Chapter 8

"What are we waiting for, Mandy?" Lola demanded irritably.

"We're waiting, Lola, for you to make up your mind," Mandy said just as irritably. "Anthony wants to know which car you want to have your outing in. When you decide, that's when we can leave. Anthony is partial to the Bentley. He said the Rolls is too ostentatious, the Mercedes is too ordinary, and the Jaguar is tacky since Ford took it over. He also said if we're going *undercover,* he can call and rent a *station wagon.*"

"The Bentley will do just fine. Tell me again why we're dressed like this?" Lola said, pointing to her bib overalls and fishing cap.

"So we blend in with the citizenry, that's why. This is no time to look like a movie star. *Herself* says we should take the Bentley, Anthony!" Mandy bellowed into the intercom.

"Where's our *gear?*"

"I gave it to Anthony. This is not a safari, Lola."

"Let's pretend it is. I know what to do on safari. Remember, my fourth husband was a big-game hunter. What *was* his name? Oh well, it doesn't matter, he's dead."

Anthony was acting as chauffeur, even though it was supposed to be his day off, just the way he acted as butler and anything else Lola could pin on him. He gave the whistle Lola made him keep in his pocket a sharp blast. "Time to go! This is exciting, isn't it, Mandy?" she said, squealing like a schoolgirl.

"You aren't going to think it's so exciting if our respective asses land in the clink. Cady said the place is posted. She said there are eleven signs."

"Oh, Mandy, when *are* you going to learn to think ahead. That's the very reason we're bringing Anthony. He's going to take the signs down and hide them. If there aren't any signs, we can't possibly be arrested. That's why we brought the gear. We have to be prepared for any and all possibilities. I learned that from what's his name. Why can't I think of his name? He's the one who liked garter belts. Actually, he *loved* garter belts," Lola dithered. "He let me shoot the elephant gun many times. I told you, I know what to do. Did you bring the food?"

Mandy twisted sideways in her seat. Her eyes flashed dangerously. "What food, Lola?"

"You always take food when you go on safari. Stuff you eat with your fingers. What's-his-name always made sure we had crackers and caviar. Anthony, we're going to have to turn around and go back home for some food."

"Why don't we stop at the Super Dog Haven and get something in a bag?" Anthony called over his shoulder.

"That's a splendid idea. Yes, let's do that. We'll save time that way. See how easy that was, Mandy? Are your knees bothering you again, dear? You always get cranky when your knees bother you."

"Shut up, Lola. Everything is bothering me. I'm thinking this is a stupid thing we're doing. You know why I think it's stupid? Let me tell you why I think it's stupid. The minute I saw you haul out that elephant gun, I knew we were in trouble. That thing hasn't been fired in forty years. Your hands shake. I can't even lift it, so you get no help from me."

"That's why we brought Anthony along. Stop being such a curmudgeon."

"Anthony is seventy-nine years old. He *creaks* the way you and I creak. He's *old*. Like we're old. We're just going to *look* at a site. There are no invaders or wild boars that we have to take out."

Lola looked down at her feet. She couldn't ever remember wearing sneakers. "These are lovely," she said, pointing to her feet. "Where did we get them again, Mandy?"

"Shut up, Lola."

"We're at the hot dog place, Miss Lola. What would you like me to order?" Anthony queried good-naturedly.

"Three of everything. Ask them if they can box it up to look like a picnic basket. That will make this outing so much more authentic," Lola chirped from the backseat.

Fifteen minutes later, Anthony parked the Bentley inside the entrance to the Judas Grove but far enough away from the main road so it couldn't be seen.

"Ohhh, I feel so invigorated," Lola said, getting out of the car. "We're going to set up camp while Anthony takes down the signs. That orange fence is terribly ugly. Take it down, too, Anthony."

"Yes, ma'am," Anthony said, saluting smartly.

"Mandy, get the machetes out of the boot."

"What machetes?" Mandy squawked.

"The machetes we're going to use to hack down these weeds. That's what you do in the jungle. We want to see where we're walking. Don't you understand, Mandy? We have to make this place look the way it did that day twenty years ago."

"When are we going to eat? We should eat now while the food is hot," Mandy grumbled.

"We'll be sluggish if we eat. We need to be alert and vibrant. We have to keep our eye on the ball. We're calling this square one. This is where the rubber meets the road. What's-his-name would be so proud of me that I remembered all that stuff he taught me. I haven't had this much fun since . . . since . . . a long time ago," she said at length.

"You know you aren't supposed to do anything physical. You could break a bone. Then you'll get laid up in bed, and I'll have to wait on you hand and foot."

"You love it, so stop whining. I feel good. When I feel good I want to do what I can do. When I don't feel good, I go to bed or the wheelchair and let you boss me around. When I feel good I get to boss you around. Now that we have that all straightened out, let's get to it. Watch me; this is how you hold the machete, and this is how you swing it. My goodness, it does cut a wide swath, doesn't it. We should be done in no time."

No time turned into two hours. Both women were exhausted as they stretched out on rubber mats under the Judas tree while Anthony continued the job they had started. "I'm going to give him a raise," Lola chirped. "I'll give you one, too, if you want it."

"Shut up, Lola. Can't you see I'm dying here? If I'm dying, what good is a raise? Don't talk to me, and the next time you get one of your brilliant ideas, forget you know me."

"You really *are* a curmudgeon. Have you noticed that you're the only one complaining? This is the tree that's cursed? Maybe we should move somewhere else," Lola said, looking up at the colorful Judas tree.

Mandy sat up. "Why is this tree cursed? You didn't say anything before about this place being cursed."

"Oh, a dozen or so people hanged themselves here. The story goes someone is buried under the tree. Then there's another story that went around back when I was a teenager that a young girl gave birth under the tree and the baby was a stillbirth. Somebody else said there were druids here. There probably isn't an ounce of truth in any of it. Parents just wanted to keep their kids away from here because of the pond and the fear that they might fall in and drown."

"I wish you hadn't told me that, Lola."

"Then why did you ask me?"

"Ladies, I'm done. How does it look?" Anthony called from the bottom of the embankment.

Both women cupped their hands around their eyes to ward off the sun. "Absolutely beautiful, Anthony. You do good work. How would you suggest we get down there, Anthony?" Lola called cheerily.

"I've got that figured out, too. See that strip of fencing? Sit on it and slide. You can both fit on it. It will be like sled riding. I couldn't cut the weeds all the way to the root, so it will slide easily. I can come up there and guide you down if you're afraid."

"For heaven's sake, I think we can manage to sit down and slide. Don't look at me like that, Mandy. It's my ass, and it's just as skinny as yours is. We aren't going to *whiz* down, we're going to *glide* down. If you're afraid, I'll hold your hand."

"Shut up, Lola. Just shut up right this minute. I'm not afraid for myself. I'm afraid for you. All right, all right, sit down."

"Will you please try to have some fun with this, Mandy. When was the last time we ever did anything more than go out to eat? All we do is sit around watching television. Or we fight just to get a rise out of one another. Push with your feet and yell, wheeeeee!"

"Now, wasn't that fun, ladies?" Anthony asked, cackling, when they hit the bottom to land at his feet.

"I think that was more exciting than the night I married my sixth husband."

"And what was he into?" Mandy whispered.

"You don't want to know. You couldn't handle it," Lola whispered in return.

"How about handling this . . . take a look at that embankment and tell me how in the hell we're going to get back up there. It didn't look that steep from the top."

"We'll worry about that later. Oh dear, we left our gear at the top and our lunch. Anthony, can you get it? Just toss it down. Mandy and I will catch it."

"Shut up, Lola. Just shut up. I'm not catching any camp stools, and neither are you. Wherever did you get the idea I would sit on a *stick?*"

"You sit on a camp stool around a fire on safari. I knew you'd pitch a fit, so I had Anthony put aluminum deck chairs in the car." The moment she finished speaking, three aluminum chairs slid down the embankment.

"We'll leave them here when we leave just in case we want to come back. You have to hide the last piece of fencing, Anthony. Be careful with our lunch, dear."

"I hate you, Lola."

"I hate you, too, Mandy. I adore Anthony, though. He's a good sport, unlike some people I know. Now, let's see what delectable goodies we have here? Weenies with chili and onions. Hmmmm. Potato skins. Hmmmm. Eat, Mandy, or I'm jamming it down your throat."

"Why are you being so mean to me, Lola?"

"Because, damn it, you're raining on my parade. Eat! We have work to do. These are so *good*, Anthony," Lola said as she wolfed down her hot dog. What do you call this stuff in the plastic cup?"

"A root beer slush."

"Wonderful, just wonderful!"

Thirty minutes later Lola held up her hands, palms outward. "It's time to do what we came here to do. I didn't sleep much last night because I was thinking about how we were going to figure out what happened here that day to my granddaughter. Originally, I thought that being an actress and Mandy being a stuntwoman and Anthony being a director, we could pool our brains. I had to fall back and regroup because, as hard as I tried, I couldn't put myself in a child's mind. I think we now need to think in terms of a director and a producer.

"Let's say we were casting for a film to be made here with that stunt the children pulled. It's all here, we don't even need props. We have a bully and the bully's friend. Then we have the four good kids. The object that day must have been for Cady to ride the zip line. She was the only one of the four who had never done it. Cady said the bullies rode the zip line, too.

"She has no clear memory of that day at all. All she could tell me was she had never done the zip line, and she wanted to do it before she moved away. She came here. The question is, did she come alone? We can't discount the fact that she might have wanted to do it when no one else was around so if she chickened out, there would be no one to see her fear. Now if I were directing this film, I'd want other children in the scene, wouldn't you, Anthony?"

"Not necessarily, Lola. If we built the scene around her fear, that fear could carry the scene. You said she couldn't swim. Would she take a chance on the zip line possibly breaking and her going into the pond? It brings us back to the fear. To your knowledge, did Cady ever come here by herself?"

"Oh, yes, many times. But if the others weren't here, she went home. She said she was afraid to stay by herself. Maybe the others were late, or maybe Cady was late. The others left, and she was alone. Maybe the bully was waiting for her. Maybe both bullies were waiting for her. Two against one would drive up the suspense, don't you think, Anthony?"

"Yes, it would. Especially if she didn't know they were lying in wait for her. It was going to be her last time at this place. Maybe she finally got up the nerve to do the line, knowing she could take that memory with her. Children, especially children her age, are all about not being chicken or having others *think* you're a chicken. Sometimes children can be brutal to one another."

"Think about this scenario," Mandy said. "She climbs the embankment, the bullies confront her. She can't go up, and she can't go down. Maybe she thinks the zip line is her only way out. They'd cut off her hair once. I know that had to leave some kind of lasting impression on her. My God, she was just a little girl, so my thinking is she would be deathly afraid of what they would do next if they caught her. Gutsy or not, she had to be petrified. Maybe she went up the tree, or maybe they chased her up the tree. There she is, crying and shaking, afraid to let go. She's out on the limb, and they go out after her. What recourse does she have? She's probably thinking they're either going to push her off the limb, whereupon she hits the water, or, being as gutsy as she is, she reaches for the zip line that will take her to ground at the bottom where she has a fighting chance at safety. If she lets them push her off the limb and into the water and doesn't know how to swim, she could drown. She has a chance to get to safety with the zip line." She looked around expectantly to see what the reaction was to her theory.

Both Anthony and Lola nodded.

"That's the end of the scene. It's not dramatic enough," Anthony said. "Let's try this one. Cady is out on the limb. Bully Number One is behind her. Where is Bully Number Two, and what is he doing? They never recovered the zip line. How did the authorities even know there was a zip line? Do we know the answer to that?"

"Yes. Cady told them. The police talked to the other children, and they agreed with Cady that they had all played on the line over the last two years. So, either Bully Number Two took the line, or the other children were there and they took it. Somebody took it because it was gone. When they couldn't come up with it, the authorities decided Cady and the King boy fell off the limb," Lola said.

"That doesn't compute. How did Jeff King's head get smashed? How did Cady get injured? The doctors said her spine had been hit with a blunt instrument of some kind. She was found on the edge of the pond. So was the King boy. How did they get to the edge if they fell into the water?" Mandy asked. "I think I want to know what happened to the zip line."

Anthony frowned. "Filming today is so different from when we were making movies.

Today they go for the shock value. With that in mind, I'd have to say, the other children were here. My guess, and this is just a guess, would be this — they were all in it in some way. Knowing the way kids are, I'd say they were pitching rocks. Take a look around, some of these are pretty big," he said, pointing to a wide array of rocks around the edge of the pond. "They could have pitched them in the pond afterward, or they fell into the pond. Do you know if they drained the pond?"

"No, they didn't drain it. There was no need they said, since both children were on the edge," Lola said. "The boy's parents said Cady hit their son with a rock. They also said their son would never hit a girl, much less hit her in the back so that she would become paralyzed. Where was Bully Number Two? What part did he play in this?" Lola said.

"Maybe he wasn't here that day," Anthony said.

"My suspicion is they were all here that day. The Hollister twins and Pete Danson were only ten years old. They would have been petrified at what happened. Boomer Ward, Bully Number Two, was Jeff King's shadow. They were always together. He was three years older, the same age as the dead boy. Cady said Boomer was never mean to her. She said he always tried to get the King boy to stop tormenting her," Lola said.

"I think they're a bunch of little liars is what

I think," Mandy said fiercely. "You know what else I think? I think they're all still scared out of their wits that Cady is going to remember and that the truth will come out. If what we're thinking is true, where will that leave them?

"Think about it, they're all white-collar professionals. They all have positions to maintain in the community. Amy is a mother, belongs to the PTA, and is probably actively involved in everything pertaining to her children. She certainly wouldn't be up for a Mother of the Year award if this came out."

"There's no proof," Anthony said. "All we have are theories. If this was my movie, I'd have all the kids in it. You have anger, jealousy, fear, and possibly murder, not to mention Cady's medical condition. We should probably toss childhood infatuations into the mix. Thirteen-year-old boys are starting to look at girls in a different way. Ten-year-old boys are becoming aware of girls. It has everything a film director could possibly want. I'd stake my reputation and my life on the fact that they were all here that day, Lola."

"I've always felt the same way. Mandy did, too. If only Cady could remember. You don't think she's in any danger, do you?"

"No," Mandy said.

"Absolutely not," Anthony said.

"You're both lying."

"You down there!" A voice from the top of the embankment bellowed. "Stay right there and don't move. Don't even twitch. What the hell did you do here?"

Lola stared up at the police officer, who appeared to be ten feet tall. "Why, Officer, whatever do you mean? We're just sitting here having a picnic. Why are you shouting like that?" Lola said, batting her false eyelashes under her fishing cap.

"Where are all the signs? Where the hell is the fence? Who cut the weeds down?"

"What are you talking about, Officer? What signs? What fence? What weeds are you referring to?"

"You homeless people are starting to get on my nerves. I'm going to run you all in."

"Homeless people!" Mandy shrieked. "Run us in for what? We're sitting here having a picnic. You can't take us to jail for having a picnic. Don't even *think* about it."

"Who cut the grass and weeds?" the officer bellowed again.

"Do we look like we cut grass? I have a gardener who does that. I'm Lola Jor Dan," she said imperiously.

"I don't care if you're Daisy Duck. Somebody cut this grass. It was overgrown yesterday. There were eleven signs here yesterday, too, and at least a mile of plastic fencing. It surrounded the entire pond. Where the hell is it?"

"What's your name and badge number? I don't have to listen to your abusive language, young man. Now, skedaddle, and stop bothering us. Are you drinking on duty or sniffing that . . . whatever it is you young people sniff?" Lola demanded.

"This is a no trespassing area. It's been posted for twenty years. There's a fine for trespassing. Don't even think about getting smart with me, lady."

"Where's the sign? Show me a sign that says we can't be here. Ha! You see, you can't produce one sign. We aren't budging." Lola looked from one to the other. "This might be a good time for us to lawyer up. You know, have our lawyer *come here*. And, I'd like to see the police chief come out here, too. Anthony, you have your cell phone with you. Make the calls. I think we just put our ball into motion. I'm all atwitter. Are you all atwitter, Mandy?"

"Shut up, Lola."

"Don't any of you move. I'm calling this in. Stay put and I mean it."

"I've never been arrested before. Another little scenario for my memoirs. This is just too delicious for words," Lola said happily.

"Think about this, Miss Movie Star. Your picture is going to be in the paper in that getup you're wearing," Mandy said sourly.

"A star is a star, Mandy. I'm preparing for my role in the movie we're going to be making. I'm playing a character part. My public will love it.

"Now, I want you two to listen to me. Anthony, try to look feeble. Drooling will help.

Mandy, say stupid things like you aren't too bright."

"We would do this . . . why? And what are you going to do, oh fearless leader?" Mandy said, a murderous expression on her face.

"I'm going to sit here and watch my ever-faithful servants to make sure they don't screw up. Where did you hide the signs and fencing, Anthony?"

"I pitched them into the pond along with the weeds. Vandals do things like that. It's all about getting into the part and mind of a vandal. You know, method acting."

"Yes, they do," Lola said smartly. "And the machetes?"

"In the boot under the spare tire."

"You two are such treasures. You are the wind beneath my wings," Lola gurgled.

"Shut up, Lola." Mandy clenched her teeth in pretended anger. What she really wanted to do was laugh out loud and smack Lola on the back.

Mac Ward and Pete Danson arrived at the same time, tires screeching, the siren on the chief's patrol car blasting and flashing. The two professionals exited their respective cars and stood at the top of the embankment talking to the police officer. The trio at the bottom, lounging in the aluminum chairs, watched them curiously. The trio at the top of the embankment eyed the trio at the bottom as they made their way down to join them.

"Miss Jor Dan, I'm Mac Ward, the new police chief. I believe you know Pete Danson since he just informed me he's your attorney. This is Officer Conroy. I'm sure we can set matters straight without resorting to drastic measures. This property has been posted with no trespassing signs. The pond was fenced off as late as yesterday. The weeds were as high as my waist as of yesterday. Was it like this when you got here?"

"It's all right to answer, Miss Jor Dan," Pete said.

"Call me Lola, Peter. I'm Lola to all my fans. I do hope you're a fan, Chief. This . . . this officer," she said, pointing to the patrol cop, "said he didn't care if I was Daisy Duck. I took offense at that, Chief. Daisy Duck is a cartoon character. I think he should apologize. But to answer your question, it looks the same to me."

"Uh-huh."

Lola watched both men carefully, the outrageous false eyelashes and fishing cap shielding her eyes. Their expressions were wary as they tried to figure out what was going on.

"Your officer as much as said he thought we took down your signs and cut this grass. Now I ask you, Chief, do you think we could do that? As the young people say today, get real. We're just sitting here having a little picnic discussing how we're going to put the movie together. Anthony used to be my director. He's retired now, but I rely on his input. This part of the movie is

187

going to be vital since it will basically be the conclusion. We didn't touch anything. We didn't go near the water. What is your problem with us being here?"

"Come on, Mac," Pete said. "It would take some intense effort to cut all the brush and weeds and rip up that fencing. Those signs were posted pretty deep, too. Surely you can't think my client had anything to do with that. My guess would be a bunch of high school kids out for a romp last night with maybe a couple of six-packs."

"Did you know, Counselor, that your client tried to buy this property this morning?"

"No. Is that important, Mac?"

Lola waved her arms to get their attention. "I tried to buy this property because we'll be filming here. It's easier to own something as opposed to leasing or renting from town officials. When you do that you have to let their grandmothers, their grandchildren, and everyone they know have parts in the film. You have to get releases, you have to have signed contracts, all manner of things. It was simpler to try and buy it. We can fashion a set in Hollywood or perhaps go to Canada to film, but that's costly, too. They tried to hold me up for more money. I won't tolerate doing business like that. Your Mr. King cost your town a million dollars, and I'm keeping in mind that his son died right here in the grove. I don't think you have a leg to stand on. Does he, Peter?"

"No, ma'am, he doesn't."

"Then we'll just stay here until we're finished. We aren't finished."

"Conroy, go get a sign and post it. Ma'am, you really have to leave. If I let you stay, the town will say I'm playing up to your celebrity."

"He has a point, Lola," Pete said. "However, until that sign is posted, you can stay."

"You're pushing it, Danson," Mac said.

"Yeah, I am."

"What about my apology?" Lola demanded. "Oh, my, who's that?" Lola said, pointing to a car that had pulled next to the chief's. "Why, I do believe it's that journalist, Larry Denville."

"Just what we need right now," Mac groaned.

"I just love the press! The press has always been so good to me. Yoo-hoo, Larry!" Lola said, flapping her arms for attention. "Come down here, sweetie. I can give you tomorrow's headline if you need one."

The reporter slipped and slid his way to the bottom. He reached for Lola's hand and smacked it with a big kiss. "I was on the scanner and heard there was a ruckus over here. Wow, the town finally decided to clean up this place. Was that your first priority on the new job, Chief? Can I quote you? How's it going, Pete? Hey, what's going on?"

Lola clucked her tongue. "Gentlemen, gentlemen, let me tell him. They want to arrest us. Now, can you believe that! As you can see, we're just sitting here trying to get a feel for the place. A sense of place is terribly important when you're doing a film. Would you like to be in the movie, Mr. Denville? As yourself, of course. We could make you into a real news bloodhound, couldn't we, Mandy?"

Mandy's head bobbed up and down.

"I tried to buy this place from the town this morning but *Mister* Cyrus King tried to hold me up for more money. You need to let the folks in this town know he cost them a million dollars. We'll just make a set in Hollywood. You aren't writing any of this down, Larry. Why is that?"

The pudgy reporter patted his shirt pocket. "No need. I always keep my recorder on."

"You're drooling again, Anthony." Lola handed him a napkin from the food bag. "They said we were trespassing. There are no signs. I rest my case. I'm not even going to go into that Daisy Duck business."

"I wish you would. I could do a follow-up article on the one I did for Sunday's paper. I think the readers would like that. What do you say, lovely lady?"

"I say that's a smashing idea. Mandy, Anthony, what do you think?" Lola gushed.

Anthony's head bobbed up and down as he dabbed at his mouth. Mandy socked her clenched fist into the palm of her hand as she muttered, "good, good, good."

"If they had a brain between the three of them, they might be considered dangerous," Officer Conroy mumbled.

"I heard that," Lola snapped.

"I did, too!" the reporter said, pointing to his shirt pocket.

"Oh, shit," Pete Danson said.

"Get the hell out of here, Conroy. Bring back the damn sign and post it." The chief turned to face Lola. "We aren't going to give you a ticket. The minute that sign goes up, you have to leave. Is that understood?"

Mandy scratched at her skinny rear end while Anthony stared at the clouds, his mouth slack.

"Whatever floats your boat, Chief," Lola said breezily. "But at what point can I expect my apology? I might be old, young man, but I'm not feeble, like these two sitting next to me. Age deserves respect. So, to answer your question, I will leave when I get my apology. I don't care to discuss this any further. I have to take care of my friends here. I'm truly sorry we had to meet under such ugly circumstances." She turned to the reporter. "Did you get that? Use the word *ugly*. People relate to that when old people are involved. Larry, why don't you come to dinner this evening and we can *really talk*."

Mac Ward turned on his heel to follow Pete Danson up the embankment. At their respective cars, they stared at one another. "You a betting man, Pete?"

"Depends," Pete hedged.

"I'd say the dark stuff is going to hit the fan soon. What's your take on all of us getting together and talking this out?"

Pete shrugged. "I guess that means you want me to call Andy and Amy, eh?"

"It's a place to start, Pete. Get back to me, okay? That client of yours is something else. Guess you know that already."

"She loves her granddaughter. She wasn't just blowing smoke down there. The lady means what she says."

"I figured that out from the git-go. See you around."

"Yeah," Pete said, climbing into his car.

Chapter 9

Cady looked up from the scrapbook she was perusing on the first-floor terrace just as Anthony let the Bentley come to a full halt in front of the six-car garage. Her jaw dropped when she saw him open the back door for her grandmother and Mandy. Atlas barked sharply to let her know he was also aware that something strange was going on. She blinked. They looked like farmers. She didn't know if she should laugh or not.

"Oh my God, she beat us home," Lola muttered. "I thought she would be out the better part of the day. Try and look like this is a daily occurrence, Mandy. You, too, Anthony."

"Did you have a nice day, Cady?" Lola asked as she swished past her, the fishing hat she was holding slapping at her side.

"Nice but strange. Boomer asked me to dinner this evening. I said yes. Pete asked me to dinner tomorrow night, and I said yes to his invitation. Amy almost kicked me out of her house, and Andy just waved in passing. How was *your* day?" she said, eyeing the getups the little group were wearing.

"Routine, sweetie, routine. Mr. Denville is coming to dinner. We more or less . . . ran into him, and Mandy thought he looked like he needed a home-cooked meal. I'm sorry you won't be joining us. Hello, Atlas, I missed you this morning. Come into the house, and I'll give you one of those jerky treats you love so much," Lola called over her shoulder.

"I was just going to make some coffee. Would you like me to bring some up to your suite, Lola?"

"Coffee? Good God, no. The sun is almost over the yardarm. We'll have a drink on my terrace. Forty-five minutes."

Cady blinked as she stared after her grandmother. "Okay," she said. Whatever the group had been up to, it was obvious they had accomplished their mission. They positively exuded victory. This must be one of Lola's *really* good days.

Even though she'd been there almost three weeks, she already knew it didn't pay to question her grandmother. If Lola wanted her to know something, she would tell her, but only when she was good and ready.

Atlas returned with a rawhide chew and a jerky stick stuck between his teeth. He settled down at her feet and proceeded to whittle away at the rawhide.

Cady leaned back in her padded chair, the warm afternoon sun bathing her in its golden glow. She should be thinking about Boomer Ward and her dinner date that evening. She should be stewing and fretting about what she was going to wear and worrying about keeping up her end of the conversation over dinner. First dates were always so awkward. She hated first dates. Then again, maybe she needed to shift into neutral and not think of it as a date but more like two old friends meeting up again.

Maybe she needed to shift out of neutral and think about Amy Hollister Chambers and her less-than-cordial welcome. She shook her head. Thinking about Amy was depressing. Better to think about and compare her old friends . . . Pete Danson and Boomer Ward. Both were good-looking. Both were tall and lean. Both appeared to be athletic. Both were successful. What kind of people had they turned into? Were they kind and caring adults? Neither had been mean or ornery when they were youngsters. Even though Boomer had hung out with Jeff King, he hadn't been ugly and hateful. What was it he had called her today? Ah, yes, little Cady Jordan. It had a nice ring to it. Almost like he'd been fond of her back then.

How very strange that, after all these years, they were all back here in Indigo Valley. In the movies, when things like this happened, they happened for a reason.

A cloud passed overhead, obliterating the sun. An omen? She shivered. "Let's go, Atlas, it looks like it might cloud up and rain. Lola's waiting for us upstairs."

The Big Three, as she thought of Lola, Mandy, and Anthony, were settled on Lola's terrace. They looked so gleeful, it was positively pitiful. She said so. "Whatever you three are up to, you better tell me now since I'm having dinner with Boomer. I'm thinking whatever it is, it just might have something to do with me or my old friends. Everyone knows a secret's no fun unless you share it."

"Darling girl, we are just trying to help and move things forward," Lola said as she up-ended her highball glass and held it out for a refill. "Sit down and we'll fill you in. Anthony, fix Cady a highball. We want to hear the details of your morning, too. Are you excited about dinner with your old tormentor? He is a hand-some hunk, that's for sure. Mandy said they call men like your friend Boomer a hunk. Men like the reporter are grown-up nerds. Your friend Boomer probably thinks of you as a hottie. Did I get that right, Anthony?"

"I think so. Young people today speak a to-tally different language from us. Why can't you say a man is handsome or a woman is beau-tiful? It's so perplexing. If we didn't watch tele-vision, we wouldn't know half the things that go on. You would not believe how much a person can learn from watching soap operas."

"Isn't he a dear? Anthony is hooked on soap operas. He fills us in every afternoon on what's going on so we don't have to watch them. I would never have been able to adapt to television. Even when I did those few guest appearances Anthony insisted on, I was so uncomfortable. I require *cameras and a set*."

"That's because your talent requires the breadth and width of the large screen, Lola," Anthony said, loyalty and adoration ringing in his voice. Cady wondered if Anthony was on Lola's list of paramours.

"Spoken like a true director," Mandy said. "Anthony was the toast of the town just like Lola was. They were Hollywood's golden couple." Her voice turned fretful. "We dwell too much in the past. It's gone, and we can't recapture it." Her voice went from fretful to defensive. "Not that we would want to. We had our day in the sun."

"Speak for yourself, Mandy. I would love to be part of this new filmmaking world. I'd give anything to direct again. I didn't think it would be like this when I got old," Anthony said.

"Well, I sure as hell didn't think so either," Lola said. "I wanted it to go on forever and ever. Stop lying, Mandy, you did, too. Thank God we still have all those old films we can watch from time to time. As you can see and hear, Cady, we're our only admirers these days. Now, tell us about your day," Lola said.

"I'm thinking you three had a more exciting day than I did, so why don't you start."

"I tried to buy the Judas Grove this morning,

but Cyrus King tried to hold me up for more money. I took my offer off the table. We thought it would be simple to buy it, then we could do what we wanted, which was to cut down the grass, dump the signs and the fencing in the pond, which we did anyway. Unfortunately, we got caught, and Mr. Denville, who listens to a police scanner, caught up with us just as we were being grilled by your friend Boomer. We then had to call our attorney, who happens to be Peter Danson. That's the end of our story."

Cady's jaw dropped. "You did . . . *what?*"

"We told a few lies, and I'm the one who did all the work," Anthony beamed. "You should have seen Lola and Mandy sliding down the embankment on that plastic fencing. I was sorry I didn't have a camera with me."

"You *slid* down the embankment! With bones that look like Swiss cheese!"

"Why do you think we're drinking ourselves silly? It was such an adventure," Lola said. "I am having a *really* good day, Cady, so please don't rain on my parade."

"You're like a minimob," Cady said. "What would you have done if they'd hauled you off to the slammer?"

"That's why we called Peter. How's that going to look in the papers? They never arrest old people. They chalk us up as being eccentric. You'd be surprised what you can get away with when you're old."

Cady shrugged. Lola had a point. "What did you accomplish, if anything?"

"We decided all your friends lied about not being at the Judas Grove the day of the accident. We all believe they were there that day, and we believe they were the ones pitching rocks at you and the boy. We just aren't sure if they panicked or not. We played out different scenarios. Anthony played director. I played a role, in my head, of course, and Mandy viewed it all from a stuntwoman's perspective."

Cady sat back and hugged her knees as she stared at her grandmother. "Why would they lie? Does that mean Boomer was there, too?"

Anthony nodded. "They were all there. I'd stake my life on it. But to answer your question, fear would be my response. Children are fearful. You were all doing something you weren't supposed to do, hence the fear. I'm sure the parents of the children stepped in and wouldn't allow the authorities to question their kids, so the kids got away with their lies. After all, they were only ten years old at the time, more or less babies. One of them had the good sense to call the police. That's on the record. Your coming back to town has upset their safe, secure lives. It's not that they can be blamed for anything, they can't. But, in the court of public opinion, they might as well kiss good-bye those safe, secure lives they've been leading for the last twenty years."

"Cady, please try harder to remember. I

know it's easier said than done. If you think about it, it's the only explanation that makes sense. I would really like to know if the police tried to play it out the way we did or if they just accepted things. Hopefully, over dinner, we might be able to ferret something out of Mr. Denville. Anthony is quite skillful at doing things like that. If not, we'll put a bug in his ear, and he might come up with something after he does a little research. Life is suddenly taking on new dimensions. By the way, what are we having for dinner, Mandy? I'm thinking we need to impress Mr. Denville. Why don't we also arrange to have a few friends visit sometime soon. Whom do you think he would relate to?"

"We'll ask him at dinner. I need to head for the kitchen so I can get dinner preparations under way, since technically it's Anthony's day off."

"You wouldn't have to do that if you'd let me hire a real cook."

"Stop right there, Lola Jor Dan. You won't eat anyone else's cooking but mine and Anthony's, and you know it. Besides, I love to cook. When people eat it, that is," she mumbled.

"Who do you think called the police that day?" Cady asked.

"I think it was Peter Danson," Lola said.

"I think so, too. Mainly because you had such a good relationship with him. He's a lawyer, and I think he must have had a strong sense of right and wrong back then that carried him toward the law. Do you have an opinion, Cady?" Anthony asked.

"I was leaning toward Pete, too."

"Are you anxious about your dinner date with Boomer?"

Cady grimaced as she stared at her grandmother. "Yes, actually I am. I've been more or less out of circulation for a while."

Lola glanced over at Anthony and nodded sagely. For his benefit she explained, "What that means, Anthony, is this. Cady hasn't had a date in a long time because she burrowed in and had her nose in books all these years. Relationships pose a risk to one's mental processes. If one doesn't put one's heart out there, then one doesn't get it broken. Am I right, Cady?"

"Yes . . . no, men asked me out, but they weren't men that interested me, so why should I take up my time or their time when it wasn't going to go anywhere? I'm not one of those females who feels she needs a man to make her life complete. I can stand on my own two feet and take care of myself. I know how to open a drain and change a fuse, and I even know how to change the oil in my car. I mowed my own lawn and took out the trash. I also don't hop into bed with the first guy that takes me out. That's what they expect. Then they get all *pissy* when you ask them if they've been *tested*. That's providing the relationship has progressed to where you are at the thinking stage of going to bed with them."

"I think that was more than Anthony and I needed to know, dear," Lola muttered.

Cady delighted in the fact that her grandmother and Anthony looked flustered.

Lola shooed her away with her hands. "You should take a nice bubble bath now and start getting ready for your big evening. It takes at least three hours to get ready. Remember what I told you. When you look good, you feel good. Looking good and feeling good at the same time enables you to control situations. Like dinner this evening. If you think you're nervous, imagine how Chief Ward must feel."

"Three hours!" Cady yelped. "I can be ready in ten minutes. And who said anything about me being nervous. Being jittery isn't the same as being nervous. Is it?"

"Wrong! The old Cady could be ready in ten minutes. The new Cady needs three hours. Jittery and nervous are the same thing. Go!"

"Yes, ma'am," Cady said smartly.

He's good-looking enough to pose for a Gap or Banana Republic ad, Cady thought as she watched Boomer Ward make his way up the walkway to the front of the house, where she was waiting with Atlas. Even from where she was standing she could see the look of approval in his expression. After an hour's deliberation, she'd finally chosen a misty green shift with three-quarter sleeves and a huge yellow sunflower appliquéd on the patch pocket. If the evening turned cool the way it did sometimes in the spring, she didn't have to worry about a shawl or a sweater. The pearls Lola had given her on her sixteenth birthday were her only jewelry.

Atlas growled at her feet.

Boomer looked better than great in his perfectly cut jeans and crisp white button-down shirt, with the sleeves rolled up to his elbows. For some reason she'd forgotten that his dark hair was curly. It was slicked back now, but eventually the tight curls would escape whatever he used to plaster them down. She couldn't remember if he'd had curly hair when they were kids because he'd always worn a Pittsburgh Pirates baseball cap. She did remember his eyes though. They were dove gray. *Twenty years ago those dove gray eyes had always looked worried. Just like now.*

He smiled. Her heart fluttered. She smiled back. Atlas growled and stepped between them when Boomer reached the porch.

"I thought I was supposed to ring the bell to make it official." The smile turned into a wide grin. It disappeared when Atlas nosed him backward. "Is this the killer dog I heard you brought with you?"

"Where did you hear a thing like that?" Cady demanded. What *was* wrong with Atlas?

"In town. I was having lunch in the diner one day, and I overheard two women talking. One of them either owns or works in the bakery. Your dog doesn't appear to like me right now. Were you by any chance planning on bringing him along?"

That hadn't been her intention at all. "Actually, I was. My grandmother is having a guest for dinner, and I didn't want him to be in the way. He's very attached to me. He gets separation anxiety when I'm not around. Are you saying it will be a problem if we take him?"

Boomer rubbed at his jaw. "My dog is in my car. I don't see it working. Do you?"

"If your dog is as aggressive as he looks, then, no, I don't see it working. My dog is just very protective. I suppose I could follow you in my car with my dog. Or we can reschedule for another time." She smiled when she saw Atlas react to her tone of voice and nose Boomer back two steps until he had to step down to the third step from the porch.

"Let me get Ozzie and see how these two guys act toward each other before we make any hasty decisions." He reached into his pocket for a small remote. He clicked it. The door opened, and the police dog charged up to his master and skidded to a stop. Both dogs eyed each other, their tails dropping down between their legs. Atlas's ears went flat against his head as he sniffed the interloper, who was also busy trying to sniff out his adversary.

Cady took a step forward just as Boomer lifted his foot to step up to the porch for a more secure footing. Both dogs moved at once, each taking a position in front of their masters. If her intention had been to reach for Boomer's arm, the dog would have sprung. Atlas showed her he would have done the same thing. She started to laugh. "Your dog doesn't want me near you, and mine doesn't want you near me. I think it's going to be a little difficult for us to go to dinner. What's your opinion?"

Boomer guffawed. "The same as yours. He's never done this before. Maybe you're wearing something he doesn't like. Dogs are sensitive to smells."

"Are you saying I stink?" Cady asked, sudden indignation ringing in her voice. "I guess you must be wearing the same thing then, because Atlas is acting the same way about you."

"No. Jesus, no, that's not . . . how could you think . . . what I meant was . . ."

"What you meant was your dog doesn't like the way I smell; therefore, I stink." Indignation continued to ring in Cady's voice when she said, "I'm wearing French perfume. *Expensive* French perfume, and it does *not* stink. I think maybe your dog has smelled too many lowlife, smelly criminals and whatever else you use him to sniff out, so he can no longer appreciate the finer things in life. My own dog, as you can see, has no problem with how I smell. I don't think he cares how you smell, he just doesn't like you. Period."

Boomer ran his hands through his hair.

"We're having a fight, and we didn't even get off the porch. You were a scrapper back when we were kids. I see that hasn't changed."

"You were a bully back then, and I see you haven't changed either," Cady snapped in return.

"*Touché*," Boomer said.

Only God in his infinite wisdom knew what happened next. Cady reached for Atlas's collar, and Boomer moved slightly forward. The dogs went wild in an instant. Cady felt like her dress was being ripped from her body as Atlas sprang forward to lunge upward, slamming Boomer backward against one of the white pillars holding up the verandah. He clamped his teeth on one of Boomer's ears and hung on.

Larry Denville, arriving for dinner with a bouquet of flowers and a box of chocolates, dropped them to the ground and snapped a picture with a pencil-like camera from his shirt pocket.

"You print that picture, you son of a bitch, and I'll lock you up and throw away the key. Get this damn dog off my ear before he rips it off," Boomer roared.

"Look what your dog did to my dress! My neck is bleeding. Bloodstains. Kiss my ass, you . . . you . . . you cop! You're *supposed* to be a cop, get him off yourself. Atlas, come."

"Can I quote you guys?" Denville shouted.

"Hell yes," Cady shrieked. She turned around, her dress hanging in strips. She felt pleased to see blood dripping down Boomer's neck.

"Nice underwear," Boomer said.

Something snapped in Cady. She ripped and gouged at her tattered dress until she was standing in her gossamer thin underwear. "There," she shrieked again, "take a good look." Her head high, she swiveled around. "Obviously we are not going to dinner. Nor are we *ever* going to dinner. Take that ill-mannered dog of yours and leave these premises. Now!"

Inside the house by the front window, the three oldsters crowed their delight. "She told him to kiss her ass!" Anthony said, his eyes wide with shock. "You used to say that all the time, Lola."

"She disrobed," Mandy said, her eyes wide with horror!

"That's my girl!" Lola cackled. "Oh, oh, here she comes. Pretend we were just walking by. We don't want her to think we were spying."

Inside the house, Cady stared at the trio before she cupped her breasts in her hands to give them a boost upward. Breathing hard, she said, "I should have kicked his ass all the way down the steps. I could have done it, too. I want to send him a bill for the dress. I loved that dress. Atlas and I will be joining you for dinner after all. Mr. Denville is standing on the porch. He took pictures!"

"I can't tell you how impressed I am," Lola said, smacking her hands together.

"I'm pissed now," Cady said, stomping her way to the elevator. "If that . . . that bully calls to apologize, tell him I left the country."

The doorbell rang. Anthony opened the door.

Cady's torn dress under his arm, the flowers and candy in his hands, Denville entered the foyer. "This is all so dramatic. I can fill up tomorrow's paper just from everything that happened today."

"Come in, you sweet thing," Lola said. "Dinner isn't quite ready yet, so let's adjourn to the solarium and have a drink. We need to talk about what you're going to write for tomorrow's edition."

"I didn't think Cady was such a spitfire," Denville said as he allowed himself to be herded along.

"What the hell happened back there, buddy? You just up and blew my evening for me," Boomer said, barreling down the road in search of a fast-food haven where he could park and lick his wounds. The big dog sitting next to him on the passenger side of his Rover stared at him with contrite eyes. "I should swat your ass for that little stunt. I should also take you home and leave you there. Better yet, I'm taking your doll baby away for a whole week. You got that, a whole week. You destroyed the girl's dress. I'm going to have to pay for that. On top of that, she told me to kiss her ass. This is not a good way to start winning friends and influencing people. How in the damn hell could French perfume offend you?"

"Woof."

Boomer skidded to a stop, stared up at the fast-food menu, and proceeded to call his order in to the mesh grille where some unseen person lurked. "Eight soft tacos with the works, two fries, one chocolate milk shake, and one bottle of water with a plastic cup."

He was on his third taco when a car pulled alongside the Range Rover. One quick glance told him he should recognize the occupants of the car, but he didn't. Other than the fact that they looked vaguely familiar, he had nothing else to go on. He'd met a lot of people in the last two weeks. Normally he was pretty good about putting a face to a name, but not that night.

"Boomer?"

"Yeah. And you are?"

"Do I look that different? Amy Hollister. It's Chambers now. This is Andy. My kids are at choir practice, and Arnie's working late tonight, so Andy and I thought we'd do dinner the easy way. I've been meaning to call you. I guess you heard Cady Jordan is back in town."

"Actually, I just came from her grandmother's house. Cady and I were supposed to go to dinner this evening, but things went awry. Have you gotten together yet?"

"She stopped by earlier today, but didn't stay

more than a minute. Andy met her just as she was leaving. We need to talk, Boomer. All of us."

"About what, Amy?" Why the hell wasn't Andy saying something.

"You know what. *That day,*" Amy said emphatically.

Boomer could feel the fine hairs on the back of his neck start to move. "I, for one, don't want to talk about that day or even remember what went on."

"Is that because you're the new police chief? All kinds of rumors are starting to float around this town. They're making a movie, and one of the scenes they're going to film is out at the pond. Everyone is talking about it. Cyrus King is calling for a special town council meeting. That movie star grandmother of Cady's tried to buy the property this morning, but Mr. King stopped it. Someone went out there and took down all the signs and the fencing. They cut down all the weeds, too. Who do you think would do something like that?"

He suddenly realized that he had forgotten what living in a small town was like. News spread like wildfire, and gossip moved at the speed of light.

Boomer summoned up a nonchalant laugh, though he was far from feeling nonchalant. "Probably a bunch of kids with a couple of sixpacks out for some fun," he said, repeating Pete's assessment of what had gone down at the pond. "That and the gossip is just a coincidence would be my opinion."

"Are you saying you're excluding yourself from the past? We need to get together and talk. What we really need to do is get our stories straight. You were there like the rest of us were there. Don't pretend you weren't."

"Well, hi there, Andy," Boomer said, sticking his head out the car window. "Cat got your tongue?" Amy had always been the leader of the twins. It was obvious she was still playing that role.

"Amy's right. We all need to get together and talk," Andy mumbled.

"With or without Cady?"

"Cady went to the grove and got a ticket for trespassing. She paid it, too. Now why would Cady go to the grove after all these years? Let me tell you why. It's one of two things. One, she still doesn't have her memory, or two, she got her memory back and went there to play it over in her mind before she comes after us. We left her there to die, for God's sake. We all thought she was as dead as Jeff." Boomer reared back at the snarl in Amy's voice.

"Maybe you left her there to die, but I didn't. I didn't turn tail and run like you three. I was so damn scared, but I made myself go back down the embankment. Cady was alive. I knew Jeff was dead because I could see his brains. I pulled them both out of the water. I ran home and called the police. If Cady regained her memory, she knows I pulled her to the edge and knows I told her I was going for help. If she hasn't regained her memory, she will, and then she'll remember. So, you see, there's no reason to meet or to talk."

Damn, hadn't he just suggested to Pete that they should all get together? He couldn't think straight anymore.

"Oh, no, Boomer Ward, it doesn't work like that. You were there just like we were there. You're as responsible as we are," Amy sputtered angrily.

"Have it your own way, Amy. I can make my own case, thank you very much. I am a cop, remember?"

Boomer put the car in gear and backed it out, knowing Amy's and Andy's eyes were boring into him.

Back in his apartment, he called the station to see what was going on. He was told crime was at a standstill in Indigo Valley for the night. He kicked off his sneakers, popped a beer, and settled himself in front of the television.

He thought about the Hollister twins. He hadn't liked them very much back in the old days. He'd liked Pete and Cady, though. Hell, he'd become a cop because of that day in the Judas Grove. His parents could never understand why he wanted to major in criminal justice. When he tried to explain without giving explicit details, they just shook their heads and said they couldn't imagine having a cop in the family.

He leaned back in his favorite recliner and closed his eyes. A vision of Cady Jordan in see-through underwear attacked his eyelids. He bolted upright. Little Cady Jordan was all grown-up.

There was no point in thinking about Cady Jordan. His dog had just taken care of that.

Damn, maybe he should call and apologize for his dog? No maybes about it. That's exactly what he would do.

Chapter 10

Amy Chambers watched as Boomer Ward drove his hunter green Range Rover out of the parking lot. "Did you hear that? Well, did you? Who does he think he is? Damn it, Andy, he was there. All of a sudden he's off the hook like he wasn't part of it. Do you believe him? Why aren't you eating, Andy?" She bit into her taco, the filling dribbling down the front of her plus-size tee shirt.

"You really are a sloppy eater, you know that," Andy said, disgust ringing in his voice. "As usual, you didn't ask me if I wanted a taco, you assumed I did. You always assume, Amy. Once in a while I like to make my own decisions. He sounded to me like he was telling the truth. I don't think the guy would take on the job as police chief unless he felt comfortable with what happened that day. Boomer never really did anything. He was just *there*. When I think back on it, he tried to look out for Cady in his own crazy way, the way we all did."

"Cady, Cady, Cady! I'm sick of hearing how everyone wanted to watch over little Cady. If you tell me you felt that way, too, I'm gonna puke." Amy squished up the paper from her taco and opened a second one. "If you aren't going to eat yours, I'll take it home for Arnie. What are you going to eat?"

"I'm meeting Jill later to discuss things. I'll probably pick up a pizza or something."

A chunk of cheese dropped to Amy's ample bosom. She pierced it with her fingernail and popped it into her mouth. Andy looked away. "Did you *really* believe him, Andy?"

"I told you, he sounded like he was telling the truth. I always thought Pete was the one who called the police. But that doesn't compute because he was with us all afternoon at the park. How could he have called?"

"I'll tell you how," Amy said, her mouth full. "He had that paper sack, and he said he had to take it home. Don't you remember how secretive he acted about that sack? You asked him what was in it, and he told you to mind your own business. We waited for him to take it home and come back. He could very easily have called when he went home."

"Then why didn't he tell us he called? I never even gave it a thought, and I know you didn't either. We were too damn scared that day to even think about making a phone call. Pete wasn't that much smarter than we were. Boomer was three years older, so he had some brains. I think he did make the call. We were just damn lucky Cady didn't die. God, do you have any idea how badly I wish this was all over? You aren't helping matters any either, Amy. I think we should go to Cady and tell her what happened. I want to get it off my chest so I can *breathe* again. Jill is going to blackmail me into reconciling with her just the way you said she was going to do. One way or another, this is all going to come out. Let's just do it and be done with it."

"No!" The single word exploded from Amy's mouth like a gunshot.

"Don't tell me no, Amy. And if you think for one minute Pete is going to listen to you, you're nuts. I'm damn sick and tired of you running my life. Half my problems with Jill can be laid on your doorstep. I can't live with this guilt anymore. I lie awake nights trying to figure out what I'm going to do if and when this hits. I have some savings that will tide me over if the business goes into the crapper. I'm prepared to move, to relocate and start over. God, Amy, I just want to be me again. I don't want to keep hiding from Jeff King's parents every time I see them because I feel so guilty. I feel like a real *wuss*. I don't know how you deal with it, Amy."

"I deal with it because the alternative doesn't bear thinking about. We aren't saying anything until . . . until we have to. Every time you don't listen to me something terrible happens, then you expect me to fix it for you. Don't tell me I run your life either. If you were capable of running it yourself, I wouldn't have to step in.

We're twins," Amy said, as if that was all the explanation her brother deserved.

Andy wilted under her attack the way he always did. He yanked at the gearshift and backed up so fast, Amy was jolted forward. "I'm not finished eating. I can't eat in a moving car. I'll get sick."

"Even a truck driver doesn't eat five tacos. You need to look in the mirror and stop eating all that junk you stuff your face with." Andy risked a glance at his sister out of the corner of his eye. His words had gone right over her head. He threw in the clincher. "You and Cady were the same size. I think you were skinnier, though. She sure turned into a sizzler."

Amy burst into tears. "You are so hateful, Andy Hollister. I would never say anything like that to you. Never, ever!"

"Like hell you wouldn't. You've been running my life and telling me what to do and when to do it for so long I feel like I don't know who I am anymore. From here on in, butt out of my business. If I fuck it up, I'll know who to blame. I mean it, Amy, stay the hell out of my business. Take all your trash with you. I don't want my car smelling like greasy tacos. Look, your husband is home waiting for you," Andy said, swerving into the Chambers's driveway.

"I hate you sometimes, Andy. I really do. If you tell, I'll call you a liar. Who do you think they'll believe, me or you?" Her voice rang with such venom, Andy felt his insides start to shrivel.

"You're sick to think like that. Sometimes I hate you, too. Don't call me, I'll call you."

"When?" Amy blubbered.

"Probably never," Andy said as he backed his car out of the driveway.

He drove aimlessly, up one street and down another just to kill time until his meeting with Jill at the Barb Wire. He'd been the one to choose the Barb Wire because no one paid attention to you in the back room. You were lucky to get waited on. If Jill pitched a fit, no one would care. He continued to drive, his thoughts going in all directions.

He hated fighting with Amy. He hated her know-it-all attitude in regard to him. Hated it when she belittled him in front of other people. Yet, he had allowed it, so it was his own fault. Amy liked to blame things on other people. She was sly and manipulative and always managed to get her way even if she had to lie to do so. He lost count of the number of times he'd gotten his ass whipped or was punished because Amy managed to convince their parents he'd done whatever it was they were blamed for. He really was a *wuss*.

The dashboard clock told him it was time to head for the Barb Wire.

Jill was already in the booth with a bottle of beer in front of her. There was one sitting next to his seat, too. She looked different. He frowned, trying to put his finger on what it was that was different about his wife. Maybe it was her face that was clean and shiny, devoid of makeup. Her eyes were red-rimmed, as though she'd been crying. She looked pretty with her ponytail, jeans, and striped shirt. She looked the way she'd looked the first time he met her. He sat down, his eyes wary.

Jill struggled to get past the first awkward moments. "I don't want a divorce, Andy. I'd rather try seeing a marriage counselor first. Or, we could try and talk out our differences. I'm willing if you are." She leaned across the table, looking miserable. "Andy, for every action, there is a reaction. Each of us reacted to the other and what we said and did. I'm willing to take my share of the blame, but you have to do the same thing. A lot of the things you said the other night were true, and a lot of other things were not true. What I'm trying to say here is we're both at fault. Will you at least listen to what I have to say?"

"Go ahead, Jill, I'd like to hear what you have to say." Like he was really going to listen and pay attention.

"Good. Our problem is your sister. No, no, let me finish. You harped and harped on the fact that on our honeymoon I called my mother five times a day. That's true, I did. Because . . . Andy, your sister called five times a day. She called you to get up in the morning. She called you to say good night. She called you to ask you what you had for lunch. She called to ask if you got sunburned. I didn't know what to do, so I called my mother. Your sister is the one who ruined our honeymoon, Andy. I waited for you to tell her to stop calling, but you just talked away, sharing our private business, laughing, and joking. Then you got ticked off at me when I called my mother, who, by the way, said your sister was suffering from separation anxiety. She told me to be patient. Am I right or am I wrong?"

He nodded. "You never said anything about that, Jill."

"It was your place to straighten out your sister, Andy. She hated me from day one. I think I knew we were doomed from the beginning, but I hung in there because my mother told me that's what a wife is supposed to do. And, no, I didn't go running to my mother over every little thing. She has eyes and ears, and she's a sharp lady. She also goes to the hairdresser that Amy goes to and got one earful after another.

"My mother is not a shiftless freeloader like you implied. You just parroted words you heard Amy say. Yes, you sent her a check every month. She told you to stop. I told you to stop, and you didn't listen. You just kept sending those checks because it made you feel good to do it. Mom had two bad months after my dad died, when she couldn't take money out of the bank. She is more than solvent. Here," she said, tossing a check across the table. "Mom gave it to me this morning. She just put it all in an account, she never touched a penny of it. You never supported my mother, and I resent the implication that you did. Those are Amy's words, and you damn well know it."

The beer was going to his head. He should have eaten something. "It doesn't matter anymore, Jill. We should have done this a year ago, two years ago. Hell, we should have done it on our honeymoon. You said you hated my guts, and now all of a sudden you want to save this marriage. Why? Because you might have to go to work to actually earn a living?" *God, did I just spout that crap?*

"We were both childish, hurling hurtful words at one another. I knew it wasn't you saying those things. Yes, you were saying them aloud, but Amy is the one who put the words in your head. Like I said, I reacted. It's true, Andy. Why can't you see it? Why are you being so stubborn? Another thing, did you or did you not forbid me to get a job? You wanted me to stay home like Amy. I'm a damn good graphic artist, Andy. I can get a job at the drop of a hat. I did what you wanted, but I was bored out of my mind. I picked on you to get a rise out of you. It was the only way we communicated. Then what did you do? You ran to Amy, got her spin on it, then came back, and we'd go a few more rounds. Amy is our problem, Andy. We could make a go of this marriage if we both worked at it. That's why I want us to go to a marriage counselor. I don't want you to come back to the house unless it's what you want. If divorce turns out to be our answer, I don't want anything from you. I'll move in with Mom until I can get settled. I'm going to leave now, and I want you to think about everything I just said. If you want to go ahead with the divorce, then that's what we'll do. Just make sure in your heart it's what you want and not what Amy wants. You know where to find me."

She was almost to the door when Andy ran after her. "Come back for a minute. I want to ask you something."

Jill slid into the booth. She cupped her hands around the beer bottle in front of her and waited.

"Do you remember my telling you about that time at the Judas Grove?"

"Of course I remember. I don't think you ever got over that, Andy. You used to talk about it in your sleep. Is it still bothering you?"

"Did you tell anyone?"

Jill's eyes never left those of her husband. "Of course not. Why would I? That was a tragic time in your life. I would never tell something like that to anyone. Has something happened?"

"Cady Jordan is back in town, and so is Boomer Ward."

"And . . ."

"If it gets out, we'll be ruined. All of us."

"You should have fessed up, Andy. I told you

something like this would happen someday. Secrets like that are a terrible burden for anyone to carry. Do you have any idea how good you would feel to get that off your chest? People are forgiving, Andy. It was a long time ago, and you were just little kids. What do the others say?"

Andy dropped his head into his hands. "Boomer doesn't feel he has anything to confess since he was the one who went home to call the police. I thought Pete was the one who called. Pete said he was all for confessing. Amy said . . . Amy said . . . she would lie if I decided to own up."

"I think I'll leave right now, Andy Hollister. You just made my case for me. Be the good person I know you are and do the right thing. Good night, Andy."

Andy leaned back in the booth and stared at the check lying on the table. *Christ Almighty, how did it come to this?* He felt like crying for his own stupidity. *Jill is right about everything. Why didn't I see it? What the hell is wrong with me?*

Do the right thing. The right thing for whom? Himself? Cady? Pete and Boomer? Amy? Had he just been spouting words to make himself feel better, or was he man enough to stand up and tell the truth? The minute he made that decision, his life was going to change forever. Did he have the guts to face that change? Amy would cease to be a part of his life if he did the right thing. Could he handle that?

Rage unlike anything he'd ever experienced in his life coursed through him. He grabbed the check off the table, slammed down a ten-dollar bill, and ran from the room out to the parking lot, where he opened the trunk and fished out his sneakers. He tossed his loafers into the trunk, put on the sneakers, and started to run, yanking at his jacket, which he tossed into some bushes. His tie sailed over his shoulder before he ripped at the buttons on his dress shirt. His arms pumped as furiously as his legs, his shirt flying through the air.

He knew that if he were running the way he did on the treadmill at the gym, he would be running at around 5.0. He broke a sweat after the first half mile, perspiration dripping down his neck onto his chest. He continued to run, his body protesting with each long stride until he collapsed along the side of the road, where he lay panting and gasping for breath. He cried then because he didn't know what else to do.

Jill Hollister drove around for almost an hour before she brought her car to a stop in front of her sister-in-law's house. Her back was ramrod straight when she climbed out of the car. She should have done this a long time ago, but Andy had always said Amy was off-limits. *Not anymore she isn't,* she thought grimly.

Even from this distance she could see Amy curled into the corner of the swing sniffling into a wad of tissues. According to Andy, crying was one of Amy's favorite pastimes. She squared her shoulders and marched up to the front porch. "Amy, it's me, Jill. I want to talk to you."

"Well, guess what, I don't want to talk to you." She made a move to uncurl her legs, but Jill pushed her back into the corner. "Right now, Amy Chambers, I don't much care what you do or do not want. I'm here to get a few things off my chest, and until I do that, you're going to sit there.

"For starters, I don't like you any more than you like me. I do, however, love Andy. If you hadn't stuck your nose into our business and tried to run Andy's life, I wouldn't be here right now. You are the cause of all our problems. You, Amy Chambers. For the first time tonight, I think Andy finally saw how manipulative and conniving you really are. I don't want a divorce, and I don't think Andy does either. I'm trying to get him to go for marriage counseling. When and if we do that, all kinds of stuff is going to come out. I came here to warn you. So, be prepared. An unbiased counselor will be able to help Andy and show him what a control freak you are. You must be one miserable woman to try and ruin your brother's life. I'm not excusing Andy in all this. From the time you were little kids you ruled his life. He thought that was the way it was supposed to be, so he never kicked up a fuss.

"I want you to listen to me very carefully. I'm

going to do everything in my power to save our marriage. If I have to chop you off at the knees, I will. From here on in, stay away from Andy. Let him make his own decisions, his own mistakes. Didn't you see what you were doing to him? How could you be so blind? Andy has been eating himself alive over that old childhood business. I told him to do the right thing. I'm going to keep encouraging him, too. My bottom line here is, I want you to leave us alone. This is between Andy and me. It's our marriage, not yours. Let us try and work it out. I said everything I came here to say. Good night, Amy."

"Who the hell do you think you are to come to my house and talk to me this way? If you aren't woman enough to hold your husband, don't try blaming it on me. I didn't tell Andy to get a divorce. He came up with that all by himself. He came here every day to complain about how lazy and shiftless you are. He said you're just like your mother. All you want to do is spend his money, money he works hard for. You don't want kids because you don't want to ruin that skinny figure of yours.

"I know everything there is to know about you because Andy couldn't wait to tell me. You're nothing but a slut."

Jill had one foot on the step in preparation for leaving. She turned around and walked back to the swing. "And I am a slut because . . ."

"Because you are. Everyone knows it. People in this town talk."

Jill dropped to her haunches so she was eye level with Amy. "People can only talk when other people give them something to talk about. I lived in Pittsburgh before I met Andy. I didn't know a soul in this town when we got married. I was never unfaithful to Andy. If rumors are going around, then my guess would be that *you* spread them. I'll get to the bottom of it with the help of my mother, and then, if I find out you're the one who started those rumors, I'll slap a lawsuit on you so fast your head will spin. Don't think for one minute I won't do it, because I will.

"Do you know something else, Amy Chambers? I think I'm going to make it my business to visit your old friend Cady Jordan. You see, I know all your little secrets, too."

"I'm glad Andy is divorcing you. He's too good for you," Amy blustered, completely taken off guard by her sister-in-law's words.

"Stay out of my life, Amy. If I have to come back here, I'll come when your husband is here, then you'll regret it. Leave Andy alone, too, until we can settle matters between us."

"Is that a threat? That sounded like a threat to me," Amy blustered again.

"That was no threat. That was a promise, and one you better hope I don't have to keep."

"Bitch!" Amy seethed under her breath.

The minute Jill's taillights faded into the night, Amy jumped off the swing and ran into the house. She dialed Andy's cell phone number and waited. She almost swooned when she heard her brother's voice. "Andy, that tramp of a wife of yours was just here. She threatened me. You need to come over here right now. What do you mean you aren't coming over because you just ran ten miles and you're exhausted? Stop lying. You couldn't run ten miles if there was a pot of gold at the finish line. On top of that, you're lazy. It's not that late. Going for counseling is the dumbest thing I ever heard of. When something is over, it's over. I refuse to believe you are even considering trying to rectify things with Jill. I told you in the beginning she wasn't the one for you, but did you listen to me? No, you did not. This is what happens when you don't listen. I should cut you loose and let you drown in your own stupidity. All right, all right, I won't call you anymore. There, does that make you happy? Remember what I said, if you decide to go noble on me, I won't go along with it. Go to hell, Andy, I'm sick of wet-nursing you. Do whatever the hell you want. Just know this, brother dear, your wife said she was going to talk to Cady Jordan."

Amy slammed the portable phone so hard into the phone tray it bounced back out and fell to the floor. She eyed it before she kicked it across the room.

Amy sat down at the table and folded her hands. Andy had never spoken to her like that in his life. Where, all of a sudden, was he getting his nerve? Did he really think he could handle the fallout if he confessed? If she couldn't handle it, how could he? Was Jill his backbone?

She closed her eyes and tried to think what her life would be like without Andy in it. If he patched things up with Jill, that meant she was out in the cold, with just Arnie and the girls. She would have to avoid her parents because she wouldn't be able to stand their harping and whining.

God, it was such a mess.

And all because Cady Jordan was back in town.

"I have to go to Squirrel Hill this morning, Amy. No breakfast for me. I'll just take a coffee to go. If you want, I can drop the girls off at school and save you a trip. What's wrong, honey, you look tired? Didn't you sleep well?"

"Hardly at all. It's that time of the month," Amy lied to her husband. "The girls love it when you drop them off at school. They're on the front porch waiting. Thanks, Arnie. I think I might go back to bed and see if I can get rid of this headache. Have a nice day," she said, pecking him on the cheek.

Amy walked her husband to the door, kissed him again and her daughters before she picked up the morning paper. She waited until the car was out of sight before she went back into the house. This was her favorite time of day, after everyone was gone and she could sit in the breakfast nook with the sun streaming through the window.

She poured her coffee, added four sugars and cream before she shook out the *Indigo Sentinel*. Her eyes almost popped out of her head when she saw the picture of Cady Jordan in what looked like either a very daring outfit or her underwear. She gasped in horror as she tried to imagine herself caught in the same circumstances. The three rolls of extra flesh under her bosom and her cellulite probably wouldn't photograph well.

Even in her underwear, if that's what she was wearing, Cady Jordan looked like a million bucks.

Amy read every single line in the paper not once but twice before she ran upstairs to shower and dress. She was out of the house in less than fifteen minutes and on her way to the bakery, where she knew Julie Ambrose would have the latest scoop. Probably half the town would be in the bakery discussing the contents of the morning paper. Just about every businessman in town stopped at the bakery for their morning coffee and Danish. All she would have to do was sit and listen.

Chapter 11

Cady squinted at the bedside clock. Seven o'clock! She'd slept in, something she rarely did. She hadn't been able to fall asleep until well after three o'clock, worrying about the morning edition of the *Indigo Sentinel*. She bolted out of bed, grabbed for her robe, and literally galloped down the steps to the kitchen.

They were waiting for her, Lola, Mandy, and Anthony, their eyes sparkling with excitement. In the middle of the table was the morning paper. "Honey, you photograph better than a model," Lola gushed. "This is priceless, just priceless."

"I imagine that Indigo Valley's new police chief is cringing a bit this morning. Wouldn't surprise me at all if they don't call a special town meeting to discuss his . . . behavior," Mandy said, stifling her laughter.

"Darling girl, you will be the topic of everyone's breakfast conversation. Eggs or pancakes?" Anthony asked.

"Toast and coffee. Oh myyyy Godddd," Cady yelped when she stared down at her likeness in the morning paper. "It's in *color!*" she shrieked.

"So it is," her grandmother responded as she brought her coffee cup to her lips. "The article is extremely interesting, too. It mentions the trespassing ticket that you paid, and it also mentions our . . . our little visit to the pond and, of course, my offer to buy the property. Mr. King is portrayed as a greedy mogul. I didn't know we had any moguls in Indigo Valley," Lola sniffed.

"The best part is that young man, Larry Denville, is going to reopen the newspaper's file on the old case and do some investigating. Now that everyone is all grown-up, he's going to do what he does best, ask questions. We told him what we suspected and how we went to the pond for a reenactment. If you had come down to dinner, you wouldn't have to read about what we all discussed. Is your headache better, dear?" Mandy asked with concern in her voice.

Her eyes were wild when she looked around at the Big Three. "It was gone when I woke up, but it's back now," Cady all but snarled. "I don't know if I can handle this."

Lola waved her hand airily. "Of course you can handle it. Just pretend you're acting in a movie like I do. If you go with make-believe, you can handle anything. Trust me. I'll have the pancakes, Anthony."

Her eyes going wilder by the minute, Cady looked from one to the other. There was no way in hell she was going to read the article in

232

the paper. No way at all. "Did Boomer call?"

The trio shook their heads in unison.

"Then that means I have to go to the police station. I have to make last night come out right. I thought about it all night long. I even dreamed about it. It was both our faults, and we both reacted. At least I did."

"Make sure you dress for the occasion," Anthony quipped.

"Shut up, Anthony," Cady barked, her eye on the color photo staring up at her.

"And she's got spit and vinegar this morning, too," Lola said happily. "Darling girl, you do not have to go to the police station. You have nothing to apologize for if that is your intention. Wait him out. Pass the time today getting ready for your date with Peter Danson this evening."

Cady continued to stare down at her likeness in the paper. She felt her face grow hot. "Maybe people will think it's a costume," she said.

"It says in the article it's your underwear," Mandy said. She gave a slow wink in Lola's direction.

"Oh, shit!"

"My advice in case anyone is interested," Anthony said imperiously, "would be to go into town and shop. Go to that bakery that is a hellhole of gossip, the drugstore where they try to sell you pots and pans, then to the hardware store where all the retirees gather to gossip. At each place mention the movie we aren't going to make. Really give them all something to gossip about. When you do things like that it keeps everyone on edge. Then they get careless wondering what's coming next, and that's when someone will make a mistake. Trust me. I directed this same film a dozen different times. Oh, and make a stop at the cemetery, but be sure to take some flowers. We need to keep you front and center so everyone gets rattled, and by *everyone*, I mean your old friends and the King family."

The fine hairs on the back of Cady's neck started to itch. "All right, all right. I'll get dressed and head for the bakery. Will that make you all happy?"

"Absolutely," Lola said.

"Definitely," Mandy smiled.

"Go for it," Anthony said as he expertly flipped a pancake.

Cady ran her fingers through her hair. "Do the three of you trust me to dress myself?"

The trio nodded again, as Cady made her way out of the kitchen and up the stairs to her room, where she stared at Ginger Rogers's dancing shoes. Did Ginger dance her way through life, or were the shoes strictly for dancing on a stage? She wished Fred's shoes were alongside the sparkly heels in the glass case.

Atlas stood guard outside the bathroom door while his mistress showered. He sniffed when she powdered up and sprayed on deodorant.

He was ever watchful as she slipped into a silky yellow dress with buttons down the side that were the size of quarters and a brilliant lime green color. The slit going up the side of the dress was generous and showed just enough of Cady's lightly tanned leg to make the outfit even more interesting. Sandals, the same shade as the buttons, were the last thing to be fished from the closet.

Cady was almost to the top of the steps when she turned around and went back to her room to put on a shimmering strand of pearls and pearl studs in her ears. Now, she was dressed.

Downstairs she paraded through the kitchen and waited patiently while Mandy tied a tartan neckerchief around Atlas's neck. The neckerchief matched the leash hanging on the hook by the back door.

Lola clapped her hands in delight. "And the show goes on," she said.

"Give 'em hell," Mandy said.

Not to be outdone, Anthony said, "Break a leg!"

"You make it sound like I'm going . . . oh, never mind. Do I look all right?"

"You look fabulous, sweetie. Remember what I said, when you look good, you feel good, and you come out on top. Plus, you smell heavenly."

"That's all fine and well and good, but what is it you think I can accomplish? Why am I doing this again?"

"Go!"

Atlas barked as he was led out the kitchen door. The time was 7:58.

"Now we wait," Lola said as she poured warm syrup over her pancakes.

It was eleven minutes past eight when Cady walked into the bakery. The place was jammed, so much so she had to take a number. The soda-fountain tables were filled with mothers who had just dropped their children off at school and were there for two reasons only, to gossip and to eat the sugary sweets. The double line at the bakery counter was full of businessmen dressed in suits and ties and late-morning joggers in sweats and sneakers. She waited patiently, aware of eyes boring into her back. The big question was, what to buy. It wasn't until she placed her order and was about to walk over to the cash register that she realized she hadn't brought her purse with her. Her face turned fire red.

"Allow me. It's the least I can do," Boomer Ward said quietly.

"Boomer! Oh, thank you. I can't believe I left my purse in the car. If you follow me outside, I'll give you back the money. Hey, I'll share what I bought. My dog's in the car, though."

"Ozzie is in my car, too. We could sit on a bench outside and eat these great-looking apple turnovers. One more coffee," he said loudly.

"That sounds like a plan. Oh, look, there's Amy." She smiled and waved, as Amy glowered.

She did wave a limp hand in her direction, however.

Outside in the early-morning sunshine, Boomer cupped her elbow in his hand and guided her to a bench outside the bakery. "Listen, I'm sorry about last night. I don't know what the hell got into Ozzie. Tell me how much I owe you for the dress, and I'll give you the money. By the way, you don't stink. You smell as good as you did last night. I really am sorry, Cady."

"It's okay, Boomer. We both reacted to whatever it was with the dogs. I'm having a hard time thinking of you as Mac. I think you'll always be Boomer to me."

"Boomer's fine. I like apple turnovers. The bakery has the best coffee in town. So, what did you think of the article in the paper?" He jerked his head backward. "They're all buzzing in there, you know."

Cady laughed. "I know."

"I'd love to stay here and talk to you, but I have a meeting. I imagine they're going to chew me out about the picture and want a detailed accounting of what went on last night. How about dinner tomorrow. I'll leave Ozzie home if you leave your dog home. Now, how much do I owe you for the dress?"

Cady knew paying for the dress was a matter of honor with Boomer. "Eighteen bucks," she said smartly.

"Sounds reasonable," Boomer said, handing

her a sheaf of bills. "I thought you were going to say something like eight hundred bucks. So, is it a date?"

"Sure. Hey, wait, I have to give you the money for the apple turnovers and coffee."

"They're on me. See you tomorrow."

Cady smiled all the way to her parked car. She was grinning from ear to ear as she drove the block and a half to the town square, where she parked the car and headed for the drugstore and hardware store. This time, though, she walked Atlas on his tartan leash, humming under her breath. Boomer was *so* good looking.

"Whew! Is it my imagination, or was this store the busiest you've ever seen it?" Julie Ambrose asked as she sat down on a spindly chair across from Amy Chambers. "We're out of everything. That Cady Jordan is gorgeous. In a million years I could never look like that. I loved that dress. She has a tan, too. The new police chief looked to me like he was staking out a claim on her. Did you see him pay her bill?"

"I saw," Amy snapped. "Did you see the morning paper? What are people saying?" Amy swigged from her coffee cup and bit into a cinnamon bun.

"Of course I saw it. We sell the paper, remember. Actually, we sold out. I was so busy, I only heard bits and pieces. One group is pissed because Cyrus King squelched the sale of the property. Hattie Brisbane said she wanted an outfit like Cady Jordan's. Melba Logan said she was a show-off. Meaning Cady. Said she was probably going to do a commercial for underwear or something like that for Victoria's Secret. The men were smirking, envying Boomer Ward. I would kill for that girl's shape," Julie prattled on.

"She wouldn't look like that if she'd had kids, like you and I," Amy snapped.

"Yes, she would, Amy. You can tell just by looking at her that she thinks appearance is important. You and I . . . we're on the go, we don't have money for fancy designer clothes and the like. We don't have time for the gym. At least I don't. I have to work to make ends meet. Of course, if I didn't eat half the stuff that comes out of the oven, I *might* get my weight down. You sound like you don't like Cady. Did something happen?"

Amy licked her fingers. "I thought that picture was disgusting. I'm going to write a letter to the editor about it, too. Nothing happened. Why do you even ask?" She eyed the last cinnamon bun on the paper plate in front of her. "Cady stopped by the other day. The house was a mess, I was a mess, and she looked like she just stepped out of a bandbox. I felt like crawling into a hole and pulling a cover over it."

"Sounds to me, Amy Chambers, like you're jealous of your old friend," Julie sniped.

"I am not jealous. Where is it written that I have to fall all over her just because we played together when we were ten years old?" She reached for the cinnamon bun and bit into it just as Pete Danson entered the shop.

"Hi, Amy."

"Hi yourself," Amy responded.

"The only thing left is one jelly donut and two cinnamon twists," Julie said, getting up to go behind the counter.

"I just came for coffee. I'm on my way to the courthouse."

"You just missed Cady and Boomer," Amy said, wiping the sugar off her mouth with a paper napkin.

"Really. That's okay, I have a dinner date with Cady this evening. I can see Boomer anytime. Take it easy, Amy. By the way, I was sorry to hear that Andy and Jill are having some marital difficulties. That's too bad. Jill's a nice girl."

"Now why did I know you were going to say that?" Amy muttered as she gathered up her plate and paper napkins. The table was littered with granules of sugar that she brushed onto the floor with her arm. Pete looked away, but not before Amy saw his look of disgust.

Amy waited five minutes before she left the bakery. She ran around the corner and down the block to Lupinsky's Gymnasium, where she signed up for a training program that would start within minutes.

★ ★ ★

Cady walked into Devine's Pharmacy and blinked. It looked like a Dollar Store, with its shelves of toys, kitchenware, plumbing supplies, and general bric-a-brac. She looked for the pharmacy section and the notions, and finally found them tucked away in a corner in back of the store, where there was a small soda fountain with tables and chairs that were full of elderly men and women reading the morning's paper. Everything smelled like Johnson's Baby Powder.

Cady sauntered over to the counter, aware that the men and women were staring at her. What was she supposed to do? *Be seen,* Lola said. She sat down and ordered a cup of coffee. She could hear the buzz of conversation behind her. When she felt a poke to her arm, she looked up at a little white-haired lady.

"Is it true, they're going to make a picture show right here in Indigo Valley? I saw your picture in the morning paper." She waved her arm to indicate the oldsters behind her. "We were wondering if we could be extras."

"I'll ask my grandmother," Cady said.

"That would be nice. We don't have much to do but sit around and read or gossip. That's what happens when you get old. You don't look like that old picture of you from that accident. I never for one minute believed you had anything to do with that boy's death. None of us believed it." She waved her arms again to indicate her friends behind her.

"Thank you for telling me that. I can't remember the accident, but I don't think I would have done anything like that."

"The boy was a bad seed. He used to uproot my prize geraniums just to be nasty. He put frogs in buckets with lids on so they couldn't breathe, and he was forever smashing pop bottles on the roads so people would get flat tires. He chased cats, and the Lord alone knew what he did to them when he did catch them. Anyone who is mean to animals is someone not to be trusted. I called his father, Cyrus, and the man said the boy was just being a boy. It was nice talking to you. My name is Millie Donovan." She offered up a gnarled, blue-veined hand. Cady shook it gently.

"You tell your grandmother we all watch her old pictures. Now, she was an actress. Not like these *flibbertigibbets* today."

"I'll be sure to tell her. It was nice meeting you, Mrs. Donovan."

"You're just as pretty as a picture, young woman."

Cady smiled. "Thank you." She went back to her coffee, finished it, paid for it, and left the store. She looked at her watch. Nine-thirty. Time to hit the hardware store.

Lattimer's Hardware Store was just like every other hardware store in a small town. Six rocking chairs lined the sidewalk next to the bags of fertilizer and peat moss. A dozen or so brooms were stacked, ends up, in a wooden barrel. Next to the barrel of brooms were dozens of bright green Weed Eaters. A blazing red sign taped to the window said everything was 10 percent off if you were a senior citizen. Sitting on all the rocking chairs were elderly men with newspapers on their laps, coffee cups from the bakery in their hands.

"Good morning, gentlemen," Cady said brightly as she sashayed into the store, where she bought a roll of duct tape just to have something to buy. She was sure Anthony would find a use for it in the garage.

The clerk rang up her purchase as she stared at Cady. "We went to school together, Cady. I recognized you from your picture in the morning paper. I'm Marie Lattimer. Do you remember me?" At Cady's blank look, she said, "It was a long time ago. We were snowflakes together in the Christmas pageant when we were nine." Cady smiled again. "You were best friends with Amy Hollister. She's married now."

"I just saw Amy in the bakery a little while ago. Everyone has changed so much. I guess I have, too. Are you married, Marie?"

"Sure am. I have a little boy named Zack. I married Ted Oliver. I work here two days a week to help out my dad. So, what do you think of Indigo Valley now that you're back? I bet you hardly recognize it, huh?"

"It's a nice town. It certainly has grown a lot

since I was here last. I like it, though. Obviously you do, too, since you stayed here."

Marie's dark curls bobbed up and down as she shook her head. "It's a great place to raise children. I like small towns, where you know everyone, and everyone helps each other. Is it really true that they're going to make a movie of your grandmother's life?"

"I think so."

"The whole town is buzzing about it. Ted told me last night that Cyrus King is opposed to the movie. He said he doesn't want that whole ugly episode brought up again. Ted works at the DMV, and Cyrus was there renewing his driver's license yesterday. I guess he had some advance information, seeing as how the article was just in this morning's paper. I don't care what that man says, I know you didn't have anything to do with their son's death."

Cady turned when she felt a presence behind her. "Uh-oh, you have another customer. It was nice seeing you again, Marie. Perhaps we can get together sometime for lunch."

"I'd really like that, Cady. Call me, okay?" the freckle-faced Marie said.

Cady made a mental note to call the smiling Marie.

Outside, Cady untied Atlas's leash from one of the broom handles. "Have a nice day, gentlemen," she said.

Inside the Mountaineer, Cady took a deep

breath. Mission accomplished. Now it was time to go to the cemetery. She'd never been to a cemetery for the simple reason she didn't know anyone who had died, thus eliminating the need to go to a cemetery. She dreaded the prospect.

She slipped the car into gear and drove off, back through town to the outskirts where she knew St. Andrews Cemetery was located. She was halfway to her destination when she remembered that Anthony's instructions were to buy flowers. She waited for a turnoff, turned around, and backtracked to a Giant Super Saver, where she purchased a bouquet of brightly colored Gerber daisies mixed with wild fern and baby's breath.

Ten minutes later she parked in Guest Parking next to a shiny red Mustang. Atlas growled as she attached the tartan leash to his collar and exited the car. Where to go. How was she supposed to locate the spot where Jeff King was buried? She vaguely remembered Anthony saying there was a site map of the Memorial Garden near the main entrance.

Atlas continued to whine and growl deep in his throat as they walked along. She shivered in the spring sunshine and wished she'd had the foresight to bring along a sweater.

Not only was there a site map, there was also an alphabetical listing of those interred. Cady let her gaze sweep down the long list of names until she came to the K's. Her heart slammed against her rib cage when she saw the name, Jeffrey Matthew King.

Next to the site map was a plastic box with maps and directions. Cady tucked the bouquet of flowers under her arm, her hold on Atlas's leash secure while she opened the box to take a copy of the map.

She wished she could be someplace else. Anywhere but there. It was pretty in an eerie kind of way, she thought, if cemeteries could be called pretty. The grass was emerald green, mowed and clipped with no sign of a weed to be seen. The oak and maple trees were in full dress, their leaves shiny and deep green. Grave sites under the magnificent trees were probably at a premium.

Cady stepped off the path to follow the arrows marked on her map, aware that the sparkling dew on the grass under the trees was starting to dry up.

She walked for a good ten minutes, stopping to gaze at some of the elaborate headstones or to read a name or a message carved in the granite. She saw the elegant stone from a distance and knew it belonged to the King family. She didn't know how she knew, but she did. Her steps slowed as she tried to take in the ornate stone with the three angels in flight, their chiseled wings works of art. She looked around. It was the tallest stone in that section of the cemetery. A picture of Jeffrey Matthew King was set in the middle of the stone with a protective covering. She bent down to stare at her old tormentor.

Jeffrey Matthew King and underneath his name the words, Beloved Son. It was hard for her to imagine Jeff King as anyone's beloved son. What was she supposed to do? Drop to her knees? Say a prayer? What? She placed the bouquet of Gerber daisies at the base of the gravestone and stepped back.

Cady narrowed her eyes, willing her mind to remember something. Anything. Why wasn't she feeling something? She'd hated the boy resting beneath the stone. Surely she should feel something, even if it was hate or anger. Where had all those feelings gone? Maybe she needed to sit on one of the little benches under the maple tree. If she did that, maybe something would come to her.

To her surprise, a young woman about her own age was sitting on the bench, a wad of tissues clutched in her hand. *She must be the owner of the red Mustang,* she thought.

Cady smiled and sat down, her gaze sweeping the long line of tombstones ahead of her. The three angels in flight blocked her view of the cobbled path and the velvety expanse of lawn that was being mowed by the caretaker.

She's pretty, Cady thought. *And so very sad.* "This is the first time I've ever been to a cemetery," she volunteered.

The young woman stared at her. "That makes you a very lucky person. My dad is here.

I try to come at least once a week. I always think something miraculous is going to happen when I come here, but it never does. I don't know why I come here because I never feel better when I leave. I don't pray when I come here either. I do that in church. Sometimes I talk, but I know that's pretty silly. It's just to make myself feel better, only it doesn't work either. Mostly, I just sit here and stare at the stone and think about the past. My mother never comes here. I don't know why that is. Is someone in your family buried here?"

"No. Just someone I used to know. I brought some flowers."

"That was a nice thing to do. I always bring flowers, too. I think I come here hoping to find answers. When you say it out loud like that, it sounds silly, too. It's peaceful here, no televisions, no ringing phones. Just the quiet. I guess you could say it's the end of the road. I bet no one visits half of these graves. There's never anyone here when I come. I was shocked to see you. By the way, my name is Jill."

"Hello, Jill," Cady said, extending her hand. "I'm Cady Jordan."

Jill laughed. "You look better in person than that picture in the morning paper. Ah, now I see why you're here. You came to the boy's grave site."

"Yes. I don't know what I expected. I don't understand why I don't feel something. I guess you know the story then. Did we ever meet?

Did we go to school together?"

"No, we never met. I was born and raised in Pittsburgh. I moved here shortly after my parents moved here. I got married, then my dad died suddenly. It was a bad time. I know the story, though, because I married Andy Hollister."

Cady blinked in surprise. "No kidding. How is Andy these days? I saw him the other day, and we waved in passing. He was on his way to Amy's house." Wait till she told all of this to Lola, Mandy, and Anthony.

"Andy and I hit a bit of a rough patch recently. He moved out and stayed with Amy for a day or so, then got an apartment of his own. We're going to try and work at it to see if we can't make things right. At least I'm hoping we can work at it. I'm willing but Andy . . . Andy . . ."

". . . Andy allows other people to run his life. When we were kids, Amy called the shots. We always did what Amy wanted when she wanted it. I guess some things never change." Cady sighed. "I hope you work things out. Don't give up would be my advice."

"I could always talk to my dad and tell him things. He'd think about it, and somehow or other, he always came up with just the right answer. I was talking to him before, but of course there were no ready-made answers. I'm going to have to work this out myself. You look to me like you're trying to work something out yourself."

"I am. I'm trying to remember what happened that day."

"Listen, I don't have anything to do. Let's you and I go to breakfast. My treat. We can talk about our hairdos, the latest fashions, those dumb TV shows, or we can sit and eat our breakfast. You can tell me all about the movie they're going to make, and I can tell you what a miserable bitch Amy Chambers is. What do you say?"

"I say that's a great idea. Let's go Dutch, though."

"Okay. I'll meet you at Eva's. She makes the best potato, cheese, onion casserole in the state, and her bacon is to die for. The eggs aren't bad either. She grinds her own blend of coffee, too."

"Sounds too good to pass up. I'll meet you there, but give me ten extra minutes. I want to drop my dog off at home. I hate for him to sit in the car."

"You got it," the long-legged woman called over her shoulder.

Cady parked the Mountaineer next to the red Mustang and climbed out at the same moment Jill Hollister exited her car. Jill laughed when Cady offered up a snappy salute, at the same time looking at her watch. "Eighteen minutes. Sometimes I amaze myself."

They walked through Eva's parking lot, which Eva shared with Lupinsky's Gymnasium customers just as Amy Chambers huffed and puffed her way to the car.

It all happened in the blink of an eye. Jill, her head down, was pretending to play hopscotch, wiggling and weaving her way between the parking lines as Cady cheered her on, laughing so hard she doubled over. Amy stopped in midstride, stared at both laughing women as her color turned from red to white to pasty gray.

"God, how I hate you!"

"That wasn't for you, Cady, that was for me. Don't let it bother you," Jill said, sobering instantly.

"I'm not so sure of that, Jill. Why do you think she hates you?" Cady asked.

"Because I took her brother away from her. Amy likes to control things. I'll deal with Amy in my own way. Let's not let her spoil things. We're just two girls going to breakfast, right?"

"Right."

Cady turned and waved. If Jill hadn't pulled her out of the way, Amy would have run her over.

"Now, *that's* a bad-ass attitude if I ever saw one," Jill muttered. "All she has to do is *appear*, and things get ruined. We aren't going to let that happen, are we, Cady?"

"No, we are not going to let that happen. Let's eat. I'm starved."

Rage rivered through Amy as she drove home. Her jaw was clenched so tight, she thought her teeth would crack in two. The minute she entered the house, she slammed the door shut, locked it, and raced upstairs, where she showered and dressed. The rage stayed with her as she fussed and fumed with her curly hair, one eye on the unmade bed and the piles of dirty clothes scattered everywhere. Her world was coming apart, and she didn't know what to do about it.

Everyone was sucking up to Cady Jordan. Everyone but her. Were they stupid, or was she the stupid one? Pete Danson had a date with Cady this evening. Boomer paid for her coffee and pastry this morning, then sat on the bench with her. They'd had a date the night before. Jill appeared to be Cady's new best friend. Andy wanted nothing to do with her. Where did that leave her, Amy Chambers? Out in the cold, that's where.

"Like hell," she mumbled as she trundled down the hall and up the steps to the attic, where she stood looking around in dismay.

The attic, like the rest of Amy's house, was a mess. Ripped lamp shades, rusty bikes, and skates were scattered about, as were doll buggies minus wheels. Wagons minus their pull handles leaned drunkenly in the far corners. Boxes of junk, broken toys, and rusty tools, along with bags of old clothes, were everywhere, forcing her to kick things out of the way to get to the trunk where the mementos of her youth were stored.

She yanked at the Flexible Flyer sled with

rusty runners hanging from its hook on the wall and sat down on it. Did she really want to open this trunk? Did she really want to look at the pictures she'd taken that day so long ago? What would the pictures prove? Nothing. Only that Jeff King was on the zip line a few feet from Cady. That, as far as she could remember, was the last picture she'd taken. She'd dropped the camera when Andy shouted to her to start throwing rocks because she was the one with the best pitching arm.

She was the one who hit Jeff King in the head, killing him. She was the one who hit Cady in the middle of the back. Not that she meant to hit Jeff. Her aim had been off when Jeff collapsed against Cady; otherwise, the rock would have gotten him on the shoulder. There was no point in lying to herself any longer.

She'd always been jealous of Cady. She'd just wanted to scare her, to make herself feel good that day. Jealous because Pete liked Cady better than he liked her. Even Andy liked Cady. Boomer Ward liked her, too, she could tell. Jeff picked on her because, in his own cockeyed way, he'd liked her, too. The devil was in her that day.

Guilty as sin.

She bolted off the Flexible Flyer and raced down the steps to the bathroom, where she lost everything she'd consumed earlier at the bakery.

She wished she could just lie down and die.

Chapter 12

They were waiting for her just the way they waited earlier, only this time they were on Lola's terrace. A pitcher of ice-cold lemonade and a plate of warm cookies sat in the middle of the table off to the side of Lola's chaise lounge. The cookies were Anthony's contribution, the lemonade, Mandy's. Lola just indulged.

Cady kicked off her sandals as she ran out to the terrace. "Wait till you hear! Just wait till you hear! Oh, this is so nice," she said, as Anthony rolled out the retractable awning to shade the third-floor terrace so that Lola wouldn't be sitting in the direct sun.

"Don't keep us in suspense, child, tell us. Anthony, pour this darling girl some lemonade. The cookies are still warm. They're your favorite, peanut butter."

"I bought you some duct tape, Anthony. I had to buy something at the hardware store. I think I met a new friend in Marie Lattimer. Her father owns the hardware. She said we were snowflakes together in a school play. I can't remember that. Anyway, everyone in town knows about the movie. Everyone in town knows Cyrus King scotched the sale. Boomer paid for my baked goods and coffee at the bakery because I forgot my purse. Amy was there stuffing her face with pastries. Boomer and I have another date tomorrow. He forked over eighteen bucks for my dress," Cady said breathlessly. She gulped at the tart lemonade, then added four sugar packets, to Mandy's chagrin.

"What! Eighteen dollars wouldn't cover the cost of the thread," Lola squawked.

Cady rolled her eyes. "Guys don't know anything about women's clothes. He said he was worried it was going to cost him eight hundred bucks. I was being nice."

"Very nice." Mandy grimaced.

Cady took a deep breath and continued. "I went to the cemetery, and yes, Anthony, I took flowers, and who do you think I met there?"

"Cyrus King," Lola said triumphantly.

"Wrong."

"The boy's mother. I think her name is Marilyn or Mary Ann, or maybe it's Maxine," Mandy said.

"Wrong again."

"The mayor or maybe an angel," Anthony said.

"Wrong again. Jill Hollister, Andy's wife. We even went to breakfast together. She offered to pay for it, too. On our way into Eva's, and boy does she make good bacon, who do you think tried to run me over in the parking lot? Amy Hollister Chambers, that's who. If Jill hadn't pulled me out of the way, she would have mowed me down. She said, and this is a quote now, 'God, how I hate you!' Jill said it was meant for her, but I'm not so sure." Cady gulped again at the cold drink before she added two more packets of sugar. She stirred her drink vigorously, her eyes on the bug-eyed Big Three.

They looked like three wise old owls as they stared at her. "And you think this means . . . what?" Lola asked, a frown starting to build between her brows.

"I don't know. I thought surely one of you would have a clue. For God's sake, she tried to run me down, Lola!"

"You could file a complaint with the new police chief," Anthony said.

"I don't want to do that. Whatever is bothering Amy is Amy's problem. I'll be careful, don't worry. I wish you could have seen Jeff King's tombstone. It has three huge carved angels in flight. It's the biggest one in the cemetery. It was rather awesome. Almost like someone was trying to make up for something by having the biggest and the best in the whole garden."

"Did the visit to the cemetery trigger any memories, Cady?" Lola asked.

"No, unfortunately. I didn't feel anything. I

should have felt something. Anger, sadness that a young boy died. I felt nothing. Jill was crying, but then it was her father buried there. I can understand her sadness and the tears. She's nice, I liked her. She might become a friend if Amy doesn't screw it up."

"Now if this was a movie I was directing, my instincts would lead me to Amy as the person to watch out for. Am I wrong, Cady, in assuming that as children, she was the ringleader and the rest of you were followers?" Anthony asked.

"She always had the best ideas. At least the most daring ideas. It was her idea to rig the zip line. She read about it in a comic book. She always got to be Maid Marian when we played Robin Hood. She would only agree to play if she got the part of Marian. She always got the red checkers, too. If it wasn't her idea, she didn't want to play. She was like that in school, too. One of our teachers used to say she was bossy."

"It would seem that trait followed her into adult life. Traits like that become obsessive later on. Perhaps she sees herself losing control over her brother with his wife. You're back in town, and I think we've all agreed, she doesn't like you very much. Then there's the secret they've kept all these years. Assuming," Lola said, holding up her hand to ward off protests, "they were all there that day, which we assume they were. Now, Cady threw in her little clinker the day she went to Amy's house by asking her why she lied. That might be heating things up a bit."

"Where does that leave us?" Mandy demanded.

"Exactly where we were earlier this morning. We're in a holding pattern. Mr. Denville said he would get back to us today after he interviewed the Kings and a few other people. He said he tracked down the old police chief, who retired a good many years ago." Lola glanced down at the diamond-studded watch on her bony wrist. "Actually, he's probably speaking with the old chief right this very minute. Isn't it lunchtime, Anthony?"

"In about two hours. Now if you want to get rid of me, just say so. I know all about girl talk."

"No. I'm hungry. Let's have something scrumptious. Shrimp scampi sounds good. A nice crisp salad and some garlic bread. A *big* glass of fine wine and some Kona coffee, and, if it isn't too much trouble, a cobbler of some sort. Not those frozen ones. A *real* one. Two hours from now will be fine."

"What are you going to do, Cady?" Mandy asked.

"I think I'm going to change and go running. Atlas could use some exercise. When I get back I'm going to pore over those scrapbooks until it's time to get ready for my date with Pete. Is there anything you want me to do?"

"Run along, dear. We'll just sit here and reminisce the way us old people do. Enjoy your run," Lola said.

The chubby reporter chugged his way up the Kings' driveway, then cut across the lawn to the front door of the house. He jabbed at the bell as he marveled at the tidy borders of flowers every color of the rainbow. He'd met Maxine King, and he seriously doubted she was the one who had planted the flowers. He'd bet a week's pay she wasn't the one who watered them either.

A maid wearing a gray uniform with a pristine white apron and little white cap on her head looked at him inquiringly when she opened the door. Denville handed her his business card, while he whipped out his press credentials from his shirt pocket with his other hand. "I'd like to speak to either Mr. or Mrs. King. It's about the death of their son. The paper is going to do a feature article on the old case now that a movie is going to be made on the life of Lola Jor Dan."

The maid stared down at the card, which had his picture on it. "Wait here," she said coolly.

She returned in five minutes, and said, "Mrs. King said to tell you she has nothing to say that hasn't already been said."

"That sounds evasive to me. I guess I can quote you on that, right?"

"On what?" the maid said, clearly flustered.

259

"That she's evasive and has nothing to say that hasn't already been said. I would think a mother would *always* have something to say about her child's death no matter how many years have gone by, don't you agree?"

"Well, yes, but I'm not . . ."

"Can I quote you on agreeing with me?"

The door suddenly jerked backward and Mrs. King appeared. "Why are you harassing my maid, Mr. Denville?"

"I wasn't harassing her. I simply asked her a few questions. She was agreeing with me, and I just wanted to make sure I got it straight. You have to do that when you write for a newspaper. It's a rule. Did you change your mind about talking to me, Mrs. King?"

"This is all because that girl has come back to town. I knew this would happen. Don't the dead deserve to rest in peace?"

Denville knew what the word *haughty* meant. However, he'd never come across anyone to whom he could apply it. Until now. Maxine King was haughty from the top of her well-coiffed head to the tips of her pointy-toed shoes. She was pencil-thin, with stringy arms and skinny legs. Her waist, he surmised, was probably eighteen inches, not a tad more. Her eyes were so green he knew their color had to be artificial. No one had eyes as green as the grass on a golf course unless they wore tinted contact lenses. And he surmised that that must be collagen in her lips. They were way too puffy for her skinny face. The word *ghoul* came to his mind.

"Well?"

"Well what, Mrs. King?"

"I asked you if the dead didn't deserve to rest in peace."

"I agree with you that the dead should rest in peace. However, think about how much more peaceful your son will rest if we manage to right an old wrong. Back then you and your husband made some very strong statements about Cady Jordan. Since Cady herself was badly injured, as I'm sure you know, and she temporarily lost her memory, and there were no witnesses to the accident, there are grounds for slander. Now, I'm not saying Cady Jordan is going to up and sue you and Mr. King, but she might. I, for one, certainly wouldn't want to go up against the battery of lawyers her grandmother will bring in. I'm going to talk to everyone in this town until we get it right. Now, I'd like a comment from you, Mrs. King."

Maxine King's gaze swept past the chubby reporter to her husband, who was coming up the walkway. Her green eyes turned to hard polished glass as she stared at her handsome husband.

"Denville," Cyrus King said curtly. "What are you doing here?"

"I came out here to get a comment from you and your wife concerning the tragedy of your son's death. And to get your explanation of why

261

you squelched the sale of the land to Lola Jor Dan. She's not a lady you want to make an enemy of. I think you might have done that."

Years ago, Cyrus King had been a dashing hunk of a football player, with girls fawning all over him, according to Larry's father. His father also said he was dumb as dirt when it came to books but hell on wheels when it came to partying and sleeping with other people's wives or girlfriends. His father had gone on to say he'd been arrogant, selfish, and downright disrespectful of everything and anything and only concerned with the good life. He'd managed to get himself thrown out of five colleges before he settled down, married Maxine Columbus, and went to work in his father's glove factory. The threat of being disinherited had worked wonders. Or so said his father.

"My wife and I really don't have anything to say to you, Mr. Denville. The past is behind us. We can't undo what happened. Our son is gone. Why do you people have to dredge it up over and over again? As for the land, it was appraised at far more than Miss Jor Dan's offer. Yes, the town could use the money, but we can't kowtow to her celebrity. Let her go make her movie somewhere else. That's all I have to say on the matter."

"Mr. Denville said Cady Jordan might sue us, Cyrus," Maxine said. "He said we made some strong statements and accusations."

"Don't you mean *you* made some strong accusations and statements, dear?"

"I didn't say accusations, Mrs. King. I said strong statements," Denville hastened to clarify.

All of a sudden, the pompous Cyrus King looked like he'd been hit with a Mack truck. He seemed to deflate right in front of the reporter's eyes. His wife looked smug. "She won't sue us, will she, dear?"

I just missed something, Denville thought. *What the hell did I miss.* "That's it? That's all you care to say?"

"My husband and I will sue if that movie star portrays our son as a bully. You can quote me on that."

"I will, of course. However, if others come forward and attest to having had run-ins with your son and will swear he was a bully, then he's going to be a bully in the movie."

"Cyrus, tell this man we mean business. I will not tolerate this, do you hear me?" Her voice was so shrill, Larry felt the urge to clamp his hands over his ears.

"Half of Indigo Valley can hear you, Maxine. No one is going to sue anyone. Good-bye, Mr. Denville."

Denville wished he could become invisible and follow the couple into the house. Oh, to be a fly on the wall. He knew in his reporter's gut he'd missed something. Maybe it wasn't words but looks or a movement. Something. Cyrus King said there would be no lawsuits. Maxine

King said there would be. If he was a betting man, he'd bet on Maxine King. It was obvious to him that Maxine King ruled the house, and Cyrus King did exactly what she said when she said it. How, he wondered, had that happened, given what his father had told him about Cyrus. He shrugged as he made his way back to his car. He knew they were watching him from the window, so he put on his own show for their benefit by taking his recorder out of his breast pocket and putting it up to his ear. Then he made some notes on a pad he kept in the car before he drove off.

His next stop, ex-chief Harry Wallaby.

Harry Wallaby was a rotund little man with the sharpest eyes Denville had ever seen. He was a cabinetmaker these days, spending his retirement in a little shop sandwiched between a tire store and a small bead factory. He was fond of saying he worked just enough hours to keep him out of his wife's hair and himself out of trouble.

Denville had gone to school with Harry's youngest son, who now lived in Scranton. He'd had many a spaghetti dinner at Harry's kitchen table, listening to the police scanner, which was always on, to Mrs. Wallaby's dismay. The amenities over, Denville got down to business. "Tell me everything you can remember about the accident out at the pond. Any little thing that maybe didn't sit right with you. You were a good cop, everyone said so. I'm thinking there was stuff that maybe didn't get into the papers or was never talked about. Help me, Mr. Wallaby. Cady's back in town in case you haven't heard. I know it's late in the game, but my dad always said it's never too late to right a wrong. Her grandmother told me about those three years she suffered. Somebody should have to acknowledge or pay for what happened to her."

"It was all in the paper, Larry. We didn't hold anything back. Cyrus now, he was like a wild man at first. His wife, now, she was a different story. She never once asked about the girl. 'Course she'd just lost her son, so maybe that's understandable. Cyrus backed off early on and let his wife do all the talking. She's the one who said Cady killed her son. Hell, the woman said a lot of stuff, none of which could be backed up. Her son was an out-and-out bully. The worst kind. We tried to tell her that, but she didn't want to hear it. I wanted to laugh when I saw those angels she had carved over his tombstone. She goes out there every week, never misses. Cyrus now, he never goes. How I know this is because John Bishop, the caretaker, told me.

"Now if you're asking me if I had any *private* theories, well, son, I had a whole bagful back then. I always figured those kids were there that day. I don't mean just Jeff and young Cady. There was the foil from a roll of camera film that was fresh. Forensics told us that. We were dealing with ten-year-olds, and you can go just so far.

"The parents were up in arms. They wouldn't allow us to question the kids after the initial go-round. They were in the park, and that was that. Those twins stood right there and lied with the straightest faces I've ever seen. My gut said they were lying, but gut feelings don't hold up in an investigation. Pete Danson, now, he was different. That boy did his damnedest not to cry. He was really shook up, but he stuck by his story. His old man was a drunk, and you know how they get. His mother, well, poor soul, she was orbiting Mars or something around that time. I tried talking to him on the Q.T., but he didn't budge from his story. Hell, the kid had enough on his plate without me digging at him. Boomer Ward got shipped off to some relatives that summer. This is just a gut feeling again, but I always thought it was Boomer that called the police that day. My deputy thought it was Danson. I know it was one or the other, and not the Hollister boy."

"The girl never got her memory back, is that it?"

"No, she never did.

"You know, we rigged up a line, used dummies with the kid's approximate weights and tried to do a reenactment of that day. We pitched rocks, we played with the tie lines. We did it all. The final result was death by misadventure. I will say one thing, though. Whoever threw those rocks had one hell of a pitching arm. Even some of my guys couldn't whack the dummies we had sliding down that zip line. If you're going to ask me if it was an accident, my answer would be, I just don't know. This town was in such an uproar, we had to bring closure as fast as we could. To this day I don't know if we were right or wrong. I never want to see anything like that ever again.

"How are you going to write that all up, son?"

"I don't know, Mr. Wallaby. The camera foil, did it have fingerprints on it? Where is it? Did it go into an evidence bag?"

"It was smudged, no prints could be retrieved. I'm sure it's been filed away somewhere. We never threw evidence away," Wallaby huffed.

"If you were me, where would you look? Who would you home in on?"

Wallaby didn't have to think about his answer. "The twins. The girl especially. The boy was pretty wimpy as I recall. That little girl had a mouth on her that was downright sinful. She was bossy as all get-out. That first day we had the three of them together, and she called the shots. She answered for all of them. I think, mind you, this is just my opinion, it was so they could all get their stories straight. What really amazed me was they didn't buckle. Little kids as a rule are afraid of the uniform. When it was his turn, the Ward kid just stood there next to his parents and gave us his story real straightforward, and that was that. He said he was at the pond earlier with Jeff King, and no one else was there so they went home. If he was lying, I sure couldn't tell. What good is this going to do if you dredge it up all over again?"

"Don't you think Cady Jordan deserves to know what happened?"

"Sometimes the truth is bitter, Larry. It's that old let sleeping dogs lie thing, if you know what I mean."

"You know what, Mr. Wallaby, she has a right to know the truth, even if it is bitter. She's all grown-up now, and I think she can handle it. How would you like to go through life with everyone thinking you'd had something to do with a friend's death? That has to lie pretty heavy on a young person's shoulders. She has to be able to get past it. Otherwise, how can she move on with her life?"

"Yes, I guess you have a point, Larry. The fallout, I'm thinking, is going to be horrendous."

"I guess everyone involved will just have to deal with it, won't they? The next time you talk to Ross, tell him I said hi. Is he coming home for Memorial Day?"

Wallaby shrugged. "He never tells us until the night before. Probably not, since he's got himself a new girlfriend."

The reporter looked at his watch. Who

should he tackle next? Pete, Boomer, or the Hollister twins? He opted for Amy for one reason only. He didn't like her. He'd asked her to the junior prom, and she'd refused. Even now, all these years later, he could still cringe at her biting refusal. She'd put her hands on her hips and stared at him. Then she'd burst out laughing and said she'd rather stay home than go with him. She hadn't stayed home, but she didn't have a date that year either. Her twin brother had taken her. Larry had taken Emily Jackson and actually had a good time.

It was his turn now.

Payback time.

She was home. That was good, Denville thought, when he pulled alongside Amy's van twenty minutes later. Notepad in hand, his recorder turned on, he exited his car and walked up the walkway to Amy's small front porch. He rang the bell and waited.

And waited. He rang the bell a second time.

"All right! All right! I'm coming!" The voice came from the second floor. She sounded like a herd of elephants as she bounded down the steps.

Amy Chambers peered through the screen door. "What do *you* want? If it's about your taxes, go to Arnie's office."

"Nope. I want to talk to you, Amy. The paper is doing a story on the old Jeff King case. I want some comments from you."

"Well, guess what, Larry Denville, I don't want to talk to you, and I sure don't have any comments. I wasn't there that day, and I have nothing to say. Go bother someone else. I'm busy. Isn't there something interesting going on in this town that you can report on? No one wants to read about all that old crap."

"Crap?" Larry scribbled the word in his notebook. "I guess I can quote you on the fact that you think Jeff King's death was, or is, crap."

"I didn't mean it that way, and you know it. I meant this circus you've been conducting. First it was all those articles in the paper, the film of the famous movie star, then the thing at the pond, and now *another* article. What are you trying to do? And no, Jeff's death was not crap. It was a tragic accident. Everyone said so, even the police. Your own paper said it was a tragic accident."

"Says who? They just said what the town wanted them to say. I spoke to Chief Wallaby, and he told me something they never put in the paper. That day they found a foil wrapper from a roll of film. It's still in the evidence bag at the police lockup. Back then they didn't have the new methods we have today to retrieve finger-prints. What was on there was smudged, but they did preserve it nonetheless. Don't you watch that television show *CSI*? Forensics these days is amazing."

It was hard to tell by looking at her through

the screen door, but Denville thought she looked whiter than snow.

"Is that supposed to mean something to me, Larry Denville?"

"It sure as hell means something to me. It means I remember you back then, and you always had a camera with you. You kept it in the basket of your bike. You always said you wanted to be a photographer when you grew up. I imagine the others will remember that."

"Obviously I changed my mind about photography being my life's work. I'm very content being a homemaker and raising my children. I don't live in the past, like some people in this town. Life goes on. Why can't you just leave it alone? I can't imagine the Kings being very happy with you."

"News is news. Now, let's have a comment. Are you sticking by your story that you weren't at the pond the day of the accident? Remember now, forensics can pin stuff down to the minute these days. You really need to start watching that show, Amy."

Amy brushed at her hair with a shaking hand. "Why does that sound like a threat, Larry? Furthermore, I can't even begin to imagine why you would think I'd have a comment after all these years. Hashing and rehashing that story is all about selling papers, and you know it."

"Nah. I really studied the police reports, and I can recite the old newspaper articles by heart.

There was something funny about all of that, and I'd bet my press badge that you and your buddies had something to do with that accident."

"Then you'd lose your press badge. Now go bother someone else. I have things to do, and they don't include talking to you about the mess you're creating. Don't you dare say I made any comments in that rag paper of yours either. If you do, I'll sue you. I mean it, Larry."

The reporter slapped at his forehead as he stared at Amy. "I would think you'd be the first one who wanted to make a comment. Everyone said Cady Jordan was your best friend. You sure don't sound friendly to me, Amy. I sure hope the others back up your story. Do you want me to let you know about the film wrapper?"

She responded by slamming the door in his face. He shrugged as he made his way to the car, knowing that Amy Chambers was watching him through the window as Maxine and Cyrus King had. He made a show of adjusting his pocket recorder before jotting a few lines in his notebook. "You were there, Amy. I know it as sure as I know I'm going to write this story," he muttered as he slipped the car into gear and backed out of the driveway.

Next on his list, Andy Hollister.

Denville looked at his watch. One o'clock. Andy Hollister was a creature of habit as everyone in town knew. He ate lunch at Martine's

Café every day of the week. Mainly because of their health-conscious menu, and it was only two doors away from his insurance office.

Two down and three to go. Four if you counted Cady Jordan. Six if he counted the twins' parents and Boomer's parents. Then again, maybe it was seven if he wanted to get in touch with Cady's parents. The forgotten people in that long-ago tragedy. He wondered if the paper would spring for a trip to wherever it was Cady's parents lived.

Amy watched from behind the blinds in her living room as the reporter drove away. She was so light-headed from the verbal confrontation, she tottered over to the sofa, where she sat down and put her head between her legs.

Her world was falling apart. Her thoughts ricocheted wildly as she wished for Larry Denville to get run over by a steamroller on his way back to the office, and for her brother to come crawling on his hands and knees up her driveway begging for her to take him in. Her thoughts careened to Pete Danson, her brother's wife, Jill, Cady, and Boomer. If they would all just die, she would be totally happy. *God, what is happening to me? When did I turn into this ugly, hateful person?*

When Cady Jordan came back to town, that's when.

She bounded off the sofa, searched for her car keys and purse. She needed help, and she knew it.

It wasn't exactly the wrong side of the tracks, but it was a shabby neighborhood. It was where she'd grown up and where her parents still lived. The houses were tract houses, ranch style, with very little lawn, no porches, and a small concrete slab off the kitchen that posed as a patio. Her parents were not into outside maintenance. They weren't into inside maintenance either. Occasionally, the lawn got mowed, usually when the grass and weeds were ankle high. Andy used to mow the lawn with an old, rusty, push mower. Inside, the furniture and the walls were the same as when she used to live there.

Alma Hollister had more important things to do with her time than keeping house. On Fridays she had a general waxing and got her hair done. Saturdays were for nails and pedicures. Sunday was designated for canasta and a brunch, usually something that could be microwaved. Monday was for garage sales, Tuesdays was girls' day out with her friends, Wednesday was appreciation day, where Alma and all her friends appreciated each other in great detail. Thursday was considered a lazy day, a day to catch up on the soap operas and read the trashy tabloids.

Fred Hollister still worked at the school as the head janitor. After work, he hung out with his cronies, either playing cards or swigging beer. It was a seven-day-a-week lifestyle that didn't leave room for much else but sleeping.

Amy hated going there, and she did so as

rarely as possible. She liked going to Arnie's parents' because they were normal people, and they liked their grandchildren.

Amy opened the screen door and shouted to her mother.

"I'm out on the patio," came the response.

Amy backed out of the door and walked around to the back, where her mother was repairing a broken nail. "How are you, Mom?"

"I'm fine, as you can see. If you'd call once in a while, it would be nice. The last time you were here was Christmas."

"The kids keep me busy, Mom. You're never here anyway. You told me you didn't like it when I popped in and disrupted you and your friends. By the way, where are they today?"

"They all went on a cruise. Your father couldn't get off work so I couldn't go. It was for senior couples . . . as in two." Her voice was so bitter-sounding, Amy cringed.

"You musta come out here for a reason, Amy, so spit it out."

"Mom, I think I might be in some trouble."

"Well, what do you want me to do about it? You have a husband. When you left this house, my responsibility ended."

Something in Amy snapped. "What responsibility are you talking about, Mom? You didn't raise Andy and me. We raised ourselves. Actually, I raised Andy. Half the time you didn't know we were alive. We came and went and did whatever we felt like doing. We didn't have a set bedtime. I got us up for school. I didn't know what a hot breakfast was till I went to college. Andy and I worked and bought our own clothes. Half the time we bought our own food. That's probably why I have high cholesterol at such a young age. It was all that fast food and grease."

"Are you saying I wasn't a good mother?" Alma Hollister screeched, her cotton candy hairdo moving in her own breeze.

"You weren't *any* kind of a mother. One time I wore the same underwear for a week because you didn't wash clothes. I had to ask the neighbors how to work the washer, and from that day on, I did my and Andy's clothes. You didn't take care of us when we were sick either. I used to steal money out of your purse to buy cough medicine for me and Andy in the winter. No, you weren't a mother.

"Did you know people in this town used to call us white trash? That's pretty hard for a kid to live down."

"You survived, didn't you," Alma snapped. "If I'm such a lousy mother, what are you doing here?"

"I don't know. I thought . . . I don't know what I thought. I guess I wanted you to look at me and show some concern. I wanted you to ask me what was wrong and if there was anything you could do to help me."

"I have problems of my own, Amy. You've really *porked* up since Christmas, haven't you?

If your husband is having an affair, that might be the reason. Men like thin women, women who take care of themselves."

"My husband likes me just fine the way I am, and no, he is not having an affair."

"The wife is always the last to know," Alma sniffed. "So, what kind of trouble are you in? Did you bounce a check or something?"

"No, Mom. Do you remember Cady Jordan?"

"I certainly do remember her. Nicest little girl you could ever hope to meet considering those parents she had. They were a bad lot. Begging for money all the time. I saw her the other day. She was just as nice and sweet as she was when she was little. Saw her in the drugstore. I always hoped she would rub off on you, but I guess that was too much to hope for."

Amy sucked in her breath. "Mom, did you ever love me and Andy?"

Alma Hollister had to think about the question so long, Amy started to cry. "Mothers are supposed to love their children."

"Well, Miss Smarty Pants, it's pretty hard to shower love when you don't get sleep and you have two squalling babies who think night is day and day is night. I went through two washing machines that first year. Of course I loved you. Not that kissy, coochie coo love nonsense. I was always too tired to go overboard with all that, and your father was no help at all. Don't you love your kids? Is that what this visit is all about?"

Amy stared at her mother in her pink pedal pushers and matching top and thong sandals. "I didn't love you. I don't think Andy did either."

"Well la de da. If you're done attacking me, you can leave now."

The urge to cry again was so strong, Amy bit down on her lip. "What was it you liked so much about Cady, Mom?"

"She was respectful. She called me ma'am. She said please and thank you. She was always clean even though her clothes were mended, and she had the prettiest pigtail. I remember one time she came over here on her bike for you, and she brought me a bunch of daisies from her yard. She was a sweet little girl. Andy liked her a lot. He wanted to give her a going-away present, but I was short that week and didn't have any extra money. If I had it, I would have given it to him. Then that accident happened. I felt bad that he didn't have a present to give her. She had a hard time of it. I wish you had been more like her. I wish Andy had been more like Pete. He was a nice boy. You two were hellions. You were so out of control, your father and I just gave up on you."

"Just like that you gave up on us."

"After that accident that probably wasn't an accident, your father and I talked. We knew you two had something to do with it. I know you did. I don't want to know about it, Amy. Isn't it time for you to pick your kids up from school?"

Amy looked at her watch. Her mother was right. The girls would be screaming their heads off if she arrived late.

"Bye, Mom."

Alma waved as her daughter took off running.

Chapter 13

Cady stared at her reflection in the mirror. She practiced smiling, grimacing, rolling her eyes, then laughing out loud. Atlas barked, not understanding what she was doing. She dropped to her knees to fondle the dog's ears. "I was just staring at myself wondering how I lived in that cocoon for so long. It was a gray life, with no color. That's all different now. Just look at us. You aren't in a cage anymore, wondering if you're going to eat today. I'm not in a cage of my own making anymore either. Lola said it was a big world out there, and we're in it now. I feel . . . elegant. I think I look nice. I never thought I could look or feel this good. I'm happy. Isn't that amazing? But, best of all, I'm not fearful like I was before we came here. Well, maybe just a little fearful, but certainly nothing like I was."

Atlas rolled over, a sign that Cady was to rub his belly. If he had been a cat, he would have purred in delight.

"If this was a perfect world, I'd go to bed tonight and wake up with my memory intact tomorrow morning. Since it isn't a perfect world, I have to keep trying to remember. Maybe Pete will say something tonight that will trigger a memory. I feel like I'm on the edge of remembering, but it just won't surface. Tonight I'm going to ask Pete point-blank about that day, and tomorrow I'm going to ask Boomer point-blank, too." She wondered what her friends back in Brentwood would say if they knew she talked to a dog. "Who cares!" She laughed.

Cady stood up, peered into the vanity mirror again. Satisfied with her appearance, she headed for the first floor to wait for Pete. Atlas whimpered at her feet. "I can't take you with me tonight, boy. I want you to stay with Lola. Go ahead, she's waiting for you." The dog obediently trotted off, as Cady made her way down the long staircase.

Anthony appeared from the living room just as the doorbell rang. He eyed her from tip to toe before he nodded his approval. "In that dress, you sashay. You know how to do that, don't you?" Cady looked blank. He demonstrated. "It's all in the hips. Quick, show me you can do it."

"I feel silly doing this," Cady said as she imitated Anthony.

"That will do for now, but you need to work on it. Think of it as art. Lola can show you tomorrow. It was one of her trademarks. There wasn't anyone in all of Hollywood who could *strut* like Lola. We'll work on that, too."

"What's that going to get me?" Cady hissed.

"A husband," Anthony hissed back a second before he opened the door.

Cady could feel a warm flush work its way up her neck. "Oh," was all she could think of to say.

When they were buckled up and the car was in gear, Pete turned to her. "What are you in the mood for?"

Once she would have shrugged and said something like, it doesn't matter. That was the old Cady. "I think I'd like some good Japanese. Hibachi style."

"You got it! So, how was your day? By the way, you look really nice. I like that color on you. What's it called?"

"Burnt orange. You look nice yourself." And he did. He wasn't overdressed in a suit and tie. He wore creased chinos, a white button-down shirt, open at the neck, and a light tweed jacket. She thought they complemented each other perfectly.

As a rule she hated blind dates. She was always uncomfortable and worried that she wasn't holding up her end of the conversation. Pete wasn't exactly a blind date, but still close to it. She said so. He laughed.

"Cady, we played together. We walked to and from school together. We were good friends. We aren't strangers."

"I know that, but in some ways we are

strangers. We haven't seen one another in over twenty years. What made you choose the law?"

"My parents. One of my teachers said he thought I was a natural. The accident played a good part in it, too. I was a senior in high school trying to make a decision as to which college to go to. I was in the library, and for some strange reason, I went to the microfiche and looked up all the old articles on the accident. They threw me out of the library that night. I remember I was the last one to leave.

"Someone either very wise or very stupid had a handle on it all. It could have turned into a legal circus, but it never happened. I guess that's when I made my decision. My original intention was to become a public defender, but they don't make much money, so I opted for private practice."

"Money's important," Cady said. *So, he's into money.*

"Especially when you never had any. Two of my college classmates went on to get medical degrees. They went into medicine for the money. Strictly for the money, no other reason."

"I don't much care about that sort of attitude. I hope they're good doctors."

Pete threw his head back and laughed. "Marty Engleman is in nuclear medicine. He's on his third wife, and paying out so much alimony and child support he's struggling like the rest of us. Zack Bancroft went into dermatology so he could work nine to five. He misdiagnosed a case a few years into his practice and got slapped with a malpractice suit. He'd let his premiums lapse and got taken to the cleaners. His wife left him, and he's floundering."

"That's terrible," Cady said.

"In a way I guess it is. They were greedy. That's the bottom line. When you go into private practice, you need to think and plan for the future. You plot your course, and you stay on it. We're here," he said, turning into a crowded parking lot. "The food is really good. What I really like about this place is they have several small tables where you aren't sitting with strangers. I think you'll like it. They have some great plum wine, but I usually have the Japanese beer. Which do you like?"

"Beer."

Cady opened the car door just as Pete walked around to open it for her. "I'm supposed to do that," he chastised.

"You can do it next time. I'm used to doing things for myself." This might be a good time to *sashay,* she thought as she stepped ahead of Pete on the narrow walk leading to the entrance of the restaurant.

"Wait a minute, Cady. What's wrong? Why are you walking like that? Did you hurt yourself getting out of the car?"

Cady turned around and burst out laughing. "I was practicing sashaying." At his dumbfounded look, she said, "For the movie."

"Oh. Why?"

"I don't know. It's required. I have to learn how to strut, too."

"Oh. Is that for the movie, too?"

"Uh-huh," Cady said, trying to hide her smile.

Inside the restaurant, with bottles of beer in front of them, Cady relaxed as the chef proceeded to put on his fire-and-knife show for their benefit. Only when he got down to the serious business of cooking did they resume their conversation.

"How's your grandmother doing, Cady?"

"Actually, she's doing really well. Mandy said she's better than she's been in over a year. Before I got here, she was just muddling through the days. Now, with me getting ready to do her memoirs, and the movie, not to mention me being here, it's like she has a reason to join the living again. She's really a funny lady, with a wicked sense of humor. Did you like her?"

"Very much so. I inherited your grandmother's account from an old friend who gave up on the law. The yearly retainer is more than I earn in a year here in Indigo Valley. I didn't solicit her business. I have to tell you, Cady, I was stunned at the size of her estate. It's rare today to find a person so well-off with such a well-managed portfolio. I won't be doing any of that, just overseeing the legal end of things," he added hastily.

Cady looked over at Pete and thought she saw dollar signs in his reading glasses, which were still perched on his nose. She blinked the vision away just as Pete removed the glasses and slipped them into his jacket pocket. *Always go with your first instincts.* It was one of Lola's rules.

She ran with it. "Guess you like money, huh?"

"Love it, love it, love it!" Pete laughed. "Your grandmother had me review her will and, as you know, she's leaving everything to you. I'm not breaking a confidence here. She told me she'd already informed you that you are her beneficiary."

"I really don't want to talk about that. I hope Lola lives to be a hundred and more if she has a good quality of life. The money isn't important to me."

Pete leaned across the table. "How can you say money isn't important?"

"I can say it because it isn't important to me. I'm young and healthy. I can work. I can take care of myself. Money is nice. Actually, it's very nice, but it doesn't make my world go 'round. I get my satisfaction out of earning my way."

"Maybe that's because of your past and your father. You used to hate the way he begged for money. Those are your words, not mine, Cady. Whatever . . . you'll never have to worry about where your next meal is going to come from."

Was it her imagination, or did Pete's voice

sound a tad too bitter? And why did his jaw look so grim? *Throw out some bait.* Another favorite ditty of Lola's.

"I think I'm going to donate it all to the Aging Actors Guild Lola set up about ten years ago. There's certainly enough money to fund it almost forever."

The fork in Pete's hand speared a succulent pink shrimp off his plate. He popped it into his mouth as he wiggled his eyebrows for her benefit. "Good idea, but I'm sure you'll change your mind along the way. If your grandmother wanted the Aging Actors Guild to have the money, then she would have made a provision in her will. Instead, she's leaving it to you. You need to think about that before you make any rash decisions. It always pays to do what the deceased wants. Otherwise, it's bad luck."

"Okay," Cady said agreeably. *I know what you're all about, Pete Danson,* money, she thought.

Cady looked down at the mound of rice and vegetables on her plate. How was she ever going to eat all this? Pete was chowing down like he hadn't eaten in a week, and he was using chopsticks in the bargain, ignoring the fork he'd started out with.

"Pete, tell me about the accident."

Here it was, the question he'd been dreading. The lawyer in him kicked in as his eyes took on a new alertness. "I can only tell you what the papers said. I'm sure you read them all by now.

Your parents and grandmother must have talked it to death."

"No. No, they didn't. They would never talk about it. In the end, I simply stopped asking. It changed my life so profoundly. I want to remember, I really do. I *need* to remember. I never would have stayed at the pond alone. Either I was late, or I was early. Why weren't you and the twins there? Usually, if I got there first and the rest of you weren't there, I always left. I never stayed because I was afraid of that place. You know, the tree and all. Plus I didn't want to get caught with Jeff and Boomer and be alone with those two. The two of them scared the daylights out of me. Not Boomer so much, but Jeff sure got me rattled. Who do you think gouged out my initials in the Judas tree?"

The lawyer in him was still at work. "You had said good-bye to all of us the day before. I guess we all knew you weren't going to ride the zip line. We were in the park. I don't know who gouged out your initials. Someone who didn't like you would be my guess. Maybe Boomer."

"How about Amy or Andy? Boomer was always *just there*. He never did anything mean to me. In fact, he tried many times to get Jeff to leave me alone. I feel like I'm right on the edge of remembering, then it slips away. So, what you're saying is you and the others didn't go to the pond that day."

Pete's heart slammed against his rib cage. He laid down his chopsticks and stared across the table at Cady. "Are you asking me if I lied? I was at the park. Other people saw us."

Cady stirred the rice into the vegetables, which were supposed to be eaten when they were crisp and crunchy. They were soggy now. "I didn't ask you if you lied. I asked you if you and the others went to the pond that day. You could have gone to the park before or after. I would never have gone to the pond that day knowing you and the others wouldn't have been there. I know that about myself, Pete. Did you or didn't you go to the pond that day? It's a simple question, Pete. A yes or a no answer will do just fine."

The ten-year-old boy inside Pete pushed the lawyer aside and responded to the question. "No." If he'd said yes, there would go his dreams of possibly marrying Cady at some point. If he'd said yes, there would be no fortune to manage and possibly inherit. If he'd said yes, he would have to kiss his standing in the community good-bye.

"Why doesn't your response have the ring of truth to it, Pete? Plus, your ears are turning red. Your ears always used to get red when Amy would come up with some daredevil adventure the rest of us were afraid of. They would stay red, too, until we either did what she wanted or we talked her out of it. I think you were all there that day because I was supposed to ride the zip line. Sooner or later I'm going to remember, Pete. If there's one thing in this life

289

that I hate, it's a liar. You were supposed to be my friends. I know a lot of years have gone by, but that shouldn't make a bit of difference. Real, true friends are supposed to be friends forever."

"Cady . . . listen to me . . ."

Cady stood up and reached for her purse. "I'll get home on my own. Thanks for dinner."

"Cady, wait," Pete said, slapping bills down on the table. "Damn it, wait."

Cady kept on walking till she reached the lobby, where she asked the hostess to call her a cab.

"Damn it, Cady, why are you so sure I lied? I suppose this means you're going to tell your grandmother to ax me as her attorney."

There it was, that money thing again. Cady looked up at his six-foot handsomeness and shook her head. "Years ago you would have trusted me. For little kids we were soul mates. I guess you forgot about that and how wonderful it was that we could commiserate together. I know you lied because your ears turned red. All of you lied that day. I know it in my head, in my heart, and in my gut. No, I'm not going to tell my grandmother to ax you. One thing has nothing to do with the other. I might not have much in this world that's my own, but I do have my good name and my integrity. Thanks again for dinner."

"Your cab just pulled up, miss," the hostess said.

"Thank you." Cady didn't look back as she walked past a fountain that gushed water, then whistled as a plume of smoke shot upward.

Cady cried all the way home in the taxi.

Pete felt like sixteen kinds of a fool as he made his way to his car. He'd just blown it. Big-time. *Damn, why did I lie?* He hadn't meant to. He'd rehearsed, a dozen different times, how he was going to explain it all to Cady without actually coming out and admitting they'd cut and run that day. He knew all the legalese, or at least he thought he knew it. When you were asked a yes or a no question, there was no legalese. Black was black and white was white. Where had all his ethics and honor gone? *Christ, what a mess,* he thought as he barreled down the road toward his house.

Damn it to hell, maybe it's time to get everyone together and try to make things right. His heart started to pump furiously at the mere thought.

He was in a hurry to get home. To his house, to his housekeeper, to his office. The things he'd busted his ass to get. Now, he was in danger of losing it all. *Son of a bitch! Why in the damn hell did I lie? To keep the status quo, that's why. And to feather my nest in the future.* He groaned aloud, hating himself for his thoughts.

When he pulled his car into the driveway, he cut the lights before he turned off the engine.

He stared out at the star-filled night, wondering what would happen in the coming weeks. He entered the house and went to his bedroom, where he changed his clothes. He was back in his car within minutes.

His destination — the pond. His sanctuary in the past. Maybe the magic of the place would help him in his grown-up life.

He drove slowly, his eyes peeled for local patrol cars. Satisfied that they were occupied elsewhere, he doused his lights long before he reached the turnoff to the pond. He longed for the old slatted tree house that had given him so much comfort. He could still climb and settle into the Y of the tree and feel safe with all the spring foliage. He could sleep in the tree if he wanted to. Hell, he'd probably be sore in the morning, but if he could find comfort that night, it would be worth a stiff body in the morning.

He felt exposed and vulnerable when he looked around at all the closely cropped grass and weeds. Maybe it wasn't such a good idea after all.

He sat down on the ground and hugged his knees, his thoughts traveling at the speed of light. *One incident, and all our lives were changed forever. I'm not different from Boomer, Andy, and Amy. Only Cady is different. Cady the victim. She'd looked so pretty tonight.* He'd hoped to feel some affection for her, but it hadn't happened. She was a stranger to him. A soon-to-be-rich stranger. He hadn't felt any sexual desire either, which he found strange. Guilt. Guilt did terrible things to people. Some people were just better at covering it up than others. All you had to do was look at Amy Chambers to know she lived in her own hell. Andy was so screwed up he couldn't make a move unless Amy okayed it. Boomer was a different story altogether. Boomer had his shit together.

In his gut he knew Boomer was the one who'd made the phone call to the authorities. It had to be Boomer. Making the phone call would take away his guilt. Still, if it all came out, Boomer would lose his job. That was almost a given. Unless . . . unless, along the way, Boomer had owned up and confessed his role in their activities that day. It was called cutting a deal and covering your ass.

Pete was so deep into his thoughts he almost jumped out of his skin when he felt a hand on his shoulder. He jerked around. "Jesus, you scared the hell out of me, Andy. What are you doing here?"

"The same thing you're doing. Looking for comfort, for answers. I know what I should do, I just can't bring myself to do it. I guess you're feeling the same way I am." He sat down next to Pete and hugged his knees the way his old playmate was doing. "The place looks so different. I wish they'd make a park here or something. What should we do, Pete? You're a lawyer, you must have some ideas."

"If I did, I blew them tonight. I had dinner with Cady. She asked me point-blank if I was here that day, and I lied and said no. She said she knew I was lying. It went downhill after that, and she took a cab home. I'm stuck with the lie now. I swear, Andy, I was going to say, 'yes I was there,' but no came out instead."

Andy picked up a twig and snapped it in two. "Maybe what we should do is go to Cady and tell her the truth. If she's as nice as she was when we were kids, and we explain the fallout, maybe she'll take pity on us and let it drop. We don't deserve it, but it could happen. It's a real mess, Pete."

"Yes, it is. What about Boomer?"

Andy shook his head. "I don't know. I think he came back here because he couldn't live with it anymore either. If the three of us go to Cady and explain things, it won't matter if Amy sticks with her lie. She'll have to live with it."

"Andy, you two are joined at the hip. If we do this, you'll be cutting your lifeline to Amy. Can you handle that?"

Andy pitched the broken twig in his hands into the pond. "I guess I'll find out, won't I?"

Chapter 14

Cady stomped her way into the house, a murderous look on her face. They were lined up in the foyer, three across, arms outstretched, so she couldn't pass without an explanation for her early return.

"I must be living under a black cloud or else I really do stink. Pete lied to me! He lied to my face. Of course I can't prove it, but the look on his face told me he was lying. What do you think of that?" she demanded, hands on hips, her face flushed.

Atlas barked as he crowded next to her leg.

Not bothering to wait for a comment, Cady blustered on. "Do you know what I'm going to do? I'm going into the library, and I'm not coming out until I remember every detail of that day. If you hear me banging my head on the wall, don't bother to check on me. I'll be shaking my head loose. Men! I hate men! The only thing they're good for is to make babies, and since I'm not in a baby-making mode, I give up on them. Do you hear me, I give up! On top of that, I didn't even eat! You know what else? Let me tell you what else. Since they're all lying, I'm going to lie myself. I'm going to call them all up and tell them one by one that I remember what happened that day. Then I'm going to stand back and watch the shit hit the fan! What do you think of that?"

Cady's voice was so belligerent, Atlas growled.

Lola clapped her hands.

"Good girl!" Mandy chortled.

"You're just like your grandmother," Anthony said gleefully. "Don't bang your head until I bring you something to eat."

"I'm calling my mother, too! If I have to, I'm going to fly up there and straighten her out once and for all. I know my mother knows more than she ever told me. Every time I asked about the accident she said it didn't pay to dredge up the past because you couldn't do anything about it. I know she was just repeating what my father said. After a while, I gave up asking. In my opinion, neither my mother nor my father cared if I got my memory back. I always had the feeling they preferred I not get it back. I'm going to tell both my parents I'm willing to undergo hypnosis if it comes to that. I want to remember. I don't care if they like it or not. If I decide to go back, I don't want you to interfere."

"Dear, we wouldn't think of trying to stop you," Lola assured her.

Cady shot her grandmother a dubious

glance, then turned to Anthony. "When you bring me something to eat, bring me a triple shot of bourbon on the rocks with a beer chaser. I'll see you all when I remember. If I don't remember, I'm going to a hypnotist. Start looking for one just in case. Good night, everyone."

"Water down that bourbon, Anthony," Lola said when she heard the door to the library slam shut.

"My God, she's just like you used to be, Lola," Mandy said in awe.

"Isn't she, though?" Pride rang in Lola's voice. "Let's hope she squelches the desire to visit her parents. No good can possibly come of that. However, we have to encourage her to do whatever she feels is necessary. For now."

They looked at one another like the three wise old owls they pretended to be. "This probably calls for a drink of *something*," Anthony said, heading for the bar area in the sunroom, Lola and Mandy trailing behind him.

The following morning, promptly at eight o'clock, Larry Denville hustled himself into the editor in chief's private office at the *Indigo Sentinel* just as Cady Jordan headed for the shower. Their objective was the same although neither one knew it.

"Good Christ, Denville, what is it now?" Stanley Kaminsky, the burly editor in chief, bellowed. "I hope it isn't any more of that crap with that twenty-year-old tragedy. There's too much other news going on to keep harping on that. Don't you get it? No one is interested."

"Stanley, people are interested. Lola Jor Dan is news, and when she does something, people sit up and pay attention. Why can't you trust me on this?"

"Trust doesn't sell papers. News sells. What is it you want this time, Denville?"

"Chief, do you remember what you said to me the day you hired me?"

"I said a lot of stuff," the EIC hedged.

"You told me in order to find a resolution or a conclusion to any story I was reporting on, I would have to go back to the beginning. That's what I want to do. I want to go to Vermont and talk to Cady Jordan's parents. That's my beginning. No one bothered to talk to them. After the accident they left, and Lola took over their daughter's care. I always thought that was very strange. Parents, no matter what, don't leave their kids behind, especially when they are as badly injured as Cady was. Don't you think that's strange, Chief?"

"Look, Denville, that kid's parents weren't your garden-variety parents. They were religious nuts. Everyone in this town knew there was bad blood between Asa Jordan and his mother, Lola. That was then, this is now. No one cares. The answer is no to whatever you were going to ask me."

"Two days, Chief. I'll drive up using my own car. I'll find the cheapest motel there is or sleep in my car. I'll chow down on fast food." Remembering his training, he mentally changed fast food to raw vegetables. "Seventy-five bucks, Chief. If I can nail this down, it might make the wire services. Human interest, Lola's upcoming movie. *Variety* might even show up. I want to do just what you taught me. I want to go all the way on this. My nose is twitching."

Stanley Kaminsky leaned back in his worn swivel chair and fired up his pipe. He stared at the pudgy reporter, knowing he was going to give in. The one thing he liked about Denville was that he had a feel as well as a nose for news. He sucked on his pipe, smoke billowing upward. "On one condition."

"Anything. I'm thinking a hundred bucks instead of seventy-five. Gas is expensive."

"You take Myrna with you. She understands women."

"Come on, Stanley, I don't need a babysitter. I'm astute. I can figure out things for myself. This is *my* story."

Stanley yanked at his collar as he twisted his neck to the right and then to the left. "I hate ties," he grumbled, "but the owner of this fine paper has a dress code, and ties are at the top of the list. It's Myrna or nothing, kid."

"All right, all right. It's my story, my by-line. She's just there for input. Agreed."

Stanley laid his pipe down in an overflowing ashtray to run his hands through his spiky gray hair. "I should be in the barbershop getting a haircut instead of talking to you, Denville. Go on, get out of here. Myrna!" he bellowed at the top of his lungs.

A twenty-nine-year-old Orphan Annie look-alike poked her head in the door. "We have an intercom, Stanley. You interrupted my train of thought. By the way, that's an ugly tie you're wearing. What?" she demanded.

"You're going to Vermont for two days with Denville. You can thank me later."

"I don't want to go to Vermont, Stanley. I'm right in the middle of that downtown zoning thing."

"Turn it over to Wexler. I didn't ask you if you *wanted* to go to Vermont, Myrna. The two of you need to clear out of here so I can get some work done. This better be good, Denville, or you're gonna find yourself in the tall grass. That goes for you, too, Myrna. Don't make me regret my decision."

Outside in the bright spring sunshine, Myrna Davis held up her hand for Larry to stop. "I just need to get my weekend bag out of my car."

"You keep a packed bag in your car?" His voice sounded so suspicious, Myrna winked. "You never know, I might get lucky."

"Oh."

The lanky Myrna was back in minutes, a dark green duffel bag slung over her shoulder.

"It looks heavy," Larry said.

"I require a lot of gear. Blow-dryer, iron,

clothes, prepackaged food. Essentials. You know, stuff. Everyone has stuff. I'm always ready to go at a moment's notice. I keep hoping for a big story, a scoop, where I take off in the blink of an eye. I'd have made a great foreign correspondent." She continued to babble, as Larry stowed her gear in the trunk of his car. She was still babbling when he exited the parking lot and headed for the turnpike.

Myrna took a deep breath. "So, fill me in. Don't leave anything out; otherwise, I won't be able to make an accurate deduction. Remember, we need two sources on everything." She stretched her long skinny legs out in front of her, then moved the seat back for more leg room.

"We don't need two sources. We're talking to the principals. I use a recorder. It's on at all times. If you'll shut up for five minutes, I'll clue you in to the way it's shaking down."

Myrna looked at him in awe. "Talk. By the way, I have total recall, so anything you say will automatically be recorded in my brain. Just ask me anything. Anything at all, and I can tell you back to when I was three years old. My brain is like a big catalog." Her voice rang with happiness and excitement.

"Shut up, Myrna, and listen. Don't make a sound. Not a peep. I like to think when I drive. I play music because it soothes my tattered nerves. Chatter sets my teeth on edge. Are we clear on all this?"

"Crystal."

301

It took Larry ten minutes to fill her in. He sighed when he was finished, wondering what, if anything, this strange-looking young woman could contribute.

"Cady Jordan was a year ahead of me in school. I remember her. She was kind of shy but not shy, if you know what I mean. She had spirit. I was tall for my age, gangly, a real female nerd. She said she liked my red hair. I loved her pigtail. She was a nice kid. I remember the accident because I cried. I even wanted to go to see her, but my mother said she was too sick. That accident sure didn't bother the others, though. Those four were always together. I wanted to belong, but I wasn't allowed out of the backyard. Then after the accident, they didn't see each other. Pete always ate by himself. Andy was with a boy named Carl, and Amy kind of flitted from girl to girl. I tried to be friends with her once, but she chased me away. Does any of that help?"

"Did you know Cady's parents?"

"No. I just know what I heard my parents say. They talked about it a lot at suppertime. Every day there was something in the paper. They left Cady here and went to wherever they were going. My mother said that was a sin. You know, to leave a sick child behind. That's why I wanted to go to see her.

"You're right, Larry. You start at the beginning. The parents are the beginning. What are we going to do if they don't want to talk to us?"

302

"I don't know. But you need to be quiet now so I can think. There's something buzzing around in my head, something I missed along the way. I have to put it all together and make the pieces fit."

Cady stepped into the shower feeling woozy from the lack of sleep and all the alcohol she'd consumed during the long night. She now knew the contents of her own personal scrapbook by heart. She'd always been good at categorizing and collating things, shifting things from one place to another until it screamed satisfaction. The articles hadn't done that. She knew there were things that had never been printed. There were too many gaps, too many unanswered questions in the printed articles, the most important being, why hadn't her parents stayed around long enough to demand a thorough investigation? They should have defended her as vigorously as the Kings had accused her.

Steaming water sluiced over her tired body, taking away some of the tenseness between her shoulders. If she didn't relax and unwind, she was going to get one of her hateful, pounding headaches.

She poured fragrant shampoo into the palm of her hand. It smelled like a warm ocean breeze and coconut. She lathered up, her thoughts going in all directions. Did her parents love her? She was thirty years old, and she still didn't know the answer to that question. They'd provided for her. She'd always had plenty to eat and a roof over her head. She'd had clean, decent clothes. Necessities. But where was the love? The only person who had ever hugged or cuddled her was Lola.

I hid my bike behind the holly bush so it would be the last thing to go into the moving truck. I wanted to trick Mom, so I could go back to the pond one last time. I rode down the street on the sidewalk going as fast as I could pedal because . . . because . . .

Cady bolted out of the shower, the door swinging crazily as she reached for a towel that she wrapped around her middle. Screaming at the top of her lungs, she raced down the hall, shouting to Lola and anyone else who could hear her. "I remember something! I remember. It just came to me in the shower."

She stood at the top of the steps, her hair full of shampoo, her body dripping wet and puddling on the floor at her feet. Her hands were clenched into tight fists as she squeezed her eyes shut trying to remember more. She needed to remember more.

And then they were there, jabbering and laughing, hugging her as they led her back to the bathroom. "My God, Lola, I'm really starting to remember. I was just standing in the shower thinking about how Mom never hugged or cuddled me. You were the only one who ever did that. It came to me out of nowhere. Out of nowhere. I remember that the reason I hid my bike behind the holly bush was so I could go to the pond one last time because . . . Because why, I don't know. It's coming back, little pieces at a time. I had to trick Mom. I did, too. I told her Mrs. Hollister said her cake was so heavy it could be used as a doorstop. Mom got all flustered, then I asked her what *sanctimonious* meant. She got all flustered again and went back into the house, and that's when I took my bike out of the bushes and rode off."

"We're so happy for you, Cady. The rest will come, I'm sure of it," Lola said, hugging her.

"Why didn't they kick up a fuss, Lola? How could they have gone off and left me like that?"

Lola shooed her into the bathroom. "We can talk about it later. Finish your shower and come down to the kitchen."

Even with the water running in the shower, she could hear their raspy whispers. What *were* they talking about? Did they know something they weren't telling her?

Fifteen minutes later, barefoot, dressed in jeans and a tee shirt, Cady galloped down the steps, Atlas at her side. She needed to talk to her mother. Maybe she even needed to talk to her father. Like that was really going to happen. She couldn't remember the last time she'd actually spoken one-on-one to her father.

They were seated at the table, waiting for her. She had the same feeling she'd had the day they'd gone to the pond. They were up to something now, too. Or else they had a secret only the three of them knew.

The kitchen looked particularly cheerful this Wednesday morning, with the sun streaming through the bow window. A large bowl of bright spring flowers graced the center of the table in the breakfast nook. She stared at the bright-lemon-colored bowl holding the flowers. "I was wearing a yellow shirt that day and . . . and . . . blue jeans, bib overalls, I think that came to the top of my socks. I was, Lola. That's what I was wearing. My dress to wear to the church supper was hanging on the door at home. The yellow shirt had long sleeves, and I was wearing the jeans because Mom didn't want me to get dirty. My God, that's another memory. See, see! This is what I mean. It comes out of nowhere. I'm remembering. I'm finally remembering." Excitement rang in Cady's voice as her gaze went from one to the other. "Say something," she implored. "It's happening! It's finally happening!"

Lola folded her arms over her thin chest. "I told you, it was just a matter of time. We're delighted for you. Oh, isn't life wonderful! Now, tell us what you're going to do."

Cady looked across the table as the trio stared at her intently. "I don't know if you realize it or not, but the three of you are giving off vibes to me that say you know something you haven't shared with me. This might be a good time to . . . you know . . . unload so that we're all on the same page. Well?"

"There is no well, sweetie. When you get old your face freezes into different expressions, and you have to wait for the muscles to relax. Isn't that right, Mandy?" Lola asked breezily.

"That's about the damnedest, lamest excuse I've ever heard. If that's the way you want it, be warned that I'll figure it out. I went to college! Now, do you think I should call Mom or actually go up there to see them in the flesh? Visiting is always so uncomfortable. They don't like it when I visit. The truth is, we have nothing to say to one another. However, if I call, Mom can hang up on me, which she usually does. Face-to-face, I can stand my ground. Dad can't get away from me in his wheelchair. What do you think? Maybe seeing them will trigger something else."

"I'd call," Mandy said carefully.

"I agree. If your mother hangs up on you, then you can think about visiting. Vermont is not exactly around the corner, child," Anthony said. He creaked to his feet and headed for the coffeepot. "We're having banana macadamia pancakes for breakfast, with warm banana syrup and globs of melted butter."

"Lola, what do you think?" Cady asked hesitantly, not liking the look she was seeing on her grandmother's face.

Lola cleared her throat. "I think it's one of those either/or decisions. If you absolutely need an answer, then I'd go with a phone call first."

"That's pretty much my thinking, too. As wonderful as those pancakes sound, Anthony, I'm going to pass on them. I'm going back to the library to call my mother. Then I'm going to head out to visit Andy Hollister. He's the only one I haven't made contact with. I'd like to see what his reaction is. Do you mind?"

"Not at all, dear. Take some coffee and toast with you, or Anthony can bring it in. You need something in your stomach."

"Not this morning, I don't. This tomato juice with a splash of Tabasco is about all I can handle. I'll see you before I leave. Do you have plans today?"

"A little of this and a little of that," Lola said vaguely as she looked everywhere but at her granddaughter.

"I'll see you in a bit then."

Cady ran down the hall to the study, where she motioned Atlas to sit and stay. She made no sound in her bare feet as she backtracked to the kitchen, where she stood and listened unashamedly. The voices were slightly muffled, but she could still follow the conversation.

"We need to discourage her from going to Vermont," Lola said. "Just toast for me, Anthony. Those pancakes are too rich this early in the morning. Like Cady says, we all need to get on the same page. Her father might . . . he's such a hateful man even if he is my son. He might blurt out something. It will be so devastating to that child. If she gets her full memory back, then it will be time to go to Vermont."

"You should have told her when she first came here, Lola," Mandy said.

"It's not my place, Mandy. Look how far she's come. She could go back into that safe little shell she lived in for so long. She's part of the real world now, her own person. She's beautiful, she's confident, she's articulate, not to mention independent. It's the self-confidence that's really important. She isn't afraid anymore. She has Atlas, and she has us. There's time. What do you think, Anthony?"

"I'm thinking my tongue was hanging out for those pancakes. As for Cady, one step at a time. This is not the time to push her to the edge even though I think she could handle it. Does that answer your question? Are you sure you don't want the pancakes?"

"All right, all right, make the damn pancakes," Lola snapped. "I only want one. They sit in your stomach like rocks. An omelet would be nice."

"All right, all right," Anthony snapped back, mimicking Lola. "You get the omelet, and Mandy and I get the pancakes."

"Mandy, did you tell Anthony about our phone call from Mr. Denville?"

"Good Lord, no. I was just about to tell him when Cady came running out of the bathroom." She focused her gaze on Anthony, and said, "That reporter is on his way to Vermont to see Cady's parents. He said in order to get everything straight, he had to start at the begin-ning. Agnes and Asa are the beginning. Now, make whatever you want out of that."

"Why don't we just have toast and jam this morning," Anthony said, suddenly sounding dejected as he sat back down at the table. "Is this going where I think it's going?"

"That would be my guess," Lola said.

"Mine, too," Mandy agreed glumly.

On the other side of the door, Cady could feel her shoulders start to twitch. So there was a secret after all. She tiptoed back to the library and sat down on the floor next to Atlas. She rubbed his belly as her mind churned. She closed her eyes trying to imagine what Larry Denville hoped to learn by talking to her par-ents. He probably already knew they would never have been nominated as parents of the year. If there was a secret involved, she was cer-tain her parents would never divulge it to a re-porter from the *Indigo Sentinel*.

The big question loomed in front of her. If she called her mother, should she tell her the reporter was on the way? Of course she should tell her mother. That's what a decent, caring daughter would do.

Cady squirmed around until she was able to reach the phone on the desk. She pulled it to the floor, her back to the desk, her legs straight out in front of her. She dialed the number and waited. Five rings, six, seven. She was ready to hang up when she heard her mother's harried voice. It was too damn early in the morning for her mother to be harried. "Mom, it's me, Cady. How are you?"

"I'm fine, Cady. Did you call for a special reason?"

Cady flinched. Each and every time she called, her mother asked the same question. Didn't it ever occur to her that she might just call for no reason other than to ask how they were? "I called because I want to talk to you. I wanted to tell you my memory is coming back in bits and pieces. I've remembered a few things. I'm trying to be patient, but it's hard. Maybe I wouldn't have to try so hard if you'd tell me about that day. I want to know why you left me. I know what you said, but I don't believe you. There's more to it that you aren't telling me. I also want to know why you didn't stick around long enough to kick up a fuss the way the Kings did. Didn't you care about me?"

"That's an awful thing for you to say, Cady. We did what we had to do. I told you that. Lola took better care of you than we could. She was able to get the best doctors in the world for you. We weren't in a position to do that. Your father's calling me. I really have to cut this short."

"He's always calling you, Mom. He runs you ragged, and you let him. He can do things for himself. He can do what he wants to do when he wants to do it, and you know it. You let him make a slave out of you."

"I don't want to hear you talking like that, Cady."

"Is he still claiming that he could have been the next Pat Robertson if it wasn't for Lola? I can hear him yelling. Tell him to get his own damn newspaper, Mom. You need to stand up for yourself. I bet if you told him you had enough of his abuse and were leaving, he'd sing a different song. He needs you. You don't need him. You can come and live with me, Mom. Maybe it's time we got to know one another."

"That's just rubbish, Cady. If you can't talk to me nicely, then please don't call me again. I don't like it when you degrade your father the way you do. I don't care what you say about me."

"Mom, that's the problem. You should care. Don't you want to be happy? Don't you want to be able to go out to the store or to the library or to a movie? Don't you want to be able to go to the church bingo or play cards with friends? You could do all that if you came to live with me. I can make all that happen for you. We could have a real garden. I have a dog now. I know you're partial to cats, and I'd make sure you got one. A nice, fat, furry, yellow tabby. Mom, he's screaming. Tell him to shut up. Tell him you're on the phone. Do it, Mom."

"Cady . . . you don't under—"

"No, I don't understand. I know you have to get off the phone. But before I hang up I wanted to give you a heads-up. There's a reporter from the *Indigo Sentinel* on his way to see you and Dad. He's redoing the story from that day. Those reporters dig *deep*, Mom. If you have something you're hiding, and I suspect you do, he's going to find out. I'm going to find out, too, Mom, because my memory is coming back. It's all right to hang up now, Mom. Your master is at the end of his rope. Tsk tsk, he's cussing." She imagined she could hear her mother's fear seeping through the phone wires. She didn't imagine the sound of her mother gasping, though.

"Good God, Cady, do you have any idea of what you've started? How could you send a reporter up here? Your father is going to have a stroke when I tell him."

"Then don't tell him. I didn't start anything, Mom. Why are you always so quick to blame me? You and Dad are the ones who seem to have a secret. I've never understood why you wouldn't talk to me about that day. I guess I never will. Whatever is going on, Mom, you and Dad brought it on yourselves. Furthermore, I did not send the reporter to see you. I have no control over a newspaper. If you stop and think about it, you'll realize I'm telling you the truth. I told you, reporters have noses for news, and this reporter is news hungry."

"If you didn't do it, then Lola put them up to it. She knows how to manipulate the press to her own ends. You're going to regret all of this. Why couldn't you just let things alone? Oh, no, you had to let Lola fill your head with all kinds of nonsense, and this is the result. I have to hang up now. We will not be speaking to any reporters today or any other day."

"You better think about that, Mom. When you don't talk they make stuff up and put their own spin on things. Now, that could be worse than whatever it is you're hiding." *Damn, I just made my mother cry. Damn.*

"Good-bye, Cady."

"Bye, Mom."

Her eyes full of tears, Cady hung up the phone. "You know what, Atlas, this whole thing sucks. It really does."

An hour later, Cady was on her way to town. Her first stop was the bakery, where she sat at one of the little soda-fountain tables with a cup of coffee and a Danish, the morning paper spread out in front of her. When she was finished, she tipped the waitress and walked the block and a half to Andy Hollister's insurance office.

A bell tinkled overhead. It was a nice office, small but cozy, with a receptionist's desk, three comfortable club chairs, and three small tables. Shiny green plants decorated the end tables, and a fica tree stood in the corner. Obviously whoever took care of the plants knew what they were doing. Copies of the latest *Time* and *Newsweek* and *People* magazines were in the middle of the low table along with a bowl of hard candies.

The door to the inner office opened. A tall

man stood in the doorway. Cady smiled. She would have known Andy Hollister anywhere. His sandy hair was starting to recede at the temples, and his freckles had lightened considerably. His eyes still crinkled at the corners when he smiled. Andy Hollister, grown up, looked exactly like the little boy she remembered. "I'm sorry, I didn't hear you come in. Martha is out with a spring cold. Cady, is it really you?"

Cady smiled as she stretched out her hand. "It's me, Andy. How are you?"

"Everyone in town has informed me that you were back. Tell me, how do you like Indigo Valley these days?"

"It sure has grown a lot. I hardly recognized it when I first got here. I don't think I would have recognized you if I passed you on the street. You turned into a good-lookin' guy," she teased lightly. "By the way, I met your wife the other day. She's real nice, Andy. I liked her. We met out at the cemetery, then we went to breakfast together."

Andy shuffled his feet. "I didn't know that. Jill and I . . ."

Cady nodded. "She said you had hit a rough patch. It happens, Andy, in the best of marriages. Work it out, and don't give up. Listen, I really came here to ask you about switching up my car insurance now that I'm going to be living here. Do I do the insurance first or go to DMV first?"

"I'll take care of it, Cady, but can we do it tomorrow or next week? I have to go to a meeting

315

in Pittsburgh this morning, and I'm already running late. Martha takes care of all the detail stuff."

"Sure, no problem. I'll come back the early part of next week."

"Cady, what were you doing at the cemetery? I know why Jill was there, but why would you go there?"

"I wanted to see Jeff King's grave. I'd never been to a cemetery before. I don't even know anyone who has died. I wanted to see if going there would help me with my memory. It didn't, but that's okay. It's been coming back in bits and pieces. Slower than I would like, but these things can't be rushed. Well, look, I've held you up long enough. It was nice seeing you again, Andy."

"I wanted to get you a going-away present that day, but Mom said she was short on funds that week."

Cady beamed her pleasure. "Really, Andy. I didn't think you liked me."

"Oh, I liked you all right. I hope you get your memory back, Cady. I really do. I gotta run."

"Andy, were you and the others there that day?"

Andy towered above her. He looked down at her with miserable eyes. "Please don't ask me that, Cady."

"I already did, Andy."

"I'll see you next week, Cady."

"Okay, Andy. Next week it is."

Chapter 15

With nothing but time on her hands, Cady climbed back into the Mountaineer and drove around town. Driving up and down the residential streets, she realized an hour later, was just an excuse to stave off the yearnings she felt to go to the pond. Knowing full well she could get another ticket for trespassing and possibly get carted off to jail didn't faze her at all as she made a U-turn in the middle of a residential street, drove to the end of town, and down the dirt road that would take her to the pond and the Judas tree that stood brooding at the top of the hill.

She parked the car and walked around to the passenger side to let Atlas out. He growled as he leaped to solid ground but didn't leave her side. Her heart thumped against her rib cage when she looked around. It looked almost the way it had the last time she was there as a child. Only that time Pete, Andy, and Amy were at the bottom of the hill waiting for her.

Whoa!

The last time she was there! The last time

she was there *was* that fateful day. Not the day she got a ticket for trespassing. She squeezed her eyes shut. She'd skidded on the gravel, almost falling off her bike when she arrived at the top of the hill. She'd literally slid down the embankment on her rear end. *That day.*

She was wearing a yellow shirt. Amy was wearing pink shorts and a striped top. Andy had jeans on with holes in the knees, and Pete had a paper sack in his hand.

Cady leaned back against the Mountaineer, her legs like jelly. Another memory. Would she have remembered if she hadn't come here? Was it the conversation she'd had with her mother that triggered something? Or was it Andy's response to her pointed question? Atlas whined as he dropped to the ground at her feet.

Cady kicked off her heels, leaving them behind as she scrambled down the embankment. Maybe she needed to look upward to where the zip line had been. Maybe she needed to look up at the Judas tree. Suddenly, she felt icy cold, yet she knew the temperature was in the low seventies.

Her voice shaky, her legs still rubbery, she called to Atlas to stay at her side. She looked up at the old tree that had once held Pete's tree house. If she took off her tight skirt, she could climb the tree and perch in the crook of the old branches. Did she want to do that? If she did, maybe she could get a new perspective on what happened that day. Maybe sitting in the tree would help her to remember what happened next.

Without stopping to think, she dropped her skirt and shinnied up the tree the way she had when she was little. "Stay, Atlas," she called over her shoulder. "I might be up here awhile, so stand guard."

The shepherd cocked his head to one side and then the other, uncertain what his mistress was doing. He dropped to his haunches, his eyes alert, and waited.

While Cady sat nestled in the branches of the oak tree struggling to remember the events of that long-ago day, a police patrol car called in to report to the new chief. "It looks to me like a young woman in her underwear is sitting in a tree by the pond. Her car, a Mercury Mountaineer, is parked at the top of the embankment. When I didn't see anyone, I got out my binoculars. I'm sure she's in her underwear. I see a dress or something on the ground, and there's a big dog sitting at the base of the tree. I have a healthy respect for dogs that look like that. Yes, Chief, the signs are up. You don't want me to check it out? Do you want me to fill out a report or put a ticket on the windshield of her car? Okay, Chief, you're the boss."

Mac Ward leaned back in the swivel chair. The fit of the chair was starting to feel right, like he'd really found his niche. Now he was about to blow it all to hell.

It was time to make his phone calls. He

wished now he'd done it days ago. Hell, he wished he'd done it years ago. Until now, he'd been looking forward to his date with Cady. He reached for his private cell phone and dialed Pete Danson's number.

"It's Mac Ward, Pete," he said curtly when Pete's secretary put him through to the lawyer. "Let's meet tomorrow morning for breakfast. You call Andy, and I'll call Amy. No, Pete, it isn't a request, it's a goddamn order. One of my men just called in to tell me Cady is at the pond and up a tree in her underwear. I'm assuming it's the tree where you guys had your tree house. This is just a hunch on my part, but I think she's starting to remember, if she hasn't already. We should have done this years ago. I, for one, am sorry we didn't. We all had our reasons, Pete. Those reasons don't matter any longer. We're responsible adults, or at least we're supposed to be. Seven-thirty sounds good to me. Eva's. I'll call ahead to make sure she saves us a table in the back."

The chief's next call was to Amy Chambers. He breathed a sigh of relief when her answering machine came on. He ended his message with, "Be there, Amy. This isn't a request, this is an order."

Mac Ward stared at a picture of the president of the United States hanging on the wall across from his desk. He was an honorable man. A man dedicated to running the country and keeping it safe for all the citizens. In his own way, he was trying to do the same thing but on a smaller scale. He thought about the secrets he'd lived with all these years. He wished, just as he had a million times before, that he had never met Jeff King.

Secrets ruined people's lives.

Five minutes later he was in his car. His destination, the pond. In the end, it always came back to Cady Jordan and that damn pond. Little Cady, all grown-up now. Just thinking about her made his heart pound the way it had when he was thirteen.

He whizzed down the highway before squealing to a stop at the grove. He parked his patrol car on the side of the road and walked down the dirt road to the top of the embankment. God, how he hated that Judas tree. He wished someone would take an ax to it. Back when he was a kid it had given him the creeps. His skin crawled now just looking at it. It was just a goddamn tree. Nothing more. A trunk, some branches, some leaves and buds about to bloom. Just a tree. And for some ungodly reason it scared the shit out of him.

He saw the dog, saw him stand up, saw him tuck his tail between his legs and his ears go flat against his big head. Cady's protector. He realized in that one instant that he wanted that particular job. The dog didn't move, neither did he. Instead, he called out. "Cady, it's Boomer. Where are you?"

"Up here!" came the reply.

"Okay, I'm coming down. Call off your dog. He looks like he's ready to chew me to pieces. Can you get down?"

"If I got up here, I guess I can get down. Easy, Atlas. Easy, boy. Stay. Okay, you can come down. He won't attack you. Keep your hands in your pockets so he doesn't see you as a threat. So how much is the ticket this time?"

"Double what it was the last time," Boomer shouted. "What the hell are you doing here, Cady?"

"Remembering."

"Come on, get down out of that tree and let's talk."

"I'm in my underwear. My skirt was too tight, so I had to take it off."

"Yeah, yeah. I saw you in your underwear before. Get down here!"

"Stop trying to boss me around, Boomer. I'll come down when I'm damn good and ready and not one minute before. Just stay where you are. Why can't you understand how important it is for me to remember? I'm not hurting anyone or anything. I'm not destroying anything. I'm just sitting here trying to get that part of my life back. I won't be whole until I can do that. I am remembering, Boomer. Just bits and pieces, but it's coming back."

"Will you please come down, Cady."

"All right. I'm going to keep coming back here until I remember. I'll pay the tickets."

Boomer's eyes widened when Cady lowered

herself to a branch where she could jump to the ground. Her zebra-striped underwear boggled his mind. "God, you're beautiful," he said, a flush creeping up his neck. "Back then . . . you . . . I wanted to kiss you. Boys of thirteen think about stuff like that. I used to dream about you, too."

"You did?"

"I had such a crush on you back then it was pathetic. You sneaked into my heart, Cady, and you never left. I had all these feelings back then. Back then . . . I keep saying it that way because I don't know how else to refer to that time. Jesus, I can't believe I'm telling you this." The flush in his neck settled into a ring of heat.

A blue jay swooped down out of the tree Cady had been sitting in. It flew across the pond and up to the Judas tree.

"Well, guess what. Here I am. Here you are."

Boomer backed up a step as Cady advanced a step.

Cady took another step forward. "It was an invitation, Boomer. You know, you lock your lips on mine, and I lock my lips on yours. It's called kissing. It will probably be a lot better than it would have been when I was ten and you were thirteen."

Boomer's heart pounded. Should he go for it or not? What *was* that wicked gleam in her eyes? He needed to get the hell out of there, and he needed to do it *immediately.*

And then it was too late. He felt warm, moist

lips on his. He felt her arms go around his neck, and he knew she was standing on her toes. Nothing in his life had ever felt so good, so wonderful. A low, agonized groan worked its way up to his chest and throat. He heard the bells and whistles, saw the fireworks explode in his brain. Among the bells and whistles he could hear a dull thumping warning. With all the willpower he could muster, he used his hands to push her away. His mouth felt like it was on fire when he struggled to take a deep breath. "Now, where in the hell did you learn to kiss like *that*, Cady Jordan?"

"I didn't. Learn it I mean. I was saving it up for you. I never kissed anyone like that before. You better not tell me you're complaining, Boomer Ward. Well, are you?"

"No. Kissing like that leads . . . You're in your underwear, for God's sake. I bet if you folded it up real tight it would fit in your ear." *Jesus, did I just say that?*

Cady laughed. "I was wearing a yellow shirt that day. And jeans or bib overalls that came to the top of my socks. Pete, Andy, and Amy were here. I remembered that this morning. It's all coming back. You're a good kisser, Boomer. Who knew?" she quipped.

"You should get dressed. Some patrol cop might come along. How's this going to look?"

He looked so flustered, Cady burst out laughing. "It's going to look like you just kissed me in my underwear. Too bad Larry Denville isn't here. We could have the front page again. He's on his way to Vermont to talk to my parents, so I guess the town won't be made aware of this little meeting."

"Denville went to Vermont!" He wondered if the outrage he was feeling showed in his expression.

"He's probably almost there by now. He said you have to start at the beginning and my parents are the beginning." Cady shrugged as she bent down to retrieve her skirt.

"Boomer, I have something I want to ask you. Were you . . ."

"Hold that thought, Cady," Boomer said, as his pager went off. He looked at it, whipped out his cell phone, and backed up. "I have to go. I'll see you tonight and give you the ticket then." At the top of the embankment, he stopped long enough to shout, "I like that underwear."

Cady laughed again as she zipped up her skirt. She watched him until he was out of sight. Dropping to the ground, she hugged her knees. For the first time in her life, she'd kissed a man to the tune of rockets and missiles. "Ya know, Atlas, for one little second there, I thought my head was going to spin right off my neck! Boomer Ward! Of all people." She picked up a pebble and skipped it across the pond. Pete had always been the best at skipping the stones. Andy was next, and Amy could just never get the hang of it. Once or twice she'd succeeded, and the boys had clapped enthusiastically. Not Amy, though. Amy had scowled and said she wanted to do something else.

Throw rocks! Hurry up. Get some bigger ones! Come on! Come On! Pitch! Hey!

Cady lurched forward. *Throw rocks. Hurry up. Get some bigger ones. Come on! Come On! Pitch! Hey!* She felt so dizzy and light-headed, she dropped back to the ground, her heart hammering inside her chest. There were words, but there were no mind pictures. She wanted to cry in frustration. *Why can I hear the words and not see my friends? Because your eyes were closed and you were on the zip line, that's why. Stupid, stupid, stupid.*

"Come on, Atlas, it's time to go home." The dog was on his feet in an instant, his side glued to her leg. He wiggled his head for her to scratch him behind his ears. She obliged.

At the top of the embankment, she looked over at the Judas tree. Right now, its buds looked as if they were about to bloom, but the tree didn't look pretty. She'd always hated how bare it was around the base of the tree. Nothing would grow there, not even moss, dandelions, or vines. As children they'd planted bluebells and daffodils, but nothing would flourish. A circular bench might take away some of the starkness. Then again, maybe nothing could remove the starkness from the forbidden area. She didn't mean to walk over to the tree, but she did. She searched out their childish carvings and winced as her fingers traced the thick chunks that were missing from the C and the J. Obliterated.

Cady traced her way back to the Mountaineer and climbed inside. She felt gleeful, exhilarated, and yet sad at the same time. She was coming to the end of the line, she could feel it. When she had all the pieces, what would she do? "Then I'm going to see Mr. and Mrs. King and lay it all out for them. If I have to, I'm going to take an ad out in the *Indigo Sentinel* so that everyone will know I wasn't responsible for Jeff's death. Right now, though, I'm going to think about that rip-snorting kiss and what tonight might bring."

Amy Chambers's eyes sparked as she listened to Boomer Ward's message on her answering machine. "This is not a request, this is an order," she mimicked him. "Go ahead, Boomer, issue all the damn orders you want, see if I care."

She wondered if somehow, some way, Boomer knew that Wednesdays were Amy Days, as Arnie called them. He took the girls to school on Wednesdays, and his parents picked them up so they could spend the night and then drove them to school in the morning, thus giving her and Arnie some private time. It would not be a problem to meet the others at seven-thirty in the morning, since Arnie was up and out by seven. Most Amy Days were spent lying in bed until eleven watching the early-morning talk shows. It was a nonproductive day just like all the other days of her life.

She rewound the message and played it again, getting sicker by the moment. It was all going to come out. She could lie till hell froze over, and it wouldn't make a difference. If she could convince Andy to go along with her, it would be Pete and Boomer against her and her brother. Who would people believe? And if Cady remembered, it was all over.

She'd never felt so alone in her life.

She screamed then, at the top of her lungs. "Why didn't you die that day with Jeff?" *Oh, God, what is happening to me? Am I losing my mind? Why didn't I take the ten o'clock appointment with the psychiatrist in Pittsburgh?* "Because I'm afraid," she whimpered. She knew she would never keep the appointment she had made for the first week in June.

From years of habit, she picked up the phone and dialed her brother's office number. She almost fainted when she heard his voice. "Don't hang up, Andy. I need to talk to you. Boomer Ward left a message on my machine this morning. Did he call you, too?"

"Pete called me. Boomer called him. And before you can ask me, no, I don't know if Cady is going to be there or not. What is it you want, Amy?"

"I guess I want to know what you're going to say? You know what I'm going to say."

"I'm going to tell the truth. I think that's

what this is all about. Why can't you understand what a relief it's going to be finally to get
this off our shoulders? If we go to Cady and
tell her the way it happened, she'll be the one
to make the final decision. She came to see me
this morning about switching up her car insurance. She was real nice, Amy. Just like she was
when we were kids. I don't know if she's
gotten her memory back or not. I don't care
either. I just want to be done with this so I can
move on. You need to talk to someone, Amy.
You really do."

"You keep saying that, Andy. All of a sudden
I'm crazy because I don't want my life to fall
apart. That's what's going to happen, and you
know it. I wish to God she had died that day."
Amy reared back when she heard the loud click
in her ear, and then the sound of the dial tone.

She calmed down immediately as she made
her way to the kitchen, where she opened the
refrigerator and withdrew all the things she
would need to make Arnie's favorite, meat loaf.
This was, after all, an Amy Day and she could
do whatever she pleased, and it pleased her at
the moment to make her husband a meat loaf.
She turned the radio on and tuned to a station
that played rock music. She made up words to
the beat of the music. *If you had died, I would
have cried . . .*

She watched him from the window. *He's a
hunk all right,* she thought. "Stay, Atlas. This is

329

my night, and he doesn't have his dog with him either. I won't be late. Stay with Lola. Now, behave yourself when I open the door."

She knew she looked good in her strawberry silk dress with the tulip skirt that flirted with her ankles. Danielle had promised men would drop to their knees when she wore it because it showed off each and every one of her luscious curves. She wondered if she should wait for Boomer's reaction or be satisfied with Anthony's whistle of approval. Lola and Mandy simply beamed with pride. She wondered if Boomer would be able to tell that she felt hot all over. "Hi," she said when she opened the door.

"Hi yourself. Can we go, or do I have to pass inspection?"

"Let me introduce you to my grandmother. It will take just a moment." She didn't wait to hear Boomer's yea or nay. She opened the door more widely, and called out, "Lola!"

"Over here, dear," Lola trilled. "We were just going to go into the sunroom to watch the evening news." The trio changed direction, heading for the front door.

"We'll only keep you a minute. I want you all to meet Boomer Ward, the new police chief. His real name is Mac. Lola Jor Dan, my grandmother, Mandy, and Anthony, this is Boomer."

"I'm so very pleased to meet you, Mr. Ward. I know Indigo Valley is in safe hands with you at the helm." Mandy and Anthony simply smiled and extended their hands.

"It's my pleasure, Miss Jor Dan. You are by far my parents' favorite actress. I know for a fact my mother has seen every single film you made. She's always saying that they don't make actresses like you anymore."

Lola almost swooned with happiness. "You must bring them to dinner one evening. I'll send an invitation. It was very nice meeting you, Mr. Ward."

"We're being dismissed. Bye. I'll see you all later." Cady giggled.

Outside on the porch she said, "Now, that wasn't so bad, was it? Thanks for saying that about your parents. Lola loves compliments."

"I only told the truth. My mother loves old films. She's going to go over the moon when I tell her she's invited to dinner. I hope it isn't for at least a month because that's how long it will take her to find just the right dress. You're right, though, it wasn't bad at all. I never took a girl home to meet my parents," Boomer blurted. "I knew how I felt when I had to stand in front of some girl's father, hoping I passed. Did you feel like that?"

"I never dated until I was in college. I was one of those bookworms. Then there was the fear and all that stuff. That's all in the past. We can go now."

"Hold on, Cady. I understand the bookworm stuff, but not the fear part. Are you talking about the accident at the pond? You were the gutsiest of all your friends as I recall. Sassy, too," he said, grinning.

"Yes, the accident left me with a lot of fears. I tried very hard to overcome them, but I wasn't all that successful. Back then I wasn't afraid of heights. I'm afraid of heights now, though. I didn't know how to swim back then either. I developed a terrible fear of water. I'll drive twenty miles out of my way to avoid going over a bridge with water underneath. Probably the worst fear of all is trusting people. The truth is, I don't trust anyone, not even my parents. I'm no longer gutsy. I always play it safe, no matter what I do. Depending on your point of view, I guess I'm still sassy. I really don't want to talk about this right now, Boomer. It depresses me."

"Okay. I understand. At least I think I do. Maybe together we can work on the trust angle."

He opened the car door for her just the way he was supposed to. She smiled. He was as uncomfortable as she was. She wished she was a little more worldly so she could put him at ease. He looked *so* good, and he smelled as good as he looked. She said so, and he laughed.

"Look, let's just have a good time this evening. Let's not talk about the past or about Pete, Andy, Amy, or Jeff. If you want to talk about all that tomorrow, we can do it. I'm thinking we both could use some quiet downtime. Agreed?"

"Okay. But we do need to talk, Boomer."

"Yes, we do. And we will. Will you trust me?"

What a strange question. She thought about the question until she was satisfied in her own mind with her answer. "Yes."

"I just want to run something by you, then we won't talk about the past. Is that okay with you?"

"Sure."

"I know how bad you want to get your memory back, and I understand. You need to remember on your own. It doesn't matter what Pete or I or anyone else says. How do you feel about our doing a reenactment of that day? Pete and I could rig up a zip line. I don't want you to give me your answer now, but I do want you to think about it. You have to be comfortable with it. You won't be doing it for me or anyone else; you'll be doing it for yourself. Will you think about it?"

"Okay, I'll think about it. I never learned to swim, Boomer," she said, fear ringing in her voice.

"You said you trusted me."

"I do. Okay, I'll think about it."

"Good. Now, where would you like to eat? It's the middle of the week, so we won't need a reservation anywhere. What's your favorite food?"

"Good Italian with lots of garlic bread. A nice crisp green salad with lots of onions. Cold frosty beer, and I'm a happy camper. But it has to be good sauce. Not that canned junk they doctor up."

"Ah, a girl after my own heart. I need to take you home to meet my parents. That's how I like my Italian, too. We're going to stink, you know that, right?"

Cady laughed. "Who cares?"

"Not me, that's for sure. Listen, do you have any decorating experience?"

"I think you need to be a little more specific."

"I moved into this apartment, and it looks like I just moved in. Can you help me spruce it up? My mother's house was always warm and comfortable. I can never seem to get that kind of a feel in an apartment. Can you help me out?"

"Is that the same as inviting me over to see your etchings?"

"Yeah, that, too. Am I that transparent?"

"Uh-huh. Okay, I'll take a look and see what I can do. Green plants make a world of difference, but if you aren't the watering type, you need to get silk ones. Then you just use a blow-dryer to blow off the dust. You need color. Your furniture isn't leather, is it? Leather is never cozy or warm."

"No. I'm a chocolate-brown person myself. All kinds of browns, if you know what I mean."

"In other words, dull."

"Dull's good. Yeah, dull. I had this girlfriend who was into earth tones and everything natural. She was so neutral about everything it made me crazy. I guess her colorless decorating skills rubbed off on me."

Cady felt a pang of jealousy hearing about the faceless, neutral woman who had been a part of Boomer's life. She felt herself starting to withdraw the way she always did when a man said something she didn't like. She gave herself a mental shake. That was the old Cady. The faceless, neutral girlfriend was gone. She laughed.

"Tell me something. How come you never got married?"

"Just never met the right woman, I guess. Maybe I've been waiting all these years for you and didn't know it. I feel compelled to tell you I have a thing about women who climb trees in their underwear. How about you?"

Cady knew her face was turning three different shades of red. "In the beginning when I started college there wasn't time for a serious relationship. Then as I got older and had even less time, maybe I was too picky. Then again, maybe I wanted bells and whistles. It didn't happen."

"Did I tell you I *really* like that dress you're wearing? When you move, it *slithers*."

Cady laughed again as she wiggled her eyebrows just for fun. Boomer burst out laughing.

The ice was broken. Cady leaned back and relaxed. Boomer did the same thing, almost on cue. She looked down at her watch. Seven-thirty. It was going to be a lovely evening. She could feel it in her bones.

★ ★ ★

When they exited Domingo's restaurant two hours later, Boomer groaned. "I ate too much. How about you, Cady?"

"I am stuffed. I think I ate four slices of garlic bread. Big slices."

"How would you like to walk it off? Listen, I have an idea. St. Joseph's is having their annual spring carnival. Rides, food, games of chance, that kind of thing. It's a bit of a hike since it's across town, but I'm up for it if you are."

"Let's do it," Cady said happily. She linked her arm with Boomer's. "Are you going to win a prize for me?"

"You mean one of those ricky-ticky plastic dolls?"

"Nope. I mean the big Kahuna. The giant teddy bear that seems to come with all carnivals. The one that nobody ever wins. They don't win because the games are always fixed. You being the police chief and all should make them keep the games on the up and up. Don't you have a badge you can pin on or something?"

Boomer grimaced. "Or something."

Cady's hand on Boomer's arm slipped down until they were holding hands. They walked along, their arms swinging, laughing and talking about everything and nothing.

"You're kind of dressed up for this, but how do you feel about entering the three-legged race? Father Cyril has it scheduled for nine-thirty. If you're up to it, we're going to have to run to make it. It's twenty bucks to enter. I think you're worth twenty bucks, Cady Jordan."

"You do, huh?" Cady slipped off her sandals, hiked her skirt up, and took off flying down the tree-shaded street. Boomer, even though he was in good shape, had just eaten, causing him to huff and puff his way after her. He caught up to her just as she entered the gate leading to the back end of the parish, where the carnival was in full swing.

"Hurry up," Boomer gasped. "They're lining up. This race is the highlight of the carnival. It brings in the most money because everyone enters. Quick, grab a rope and tie us together."

"If we win, what's the prize? I love prizes."

"I don't have a clue, Cady. You get your picture in the paper. Maybe you get to eat for free for the rest of the evening. One of the guys at the station told me yesterday that they gave away a phony silver dollar that said WINNER on it last year. It's a half-mile race, all around the rectory. Line up, line up!" Cady grinned at the exuberance in Boomer's voice. She felt excited herself. "Sam McInerney fires off his old musket at the starting line. He renewed his permit for it yesterday. He's also the judge."

"What's our strategy?" Cady asked, sticking her leg into the sack next to Boomer's.

"Huh?"

"How are we going to win this race? Do we start off slow, save our strength for the end sprint? Do we just burst out full speed ahead or what?"

Boomer looked down at Cady and saw that she was serious. He burst out laughing. "Hell, Cady, I never did this before. Let's just have some fun."

Sam McInerney held up his musket and waved it around. "I'm gonna fire on the count of three! If you fall, you're out of the race. One! Two! Three!"

The screaming and yelling was so loud as kids, grandparents, and the carnival workers shouted for their favorites. Dogs barked and howled as their owners struggled past the colored flags along the route to the back of the parish house.

"This is work!" Cady shouted.

"You're telling me," Boomer gasped. "Do you want to quit?"

"No. Keep going, Boomer! Keep going!"

"I'm going, I'm going."

"You said this was going to be fun," Cady said.

"It is fun! It's a lot of fun! I paid twenty bucks for us to have fun. Tell me you're having fun!"

"I'm having fun!" Cady gasped. "We aren't going to win, are we?"

"Nope! There are at least sixty-two couples ahead of us. And another sixty-two behind us. Want to quit?"

"Do you?"

"I asked you first," Boomer said through clenched teeth. "You look tired, Cady."

"You look like you're in *pain,* Boomer." She hardly recognized her own voice. Her mouth felt dryer than cotton candy. "You have to finish, Boomer. You're the police chief. How's it going to look if you bail out?"

"Oh, God, you had to say that, didn't you? Ooops, watch out, there's a pileup ahead."

Cady was struggling with each breath she took. She moved to the side to avoid the couples on the ground who were rolling to the side to get out of the way.

"We're going to laugh at this tomorrow," Boomer said.

"Ha-ha. How much farther?"

"We're almost there. Don't quit now. There goes another pileup. If we can stay on our feet, we'll finish in the top ten."

When they trudged across the finish line, Boomer tripped on something, sending them both to the ground. They rolled across the grass. Gasping for breath, they held on to each other. "Let's not do this next year," Cady said.

He kissed her then, his lips crushing hers before his tongue plunged into her mouth. She clung to him, her whole being on fire. His hands were in her hair, on her throat, on her breasts. She pressed herself against him, heard his moan of pleasure just as she sensed someone hovering nearby.

"Chief, Father Cyril would like to talk to you

for a minute. I told him it looked like you were busy, but he said he didn't care. He wants to give you a consolation prize. Sorry."

"Who was that?" Cady said as she untied their legs, then did her best to straighten out her dress and get to her feet at the same time. "I think I lost my shoes."

"That was Father Bernard. Try to look like we weren't doing what we were doing, okay?"

"Okay, Boomer."

Father Bernard, a sly smile on his face, motioned for Boomer and Cady to take their place at the finish line, where Father Cyril was handing out awards. A huge crowd surrounded the area as Tom Sanders and his wife, Cissy, walked off with the first place prize. The nine remaining winners were awarded purple ribbons with a gold seal stapled in the middle.

"I want to see you win next year, Chief," Father Cyril boomed. "It's all about practice and getting in sync."

Boomer nodded. "Did you hear that, Cady? He said we have to practice. We have to get in sync."

"I thought we were in sync," Cady said boldly. "I think I'm ready to go home now."

"We didn't go on any rides. I wanted to take you on the chairlift thing to help you conquer your fear of heights."

"Next year. Let's get some cotton candy and go home. No, no, we can't go home yet. You have to win the big panda bear for me. We still have to walk back across town and I don't have any shoes."

Boomer's mind raced. How in the hell was he going to get Cady the big bear? She didn't say he had to *win* it.

"There it is. Oohhh, it's a big one! All you have to do is throw the ball into the clown's mouth five times and you win it! You can do it, can't you, Boomer?"

"Of course I can do it," he snorted. "First I have to make sure the balls aren't loaded and the clowns aren't off center. You just stand here now while I talk to the owner of this little game of skill. I'll be right back."

Boomer skirted the edge of the booth and drew the carny outside. "Here's the deal, Mister. I'm the police chief here in Indigo Valley. My *girlfriend* wants that big panda bear. How about a hundred bucks, and I don't inspect the balls and positions of the clowns?" He fanned five twenty-dollar bills under the carny's nose.

"Deal, Mister Police Chief. Throw your balls and the little lady will take home the panda!"

"Looks like it's on the up and up," Boomer said when he joined Cady at the booth. "Let's see, all I have to do is pitch five balls. If I get all five in the clown's mouth, you get the panda."

"Five balls for a dollar," Cady said. "Oh, I hope you can do it! Lola took me to a fair once, but neither of us won a thing. I'm crossing my fingers, Boomer."

Boomer picked up the balls and, with five rapid throws, landed all five balls in the clown's mouth. Cady squealed her joy as the carny handed her the huge panda.

They made one last stop for cotton candy before they left the carnival. Their faces were sticky red with sugar when they collapsed in Boomer's car.

"Oh, Boomer, I had such a good time tonight. I think it's one of the best times I ever had in my whole life."

"Me too," Boomer said gruffly. He hoped he could keep his eyes open long enough to drive home. He reached across for Cady's hand. It felt warm and soft, like it belonged in his.

Myrna locked the car door and urged Larry to do the same thing. "Are you sure we're in the right area? I don't think I'd want to be around here after dark." She shivered to make her point.

"This is the right street. You're right about it being a run-down area. I'm stunned that Lola Jor Dan would allow her son and his wife to live in a place like this. Look, we'll scout it out and come back early in the morning. It'll be dark soon, and I don't like the looks of that gang of bikers back there on the corner. We can get some dinner and maybe take in a movie if that's all right with you."

"You mean like a date?"

"No, not a date. We're here on newspaper

business. The paper will pick up the tab. I'm not sure about the movie part, but the motel and dinner part can get expensed. We need to come up with a game plan in case the Jordans pretend they aren't home. People who live in areas like this tend not to answer their doors. If we call first, there goes our element of surprise. When you surprise people, you catch them off guard, and boom, you get stuff you wouldn't normally get."

"That's so clever, Larry. I'm so glad I came along. I have a feeling I'm going to learn a lot from you on this trip. I just hope I can contribute something. I want to be as good as you are someday."

Larry's chest puffed out. He grudgingly admitted to himself that he was glad of her company, and on top of that he liked the skinny girl with the curly hair and freckles. He liked her wicked sense of humor.

"Look, Larry, that's the house, the brown one with the missing step. I can see a ramp on the side. I wonder what it looks like on the inside. Sometimes you can't go by outward appearances. He was a preacher, right? Maybe he thinks they need to live in a place like this, or maybe he took a vow of poverty."

"He was a scam artist, Myrna. He was one of those fire and brimstone, go to hell in a handbasket and pass the collection plate preachers. He moved around a lot after he left Indigo Valley. Probably one step ahead of the law. The story that I heard was he was ashamed of his mother for being married six or seven times. Hell, look at Elizabeth Taylor. Her kids love her, and she was married six or seven times. When I interviewed Lola all she would say was they were a big disappointment to one another, so I guess it goes two ways. I couldn't find out anything about Cady's mother. She's just there, if you know what I mean."

"How do they live? Do preachers get pensions?"

"That's a damn good question, Myrna. We need to find that out. Maybe Mrs. Jordan works. We'll find out in the morning one way or another. So, what are you in the mood to eat?"

"Are we going on the cheap?"

"We need to keep it simple, or Stanley will flip us the bird. I had to beg for a hundred bucks."

"I'm a big eater. You'd never know it by looking at me. It's my metabolism. I guess we should go Chinese because they give you lots of food. I'll spring for the candy and popcorn at the movie if you buy the tickets."

"Deal," Larry said, slapping out at the palm of her hand.

It was exactly six-thirty the following morning when Larry pounded on Asa and Agnes Jordan's front door. He wasn't disappointed when there was no response. "Let's walk around to the back. We're just going to bang on the door till someone opens it. No one in this neighborhood is going to pay attention. I doubt they'll call the cops. Then again, I could be wrong. Shit, it's starting to rain."

The back door was half-wood and half-glass. The shade was rolled all the way up. He could see a man in a wheelchair sitting at the table, a coffee cup and newspaper in front of him. Standing at the stove, her back to him, was a tall, austere-looking woman. With no sign of a doorbell, Larry knocked on the pane of glass. The occupants of the kitchen turned and looked at him. He banged on the glass again and held up his press credentials.

"Go away," Mrs. Jordan said as she pulled down the shade.

"I'm sorry, Mrs. Jordan, I can't do that. I came all the way from Indigo Valley, and I need to talk to you. I'm not going to go away, so please open the door."

"Call the police, Agnes," Asa Jordan ordered.

"They know I'm here," Larry shouted. "It won't do you any good to call them. All we want to do is talk to you for a few minutes. What harm can come of talking with me? Unless you're hiding something."

"We aren't hiding anything," the man bellowed. "Leave us in peace. We aren't bothering anyone. When you report back to the woman who is my mother, tell her I have nothing to say."

"Your mother didn't send me here, Mr. Jordan. My paper sent me."

"Let me try, Larry," Myrna whispered.

"Mr. Jordan. My name is Myrna. I work for the paper, too. We want to do a human interest story on you and your mother. The way I heard it, you could have been the next Jerry Falwell. There's a rumor going around that she didn't like that idea and spoiled your chances to move ahead in your . . . your calling. Others are saying your daughter's accident had something to do with it. We just want to talk."

Larry looked at the girl standing next to him in awe. He almost jumped out of his skin when the door opened suddenly. "Ten minutes," Mrs. Jordan said.

"We need more like thirty minutes," Myrna said, crowding close to Larry to get into the house. "Talking to a reporter is really very interesting. The time goes by rather quickly, then you get to see what you said in print. We'll overnight you a copy of the paper when the article comes out," she babbled.

Agnes Jordan motioned for the two of them to sit down. "Would you like some coffee?" Both reporters shook their heads. Asa Jordan scowled at his wife.

"Let's start at the beginning . . ."

Myrna let her mind race as she gazed from Asa Jordan to his wife. *Downtrodden* and *beaten* were the words that came to mind regarding Agnes. Asa, in her opinion, came across as bitter and hateful. Perhaps his attitude had something to do with being in a wheelchair. On the other hand, from the look of Agnes Jordan, she'd almost bet her next paycheck that Asa had always been a bitter, hateful man.

She listened with one ear as Larry questioned Cady's father. She decided to engage Agnes in conversation in the hope she would give up something Larry could use. "I went to school with your daughter Cady, Mrs. Jordan. I always liked her. I was really sad when the accident happened. And then her losing her memory on top of that must have been terrible for all of you. She is getting her memory back, though. That's wonderful, isn't it?"

Agnes simply nodded. The woman wasn't going to give up anything.

"I never liked Jeff King. He was such a bully. He terrorized everyone in school, especially the girls, but he really hated Cady. Did you ever talk to his parents about how he bullied her?"

"No. Children have to learn how to get along. Cady never complained."

Agnes Jordan crossed her arms over her chest.

"It probably wouldn't have done her one bit of good if she had complained. The whole town is so excited that they're going to be making a movie of your mother-in-law's life, right down to when she came back to Indigo Valley to live. The tragedy is going to be included. Do you know who will be playing the parts of you and your husband?"

"No, I don't know anything about it."

"They're going to be playing up the part of your husband real big. Playing him off against his mother and all. Her being famous and his estrangement from her." At Agnes Jordan's fearful look, Myrna said, "You know, Lola Jor Dan's decadent lifestyle and your husband's religious background. Where do you fit in the mix? Cady, of course, will play a huge part, or her stand-in will. All those years of suffering, and she was so young. You must have been devastated. Was it hard to leave her behind? People aren't going to understand that part at all."

Agnes shrugged, her eyes on her husband. *I'll bet she was pretty when she was younger.* Even now, under the shapeless clothes, Myrna could tell that the woman had kept her figure. Makeup, a new hairstyle, and she would still be an attractive woman. *She's afraid of us,* Myrna thought with a jolt. *There's a secret here, and she's afraid we're going to figure it out.*

Her brain shifted and collated the facts as she remembered them. Agnes had been home with the moving men at the time of the accident. Asa had been at his makeshift temple or whatever it was where he preached, and there had been witnesses. That had to mean whatever their secret was, it had nothing to do with the accident.

Maybe it had to do with Lola Jor Dan. "Are you and your husband fans of Lola's?"

Asa Jordan's wheelchair whirled around so fast, Myrna thought he was going to smash it into his wife. "No, we are not fans. My wife and I do not approve of my mother's lifestyle. Six marriages is ungodly. A man takes one wife for better or worse, and you live your life," the ex-preacher snarled.

Aha. "But, Mr. Jordan, your mother didn't divorce her six husbands, they died of natural causes. Surely that makes a difference."

"You take one man for your life's partner. You grow old together and forgive each other's sins. Isn't that right, Agnes?"

Instead of speaking, Agnes nodded. A second later she was on her feet pouring coffee into her cup. She carefully avoided looking at her husband.

"I guess that means you consider your mother a sinner to end all sinners. Can we quote you on that?"

"No," Agnes said.

"Yes," Asa said.

Out of the corner of her eye, Myrna could see Larry shrug.

"If you had made it big like some of the other televangelists, do you think that would have changed your thinking, or possibly changed your relationship with your mother?" Larry asked pointedly.

"My mother wanted no part of my faith," Asa said bitterly. "She could have helped me along the way, but she chose to ignore me and God."

"What about Cady. Did she embrace your faith?"

"She did until my mother got hold of her. When she came back to us, she wasn't the same. She had ideas, plans, and wanted to do things we didn't approve of. We had to keep a tight rein on her. She was a bad seed just like her . . ."

"Just like who, Mr. Jordan?" Myrna said, pouncing on his unfinished sentence.

"Just like all sinners." The wheelchair whirled around again until the preacher was once more facing Larry.

Myrna looked up at Agnes Jordan and was stunned to see tears in her eyes. She was shaking from head to toe. She threw her head back, and shouted. "Say it, Asa! Go on, say it! Tell these people our dirty secret! I can't take this anymore. I'm leaving. Cady called me yesterday and invited me to live with her. I hate you! Do you hear me, I hate you! I've always hated you!"

"Shut your mouth, Agnes. You need to repent. Get down on your knees and repent. Do it now, woman, or you will burn in hell with all the other sinners!" Asa bellowed as he turned the chair he was sitting in so that he could face her.

"I've lived in hell from the day I met you," Agnes screamed, the veins in her neck bulging with fury.

Myrna and Larry stood stupefied as Agnes Jordan let loose with all the venom stored in her body. As she cursed her husband she smashed everything in sight. When she was finally exhausted, she turned to the two reporters. "I'm sorry you had to witness this outburst. You should probably leave now. I think you have enough to write about. I'll be leaving myself in a few minutes."

Myrna felt out of her depth. Womanly instinct led her to the woman's side, where she wrapped her skinny arms around her shoulders. "Can we help you? Can we take you somewhere?"

Agnes Jordan squared her shoulders. "I have an old car. I think it will get me to Indigo Valley and my daughter. I should have left a long time ago. Go now."

The two reporters backed out of the kitchen door. When it closed behind them they could hear Cady's mother shrieking, "I will not repent! Do you hear me, Asa! I know there's a place reserved for you in hell because that's where you're going. And, hear this, Asa Jordan, if there was a way for me to send you there, I would!"

And then there was silence.

"Jesus, Mother of God! What the hell was that all about?" Larry said, beelining for his car, Myrna on his heels.

"This is just a guess on my part, and it has nothing to do with my fine reporting skills, but I'd say Mr. Asa Jordan considers his wife and daughter sinners. Possibly bigger sinners than his mother. He's a whack job, Larry. Come on, let's get out of here."

351

"What about her? What if he does something to her?"

"He's all mouth. He's a bully just the way Jeff King was a bully. That woman has lived in fear all her life. Couldn't you see that? We just did her the biggest favor of her life. She's going back to Indigo Valley, to her daughter. I think that's pretty wonderful, if you want my opinion. Are you going to write about this, Larry?"

"Jeez, I don't know. I'm not one of those tabloid reporters who goes for the jugular and ruins people's lives. I want to see how this plays out. I'm not going to expense this trip because if I do, then I'm duty-bound to report what happened."

"I'll split the expenses with you. Hey, how about taking in a movie tonight. A date. We could go Dutch."

Larry laughed. "Okay. You're a real trouper. I was listening to you talking to Mrs. Jordan. You did real good."

"If that console wasn't between the seats, I'd wiggle closer and hug you. That's one of the nicest things anyone has ever said to me."

Larry smiled. He thought he just might have, sort of/kind of, found a girl.

Chapter 16

Cady opened one sleepy eye and looked down at the man next to her on the couch. She could feel his body warmth against her side. Six o'clock. They'd talked all night long about everything and nothing. Where had the hours gone? She smiled in the early-morning light as she stared down at her old childhood protector. Something stirred in her. Something she'd never felt or experienced before. She liked the feeling.

She shook his shoulder. "Boomer, wake up. It's six o'clock, and I have to go home. I guess we fell asleep."

Boomer bolted upright. "Six o'clock!" he said incredulously.

"Yep. We spent the night together." She found herself smiling from ear to ear and wasn't sure why. "I can call a cab. You better hit the shower, or you're going to be late for work."

"I'm off today, but I have a meeting I can't blow off. Why don't you take my car, and I'll use my truck. I keep it for camping and fishing trips, and there's more room in it for Ozzie. You can bring it back later after you get cleaned up. We can spend the day together if you want to." He ran his hands through his hair, then matched Cady, smile for smile. "We really did spend the night together, didn't we?"

"Yep. Hey, before I forget, I never knew the pond was the local lover's lane. I meant to ask you last night how you came by that information, but you got beeped, and then I forgot."

"In the bakery, where else? That place is one hotbed of gossip.

"There were all kinds of stories that were told about the Judas tree, the pond, the entire area. When we were little kids, it was one story, when we were teenagers, it was another story. Hell, I used to park there with Cassie Denvers in my senior year on a regular basis. Someone started a story about the Judas tree. It grew legs with the telling. There are other Judas trees in the area but none as big or as pretty as that one. It seems they all bloom around the same time in the late spring with the exception of the one at the pond. It's a late bloomer for some reason. Maybe there's too much shade from the oaks and maples or something. The fact that it was a late bloomer just added to the mystique of the tree and the place."

"That is so interesting. Yes, I would very much like to spend the day with you. Let's do a picnic down by the pond. I'll pay the ticket, and I'll even bring the food."

"That sounds like a plan to me. You look nice when you wake up," he said.

Cady grinned. "So do you."

"Everyone is going to think . . ."

"Yes, they are." Cady smiled. "What time should I be ready?"

"Let's say ten o'clock." Boomer tossed her the keys to his Toyota.

Reading his intentions, Cady said, "I don't think you should kiss me."

"I don't think so either." He shuffled his feet, his face flushed. "I think I loved you all my life. I probably shouldn't say something like that. You must think I'm nuts."

"No, I don't think you're nuts. I wish I had known. I don't know if it would have made a difference in my life or not. It makes a difference now, though. I've never been in love," she said honestly. "I find myself wondering . . . I think I better leave right now."

"I think so, too. I'll see you at ten. No dogs, right?"

"Right. Just us," she twinkled.

Boomer groaned as he opened the door for her. He groaned again as she blew him an airy kiss. A cold shower was exactly what he needed.

"I hear a car," Anthony said excitedly.

"Thank God. I used to come home around this hour when I was younger," Lola said, her eyes on the clock. "Remember now, we *did not* sit up all night waiting for her. Anthony, bang some pots or something. Mandy, set the table!" Lola ordered. "This is not out of the ordinary. This is . . . it is . . . well, it's what it is."

"Cady, sweetie, did you go out to the bakery to surprise us?" Lola said, peering at her disheveled granddaughter the minute she walked through the kitchen door. "Is that a strange car I see in the courtyard?"

Cady eyed the occupants of the kitchen. A grin stretched across her face. "You've been up all night waiting for me, haven't you?" She winked at Anthony, who flushed a rosy hue.

"We did no such thing. You know we're early risers. Anthony promised to make us eggs Benedict. Mandy and I couldn't wait. Why am I getting the feeling you don't believe me?" Lola fretted.

"You're so full of it, the three of you. Besides, you are all transparent as hell. You're wearing the same clothes you were wearing when I left. You look as messy as I do. Eggs Benedict, huh?"

"Yes, eggs Benedict," Anthony said, banging a fry pan for emphasis.

"You need ingredients to cook, Anthony. I guess you want to know what happened," she teased. She sat down and stretched her legs out. "Coffee would be great right now," she hinted.

"Only if you want to tell us," Lola said, looking about the kitchen, her demeanor off-hand.

They pinned her with their respective gazes. "Nothing happened."

They were aghast. "*Nothing!*" the trio said in unison.

"How can that be? We gave you detailed instructions. We did everything but give you a blueprint."

Cady rolled her eyes as she accepted the cup of coffee Anthony held out. "We talked all night and fell asleep on his couch. He is a . . . magnificent kisser in case you're interested. When I tell you he can make my blood sing, you can believe it!"

Lola clapped her hands in delight. "I just knew it. He has *that* look. Never mind, I'll explain it some other time," she said to Anthony and Mandy, who blinked in surprise at her statement. "Such restraint! I think we like him." Mandy and Anthony nodded in agreement.

"He said he's loved me all his life. What do you think of that?" She hoped it was the bombshell they were hoping for. She hated to disappoint them.

Anthony sniffed as he oiled the fry pan. "Men say that all the time. It's to disarm you and make you feel vulnerable so you let your guard down, then they *pounce*. I'm a man," he said, as if that was all the explanation needed.

"Anthony, you're raining on my parade. He wants me to meet his parents. Well, not right away but sometime."

"That's another bone men throw at you." Anthony sniffed again. "You can't trust men. I certainly hope you didn't respond in kind."

"Anthonyyyy," Cady wailed. "Well, we didn't have sex, if that's what you mean. I was up for it. He seemed a little nervous." She threw her hands in the air. "We're going on a picnic today. I'm going to bring along a blanket. A blanket, Anthony. Can you make some food for us? I'm going to pick him up at ten o'clock. Are you saying I did it all wrong?"

"Dear girl, you did it all just right. He's panting. When men pant, things happen. Anthony doesn't know what he's talking about, does he, Mandy?"

Mandy's head bobbed up and down. "Anthony is just a man. He knows how his stuff works. He doesn't have a clue as to how yours works. You did fine, Cady. We have the most delightful, soft, cushiony, wonderful, yellow, fuzzy blanket in the linen closet. It will caress you, hug you to its fibers, and engulf you in warm, cozy feelings."

"Enough!" Lola shouted. "She doesn't need any advice. Well, maybe just a little. Whip up something wonderful, Anthony. The way to a man's heart is through his stomach and not through sex, like everyone believes. No fried chicken and hard-boiled eggs. They give you *gas!* Fix something delightful, and make it look delicious. A good wine. Crystal glasses, of course. Use that wonderful picnic basket.

Linen napkins, to be sure. Be certain they match the picnic cloth. I'll have some toast and fruit now, Anthony."

"I think I'll just meander upstairs and get ready. If you have any more suggestions, make a list, but I think I have it covered. Oh, my God, I forgot to tell you or did I tell you?" Cady dithered. "I remembered something else. I was wearing a yellow shirt that day. They were there, all of them. I even know what color Amy was wearing: pink. Pete had a paper sack in his hand. I remembered. It's all coming back. I heard them talking, but I couldn't see anything. I think it was because I was on the zip line and my eyes were squeezed shut. I can't be sure, though. I'm just happy that I'm remembering. I feel so . . . *so alive!* Maybe today I'll remember the rest of it. We're going to picnic at the pond. My expectations are running high." She ran over to her grandmother and hugged her so tightly Lola squealed for mercy.

"Darling girl, I knew it! I just knew it! Go. Remember, scented soap first, then use the matching lotion and body powder, then perfume. Hurry, it's not good to keep a man waiting. We'll have everything ready for you when you get back down here."

Anthony slapped two pieces of toast in front of Lola and handed her a banana. She looked at it in dismay. "Now, what should I concoct to drive Mr. Boomer insane?"

They squabbled good-naturedly as they suggested, rejected, and finally came to an agreement. The picnic menu would consist of stuffed artichokes, shiitake mushrooms filled with goat cheese, cherry tomatoes stuffed with smoked salmon and cream cheese, asparagus spears wrapped in Prosciutto, duck pâté with crackers, and, for dessert, strawberries dipped in chocolate. It was left up to Anthony to choose the wine.

"Ah, we work so well together," Lola said happily.

The kitchen took on an air of conspiracy as the Big Three set to work.

Heads turned when Boomer Ward walked into Eva's restaurant. He didn't notice, as he headed for the table in the back that he had reserved. He was the first one to arrive. A bustling waitress in a yellow uniform with a brown-checkered apron approached with a carafe of coffee and poured. "Bring a pitcher of orange juice, a bowl of fruit, and a plate of croissants. A large pot of coffee. There will be four of us," he said.

Eva's was a small-town restaurant favored by just about everyone in Indigo Valley, just the way the bakery was. He loved the smell of fresh coffee and the pastries that were baked on the premises. As a child, his parents had brought him to Eva's every Saturday morning for breakfast. His dad always had a big stack of buttermilk pancakes with a side order of scrambled eggs and six slices of bacon. His mother had a fruit cup and a blueberry muffin. He almost laughed out loud when he remembered the day when he was twelve or so and gave Helen, the waitress, his order, which was the same as his father's. She'd winked at him to show he'd grown up. He'd eaten every bit of it, too, to his father's and mother's dismay.

Memories were wonderful. Especially the good ones. He poured himself a second cup of coffee from the carafe. His thoughts weren't on what would soon transpire but on Cady and the evening they'd spent together. Today might be the last time she would want to see him once she knew what had really happened that day. He was glad now that he'd told her how he felt. He was glad, too, to have finally said the words out loud.

First love. He found himself smiling at the thought. He looked up to see Pete Danson headed his way. He slid into the booth and reached for the carafe.

"How's it going, Boomer?"

"I guess it's going as good as can be expected. How's it with you?"

Pete shrugged. "I feel like I'm about to fall over a cliff onto the rocks down below. Andy said he'd be here, but he might be a few minutes late. Did you get hold of Amy?"

"I left a message on her answering machine. I'm sure she got it, but I don't know if she'll show up or not."

"I'm not counting on it. How's the police business?"

"Fairly calm and quiet. One of my guys picked up Jeb Wooster on Saturday night for setting fire to his garage. His wife said he did it on purpose. He said it was an accident. Seems she's addicted to the Shopper's Channel and stores all her purchases in the garage until she can figure out what to do with them. He figured it out for her. Dan McGruder ripped out Henry Lanson's picket fence on Sunday afternoon because Lanson painted it robin's-egg blue, and Dan said he couldn't abide the color. That's pretty much it on the crime front. What's new in the legal profession?"

"Not a damn thing. Actually, it's slower than slow. Spring is usually a busy time with divorces, according to my colleagues, but since I don't handle divorce cases anymore, that's it on news from the legal front. You know, on to bigger and better things, but this year it's been quiet. I think Andy and Jill are going to patch it up. I have a dog bite case pending and one with Harriet Barclay, who says she got poisoned by some green beans she bought at the Giant. I could write a book in my spare time."

"Larry Denville went up to Vermont yesterday to see Cady's parents," Boomer said quietly.

"No shit! Why?"

"He said you have to start at the beginning. I guess he thinks Cady's parents are the beginning. In my opinion, the four of us are the beginning. But then, he doesn't know that. At least I don't think he does. He might suspect it, but he isn't sure," Boomer said.

"He's an honest reporter. I like him," Pete said. "I just can't imagine what he thinks they can tell him that wasn't in the papers. Hell, they took off like scalded cats right after the accident. They both gave statements and had witnesses verify they were where they said they were. That kind of thing. If they have any secrets, they sure as hell aren't going to part with them to some reporter. They were both pretty tight-lipped as I recall. The only time the father opened his mouth was to spout that fire and brimstone stuff. The mother was afraid of her own shadow and never opened her mouth at all."

"Here's Andy," Boomer said. "Coffee's hot. Help yourself. Is Amy coming?"

"Yeah. She was parking her car as I was getting out of mine."

It was obvious to the others that Amy had taken some pains with her makeup and hair. She looked like most of the other women in the restaurant, chubby and matronly. Until you looked into her eyes. Boomer felt a prickle of apprehension. She slid into the booth next to him. She smelled powdery and sweet. He watched out of the corner of his eye as she leaned back in the booth and folded her hands.

Pete poured her a cup of coffee. She nodded her thanks.

"Now that we're all here, let's get to it," Boomer said. He looked around as though he expected either a dissenting remark or someone was going to get up and leave. No one said a word.

Boomer took a deep breath. "Yesterday, a call came into my office from one of my men. He said he saw Cady Jordan up in the tree at the pond. The one where you guys built the tree house. I'm sure you all know someone cut down all the weeds and took away the No Trespassing signs. They're back up now, however."

"Was she issued a ticket for trespassing?" Amy snapped.

"As a matter of fact, yes. I went to the pond myself, and there she was up in the tree. She remembered parts of that day. She knows you were all there. She even remembers what you were wearing and what she was wearing. She can remember all of you pitching the rocks and yelling and screaming."

Andy's head dropped to his hands. His shoulders started to shake. Pete sighed as he reached over to put a comforting hand on his shoulder. Amy remained impassive as she sipped at her coffee.

"Cady thinks the reason she could only hear the words you three were screaming was because she was on the zip line and had her eyes squeezed shut."

"How convenient," Amy snapped again.

"What the hell is your problem, Amy?" Pete lashed out. Andy's head jerked upright at Pete's language and his tone.

"You know what, I'm sick of all of this. It was all about little Cady Jordan. Now it's all about big Cady Jordan. If you all want to say you were there, go ahead. I wasn't there. Period," Amy all but spat.

"Cady's going to remember. She knows you were there. We know you were there. That's four against one, Amy. Why are you going to lie? It will only make things worse. For you especially," Boomer said.

"You were there, Amy, so stop lying," Andy said. "I'll swear in court you were there. So will Pete and Boomer. If you lie, you'll just make it worse for yourself and your family."

Amy broke out into a cold sweat. "Damn you," she cursed. "If I tell, Arnie will leave me."

"That's the chance you have to take. The rest of us are putting our reputations and careers on the line. Why the hell should you be any different? Besides, you had the best pitching arm in Indigo Valley at the time. Everyone knew it, and they'll start to remember. You *never* missed," Andy said. "You always hit your target! Oh, Jesus God, you didn't . . . Amy, you didn't . . ." Unable to finish what he was going to say, Andy's face turned paper white.

"What?" Boomer snarled. "Don't say something like that and let it hang in the air, Andy."

"I think what he's saying is he thinks Amy hit Cady on purpose. Andy's right, Amy had the best pitching arm. Hell, when she was ten her fastball had no equal."

Amy slapped her palms down on the table. "That's a lie! I would never do such a thing! How can you even think it, much less say it out loud? You're my own brother!"

"Because it's true," Andy said sadly. "And you know it's true, Amy."

Amy grew so calm she scared herself. "It simply isn't true. It was all twenty years ago. You're all running around like chickens without heads. Your memories can't be any better than mine. I refuse to admit to anything. You just want to get back at me because of Jill, Andy, and we both know it. Furthermore, I don't care if you are the new police chief, Boomer. You won't be for long when you tell that cockamamie story. And, by the way, just what the hell *were* you doing while your best friend was trying to hurt little Cady Jordan?"

"I was trying to figure out if the zip line would hold the two of them. In addition, Amy, I was the only one of all of us who knew how to swim at that time. I was worried about which one I would have to save. That's some pretty heavy stuff for a thirteen-year-old. Yeah, I'm the one who pulled Cady to shore. I pulled Jeff, too, but he was already dead. I'm also the one who had the good sense to call the police. If I hadn't, Cady might have died."

"Who would you have saved, Boomer?" Pete asked quietly.

"Cady. I hated Jeff King. I would have saved Cady first and Jeff second. At least I think that's what I would have done. The rest of you turned tail and ran. You didn't even stop to see if Cady was dead or not."

"Jesus, Boomer, we were ten-year-olds! I thought they were both dead. I swear to God, that's what I thought," Andy said, his voice full of anguish.

"That goes for me, too," Pete said. "I was scared shitless. We all were. You were three years older, Boomer. Hey, you lied like the rest of us. We can *almost* be excused. What's your excuse? Those three years make a hell of a difference."

"I did tell in my own way. I called the police. I took down the zip line and threw it into the pond. Don't ask me why," Boomer said.

"Well, whoop-de-do," Amy said.

"Back up a minute here. You said you hated Jeff King. And yet you were always with him just like his shadow. Hating him and hanging out with him are two different things. I think you need to explain that to all of us," Pete said.

"Yes, I was always with him. Did you *ever* see me do even *one* thing or help Jeff in any way? No, you didn't. I was there, but I never did a thing. In fact, more often than not, I tried to stop him from some of the stuff he tried to pull.

I liked all of you back then. More than anything, I wanted to play with you but . . . I got these ice skates for Christmas one year, and my mother told me the pond wasn't frozen hard enough to skate on it. I couldn't wait to try them out, so I went to the pond and fell through the ice. Jeff pulled me out. He saved my life. Jeff said I owed him and was in his debt. That's why I hung out with him. I didn't like him. I actually grew to hate him because he further tormented me by telling me his sick secret. It's not your business, so don't ask me what it was. Now, what the hell are we going to do?"

"I already lied. Cady asked me point-blank the other night, and I said I wasn't at the pond that day. Now, I'm all for telling the truth," Pete said, his voice miserable.

"She asked me, too, when she came to the office yesterday morning. My response was, 'Don't ask me that, Cady.' That means I can go either way. I say we tell her the truth," Andy said.

"That's how I feel. I think we should tell her before she regains her full memory. How about later today? I'll call you with the details. I had this idea. How do you feel about doing a reenactment of that day? If we pull together and all go there to help her, it might all come back. Every little detail. She deserves to know. Are we agreed?"

"Yes," Pete said.

"Yes," was Andy's heartfelt response.

"I think I'll go home now. I have to clean my bathrooms," Amy said.

"You aren't going anywhere, Amy," Andy said, reaching across the table to grab her arm. "You're in this, too. If you balk, I'm going to Arnie and telling him the whole story. Now, what's it going to be?"

"Amy, we can all talk to Arnie. We can make him see that it was an accident and that he shouldn't blame you. I think you might be shortchanging your husband here. If he loves you, he will forgive you when he knows the whole story. Give the guy a chance, and for God's sake, do the right thing here," Boomer said.

Amy's response was to toss a five-dollar bill on the table and slide out of the booth.

The three men looked at one another. Andy's shoulders started to shake again.

Boomer looked across the table, his gaze fixed on Andy. "Just how sure are you that Amy purposely threw the rocks at Cady?"

"As sure as I know my name is Andy Hollister. Jesus, I think I'm going to be sick," he said, barreling out of the booth in search of the men's room.

Boomer and Pete stared at one another. "I swear to good Christ, I didn't see it that way, Boomer. We were just throwing rocks to make Jeff get off the line. I had no clue Andy even thought something like that."

Boomer shook his head. "I saw you all pitching the rocks, but I was so busy with the line I didn't know who was throwing what. Imagine carrying that around for twenty years." He shook his head again, trying to clear away his ugly thoughts.

"I guess it's us versus Amy," Pete said. "You okay, Andy?" he asked his childhood friend when Andy slid back into the booth. "You still okay with all of this?"

"Yeah, I am. So, what time are we going to do the reenactment?"

"The same time as the real accident. Five-thirty. By the way, did either one of you gouge out Cady's initials in the Judas tree?"

"Oh, jeez, I forgot about those initials. Did someone do that?" Andy asked weakly as he mopped at his forehead. "It wasn't me."

"It wasn't me either," Pete said.

"I didn't do it," Boomer said. "That leaves Amy or maybe Mr. or Mrs. King, but I think that's a real stretch to even consider them."

"She's sick," Andy said. "Look, I don't know what to do. Help me here. Should I go and talk to Arnie? What?"

"I think this is one of those let your conscience be your guide kind of things. If you need either one of us to go with you, I'll be there," Pete said.

Boomer nodded. "Me too."

"I need to think about this before I make a decision. I guess I'll see you at five-thirty then."

"When I was a kid, I thought those twins were the best of the best. I wanted to be like them so bad I used to make myself sick. They had so much free rein. I had rules and time-tables and all that other junk. My mother might have been on the weird side, but she did have rules such as they were. Those two raised themselves. Maybe you and I were the lucky ones. I don't know anything anymore," Pete said miserably.

Boomer's eyes were sad. "I know what you mean."

"If you give me a dollar right now, I'll be your attorney. That means I can't ever divulge what you tell me. Tell me the secret so it stops eating you alive."

Boomer fished a dollar out of his pocket and slid it across the table. Then he told him Jeff King's secret. He watched the color drain out of Pete's face before he, like Andy, bolted for the men's room.

When Pete returned, the two men had a hard time looking at one another. "I'll see you at the pond later, okay?"

"Yeah," Pete mumbled as he made his way out of the restaurant.

Boomer felt like he was a hundred years old with the weight of the world on his shoulders when he followed Pete out to the parking lot.

The bright sun and the prospect of pic-nicking with Cady brought a sudden smile to his face. All he had to do was check in at the office, catch up on a few loose ends, and it would be time to meet Cady at his apartment.

On the way to his car he wondered how two weeks as chief of police of Indigo Valley was going to look on his updated résumé.

Cady swished into the kitchen and did what she called her twirly number to gauge the Big Three's approval. "Do I look enticing and delectable?"

"Oh, baby, on my best day, I never looked as good as you do right now. For some reason I keep saying that over and over. You look like you could break a man's heart without even trying," Lola said.

"You smell divine," Mandy said.

"If I was thirty years younger, I'd give that young buck a run for his money," Anthony said, leering at her.

"And I'd take you up on it, Anthony. Oh, that all looks wonderful. Boomer is going to be so impressed."

"Here's the blanket," Mandy said, reaching behind her to pluck a folded yellow blanket that looked to be as soft as feathers.

Cady touched it. "Ooohhh," she grinned. "I like how this feels."

"I knew you would. *Herself* here always used to travel with a yellow blanket just like this. Don't ask me why. It's one of her deepest, darkest secrets," Mandy gurgled.

Lola looked embarrassed. "I love the color of

yellow. It's bright and warm, not to mention inviting, and it's the same color as *gold,* and I do love gold. That's as much of an explanation as you're going to get."

"It'll do." Cady grinned. "So, do you like this outfit?" she asked, referring to the halter-style dress with the full swinging skirt. "I'm wearing my bathing suit underneath. You know, in case I fall into the pond. I hope it isn't too cold. Don't worry, Boomer knows how to swim. He'll fish me out if I fall in."

"Someone should take pictures," Mandy grumbled.

"You're absolutely right, Mandy, someone should. I'll stop at the drugstore and pick up one of those disposable cameras. If this is to be a reenactment, it has to be exactly the way it was that day. *Amy was snapping away like crazy.* . . . Oh, my God, I just remembered that. Did you hear what I just said? Amy was taking pictures. She used to send them away someplace because she would get a free roll of film when she got the pictures back. She took pictures! I wonder if the others remember that. It's coming back, it really is. Just a few more pieces of the puzzle. It won't freeze on me, will it, Lola?" Cady asked anxiously.

"No, baby, it's all going to come back. Every last bit of it, then you'll be the perfect Cady Jordan. No missing pieces. You'll be whole again."

Cady flopped down on one of the kitchen

chairs. She stared at her grandmother, her eyes full of questions. "Lola, what if I remember something that . . . that isn't good? What if I remember that I did something to Jeff King? How will I handle that?"

"Let's not worry about what-ifs. Let's just worry about you getting the full picture. If something like that happens, we'll deal with it. You have three allies now, and don't you forget it. Boomer will make four if we count him. I really suspect he was there that day with the others even though you don't remember that part. Yet. I don't think he would come courting you if there was some deep, dark secret about that day. I don't want you to dwell on that aspect of things because it might hamper you in remembering the rest of it. Agreed?"

"Agreed. There are no words to tell you how much I love the three of you. It's like having two mothers and a really nice father who care about me. None of this would be happening if it wasn't for all of you."

"Here's your picnic basket. You must let me know how Mr. Boomer likes my delicacies. They're all finger foods, just the way a picnic is supposed to be, and there's not one *gassy* thing in the bunch as per your grandmother's instructions."

"It's such a relief to know that you actually listen to me sometimes, Anthony," Lola said, tongue in cheek.

"Then I'm off. I don't know what time I'll be

back. You aren't going to wait up for me, are you?"

"Good heavens, no," Lola said adamantly.

"Yes, you are, but that's okay. It makes me feel loved." She hugged and kissed each of them before she tripped out of the kitchen.

Atlas howled his displeasure until Lola offered him one of his favorite treats. "We'll play ball later." Playing ball meant Lola rolled a tennis ball across the floor, and Atlas brought it back to her.

"I think we're going great guns, ladies and gentlemen. Now, what's for breakfast?" Lola asked brightly.

Chapter 17

Amy Chambers unlocked the door of her house with a steady hand. She hummed under her breath as she looked around the messy foyer and living room. As she moved toward the kitchen, she picked up toys, a stray sock, yesterday's newspaper, and two empty beer bottles from the coffee table. She continued to hum under her breath to some unheard tune as she deposited the trash into the compacter. The stray sock went into the washer.

She needed to clean.

To scrub.

To disinfect.

To sanitize.

The laundry room had a plethora of cleaning supplies. All of them rarely used. Bucket, scrub brush, Clorox, soap, Brillo pads, and a sharp knife to get the grime and gunk out of the corners got dumped into a plastic bin. She looked around for a pair of rubber gloves but couldn't find them. Her shoulders settled into a shrug as she continued to hum. The rag bag was full. Within seconds, a tattered dish towel was wrapped around her flyaway hair to keep it out of her face. She tied a huge bow on the wrap-around apron she found hanging on the back of the laundry room door. She frowned. Where in the world had she gotten an apron? She shrugged again, since it really didn't matter.

The water was scalding hot. She barely noticed. She managed to carry the bucket, a bundle of rags, and, with her elbow, crank up the radio in the kitchen. Bon Jovi filled the house with sound.

Where to start. From the top down. Like at the beginning. What exactly did that mean, start at the beginning? Did it mean when you were born? Did it mean at the onset of a special event? Whatever it meant, it was stupid. Start at the top. That meant the bathrooms, all three of them. Then she would have to scrub and polish the furniture, change the sheets on all the beds, carry the laundry downstairs or just shove it into the laundry chute and hope it got stuck like it sometimes did, eliminating the need to turn on the washer.

Water gurgled into the bathtub as she added Spic and Span to the water. The venetian blinds came down and were dumped into the tub. The toilets foamed with blue-and-white crystals. She blinked at the rust stains. She was really going to have to scrub those. The grout between the tiles on the floor caused her eyebrows to shoot upward. The cap came off the Clorox bottle, the contents spilling across the floor. Holding her nose so she wouldn't breathe the fumes, she opened the window and turned on the exhaust fan before she closed the door and set about scrubbing and polishing the bedroom furniture she shared with Arnie.

Her next task was to change the gray-colored sheets on the bed. She tried to remember the last time she'd changed them, but she gave up.

Amy looked at the sheer curtains hanging on the windows. They were as gray as the sheets on her bed. She stood on a vanity bench and took them down. The washer was going to go all day long.

Bon Jovi had been replaced with Golden Oldies, and Elvis was now screaming about his "Blue Suede Shoes" as she huffed her way downstairs to put the dusty, musty, filthy curtains into the washer.

Amy looked at the clock. It was only nine o'clock.

She whirled around the kitchen. What should she do next? She opened the refrigerator. Obviously, everything had to go. Within minutes, the trash can was overflowing. It was a short walk through the kitchen to the back patio and the three, huge, outdoor trash cans.

By ten-thirty the refrigerator was cleaned out and only a gallon of milk remained. It was so sparkly clean, Amy thought about putting her sunglasses on. The stove gleamed, and the self-cleaning oven was working to remove the burned spills on the oven bottom. The counter was clean, all the junk from empty or near-empty containers also in the trash. It sparkled, as did the words Elvis was moaning about being moody blue. It must be Elvis day, she thought. That was okay, she loved Elvis.

Eleven-thirty found the living room vacuumed, furniture polished, windows cleaned, the blinds dusted. She made a startling discovery when she wiped the dust off the face of the television set. She didn't need glasses after all. A wet rag had just saved her 150 dollars. She was so pleased with her discovery, she danced her way to the second floor and the girls' rooms.

At three o'clock, Amy removed the dish towel from her head and apron from around her waist. It was time to pick up the girls from school and take them to their dance class. Joellen Rubolotto was picking up the girls from dance class and giving them dinner since it was her turn. They wouldn't be home until seven or seven-thirty. Arnie wouldn't be home till eight or eight-thirty.

On her return, after dropping the girls off at dance class, Amy wrinkled her nose. The house reeked of Pine Sol and Clorox. She hated the smell. She looked down at her red hands with their short, bitten nails. The skin was cracking around her fingers. They felt raw from all the Clorox. She jammed them into her pockets as she walked from room to room.

"It's not clean enough," she muttered over and over. "It has to shine and sparkle. I have to wash it all away. I have to wash, too," she muttered over and over. She stripped down and turned on the shower. Steam billowed out of the stall. She stepped inside, barely wincing as the hot water cascaded over her body. She cried, her hot tears mingling with the hot water pouring out of the showerhead.

Twenty minutes later, the hot, steamy water barely lukewarm, Amy looked at her arms and her legs. She still wasn't clean. She had to keep scrubbing, but it hurt too bad. She tried to comprehend the blisters dotting her body. She continued to cry as the warm water turned cool and then cold. She hugged her arms around her chest, but she didn't move. She was going to stand there until she was clean again. Clean and innocent like she was before that day.

Lola Jor Dan's voice was fretful when she looked across the terrace at her two closest friends. It was almost four-thirty. An hour to go before the reenactment. "Do you think it will work? If it doesn't, I guess the others are going to speak up and tell the truth. At least that's what I'm hoping they're going to do. What do you two think?"

Mandy reached down to pluck a yellow leaf from a bushy geranium plant next to her chair. "I don't know, Lola. Cady has guts, I have to give her that. She's absolutely petrified of water. She told me she would drive twenty miles out of her way so she wouldn't have to go over a bridge. The fact that she's willing to go for it tells me things will be okay. I'm not sure about the others speaking up. Good intentions or not, things like that tend to go awry at times.

"I think it's going to rain. Clouds are moving in from the west. I hope it holds off till they make their run. I certainly don't want to see them postpone it. I think I like that Boomer Ward. I think I like him a lot."

"Do you now?" Lola drawled.

"I like him, too," Anthony said, not to be outdone. "He's a man's man."

"If you were directing this, Anthony, how would you play it out?"

"Just the way we did when we were at the pond. They were there. She's going to remember. The only problem that I see is this, who's going to play the part of Jeff King when they do their reenactment? Cady didn't say. I don't even know if any of them even thought about it. They're all grown-up now. They weigh more today than they did back then. When police do reenactments, they try to get it as close to the real event as possible. I'm hoping Mr. Boomer is planning on using dummies whose weight would be the same as the kids'. But" — he held up a warning hand — "Cady said she had her bathing suit on under her dress. That means, to me at least, that she's planning on doing the zip line. I wish we had asked more questions this morning."

"We could all pile into the car and go there," Lola said. "Not to interfere, but to watch. Should we give it a go? I'm on pins and needles sitting here. What if something goes wrong?"

"Stop thinking like that, Lola. It is going to rain, my knees are starting to ache, and the temperature is dropping. What do you think, Anthony?"

"What I think is we need to mind our own business. We got the ball rolling, now we have to sit back and rest on our laurels. We won't be able to alter the outcome, so what's the point in upsetting Cady and the others by showing up. Furthermore, it won't be a true reenactment if we're there," Anthony said logically.

"Someone's at the gate," Mandy said when a shrill whistle blasted out of the security monitor mounted in Lola's bedroom.

"Its probably some pesky salesperson. Don't even bother seeing who it is. We aren't expecting company. That's a damn order, Mandy."

Mandy was back on the terrace as fast as her arthritic knees would bring her. "Lola, I can't be sure, but I think it's Cady's mother. She's driving a dilapidated car. I haven't seen her in years and years, but it certainly looks like your daughter-in-law. What should I do?"

"Good God! Go! Ask who it is. Things always happen like this in the movies, never in real life. Well?" she shouted.

"She said her name is Agnes Jordan. Agnes Jordan is your daughter-in-law. Your son isn't in the car in case you're interested. Should I buzz her in?"

"Now what do you think?" Lola snapped. "It figures she would show up now. This isn't even good Grade B movie material. We need to go downstairs. Anthony, open the elevator and let's see what she wants. She has to want something."

"Lola," Mandy said, putting a hand on her shoulder, "try to be kind. Don't fly off the handle. And remember, she's Cady's mother."

"Do you think for one minute that I could ever forget that? I'm not an ogre. I know exactly who to blame for everything — my son, Asa. Open the door for her. Anthony, make some coffee. She doesn't drink. At least I don't think she does."

Agnes Jordan stood in the open doorway looking like a deer caught in a pair of headlights. "Agnes, how nice to see you," Lola said warmly. "Please, come in. We were just going to have some coffee. Would you care to join us?"

"I'd like that, Lola, but instead of coffee I'd like about six ounces of good bourbon. Straight up."

"I think we can handle that, can't we, Anthony?" *What do we have here?* Lola wondered.

"Absolutely, madam," Anthony said. "Would you like me to serve in the sunroom?"

"Yes, the sunroom will be fine."

In the sunroom, everyone perched on the edges of their seats, Lola, Mandy, and Anthony watching in amazement as Agnes Jordan downed the bourbon in three hasty swallows. Her eyes watered, and she coughed as she held out the glass for a refill. "I needed that. I guess you're wondering why I'm here."

"The thought did occur to me," Lola said dryly. "You're welcome, of course," she said, remembering Mandy's admonition to be kind.

"I was wondering, Lola, if you'd help me the way you . . . Of course I'll pay you back when I can. I left Asa. I couldn't take it one more minute. Not one more minute. The only way to explain it is, I snapped. A reporter came to see us, and he was asking questions. The young girl with him was so nice. She knew Cady when they were little. I think that had something to do with it." She gulped at the fresh drink. This time her eyes didn't water, but they were starting to glaze over.

"I hate him, Lola. The hatred is so pure, so deep, there are no words to describe it to you. Can I please stay here until I can find a place of my own and a job? Cady asked me to come. Even if she hadn't, I would have come on my own. I wish so many things, Lola. God, you have no idea what I wish for."

"I know, Agnes, I know. You're welcome to stay here as long as you like. Whatever you need, it's yours. Why in the world didn't you come sooner? I gave up trying to convince you to come here a long time ago. Why did you stay with him so long? Why?"

"I wish I knew. Guilt is such a terrible thing. I need to ask another favor, Lola. I don't want Cady to see me looking like a scrubwoman. Do you have something I can borrow?"

"We aren't the same size, Agnes. I'll take care of it. Mandy, call Rutherby's and have them send over a selection. Do we have any of that hair dye left that Danielle and Mona used on Cady? If we do, let's work some magic here. Those glasses went out of style twenty years ago, Aggie."

"I know. I appreciate this, Lola. I will repay you."

"That's not necessary. In your own way your heart is as generous as my own, and we both know it. Finish your drink and let's go upstairs. I have the prettiest bedroom that will be just perfect for you. It's very feminine, just the way you used to be before my son got hold of you."

"Do you want to know how he is?"

"No, Agnes, I don't."

"I didn't think so, but I had to ask. This is a beautiful house, Lola. I imagine Cady is very happy here. Will she be home soon?"

"Sometime this evening, I'm sure. Come along, let's get you situated. Are you hungry?"

"Lola, I've been hungry all my life. I think I'd like some meat. I haven't had meat in years. But not now, later, when it's time for supper will be fine. I'm good at waiting and being patient. I think my whole life was geared up to this moment."

Lola felt tears burning her eyes, but she blinked them away.

Lola reached out and took Agnes's arm. "Tell me this isn't a trial run or something like that. Tell me you're here to stay. I'm not going to be here forever, and I want to know Cady has someone she can count on. Wait till you see how she's blossomed. I want your word, Agnes, that you won't go back to Asa."

"I'm here to stay, Lola, as long as you and Cady will have me. I also need to think about getting a divorce. I want to do that as soon as possible."

Lola leaned over, and whispered in Agnes's ear, "You know what we have to do, don't you, Agnes?"

"Yes. I'm ready and I'm prepared. I never thought it would come to this. Am I going to go to hell, Lola?"

"Well if you are, you are certainly going to have a lot of company."

Cady rolled over onto her stomach and propped her elbows on the fuzzy, yellow blanket. "This has been a really nice day, Boomer. Do you realize that after you put up the zip line, we've done nothing but talk for" — she looked down at her wrist — "almost six hours."

Boomer rolled over, and said, "Time flies when you're having fun. Look, there's a duck in the pond."

Cady laughed. "Just one? Oh, look, there's his mate. I bet you didn't know ducks are monogamous."

"I knew that." Boomer laughed. "You aren't going to tell your grandmother we ditched that gourmet picnic in favor of Manny's Take-Out Deli, are you?"

"Absolutely not." She pointed to the spot on the far side of the pond where they'd dumped Anthony's gourmet creations in favor of greasy, finger-lickin' fried chicken, pickled eggs, big fat deli pickles, and shiny, crunchy apples. "See, the squirrels and birds have devoured most of it. I'll simply say it was all finished. It won't be necessary to say by whom."

Boomer leaned over on his side, propping himself up on his elbow. He looked up, then at the rustling in the trees. "The temperature is dropping. I think it's going to rain. When you can see the underside of the leaves, that means rain. My mom told me that when I was a kid and wanted to go somewhere when she thought it was going to rain. You're shivering. Stay here, I have an old jacket in my car."

Cady smiled as Boomer scaled the embankment and returned with a lightweight windbreaker that he helped her put on. Her heart fluttered in her chest at what she was feeling. He was looking at her as though he could read her mind. "What?"

"I was just thinking about how you've changed, and yet I can still see that little kid in you. My crush on you back then was so fierce. I'm telling you, I used to *ache*. I think my mother knew because she started lecturing me on the birds and bees and when she got done, my dad took over. They were hell on wheels when it came to showing respect to girls and women. You know something, I never did tell them about falling through the ice and Jeff King saving me. To this day, I don't know why I didn't tell them."

"Your parents sound like nice people. You were the lucky one." Cady locked her arms around her knees to bring them close to her chest, her gaze on a trio of bluebirds squabbling over one of the asparagus spears they'd spread out. "Amy and Andy's parents never cared what they did. They could come and go at all hours. They didn't have a curfew. I don't think they had even one rule they had to go by. I thought that was so cool back then. Amy used to steal money out of her mother's purse. That always bothered me. Andy wasn't like her, though. Even though they were twins, he was different. Amy was the boss. She never let us forget it either. Pete was different. He had the thing with his mother, and he did his best. Then there was you. None of us could figure you out back then. We were such misfits." She laughed. "Look at us now. I think there's a song with those words in it."

"You haven't said one word today about Jeff King. Why is that, Cady?"

Cady stared at the scudding gray clouds overhead. "I was afraid of him. I guess you never talk about your secret fears because if you say the words out loud, it makes them more real somehow. I lived in fear of him. As soon as I would spot him, I'd start to shake. One day Pete and Andy tried to figure it out for me. They asked me what I thought was the worst thing he could do to me. I couldn't tell them. I think in our own childish way we were all thinking, let him do whatever it was he wanted to do and he'd leave us alone. I guess my ten-year-old mind thought he wanted to kill me. With a father like mine I knew about hell and all that other junk he was always spouting. I think I was more afraid of Jeff King than I was of the devil."

Boomer felt sick to his stomach, recalling the secret Jeff had told him. "It's starting to rain. Run up to the car, and I'll bring the stuff. It might just be a spring shower. It's almost five, so the others should be here soon."

Cady stood up and scampered up the embankment just as a torrent of rain poured from the heavens. The wind kicked up, shrieking through the trees. She shivered. It had to be an omen of some kind.

Inside the car, Boomer looked at Cady. They burst out laughing. "You know what they say about the best-laid plans of mice and men. Maybe we weren't meant to do this reenactment," Cady said in a jittery voice. "I don't think this is one of those light spring showers either, do you?"

"Nope. We'll have to reschedule," Boomer said. "We might as well wait for the others to get here. Maybe we could all go to dinner or something."

"Now, that sounds like a good idea. All of us together for a nice social evening."

"What's your feeling about spending the night with the police chief?" Boomer asked.

"Could you be a little more specific?" Cady said lightly, as her heart slammed against her rib cage.

"This, that, the other thing." His face turned apple red. "You're going to make me say it, aren't you?"

"Uh-huh."

"Well . . . I . . . what I mean is . . . you . . . me . . ."

"As in together, sort of like a couple?" Cady prompted.

"Yeah, yeah, like that."

"And . . . ?"

Boomer mopped at his perspiring forehead in the steamy car. "Bed," he managed to say in a strangled voice.

"Bed. Is that what you said, bed? Beds are good. I have one at the house. I sleep in it," she teased, enjoying her sudden power. "Spell it out."

Boomer rattled something that was barely distinguishable. Cady frowned.

"Let me see if I have this right just so there's no misunderstanding later on. You want me to go back to your apartment where you have a bed. We are going to get *nakid* and do all kinds of wild, crazy, wonderful things, and you have a can of lick-off chocolate paint the guys gave you when you left your last job that you never used and it's flavored with almond. You want me to lick it off you or are you going to lick it off me? Then we will mess up your bed and do some more of those wild, wonderful, crazy things. Did I get that right?"

Boomer managed to look indignant and embarrassed at the same time. "I don't think I said it quite like that, but yeah, that's the drill. I guess you want to go home now, huh?"

"Boomer Ward, you are *onnnn*," Cady cried.

Boomer's eyes widened in disbelief.

"I guess we should scratch dinner with the others, huh?"

"Oh yeah," Boomer responded in a strangled voice, suddenly looking a little nervous. Cady buried her head in his shoulder so he wouldn't see her ear-to-ear smile.

At ten minutes of five, Andy Hollister waved good-bye to his secretary. "See you in the morning." He hoped it was true and he would be in shape to open the office in the morning.

His idea was to swing by his sister's house and offer her a ride to the pond. Hopefully, he could convince her at this, the eleventh hour, that it was the wise and right thing to do. Amy was stubborn, though, so he wasn't really counting on her to accompany him. Hell, knowing Amy, she was liable to kick his ass all the way to the pond, and he wouldn't have to worry about driving the distance.

Ten minutes later, he swerved into her driveway. At least she was home. Her car was sitting at the far end of the driveway and even from where he was sitting in his car, he could see the front door was open. Amy always left her doors open, to Arnie's chagrin.

He loped up the walkway and onto the small porch. He wrinkled his nose at what he was smelling as he tried to put a name to it. Maybe Amy had called an exterminator. He opened the screen door and walked inside. He stopped short and actually backed up a step to look at the house number on the white pillar on the porch. Was he in the right house?

The smell was coming from everywhere, and it was overpowering. In his life, he'd never seen Amy's house so clean. Never. He called her name as he walked through the living room, dining room, and then into the kitchen. He was stunned at what he was seeing. He opened the refrigerator and didn't know why. A gallon of milk.

He called her name again. Where were the kids? Why was it so quiet? Amy usually played the radio. Sometimes it played all night long because she was too lazy to walk into the kitchen to turn it off before going to bed.

He retraced his steps to the living room, where he loped up the steps, shouting his sister's name. The smell was stronger on the second floor. He found himself gagging. He tried to breathe through his mouth as he looked around. It boggled his mind that the second floor was cleaner than the first floor.

He thought he heard water running. He held his breath as he listened. Amy must be in the shower. He felt the fine hairs on his neck stand on end as he made his way down the hall to Amy's bedroom. He called out a second and then a third time. His heart kicked up a beat when there was no response. It was the shower he'd heard.

Andy poked his head into the bathroom doorway. "Amy, it's me, Andy. How long before you're finished? I need to talk to you." He frowned when he realized there was no steam coming out of the stall shower. "Come on, Amy, answer me. If you don't, I'm going to open that damn door. You need to grow up and start acting like the responsible adult you are. Okay, have it your way." He marched across the tile floor and opened the door a crack.

"Amy!" he shouted hoarsely. "Amy, what's wrong? Oh, Jesus!" Quickly he turned off the water and grabbed towels off the rack.

"Amy, what happened? Talk to me, damn it!" He wrapped his sister in two towels and led her through the bathroom to the bed. He switched on the light and gasped. "Oh, my God, Amy!" He rolled across the bed and grabbed for the phone. He jabbed in 9-1-1 and waited. "Now! I need an ambulance now! Something's happened to my sister. She's blistered from head to toe from a hot shower. I think it's from a shower. I just got here and found her like this. The water was freezing. I think she's in shock." He gave the address, broke the connection, and called his brother-in-law.

Tears rolled down his cheeks as he cradled his sister next to him. "Ah, Amy, why'd you do this? Why?"

He was still crying when the EMS people carried Amy out on a stretcher. He stood by helplessly as he waited for his brother-in-law.

While he waited, he dug into his pocket for his Nokia and called Pete's cell phone number. He explained the situation in a jittery voice and listened to Pete tell him the reenactment was canceled because it was pouring rain.

Andy looked outside and was stunned to see the heavy rain. *Was it raining when I arrived?* He couldn't remember. *Where the hell is Arnie? Maybe he went straight to the hospital. Did I tell him to go there or come home?* He couldn't remember that either.

Should he call their parents? Amy would say no. He said yes. His mother picked up after three rings. "Mom, it's Andy. I'm calling to tell you Amy was just taken to the hospital. She's been scalded over her entire body in the shower. I think she's in shock."

"You have to be pretty stupid to get burned in a shower. Why didn't she just get out? Let me know how she's doing."

"Aren't you going to the hospital to see her?" Andy asked, his voice so agitated he could barely get the words out of his mouth.

"And what good can I do in the hospital? That's why hospitals have doctors and nurses. You aren't going to tell me she has no insurance, are you, because if you are, your father and I are just squeaking by. We can't help."

Andy didn't bother to respond. Instead, he clicked the OFF button and sat down on the top step of the porch. Rain poured over him as he dropped his head into his hands and cried. When he couldn't cry any more, he pulled out the Nokia again and dialed his wife's number. "Jill, it's Andy. I'm at Amy's house. Can you come and get me? I need you. Please."

Chapter 18

Atlas barked just as the buzzer sounded at the electronic gate. Mandy scurried to the monitor to see Larry Denville waiting patiently to be admitted. She pressed the button that would release the gate. Atlas continued to bark but not as loudly as he had at first.

"Lola, the reporter is here, and he has someone with him. They're on their way up the driveway," Mandy cried shrilly, so that both Lola and Anthony could hear her.

"Now we'll get his spin on the way things went in Vermont. By the way, Anthony just looked in on Aggie, and she's curled up in bed sleeping. I think nine shots of liquor might have something to do with it. I expect she'll sleep through the night knowing she's safe and sound," Lola said, just as Denville rang the bell outside the kitchen door.

"This is my associate, Myrna Davis," Denville said, and proceeded to make the appropriate introductions. "We have Myrna to thank for Mrs. Jordan finally seeing the light in regard to her husband. We just stopped by to see if she arrived safe and sound. And to tell you I'm not sure I want to continue with this article and all the dredging up of the past that would go with it. My reporter instincts are telling me there are some serious private issues at stake, and I have no desire to turn into a tabloid reporter. So, if it's all the same to you, Miss Jor Dan, I'm going to put all this on hold until you tell me otherwise."

Lola's skinny hand shot out and patted the reporter on the back. "I knew I liked you for a reason. You're right about everything. Agnes is safely asleep upstairs. We'll take care of her. Now, how can I thank you for all the trouble you've gone to?"

"I'd like Madonna's autograph if that's possible and Myrna would like Brad Pitt's."

Lola laughed. "That's a pretty tall order, but I still know some people in Hollywood on the younger side who might be able to help us. Why don't you and Myrna come for dinner on Sunday."

"Oh, I'd love that, Miss Jor Dan. I've seen all your films. I think I like the black-and-white versions better than the ones they colorized," Myrna gushed.

"You are a girl after my own heart," Lola gushed in return.

"Mrs. Jordan is a nice lady. Larry and I doubled back and waited to make sure she was really going to leave. We stayed behind her all the way on the interstate in case she broke down or something. I hope it all works out for everyone. If you need either Larry or me, just call the paper, and we'll be right here."

"I love it when I can depend on people," Lola said, ushering the couple to the door. "We'll be in touch."

"She's as homely as a mud fence," Anthony said.

"No, Anthony, she's beautiful. She has a heart, and right now her heart is fixated on Mr. Denville. I saw a certain light in his eyes when he looked at her. As we all know, beauty is in the eye of the beholder. That young woman has character. I think we'll introduce her to Cady. I think they'll get on well. In addition, the young woman obviously has a brain, and she uses it. I really liked her."

"She's still homely, Lola," Anthony said.

"Not to me she isn't," Lola said.

"I agree with Lola," Mandy said.

"All right, all right," Anthony grumbled. "Are we just going to sit here and twiddle our thumbs, or are we going to do something?"

"What would you like to do, Anthony?" Lola asked patiently.

"Give me five minutes, and I'll think of something," the majordomo responded.

Lola looked pointedly at her watch as Anthony and Mandy rolled their eyes.

"I think I was sixteen the last time I made out with a girl in the backseat of a car,"

Boomer said with a grin. "Now that I'm older, I think I prefer a bed. How about you? Heavy breathing will definitely fog up the windows." He wiped one of the windows with the palm of his hand. "I think it finally stopped raining."

Cady laughed. "Hmmm," was all she said. She didn't see any point in telling him she'd *never* made out in the backseat of a car. She moved closer so he would kiss her again. Then his cell phone rang.

"Damn!" Boomer said. "Sorry about this," he said, fishing his cell phone out of his pants pocket. "Yeah," he barked. His eyebrows shot upward as he mouthed the words, "It's Pete." He listened, his expression turning blank. "Okay, Pete, we're on our way. Tell Andy to take it easy, okay?"

"What is it?" Cady demanded.

Boomer used his right hand to smear a clear spot on the steamed window. He stared out at the rain. "I'm not sure. Pete said Andy called to tell him he stopped by Amy's house to give her a ride to the pond. He found her in the shower. He said she was blistered from head to toe, but that the water coming out of the shower was ice-cold. Andy said she was out of it. He called 9-1-1. That means I have to go to the hospital. Nine-one-one means the police have to check things out." He leaned over and opened Cady's door so she could get out to climb into the front seat. He did the same with his own door.

"Was . . . was it an accident?"

Boomer looked at her sharply. "I don't know, Cady. Sometimes . . . water just . . . I don't know. I don't understand why she would have stayed in the shower."

Cady could feel her insides start to quiver. She stared out at the gray landscape. How she had looked forward to this day.

"Do you want to come with me, or do you want me to drop you off at home?"

"I want to go with you. Amy is going to need all the support we can muster up. I remember what it was like when I was in the hospital. If it's okay, I want to be there."

"Okay. You never talk about that time, why is that?"

Cady continued to stare out the window. "Because it was awful. I hate to remember the pain. There was always someone poking me, prodding me, stretching me until I would just give up and cry. Then Lola would come in and work her magic. She would tell me stories by the hour and tell me what we were going to do once I was better. She was going to take me ice-skating at Rockefeller Center in New York. We were going to go to Disneyland. She even promised a camping trip and some white-water rafting. She said she would take me around the world if I wanted her to, but I had to cooperate and do what the therapists said. I did, but all those wonderful things never happened. The day they said I was well enough to travel, my parents came and took me away. I don't know who screamed and cried the loudest, Lola or me. Does that answer your question?"

"How did Jeff hurt you on the line? I can't get that clear in my mind."

"The rocks hit me. They hit Jeff, too. I felt something warm all over my face and arms. I think it was Jeff's blood. Jeff was just hanging on, trying to shake my hands loose. He was hissing something in my ear, and I didn't want to hear it. That was before he was hit."

"Cady," Boomer said quietly, "did you hear what you just said?"

"I said, the rocks hit me and Jeff. *Jeff was telling me something I didn't want to hear. The rocks hit me and Jeff.* I remember feeling a lot of pain. I guess we both fell at the same time. I don't remember falling, though."

"What did Jeff whisper to you?" Boomer asked, his voice sounding ragged.

"I don't know. I can't remember, just the way I can't remember falling. I don't remember you being there that day. Were you, Boomer?"

"Yes, I was there. I was trying to secure the zip line. I was up and behind you."

"Why did they all lie? *You lied, too,*" Cady said, squirming closer to the door, as far away from Boomer as she could get. Suddenly she longed for Atlas. "You know what, I don't think I want to go to the hospital after all. Drop me off at the corner there by the hardware store. I'll call Anthony to come and get me.

"You all lied to me. Even you, Boomer. And

to think I was considering going to bed with you. Not in this lifetime, you . . . you . . . cop!" A second later, Cady had the door open and was on the ground running even before Boomer came to a full stop.

"Son of a bitch," Boomer seethed as he listened to cars behind him honk their horns. He bent over, reached down for his portable siren, and plopped it on the roof of his car. That would shut them up. The horns stopped as one.

He zipped through town, his siren blasting until he reached the hospital. He parked and stormed his way into the lobby, to the information desk. He whirled around when he felt a hand on his shoulder. Pete Danson. He shook his head to clear his thoughts.

"C'mon into the coffee shop," Pete said. "Andy and his wife are in there having coffee. Right now, we don't even know where they've taken Amy. Her husband is with her, so that's a plus. A couple of your men are back in the Emergency Unit."

Boomer followed blindly, aware that he was being introduced to Andy's wife. They shook hands, and a fourth cup of coffee was ordered. He sat down and looked from Pete to Andy. "Cady remembered on our way here. She got out of the car by the hardware store and started running. She remembers most of it now. She called all of us liars. I wish you could have seen the look on her face."

"Maybe I should talk to her," Jill said, getting up. "We hit it off that day when we first met. I think she might be able to use a friend about now. Which way did she go?"

"Up to the corner, toward the bakery and Andy's office. I think you're right about her needing a friend, but she's probably halfway home by now." Three pairs of eyes watched as Jill sprinted out of the hospital and down the curving driveway that led to the main section of town.

"I wonder why she didn't take the car," Boomer said.

Andy and Pete stared at him, then shrugged.

"So, she knows," Pete said.

"Yeah," Boomer said. He eyed a rack of paperback novels off to the side. He remembered another hospital gift and coffee shop like this one. His parents had brought him to the hospital when his grandfather had become ill. They'd loaded him up with licorice, popcorn, and soda pop, and told him to sit and not move until they were ready to leave. It was an everyday occurrence for a long time. Then one day his mother said they didn't have to go anymore. He'd stayed with the neighbors for a few days after that.

"People die in places like this," Boomer said gruffly.

"People also get better in places like this," Andy said. "Jesus, why would she do something like that to herself?" His voice was so tortured

Pete took pity on him.

"This is just a guess on my part, but maybe she was trying to wash away her guilt. Look, I'm no shrink. I have a little experience dealing with them because of my mother but this . . . this is out of my league. I don't think we should say anything to her husband. He's got enough on his plate right now. Do you agree?"

Andy and Boomer nodded.

"Now what?" Andy said.

"I have to go talk to my men. I'll be back," Boomer said, draining his coffee cup. "Wait for me."

"Like we have somewhere to go or anything to say," Andy mumbled. Pete nodded slightly to show he was of the same opinion.

A volunteer wearing a pink smock and a headband to match appeared and filled their cups. Neither man moved to drink the steaming coffee.

"This out and out sucks," Andy said. "I feel like I'm wading through a nightmare."

All Pete could do was shake his head from side to side. "I wish I knew more about burns. I can't believe Amy would do something like that to herself deliberately. Do you suppose she did it so we'd feel sorry for her and not tell? God Almighty, what kind of thinking is that?"

"You don't think she'll die, do you, Pete? Lately, we haven't been getting along. I said some pretty terrible things, and so did she. I feel like this is my fault."

"It's not your fault, Andy. Amy is . . . Amy has a mind of her own. She's the only one who knows why she would do something like that. If she was as bad as you said, she must have done it on purpose. When the water in a shower comes on too hot, and it does happen, you hop out of the way or jump out of the shower. At least that's what I do. She must have used up all the hot water in the tank if it was cold when you got there. That might be for the good. I think I remember reading something about ice or cold for burns. She's young, she's healthy, so it might not be so bad." Pete wondered if Andy was picking up on how lame everything he was saying sounded.

"They're transporting Amy to a special burn unit in Pittsburgh," Boomer said, sliding into the seat he'd vacated earlier. "I didn't see Amy's husband, but he is with her. The charge nurse said her condition is critical."

Andy dropped his head to the table and banged it twice.

"Just out of curiosity, Andy, what the hell good is banging your head going to do? You are not your sister's keeper. She has a husband who looks out for her and watches over her. There was no way you could have known she would do something like this, so stop blaming yourself," Boomer said, not unkindly.

"We're twins. We've always been in tune with each other. I think that's why I went over there. I knew she wouldn't go to the pond unless I made an effort to make amends with her. I should have gone earlier. Damn it, why did I wait till the last minute?"

"Okay, blame yourself then," Boomer said. This time his voice was firm and practical.

"What about Cady?" Pete asked hesitantly. He waved away the volunteer with the coffeepot.

"I think it's pretty safe to say she's fed up with all of us, and me in particular. She's got almost all of her memory back now. Just one more piece, and that's the ball game," Boomer said as he impatiently brushed his hair back from his forehead.

"Does that mean there's no point in all of us going to her and fessing up?" Pete asked.

"You can do whatever you want, Pete. You, too, Andy. She already knows we all lied. What's the point?"

"To explain. To tell her we're sorry," Andy said. "To try to make her understand we were scared out of our wits. I don't know about you two, but I want to look at her when I tell her what I did. I want to see her face, and I want her to see mine, so that she knows I'm sorry. I am sorry. I want her to know I suffered just the way she did. Not the pain part but the mental part. I can't walk away until I do that."

"What about Amy's part?" Pete asked.

"I can't speak for Amy any more than either of you can. I'll take whatever is coming to me, and, no, I will not cover up for Amy if that's your next question. I just want this to be over and done with before I do something stupid like Amy did. Now, what's it going to be?"

Pete stood up and carried the check to the cashier. He paid the bill, walked back, and left a tip on the table. "Okay, let's do it! Right now."

Boomer stood up, and so did Andy. They followed Pete to the main lobby, where Andy asked them to wait while he got an update on what was going on with his sister.

"You look pretty frazzled, Boomer. Are you and Cady . . ."

"*Were* is the operative word. She hates my guts right now. I saw so much emotion in her. She can't comprehend that we *all* lied. I have trouble believing it myself. Let's just get this over with," Boomer said grimly.

Andy caught up with them in the parking lot. "Amy's on her way to the burn center. They're afraid of pneumonia. She's not responding to anything, but it's still too early. I am hoping Arnie's with her. He told the nurse to tell me he'd call me when he knew something more. His parents are taking the girls to their house."

"Shouldn't you call your parents, Andy?" Boomer asked.

Andy snorted. "I did call them from the house. My mother said I better not be calling to ask for money because they didn't have any to give. She also said she wasn't going to the hospital because that's why they have nurses and doctors. They were never, nor will they ever be, Parents of the Year. Let's go."

They were a three-car caravan of miserable human beings as they drove through town on the way to confess their sins to Cady Jordan.

Cady looked up when she saw a shadow fall across the booth she was sitting in. "Jill, what are you doing here?"

Instead of answering Cady, Jill looked around the seedy bar called the Drop Zone, and said, "So this is what it looks like. I always wondered. Interesting clientele," she said, pointing to the bar with its tattooed, ponytailed, Harley jocks. Cady offered up a sickly smile as Jill slid into the booth. "A Bud Light in the bottle," she said to the bartender.

"You didn't answer my question, Jill. What are you doing here?"

"I came looking for you." There was no way she was going to lie to this miserable young woman she wanted to be friends with. "The police chief, the one you call Boomer, came to the hospital and told us what happened. It was my idea to come after you, not theirs. Andy called me from Amy's house and asked me to pick him up. He's a basket case right now. So are the others. If it's any consolation to you, your friend Boomer looks about as miserable as a man can look and still function."

"Good," Cady snapped. "I was actually contemplating going to bed with him tonight. He lied to me. They all damn well lied about me and to me. If there's one thing in this life I hate, it's someone who lies and takes advantage of someone else for their own benefit. I'm not really very good company, so maybe you should leave. I'm just going to sit here and drink and think. I'll call Anthony to come and pick me up when I've had enough."

"I wasn't very good company that day in the cemetery either, but you stuck with me. I was hoping we could be friends. That means friends stick together. It also means if you planned on getting soused, I'm getting soused with you. You okay with that?"

Cady thought about it. "I've already had two beers. This is my third."

"We'll play catch-up. I'm pretty much of a social drinker these days, but in college I could hold my own. You want to see someone who can put it away, you should see Amy. Andy's a beer after he mows the grass kind of guy."

"I didn't know that. I always liked Andy. I liked Pete, too. I wanted to like Amy, but it was hard. It was that twin thing. I guess if you aren't a twin, you just don't understand the closeness twins share to the exclusion of other friends."

The two women sat quietly, their eyes on the men at the bar as they drank from their respective bottles. Finally, Jill said, "I used to buy into that." She held up her empty beer bottle for the bartender's scrutiny.

Cady moved the beer bottle back and forth

on the table, creating wet circles that ran into one another. "Have you heard any more about Amy's condition?"

"Amy's doctors are having her transferred to a special burn unit in Pittsburgh. She's not doing well. I guess she isn't responding to whatever they've been doing for her here. I really don't know any more than that, Cady."

She has the nicest smile, Cady thought as she stared at the woman across from her. She'd gotten a haircut in the past few days and looked fashionable. Today she was wearing a tank top that was buttercup yellow with matching shorts and straw sandals. "So, when did you stop buying into the twin business?"

"When it started to interfere with my marriage. I'm surprised I hung in there as long as I did. Amy made me so crazy I took it out on Andy, and he would never, ever, see my side. It was like she brainwashed him. Look at me, Cady, because I want to tell you something before we both get so soused neither of us will remember. Andy told me early on in our marriage about that day at the pond. It ate at him. And I mean it *ate* at him. When you came back to town, he wanted to tell you. He tried talking to the others, but they convinced him to wait it out. He had his game plan in place. He's had nightmares our whole married life. I can only imagine what it was like before we got married. He was going to pack up and leave after he confessed. He figured his life was going to be ruined. That's what they all thought. They thought you would be vindictive and want to ruin them. If that's what you have to do to put it all behind you, then that's what you have to do.

"Amy was the one who said she would lie. She said she wasn't admitting to anything. Andy said she was jealous of you when all of you were children. I didn't know a lot of this until today, when I went to pick up Andy. You need to listen to me, Cady. I'm going to tell you what Andy told me. It's the way he remembers it. Andy is the only one who remembers this, and that's why I think he has been so tormented all these years. Amy threw the rocks *at you*. She got you smack in the back when you whirled around on the zip line trying to push Jeff away from you. She threw them at Jeff, too, but with a bad aim. Andy said the rock that hit Jeff in the head was meant for your head."

Cady started to cry. Jill handed her a napkin.

"Andy never told Amy he knew what she did until today. She, of course, denied it. They all agreed, Pete, Boomer, and Andy, that they had made up their minds to tell you the truth before you remembered on your own. The reenactment was to help things along. Amy wanted no part of it. She left and went home, and what happened is the result."

Cady digested Jill's words as she finished the last of her beer. She thumped her bottle on the table and held up her hand. "I think that's what you do in a place like this," she said. "Were they really going to tell me?"

"Yes, Cady, they were really going to tell you. Tell me what you're thinking."

"I don't know what I'm thinking," Cady said, slurring her words. "I guess I feel a little betrayed, a little angry, and yet I *almost* understand how afraid they must have been. The part I'm having trouble with is *they left me there to die*."

"How do you know that? They all said they thought you were already dead. Except Boomer. He was the one who called the police," Jill said, draining her third bottle of beer. She did what Cady did and banged on the table, holding her empty aloft.

"How do I know that they left me there to die? I just remembered it, that's how. Oh, another piece just fell into place. We need to drink to that, Jill."

"No, no, no. Didn't you hear what I just said? They thought you were dead. At least Andy did. He told me that years ago. If that's what they thought, it makes a big difference, Cady."

The two women stared at one another, each busy with her own thoughts. They continued to sit, drinking their beer. "What am I supposed to do now?" Cady finally asked. Her tone was so belligerent, Jill shrugged.

Finally, Jill asked, "Exactly how much do you care about all this?"

"About them not telling me? I don't know. I

told you, I hate liars. Didn't I just tell you that? All I want is to get my memory back. All of it. Every single little piece. They robbed me of that. I don't think I can make any decision about anything until that happens."

"Yes, you did tell me that. What happens if you don't get your memory back, Cady?"

"I wish I knew, Jill. I feel like I'm in this holding pattern. Boy, do I have to go to the bathroom. Wait for me, okay?"

"Sure. I don't have anywhere to go. Maybe we need to go outside and get some fresh air to clear our heads. What do you say?"

"Sounds good to me. I'll be right back."

The bartender with the dirty apron walked over to the table and slapped down the bar bill. Jill looked at it and suddenly remembered she'd run out of the hospital, leaving Andy with her purse. She hoped Cady had some money.

Minutes later, Cady slid into the booth and almost fell over. She eyed all the empty beer bottles on the table and then glared down at the bill. "Is he throwing us out?"

"I think he wants to be paid. I hate to say this, but I left my purse with Andy at the hospital. You have some money, don't you?"

"Nope. I left my purse in Boomer's car when I bailed out on him. What are we going to do?" She crooked her finger at the bartender.

"We seem to have a little problem, sir. We don't have any money. Can I bring it by tomorrow? What time do you open this fine establishment?" Cady batted her eyes at the bartender, who just scowled.

"Ten o'clock in the morning. There's a phone on the bar you can use. I run this business to make money. Call someone." He walked away to Cady's chagrin, his face bulldog angry.

"I guess I better call my grandmother. She'll send Anthony with some money. I hate for him to see me like this. Today was supposed to be so wonderful, and here I am in this sleazy bar, half-drunk, with no money."

"I can call Andy," Jill volunteered.

"Andy has enough problems. Don't add this to his list. That leaves Boomer and Pete. Oh, God, I don't want to call either one of them," Cady groaned. "Do you have any friends? What about your mother?"

Jill shook her head. "My mother is in Pittsburgh visiting her sister, and my friend is on a business trip. I don't have many friends, I'm sorry to say."

"Then we have to come up with something. How about if we run up to the bar and pretend like we're going to call someone and then blast out of here. That guy's kind of fat. I think we can outrun him. I'll come by tomorrow and pay him."

"You looked kind of wobbly when you came back from the rest room." Jill eyed the empty bottles on the table. "I don't think I'm any too steady myself. Hey, if you think it will work,

I'm up for it. Jeez, look at him flexing his arm with that serpent tattoo. It looks like it's *slithering*. He's trying to intimidate us."

"Well, he's doing a damn fine job of it," Cady hissed. "Okay, let's *do it*."

The moment the bartender saw the women approaching, he reached for the phone, which was every bit as dirty as his apron, and slid it along the bar. Cady looked at it, knowing she didn't want to touch it. She reached down and took her sandals off. Jill did the same thing. "On the count of three," Cady mumbled. "Now!"

Both women blasted through the fly-specked screen door and ran down the street, the bartender and several of his sterling customers giving chase as they whooped and hollered, demanding payment. At the corner of Sycamore and Chestnut avenues, a patrol car skidded to a stop. Cady dropped her sandals and ran as fast as she could, Jill right on her heels.

As she whizzed down the street she stumbled against a mailbox but kept on going, leaving half of her dress behind on a parking meter next to the mailbox. The other half fell away as she continued running.

"You lost your dress. Nice duds, Cady. Faster, they're gaining on us." Jill laughed hysterically.

"How'd that happen?" Cady asked, looking down at her bare legs.

"The parking meter next to the mailbox was

broken, and the sash of your dress caught on it," Jill gasped. "I can't run anymore, Cady. My side hurts."

"Oh myyyy God, there's that reporter that went to see my mother. Look, he's taking our picture!"

"Oh, shit!" Jill said, sitting down in the middle of the sidewalk when she realized she couldn't outrun the cop who had climbed out of his patrol car. "Don't open your mouth. Don't say a word. They allow one phone call when they arrest you. You sure do have some fancy underwear, girl. I liked what you were wearing in that picture in the paper the other day."

"This is a bathing suit. I had it on under my dress because I thought I might fall into the pond."

"That sounds good," Jill said, stretching her legs out in front of her, her palms on the concrete holding her upright.

"All right, ladies, up and at 'em," the patrol officer said.

"And if we don't?" Cady said, glaring at him.

"Then I'll have to add resisting arrest to the other charges."

"Which are?"

"Not paying me for all that beer you two drank," the bartender snarled. The serpent on his arm was wiggling so fiercely, Cady's head started to spin.

"Oooh, I'm so afraid of you," Cady said

bravely. She wondered if she was going to get sick. The patrol officer looked like he was wondering the same thing.

"Can I get a quote from you, Miss Jordan?" the reporter asked.

"Well, sure, Mr. Denville. What should we say, Jill?"

Jill's brow furrowed. "Tell him . . . tell him . . . tell him anything you want."

Cady's head jerked upright. "We think we'll reserve comment until such time as a comment is needed."

"That was good." Jill wiggled her toes for everyone's benefit.

"Get in the car, ladies," the patrol officer blustered. "Don't make me call for backup."

"My mother told me never to get in a car with strangers," Cady said.

"My mother told me the same thing," Jill said.

"I'm calling for backup."

"He's calling for backup, Jill."

Jill giggled. "Back up, pull up, sit up, hold up. Whatever."

"What happened to my dress?"

"Part of it is hanging on the parking meter," Jill said, stretching her neck to see if the dress was where she'd seen it last.

Five minutes later, backup arrived in the person of Officer Conroy. He took in the scene and grimaced. "That one has a problem," he said, pointing to Cady. "She likes to parade around and climb trees in her underwear. Haul their asses in and let them sleep it off."

"I heard that! I am not an *ex-a-bish-* . . . show-off. Neither is my friend. So there!"

"She is not one of those," Jill said, sticking up for her friend.

"Throw them both in the drunk tank with Carlyle Richards. He's been on a three-day toot and doesn't even know his name. They can keep each other company," the cop said.

"Call my grandmother, Mr. Denville," Cady shouted to the reporter, as both cops hauled and shoved them into the back of the patrol car.

"You two are a menace," the patrol officer said. "The minute you women got the right to vote, all hell broke loose."

Cady picked up her feet and jammed them against the wire mesh that separated prisoners from the driver. Jill did the same thing.

"Keep that up, and I'll add assault to your other charges."

Cady's middle finger shot in the air. Not to be outdone, Jill did the same thing.

At the police station, with his fellow officers gawking at his prisoners, the patrol officer ushered Cady and Jill into the station. He handed them over to a fellow officer just as Boomer Ward walked out into the hallway. His jaw dropped as Cady and Jill sashayed past him like they'd never seen him before.

"What the hell . . . Somebody better explain

what the hell is going on here. Why are these women here? What do you mean you're locking them up? What did they do?" He listened to the charges, his eyes almost bugging out of his head.

Larry Denville walked into the station, and said, "I need a quote. I also want to see the police report when it's ready."

Pete Danson, his eyes wild, blew into the station like a wild gust of wind, Andy Hollister behind him. "I want to see my clients, and I want to see them *now*. What are the charges?"

Boomer rattled them off. Pete blanched. "Tell me you're making that up."

"They're in the drunk tank. Go see for yourself. They're staying there, too."

"I don't think so! This is all a big misunderstanding. We need to talk about this, Boomer."

Boomer eyeballed the arresting officer, and said, "Make it good, Carpenter, or you're going to be walking the boonies and doing crossing guard duty."

"Conroy, fetch the prisoners. Now!"

"But, Chief . . ."

"*Now* means now, Conroy, or you'll be walking the boonies with Carpenter."

Boomer tried to strike a pose befitting the fine office he held, but when he saw Cady in her bikini sashaying down the hall, he did a double take, as did all the officers in the duty room. A moment later she was in his face. "Is this where you start with the thumbscrews?"

"No, this is where you go home and sleep it off," Boomer said quietly. So quietly, Cady had to strain to hear the words.

"Are we free to go?"

"You're free to go," Pete said. "I'll take care of the paperwork."

"Fine, you do that. You're fired. I hate liars." With as much dignity as she could muster, Cady stalked out of the police station. Jill followed, with Andy in tow.

"We'll give you a ride home, Cady."

"Thanks, but I think I'll walk."

"I don't think that's such a good idea considering what you're wearing."

Cady looked down at the skimpy flowered bikini and nodded. "I guess you're right."

Cady cried all the way back to Lola's mansion.

At the house, she asked to be dropped off at the gate. "I'll walk the rest of the way. Thanks for the ride. I guess I lost my shoes, too." She hugged Jill and tried not to look at Andy's miserable face. "I hope your sister is okay, Andy. If there's anything I can do for her, let me know."

The Big Three, their eyes almost popping out of their heads, stared at her. Cady took a deep breath. "This is the short version. I remembered more. Rain canceled the reenactment. Amy Chambers scalded herself today and is in a burn unit in Pittsburgh. Jill and I were arrested for all kinds of things. Drunk and disorderly, failure to pay a bar tab, disturbing the peace, resisting arrest, assault on a police officer, and a bunch of other stuff. I think I'm out on bail. I fired Pete Danson. I'm now going to bed. I'll see you in the morning. Oh, yeah, I was going to go to bed with Boomer. He has this lick-off chocolate paint we were going to try. Obviously we will never be trying it now. Good night, all."

"So much skin," Anthony said.

"I wonder if this will make the papers," Mandy muttered.

Lola's eyes sparkled. "Lick-off chocolate paint. Hmmm."

Upstairs, Cady showered in the Ginger Rogers bathroom, then crawled into bed and cried. Atlas licked her tears as he stretched out alongside her.

Chapter 19

For the first time in their respective lives, the Big Three were speechless as they hovered and glowered over the front page of the *Indigo Sentinel*.

"It says your granddaughter is a brawler. An inebriated brawler," Anthony said in hushed tones.

"A near-naked brawler. It reminds me of one or two of your more famous escapades, Lola," Mandy clarified, tongue in cheek.

"So it does. The child is incredibly photogenic. It's almost impossible to believe it's the same Cady," Lola said proudly.

"Straight to the hoosegow. The charges are . . . awesome. The way this reads, she sounds worse than Clyde's partner Bonnie. I thought that reporter Denville was on *our* side," Anthony dithered.

"He is on our side. This is human interest," Lola snapped as she read the article a second time to be sure she didn't miss anything. "He's not speculating, he's reporting facts. There's a difference. If there's one thing I know, it's how the print media works. Look, he even has a picture of her dress hanging off a parking meter. He does say it's her bathing suit, not underwear. Facts. One cannot argue with facts."

"We should have told Cady that her friends came out here yesterday," Mandy said, hoping to distract Lola from the article.

"Frankly, my friends, I don't think it would have mattered. She was . . . what's the word young people use so much today . . . ah, yes, *pissed?* She was definitely pissed when she came in last night. No, it wouldn't have mattered. I think perhaps it's time for us to . . . to . . ."

"Meddle?" Mandy snorted. "I think we should mind our own business, Lola. Match-makers we are not. We could end up making things worse."

"The path to true love never was smooth, and if it is, then it isn't true love," Lola said breezily. "The child is in love. I recognize the signs. What could possibly be wrong with us going to the police station to . . . square things away? Cady said she fired Pete Danson, so that would give us reason to go. Now, if we just happen to bump into the police chief, oh well. I know a thing or two about love, as you both know, and our Cady's heart was broken last night. We need to fix that."

"We do not need to fix that, Lola. Cady will . . . when she wakes up, view things differently," Mandy said as she eyed the coffee dripping into the pot. "You're very slow this morning, Anthony. Breakfast should have been ready an hour ago."

Anthony looked in the oven to check his cinnamon rolls. He plopped down on one of the kitchen chairs. "I quit! I'm going back to California, where people are just plain crazy. When I came here you told me we were all going to have a nice, quiet, uneventful retirement."

"That was ten years ago, Anthony. For ten years we atrophied. Now it's time we livened up a bit. Look at us, we look like three *stiffs*. Furthermore, I fired you last week, so how can you quit?" Lola demanded. "This is getting us nowhere. On top of that, we now have Agnes in the mix. Plus, I have to make some decisions where that no-account son of mine is concerned. Do we still have that campground in Oregon one of my husbands left me?"

Mandy threw her hands in the air. "I don't know, Lola. Ask your new lawyer. The one Cady fired. Let him earn that handsome retainer you pay out every year. Why?" she demanded.

"I have to . . . what I have to do is, somehow, provide for Asa. I can't let him continue to accept public assistance like it's his due. Remind me to ask Agnes what he did with all the money I sent over the years. There was no reason for them to live the way they were living. I cannot believe she hasn't eaten meat in years. There is no reason for something like that. No reason at all. Anthony, pencil in a visit to Peter Danson's office. We'll put him in charge. Asa never needs to know I'm behind his survival. Lawyers know how to be creative."

"Cady fired your lawyer," Mandy reminded her, sniffing.

"I'll just rehire him." Lola sniffed in return. "Breakfast of late, Anthony, has been a hodge-podge. I'm really hungry this morning, not to mention we have company, so we should be putting our best foot forward."

"I quit, remember?"

"You can't quit till after breakfast. Be specific, what do you want this time?"

"Nothing. I was just exercising my vocal cords. How do bacon and eggs sound?"

"It sounds wonderful, Anthony." Lola smiled. She patted his hand in a familiar way that caused Anthony's plump cheeks to turn pink.

"I know I don't tell you two this often enough, but I love you dearly. You two, Cady also, are the wind beneath my wings. These past weeks have been the most wonderful in my whole life. I just want you to know that, and I'm sorry if I turn into a curmudgeon sometimes."

Lola's little speech had the desired effect. Both old friends wrapped their arms around her thin shoulders. "Whatever you want is fine with me, Lola," Anthony said.

"I'll make a schedule for today," Mandy volunteered.

425

"Wonderful. Isn't life exciting?" Lola said, passion ringing in her voice.

Upstairs, Atlas stirred and rubbed his snout against his mistress's arm to wake her up. Cady's arm lashed out as she struggled to wakefulness.

"Oh, God, it's daylight," Cady said, rolling over on her back to stare up at the ceiling. "Even if I told you, you wouldn't believe what happened to me last night, Atlas. My head is going to fly right off my neck any minute. It's called a hangover. Okay, okay, I know you want to go out. I just need a minute, Atlas."

The shepherd waited patiently till his mistress returned from the bathroom in her flannel robe. Together they walked down the steps to the kitchen, where she opened the door for the dog to go outside. She looked at the Big Three, who were staring at her intently. Her gaze dropped to the newspaper spread out on the table. She groaned.

"I don't want to read it. Just hit the high spots. Are there pictures?" When they nodded, she groaned again. "I feel like I'm on a fast-track treadmill and can't get off. I know I have to do something, make some decisions, but I don't know . . ."

"Let us help you, dear," Lola said. She winced at Mandy's kick under the table. "At least let us offer some suggestions. By the way, dear, your mother is upstairs. She left your father and is going to seek a divorce."

426

Cady blinked, then grabbed her head in her hands to still her pounding temples. "Just like that, after all these years, she up and leaves him! She's here! I don't believe this! What happened? Don't tell me, I don't want to know. Is she all right?"

"She's fine. I'll leave it to Agnes to explain things to you."

"What about Dad? Who is going to take care of him?"

"I'm working on it, Cady. It all happened rather quickly. Social Services will look after him until I can come up with something. The bottom line is he is his normal, ugly self."

"It was that damn reporter, wasn't it?"

No one answered her question. Cady reached for the cup of coffee Anthony handed her. She gulped at it. She stared at the plate of cinnamon buns in the middle of the table. As much as she wanted one, she knew her stomach couldn't handle the sticky, sweet breakfast treats.

"Now, dear, tell us how we can help you today," Lola said.

"As soon as I get rid of this headache, I'm going out to the pond, and I'm going to ride the zip line. Boomer hooked it up yesterday, so it's still there. You can go with me and watch. Since I can't swim, I'll pick up a life preserver at the sporting good store on the way. I'm going to ride that damn thing until I remember everything. I don't care if it takes me all day, and I don't care if I get waterlogged and my skin puckers up like a prune. I'm doing it!"

"That's my girl! Of course we're going with you. We have nothing planned today, do we?" Lola said, staring at Anthony and Mandy and defying them to contradict her.

"Absolutely nothing," they responded in unison.

Cady didn't know why, but she thought the three of them were lying through their teeth. She nodded.

"Some dry toast and tomato juice with a dash of Tabasco might help," Anthony said.

Cady nodded again.

"By the way, dear, your friends stopped by yesterday. They came in separate cars, Boomer, Peter, and Andy. We had to tell them you weren't here. We could have directed them to the Drop Zone had we known that's where you were entertaining Andy's wife. We weren't really worried about you since you're all grown-up," Lola said.

"The three of them came here! Did they say what they wanted?"

"No, they didn't say. Mandy didn't open the gate. She spoke to them through the intercom. They backed up and left. It was before your . . . ah . . . arrest," Lola said, tongue in cheek.

"I don't think I'll be able to live that down."

"It will look good in your memoirs someday." Anthony beamed.

"Oh, God! Is my mother really all right,

Lola? Put that paper away. I don't want her seeing that article. She'll never understand something like that."

Lola laughed. "Dear girl, if you only knew how wrong you are. On top of that, you worry too much. But to answer your question, your mother is fine. She's probably the best she's ever been since marrying my son. She's looking forward to seeing you."

Cady made a face as she downed the glass of ice-cold tomato juice. She waited for a moment to see how it would sit in her stomach. Satisfied that her hangover was on the road to recovery, she got up, waved, and headed for the steps that would take her to the second floor. She looked back, and called over her shoulder, "Remember now, don't show that paper to my mother."

Chief of Police Mac Ward, aka Boomer, shuffled papers on his desk in between fielding phone calls. He had no idea what he was shuffling, no idea what to do or what the day would bring. He wished he was a kid again so he could bawl his head off. He toyed with the idea of calling his parents for advice, but shame stopped him. He was a man, for God's sake. On top of that, he was the police chief. That had to mean he was a man with a brain. In Cady Jordan's eyes he wasn't the police chief, and he sure as hell wasn't a man. In her eyes he was an out-and-out liar. He had to correct that misconception, and he had to do it *immediately*. Well, maybe not right that minute, since the clock told him it was only ten minutes to eight. Ten o'clock would be a decent time to make his appearance at the Jor Dan mansion.

If he had to grovel, he would. If he had to stand on his head, he would. Whatever it took, he was willing to do to make Cady understand he'd done what he could for her that awful day.

He thought about his sleepless night and how he'd prowled his apartment till he thought he would go out of his mind. He'd eaten two bags of popcorn and drunk a whole bottle of wine, hoping it would lull him to sleep. All it did was wire him up even more.

Andy. He needed to call Andy Hollister to see how Amy was. He punched his name into the computer and up came Andy's home phone number, a new apartment number, and the office number. He dialed the home number on his private cell phone. Andy answered on the first ring. "It's Boomer, Andy. Is there any news on Amy?" He held his breath while he waited for a reply.

"Arnie called around four this morning. I wasn't sleeping. He said . . . he said . . . Amy took a turn for the worse around two o'clock. I wanted to go there, but Arnie told me no. He doesn't want me there. I don't know why that is, do you, Boomer?"

"I'm sorry to hear that, Andy. Why don't you go anyway. I think you'll feel better if you do.

430

Make sure you take your wife with you. That's what I would do if I were in your place."

"I think I will do that." Relief rang in Andy's voice, hearing someone else make the decision for him. "What about Cady?"

"I'm going to take care of all that today. Don't worry about it. I'm going to do my best to make it all come out right."

"Thanks, Boomer."

"What are friends for, Andy?" He realized it was the truth. When this was all over, he was going to make sure he strengthened his friendship with both Pete and Andy. His father always said you could never have enough friends. Now, he understood what that meant. "Andy?"

"Yeah."

"If there's anything I can do, call me, okay?" He rattled off his cell phone number. "You can reach me anytime on it. Don't worry about Cady. Let me know Amy's condition."

"All right, Boomer."

A turn for the worse could mean so many things. It didn't have to mean it was as terminal-sounding as the words implied. He realized suddenly that he didn't have a good feeling where Amy Chambers was concerned.

Boomer dialed again. He caught Pete as he was walking across the yard to open his office. "I just spoke to Andy, and he said Amy took a turn for the worse around two this morning. Amy's husband doesn't want him to go to the hospital, but I told him to go anyway. Do you think that was the right thing to tell him, Pete? Now that I stuck my foot in my mouth, I'm not sure I had any right to tell him to do what I would do."

"Hell, yes, it was the right thing. You know what, I think I'm going to cancel all my appointments and go there myself. If you want to know why, the best answer I can give you is I don't have a good feeling about all of this."

Boomer sucked in his breath. It was all he had to hear. "Do you want some company?"

"Yeah. Yeah, company would be great. What about Cady?"

"Don't go there, Pete."

"Okay, I won't. I'll pick you up in fifteen minutes."

"I'll be out front."

As Cady walked into the kitchen, she stopped in her tracks, her jaw dropping, her eyes popping. "Mom! Is that really you, Mom? Gee, you look . . . you look great. Are you okay? Are you staying? Did you leave for good, or is this like a trial run or something?"

"Slow down, Cady. I'm fine, as you can see. I'm staying as long as Lola will have me. Eventually, I'll find a job and an apartment of my own. I'm going to need to do that so I can be me again. I left for good, and this is not a trial run. Your father will be fine. A Social Services person goes to the house every day and helps your father. He can do everything himself that I used to do for him. He gets around very well. He can even take his chair outside because there's a ramp for his convenience. I don't want you to worry about him."

"Why, Mom? I asked you to come the other day, and you told me no, and then you hung up on me. What changed for you in a matter of a day?"

"Circumstances. I realized I didn't have to take his abuse one more minute. Maybe I snapped. Whatever the reason, here I am. I'm not too late, am I, Cady?"

Cady shook her head. "No, Mom. Gee, you look so pretty. I really like your haircut and the highlights. You look ten years younger. I wouldn't be surprised to find out you turn a few heads here in Indigo Valley." Agnes Jordan blushed a rosy red. She smiled and winked at Lola.

She's got some spunk, Cady thought. *Something I never thought I would see in my victimized mother.*

"Did anyone call?" Cady asked, her voice ringing with hope.

"No, dear. The phone hasn't rung. Are you ready to go to the pond?"

"Yes, but first I want to call the hospital to see how Amy is. I'll do it in the library. Finish your breakfast." She hugged her mother. "I'm glad you're here, Mom."

"Me too, Cady. I wish I had done this a long time ago."

When the kitchen door closed behind Cady, Agnes leaned across the table. "What is it you want me to do, Lola? I think I know, but I guess I'm just one of those people who has to hear the words aloud. But first, I want you to know that I didn't want to rip Cady away from you after her recovery. I would have had to be a fool not to see how well she'd done with you and how much she loved you. I begged Asa to let her stay even though my heart was breaking. You need to believe that, Lola."

"I do know, Aggie. Right then is when the two of us should have popped him good. Why didn't we?"

"Because you were protecting me, and you knew he would make it worse on both Cady and me if I didn't do what he said. She had a miserable life with us. I did what I could, but I could never take your place. I used to hear her pray at night asking God to let you come and get her. She absolutely refused to accept that garbage Asa spouted as his faith. More often than not she was punished seven days a week. She didn't buckle, though."

"What happened to all the money I sent, Aggie?"

Agnes Jordan flinched. She stared out the window, her eyes filling with tears. "He gave it all away. He called it prostitution money. It made him feel good to hand out money. He didn't care if we ate peanut butter and jelly or macaroni and cheese seven days a week. It was the same with all those wonderful gifts you sent Cady. He gave those away, too. All she was allowed to keep was her bike. And books from the library. I wouldn't blame you for a minute if you hate me."

"I don't hate you, Agnes, I never did. I understood. I think you paid your dues, and it's time for you to live again just the way Cady is learning to live again. We're going to make this all come out right. You have to do your part, Aggie, and it isn't going to be easy."

"I know that."

Cady entered the kitchen and looked from one to the other. "I called the hospital in Pittsburgh. Amy is listed as critical. They said she took a turn for the worse. Her husband is with her. I feel so bad," she said, tears springing to her eyes. "If there was something I could do, I'd do it in a minute. There was a time when I thought she was my best friend. I called Boomer, and the desk sergeant said he went to Pittsburgh. I called Pete's office, and Andy's, too, but both their secretaries said they also went to Pittsburgh. I'm assuming they went to the hospital. They all went but me. Why didn't they call and tell me? I would have gone with them."

No one had an answer for her. "What should I do? Am I just supposed to sit here and wait to hear or what?" Again, there were no answers from those sitting around the table. Her voice as well as her stance turned stubborn. "So much for friends and feeling wanted. I'm ready to go to the pond. We need to make two stops. I want to stop by the Drop Zone to pay my bill from last night and I need to get the life preserver. Are you coming, Mom?"

"Only if you want me to come."

"The more the merrier. Okay, gang, let's rumble."

"We're smokin' now," Lola said, standing up, her closed fist shooting into the air.

"I hate hospitals," Pete Danson said, as they walked down a long hallway that smelled of alcohol and disinfectant. He looked around at scurrying nurses and busy doctors, all carrying clipboards, stethoscopes hanging around their necks or sticking out of their pockets. Carts clattered, and the loudspeaker blared. "I always thought hospitals, like libraries, were quiet places. You can't think in places like this with all the noise. Nurses don't *rustle* anymore. They don't wear those perky little caps either," he said fretfully. "I used to visit my mother a lot in the beginning," he said by way of explanation for voicing his opinion.

"I'm not fond of hospitals myself," Boomer said. "I think this is the burn unit. Let me check with the desk."

Pete shuddered. Where was Andy? He saw him a moment later. Andy looked like he'd been to hell and back. Pete clapped him on the back.

"Thanks for coming, Pete," Andy said, his voice ringing with pleased surprise.

"Boomer's here, too. He's at the desk. Do you know anything?"

"Only that Arnie told me to get my fucking ass out of here. He said I was the reason Amy was here. He thinks . . . he thinks that Amy's and my relationship made her do what she did. I didn't have the guts to tell him differently. He's calling the shots, and they won't let me see her. I can look through the glass because I'm her brother, but that's it. Maybe I should go home."

"You should only do what feels right, Andy. You're Amy's brother. The way I see it, you have every right to be here."

Boomer returned, his badge in his hand. "I had to use some clout," he said, hooking the badge back onto his belt. "It's not good, Andy. In fact, it's touch-and-go. The husband doesn't want you here, according to the nurse. I straightened her right out. You can stay as long as you like. Pete and I will stay with you."

"You don't have to do that. I appreciate your coming here at all. Only friends would do that. I wish there was some way Amy could know we're all here. Arnie won't even come out of the room. He's all dressed up in surgical gear and has to wear a mask. Germs. I called my mother, and she said I needed to stop being an alarmist." He threw his hands in the air. Jill led him to a chair in a small waiting room.

"Did anyone call Cady?" Jill asked.

The three men looked at one another, then shook their heads. "Well, don't you think she has a right to know? Did it ever occur to any of you that she might want to be here, too? No, I guess not." Disgust rang in Jill's voice.

"Considering the circumstances, I don't think . . ." It was as far as Boomer got before Jill interrupted him.

"I'm going to call her. The decision to come or not is hers to make, not yours. What kind of friends are you, anyway? You are so dumb when it comes to women." The anger in her voice was so strong the three men took a step backward as they tried to comprehend what she was saying. Jill trotted off in search of a pay phone.

"Leave it up to a woman to cut you down to size. She's right, we don't know anything about women. I don't think the man has been born who knows how to handle women," Boomer said morosely.

Within minutes, Jill was back in the waiting room. "There was no answer, so I left a detailed message. I'll call again later. Andy and I both left in such a hurry we forgot our cell phones."

"I can leave mine with you when we leave," Pete offered. Jill nodded.

Boomer looked around the small room and wondered how many people on average sat in the room on a daily basis. How many cried tears of sadness and how many cried tears of joy? The furniture was hard and uncomfortable, the tables more utilitarian than decorative. The pictures on the walls were Kmart specials. The chairs should be deep and comfortable, the tables full of fresh magazines and newspapers. New toys would help, too. People waiting to hear life-and-death news needed to be comfortable. A coffeepot or soda machine would definitely be an asset.

He sensed rather than saw a form approaching. He looked up. It had to be Arnie Chambers, because he zeroed in on Andy with a vengeance. Boomer braced himself for what he knew was coming.

"I told you to get the hell out of here, Andy. I meant it then, and I mean it now. If it weren't for you, Amy wouldn't be here fighting for her life. She wet-nursed you your whole life, sometimes to the exclusion of her own family. Meaning me and the girls. I never said anything because she loved you. You were her twin. She said that made your relationship special. Then you fucking turn on her for no reason other than your on-again, off-again marriage. All she did was try to help you. When she called you, you hung up on her. She would cry all night long. She couldn't eat, and she couldn't sleep. She said she failed you. You were more important to her than me and the kids. This is your fault!"

Boomer was on his feet in an instant. "Let's hold it right there, Mr. Chambers. There's no need for you to attack Andy like that. Amy's his sister, and he has every right to be here."

"Who the hell are you?" Chambers blustered.

Boomer took a step closer to Andy. "I'm Andy's friend. I'm also the police chief in Indigo Valley."

"Is that supposed to scare me? It doesn't. If my wife dies, it's his fault," Arnie said, jabbing a finger at Andy. "He'll have to live with his guilt for the rest of his life the way I'll have to live without a wife, and my children will have to learn to live without their mother."

"First of all, Mr. Chambers, Amy has not expired. I think you're a little ahead of yourself here. No, Mr. Chambers, it will not be Andy's fault if Amy dies. It's Amy's fault that she's here. Amy made the decision to take a scalding-hot shower. That's a premeditated action. You can't hold her brother responsible for something she decided to do on her own. I read the police report, and I read her chart here at the hospital. Furthermore, we all had breakfast with Amy yesterday, and when she left she said she was going home to clean her bathrooms. She was herself at that time. If something transpired on the way home or when she arrived home to make her do such a thing, none of us is aware of it. Just because you're married doesn't mean you necessarily know every little secret about each other."

"That's where you're wrong, Mr. Police Chief. Amy and I had no secrets. We knew everything there was to know about each other. It's *his* fault," he said, jabbing out with his finger again. "I'm holding him responsible. Live with that, you son of a bitch!"

It looked to Boomer like Andy was going to run after Arnie to plead his case. Pete sensed it, too, and pushed him down into one of the uncomfortable chairs.

"Someone should have told him," Jill said quietly.

"This isn't the time. Maybe it will never be time," Boomer said. He squatted in front of Andy, and said, "Andy, look at me. He's out of his mind with grief. He's looking into the future and not seeing Amy with him. He needs to blame someone. When tragedy happens, people tend to want to place blame. It's their way of getting through a particularly bad time. That's all he's doing. It's not your fault, Andy. Sad as it is to say, it's Amy's fault. You should be commended for trying to get her to do the right thing. It was her choice. Are you listening to me, Andy? Jesus Christ, how did we get to this place in time?"

"Yes, Boomer, I'm listening, and I understand everything you just said. I know Arnie is having a hard time of it. We got to this place because of our guilt. Amy's going to pay with her life for our guilt."

"*Her guilt*, Andy!" Pete said hoarsely. "She did it. Not you, not me, not Boomer. We lied, but that's all we did."

441

Jill reached for her husband's hand. "They're right, Andy. It's just going to take some getting used to." She looked at Pete and Boomer and smiled. "You two should leave. Andy and I will stay here. We appreciate your coming. If there's . . . any change, I'll call you."

Pete handed over his cell phone. "If you need us, we'll be here in a heartbeat."

"In a heartbeat," Boomer echoed Pete's words.

Neither man spoke until they were outside.

"That was some heavy-duty guilt to throw at someone," Pete said. "Lesser men than Andy Hollister would have caved under that onslaught. I think you got through to him, though."

"I hope so. Do you think we should have called Cady?"

Pete shrugged. "Hell, I don't know. Amy hated her, tried to kill her. I don't think Cady is any too fond of her either. Would she come here? Probably. That's the kind of person she is. Like Jill said, what the hell do we know about women."

The hour-long drive back to Indigo Valley was made in total silence.

Chapter 20

The bartender at the Drop Zone backed up a step when Cady breezed into his bar. He was wearing the same dirty apron and the same Harley Davidson tee shirt he'd been wearing the night before. The serpent on his burly arm was wiggling and slithering as he whipped his arms about, his eyes wary.

"I came to apologize and to give you this," Cady said, sliding a hundred-dollar bill across the counter. "It's for any inconvenience my friend and I might have caused you. I would appreciate it if you would drop the charges you filed against my friend and me. If you can't see your way to doing that, I understand. Again, I'm sorry."

"Well . . . we get a lot of bums in here. I usually get my money the minute I serve a drink. You two looked like *ladies*," he blustered. "I didn't think you'd try to put one over on me. I don't have a problem with dropping the charges. I never would have showed up in court anyway. I can't afford to shut this place down. My customers depend on me." The serpent stopped slithering and appeared to go to sleep as the bartender placed his arms on the bar.

"I appreciate that, sir."

Outside in the warm spring air, Cady took a deep breath before she climbed into the waiting Bentley. "He's one of those guys who walks the walk and talks the talk, but when it's down to the wire, he bails. He said he'd drop the charges because he can't afford to close the bar to go to court."

Lola frowned, as did Anthony and Mandy. "I was looking forward to giving a character reference in court," Lola said. "One worthy of my profession."

"You'll get over it." Cady grinned.

"So this is the place where you were arrested. It was such an interesting article in the paper this morning," Agnes said as she stared out the tinted windows at the sleazy bar.

Cady's eyes accused Lola and the others.

"She snatched the paper right out of my hand," Lola said virtuously. "Besides, I'm too old to tussle over a newspaper that will eventually go into the trash."

"I thought you were going to save it for my memoirs," Cady snapped.

"After the article was clipped, dear. Your mother does not have a problem with the article. Can we please move on here?" Lola said.

Move on they did. The Bentley slid into traffic as Anthony expertly guided the big car toward the turnoff leading to the pond.

"Should we place bets now as to whether we're going to get arrested or not?" Anthony chirped from the driver's seat.

"Arrested?" Agnes Jordan squeaked.

"You know, Agnes, orange jumpsuits, handcuffs, your Miranda rights, that kind of thing. Don't sweat it, we've done this before. Just go with the flow. Bail is a wonderful thing, and you get your picture in the paper," Lola said.

"All right, ladies, we're here. If this was a film I was directing, this is when the lead character, which is you, Cady, would throw out her chest, and say, 'This is where the rubber meets the road.' "

"It's the same thing as getting ready to rumble, Mom, or as Lola says, we're smokin' now."

"I see," Agnes said, clearly not seeing at all. "Well, I'm ready. What do you want me to do?"

"We need to gather up some rocks. Good-size ones. We're going to playact. Anthony is going to be Pete. Mom, you're going to be Andy. Mandy is going to be Amy. Lola is going to be Boomer. If Lola plays Boomer's part, she won't have to scramble down the embankment. She just has to stand by the tree checking the zip line. Can you pitch a rock, Mom?"

"I can do whatever I have to do, Cady. I cannot believe you children rode that contraption." Agnes looked up at the Judas tree and started to shake. Lola placed a comforting hand on her arm and whispered something in her ear that only Agnes heard. She calmed almost immediately. Cady wished she could have heard the magic words Lola said to her mother.

"Anthony, Pete had a paper sack in his hand that day. Andy wanted to know what was in it, and Pete told him to mind his own business. It was probably his turn to bring cookies or crackers. You need a bag. Get the trash bag out of the car. Everyone take their places, and let's do a dry run. I'm going to put on my life preserver and climb the tree. I'll position you from the tree if I can remember where everyone was that day.

"Lola, just stand at the base of the tree. I know the line is safe because Boomer hooked it up yesterday. He checked it twice. He was going to tie a rope around my waist and pull me to shore when I fell in, but I think the preserver is a better idea. Give me time to get up in the tree."

Cady's feet sought for and found toeholds in the ancient tree. Before she knew it, she was settled in the wide V of the lowest branch. She needed to go one branch higher. She marveled at the change twenty years had made in the old oak.

"Okay, the way I remember it, it was Pete's turn to bring the Kool-Aid and cookies, so I guess that's what was in the sack. Amy took my arm and told me not to be afraid. She said all your heart did was beat real fast. I just wanted to get it over and done with before Jeff and Boomer got here.

"Andy said Jeff and Boomer were there earlier, so they pretended to leave, but then they came back to wait for me. He said Amy had her camera and would take pictures and send them to me at our new address. He warned me not to close my eyes.

"I was to go on the count of five. I climbed up here and then out onto this same branch. It wasn't as thick back then as it is now. I didn't weigh as much either." She crawled on her belly along the thick branch. "I heard a hissing sound and turned around. Pete yelled to warn me Boomer and Jeff were there. Right away I tried to snake my way backward. They kept yelling at me to get down, but my overalls were caught on something."

"Are you all right, Cady?" Lola called from the base of the tree. "I mean, *really* all right."

"My heart is beating just as fast as it was that day. I'm okay. Seriously, Lola, I'm okay.

"Okay, listen to me," Cady shouted. "This is where Jeff jumped from that tree," she said, pointing to the tree next to the one she was in. "He let out one of those Tarzan yells to scare me, and boy, did he scare me."

"Where was Boomer?" Anthony shouted.

"I couldn't really see him. I think he was monkeying around with the zip line. I could hear him, but I couldn't see him. Jeff was creeping up on the branch, and I was too afraid to move. They screamed for me to jump on the line before Jeff could push me. That's when they started throwing the rocks. Throw the rocks!" she screamed.

It was no longer a reenactment. She was ten years old and consumed with so much fear she was frozen to the tree branch. She could hear Jeff's crazy laughter behind her. That and the hatred in his voice finally propelled her forward. From far away she could hear Boomer Ward shouting that the line would break if Jeff added his weight to it. She heard him bellow at the top of his lungs, "Don't do it, Jeff!"

Cady reached for the wooden handle that would let her slide to the bottom, where her friends waited. She took a deep breath, saw the rocks hurtling her way, then squeezed her eyes shut. When she pushed off she felt Jeff King's hand grab hold of her shirt while his other hand yanked at her head. He screamed into her ear just as she pushed off.

Pain engulfed her as she let go of the wooden handle and fell into the water.

"Let go, Jeff, let go!" Boomer shouted.

Her world turned black.

Cady slid down the zip line and landed on all fours. She wondered if she looked as dazed as she felt. "I did it! I really did it!"

As one, they hugged her. "Do you remember now?" Anthony asked anxiously.

"Yes. Yes, I remember. They thought I was dead. Amy told them I was dead. Pete wanted to go for help, so did Andy, but Amy said I was dead. They went to the park because they thought they would be blamed and sent away to some awful place. They left me there, and I couldn't move.

"Boomer came back and pulled me out of the water. He put his hand on my chest to see if I was breathing. I heard him clear as anything. He said he was going to get help. He told me not to move, and then he said he didn't do anything to the line, that he was trying to make it as tight as he could so it wouldn't snap. He told me not to cry and squeezed my hand.

"I woke up in the hospital. That's all pretty much a blur, with people asking me questions that I couldn't answer. Finally, they gave up." The only thing she left out of her summary were the words Jeff King had screamed in her ear.

They were at the base of the tree now, where Lola stood. Cady could see her grandmother visibly shrink before her eyes as Lola reached out for Agnes Jordan's trembling hand. Cady stared at them for a minute before she moved forward. "I'm going to walk home. I need to think," she said softly.

"Cady, it's five miles to the house," Anthony protested.

"This, Anthony, is where the rubber really and truly meets the road. Let her go," Lola replied in a voice that was barely above a whisper.

Cady walked along, barely noticing when the huge Bentley passed her by. She felt so sick to her stomach she wondered if she was going to have to dive into the bushes to puke her guts out. She swallowed hard, willing the tomato juice and coffee she'd consumed earlier to stay down.

She trudged. Cars blew their horns. She ignored them as she walked along. She needed to go someplace quiet so she could think. Maybe the Drop Zone and her new best friend, the bartender with the slithering serpent on his arm. She could probably sit there all day and even eat if she wanted some of the pickled eggs in the greasy-looking jar sitting on the counter. Her stomach heaved with the thought.

She looked over her shoulder as she heard a light tap of a horn behind her. She moved farther to the side of the road. When the car came to a complete stop, she looked up and groaned. Pete Danson was behind the wheel with Boomer Ward in the seat next to him.

"What? Are you going to tell me it's illegal to walk on the side of the road? So mail me a ticket!"

"Get in the car, Cady," Boomer said.

"Don't tell me what to do. Don't ever tell me what to do," she shot back.

"Sorry. Will you please get your ass in this car. If you don't, I'll have to get out and arrest you. What's it going to be?"

"What's it going to be?" Cady said, mimicking him. "What do you think it's going to be?"

450

Boomer opened the door and stepped out. He swept Cady up in his arms and deposited her in the backseat. "Now, it's two tickets. You were at the pond again. We set up cameras."

"Liar. Both of you are liars. I consider this a case of kidnapping, so you can just kiss my ass, Boomer Ward. Let me off at the Drop Zone."

Pete raised his eyebrows and did his best to stifle the laughter that was bubbling in his throat. He risked a glance at his passenger. Boomer looked out of his depth. Pete felt pleased for some reason.

"You are the most ornery, cantankerous, snippy female I have ever come across. What were you doing at the pond?"

"Not that it's any of your damn business, but I rode the zip line. And, Boomer Ward and Pete Danson, I remembered *everything. Everything.*"

"Everything?" Boomer said.

Pete's shoulders sagged.

"In addition to your other faults, you obviously have a hearing problem, too. I said *everything.* Everything means everything. There's the Drop Zone. Stop the car. I have friends there. I can even run a tab now that I have such good credit. Another thing, it would have not only been nice but the decent thing to do to tell me about Amy's turn for the worse. I had to call the hospital myself."

Cady hopped out of the car and made her way to the fly-specked screen door of the Drop Zone. She didn't look back.

Pete couldn't resist saying, "Guess she told you."

Boomer frowned. "If she's telling the truth, and she remembers *everything* like she said, she sure is taking it well."

Pete snorted as he talked louder to be heard over the music blasting out of the Drop Zone. "Jill's right, you don't know anything about women. She's in shock. She didn't go to the pond by herself. She probably sent the geriatric gang on home because she wanted to think."

"I'm going to get out here, too, Pete. Call me if you hear anything about Amy."

Pete stuck his head out the car window. "I wouldn't go in there after her if I were you, Boomer. You two are like oil and water."

"Thanks for the advice. Call me."

"Yeah, yeah," Pete said, putting his car in gear. He eased his way into traffic, his eyes on the rearview mirror. Boomer was standing on the corner like he didn't know what to do.

Sometimes life was a bitch.

Inside the Drop Zone, the bartender growled, "Did you forget something?"

"No, I didn't forget anything. I was wondering if you would mind if I went over there," she said, pointing to the booth she'd sat in last night with Jill, "and had a drink. I have to warn you ahead of time I have no money with me. I will come back either later or tomorrow to pay you. Is that okay?"

The bartender looked Cady over from head to toe. He finally decided she might be a good advertisement for his bar. "Okay," he growled.

"Good, I'll start with a . . . cup of tea and one of those pickled eggs." Her stomach protested just mentioning the words *pickled eggs.*

The serpent slithered as the bartender rubbed at his chin. "Tea?"

Cady's head bobbed up and down. "Tea. Four sugars, no cream. Do you have any cigarettes?"

"This isn't a grocery store, lady. Smoking isn't good for you."

"I know that. I need to think. People smoke when they think. I want to see if it works for me. Serious thinking. I'm going to need some napkins, too, in case I cry."

"Jeez, lady, maybe you should go somewhere else. Like one of those fa-cil-ities for people with head problems."

"I don't have a head problem; my problem is my heart."

"I don't know CPR, lady. No one in here knows CPR. Why don't you just go over to Eva's and sit there?"

"Just give me the tea and egg," Cady snapped. "Don't forget the napkins."

Forty minutes later, Cady was still sitting in the booth. She had three hard-boiled eggs wrapped in napkins in her pocket. She'd spilled the tea on the rough floor when the bartender wasn't looking. She didn't feel one bit better than when she'd walked in. Obviously it was time to go home. Her eyes filled. She blew her nose into a napkin and tossed it onto the soggy pile already littering the table. She looked up when she saw a shadow slide across the table.

"Go away, Boomer. I don't want to talk to you. I don't want to talk to any of you. I hate what you did. What you all did."

"I've been sitting in the corner watching you. I want you to listen to me. You don't know it all, Cady. There's more that you don't know, not that you can't remember, just that you don't know. I'm going to tell you. I want you to listen to me. When I'm finished, I'll leave, and I'll never bother you again. Is it a deal?"

He would never bother her again. She already felt her loss. Her eyes filled again as she waited.

"Pete and I didn't know this until the other day when Andy told us. Andy said Amy deliberately threw the rocks at you. She threw them to hurt you, Cady. She's the one who killed Jeff. The rock was aimed at you, but you jerked away, and it hit Jeff in the temple with such force it killed him. I saw his brains, Cady. The rock was aimed at you. Andy said Amy hated you. Andy carried that secret with him all these years. I think he managed to suppress it for a time, but it was still there. I guess you know he's a basket case. When he told Amy he couldn't take it anymore, and was going to go to you and tell you the truth, Amy went ballistic. She just kept saying she was going to keep on lying. She didn't want her husband to know, but I didn't want to get involved with that. We were all going to go to you to tell you the truth. Actually, we did go to the house, but they said you weren't there. I know now you were here.

"They thought you were dead that day, Cady. That's why they ran. They were afraid they would be blamed. Amy never said a word then or later about throwing the rock that killed Jeff. It's almost impossible for me to believe a ten-year-old like Amy would harm someone so cold-bloodedly and be able to cover up and lie about what she did.

"I waited till they left that day, and I went and pulled you to the edge of the pond. I knew you were alive."

"You told me you were going for help, and you told me not to cry," Cady said. "You squeezed my hand."

"You really do remember," Boomer said in awe.

"You also said you were just checking the line. I remember you yelling to Jeff not to get on the zip line. I know the others thought I was dead after I fell. I heard them. I don't know why I couldn't talk."

"Was it because of what Jeff said to you?"

Cady's head bobbed up and down. "It was just an instant, and I'm thinking now, that was the worst thing he could possibly have said to me. I guess that's why I blocked it out. The rest of my memory just went with it. Did you know?"

It was Boomer's turn to nod. "I wanted to kill him the day he told me his dirty little secret. God, you have no idea how much I hated that kid. All I felt was relief when he died. I'll never deny having that feeling either."

Tears rolled down Cady's cheeks. "Half this town believes I killed Jeff King. If you all had come forward, you could have corrected the situation. Damn it, Boomer, Jeff King told me I was his *half sister*. Do you have any idea what that did to me? I hated him because of how he treated me. He hated me because his father is my father, too. That's why I blocked it out. I was just a little kid. There was no way I could handle something like that."

"Cady, only the Kings believed that you killed Jeff, and now you know why."

"I don't know what to do, Boomer," Cady said, forgetting how angry she'd been with him. "I just want to put this behind me. I want to be able to accept it and move on with my life."

"Then do it."

"Just like that," Cady said, blowing her nose again. The napkin went on top of the pile.

"Yeah, just like that."

"What about Amy? How do I deal with her?"

"That's your call, Cady. Just remember, you'll have to live with your decision for the rest of your life. What good will it do if we tell the truth to the Kings? If you decide you want to go public, Andy, Pete, and I are prepared to stand up and tell the truth. Like I said, it's your call, Cady."

"Does anyone else in town know Jeff King was my . . . *half brother?*" There, she'd said the words aloud, and the world hadn't crashed down around her.

Boomer flinched at her matter-of-fact question. "I never heard a word even when I was a kid. My parents would have said something. You know how small towns are. I think your secret is safe."

"When I remembered up there on the zip line, do you know what my first thought was?" Boomer shook his head. "My first thought was that Lola isn't really my grandmother. That realization was like a stabbing pain right in my heart. Like you, I only felt relief that the man I thought of as my father isn't my father. I don't want to believe that Cyrus King, my real father, believed any of those stories about my killing Jeff. I think it was his wife who probably started the rumors. She must have found out about his affair with my mother, or else Mr. King confessed to it. Jeff was her *only* son. To lose him like that must have been more than she could bear. When a tragedy like that happens, you look for someone to blame it on. It was easy to pick on me considering I was her husband's illegitimate child. It also explains that attitude of the man I thought was my father.

He made my mother pay for her mistake every day of her life. I paid for it, too. Everything makes sense now."

"Are you ready to go home now, Cady?"

Cady looked around. The bartender winked at her. In spite of herself, she grinned. She turned back to Boomer. "I'm not sure where I belong, Boomer. Where is home?"

"You know what my mother told me. She said home is wherever your stuff is. I think she's right. I don't know how much stuff you have, but I don't have a lot. I'm willing to share my space with you.

"Cady, what are you going to do?"

Cady looked into Boomer's eyes. "Nothing. All I wanted was to remember that time in my life so I could move forward. The past is gone. I don't know about you, but I sure don't want it back. You're all safe. None of you had a thing to worry about where I was concerned. We could all have saved ourselves so much angst if we'd just gotten together to talk it through. I hope Amy recovers. I want your promise, and I don't care that you're the police chief, that you will never tell anyone what Amy did. I want Andy and Pete's promise, too."

"You have my word, Cady, and I don't think you have to worry about getting theirs, too."

"And you have mine, Boomer. I think I'm ready to leave now."

"We'll have to walk over to the station so I can pick up my car."

"I'll see you tomorrow, Henry," she said to the bartender. The serpent wiggled and slithered as he waved good-bye.

At the gate to Lola's mansion, Boomer stopped the car. "If you don't hate my guts, do you want to have dinner tonight?"

"I would like that. Do you mind if I bring my mother? I'd like you to meet her."

"Okay. I'll pick you up at seven. Does this mean we're back on track, Cady?"

Were they? She smiled and nodded. "I remember how good it felt when you squeezed my hand that day twenty years ago."

Boomer watched her walk away, his own eyes wet.

Cady entered the kitchen and looked around. Nothing had changed other than the fact that there were now four people sitting at the table instead of three. She homed in on Lola. Tears rolled down her cheeks. "None of it matters. What matters is knowing I'm not really your granddaughter. I thought I belonged to you because I loved you so much. Can I still come and visit? Can we be friends?" Hard sobs tore at her throat when she dropped to her knees to put her head in Lola's lap.

"Dear child, you *are* my granddaughter. Biology can't change that. That genealogical crap was always overrated in my opinion. Look at me, Cady. I've loved you since the day you were born. I've loved you every day since, and I will love you until the day I die and then into perpetuity. Are we clear on that? Nothing has changed except you got your memory back. With the exception of your friend Amy, only good things came of all this. Your mother is here. My son is going to have the life he always wanted, thanks to 'an anonymous benefactor.' You have made peace with your friends and made some new friends in the process. You have lightened our lives, and all of us love you dearly. We love your dog, too."

"Blow your nose," Anthony said, handing her a paper napkin. Cady noticed that his own eyes were wet, and so were Mandy's. Lola's eyes, on the other hand, sparkled with happiness. Her mother, she noticed, was smiling.

"It's time for you to meet your father, Cady. Let's just do it and get it over with. Lola, I'd like you to come along." She turned to Cady. "We can talk about this now or sometime in the future, or we never have to talk about it. The short take is, I knew I made a mistake when I married your . . . Asa. He didn't love me, and I didn't love him. He was charismatic, though. I was young enough that I wanted . . . excitement, someone to say he loved me. Cyrus King and I would meet at the Judas tree every chance we could. Back then it was a lover's lane of sorts. He was married, I was married, and then I was pregnant."

"Mom, it's okay. I'm okay with it. Let's not talk about it ever again. This is the first day of our new lives. No looking back. I've had enough of the past to last me a lifetime, and so did you. Now, are you coming to Mr. Cyrus King's house with us, *Granny?*"

"It will be my pleasure." Lola's wet eyes sparkled.

Cyrus King opened the door. Lola took the initiative, and said, "Cyrus, I brought your daughter to see you. We have a story to tell you, and I want you to listen. I expect we can all be civil about this. Invite us in, please. That's another way of saying I won't take no for an answer."

Cyrus King took a deep breath, his eyes on Agnes Jordan. He stepped aside, as his wife walked around the corner to stare at the uninvited guests.

"What are *they* doing here?" Maxine King spat.

"We're here to talk, Mrs. King. I'm not in the mood for any shenanigans, so either be quiet or leave. Cyrus?" Lola's imperious stage voice carried throughout the whole house.

"Sit down," Cyrus King said, motioning to a gold brocade sofa that looked like it had never been sat on.

Lola began, "You, of course, know Agnes. This lovely young woman is Cady, your daughter. As you may or may not know, Cady lost her memory the day of the accident. She has fully regained that memory and is here to tell you what really happened that day. The others who were at the pond that day will back up her story, so let's get to it. Cady, tell them what happened."

Cady licked at her dry lips and spoke hesitantly. Her words picked up speed as she recited the events of that fateful afternoon. "I did not kill your son, Jeff . . . my half brother. I don't know this for sure, but I have a feeling neither of you knew that he knew I am his half sister. I'm assuming he overheard the two of you discussing the situation at some point. He told Boomer Ward he knew about me and swore him to secrecy. Your son was a bully, I'm sorry to say. He made my life miserable. I lived in fear of him. So did the others. My family and I are not going to shout this from the rooftops. The only reason we came here at all was to tell you I did not kill your son." She stood up and looked at her father. "I'm sorry I never got to know you. That isn't going to change anytime soon. You and your wife have nothing to fear from us."

Was she making a mistake in not telling the Kings Amy was the one who threw the rock that killed their son? If she told them, would they believe her? The only thing that was important at this point in time was her knowing that she hadn't killed her half brother. As far as she was concerned, the Kings could believe whatever they wanted to believe. Hopefully, Amy would be able to put it behind her, too, when she recovered. Life would go on for all of them.

Maxine King cried into a lace hankie. Her husband ignored her.

"I think we can see ourselves out," Lola said.

Cyrus King stared at his daughter. Cady thought she saw approval in his eyes.

In the car, Lola turned to Cady. "Well?"

"He's just a man, Lola. The word *father* isn't etched on his forehead. He's just a man. Mom, you okay?"

"I'm just fine. I feel like I just pulled both of my feet out of quicksand. If I could sing, I would."

"What about you, dear child?" Lola asked.

"I feel . . . good. Today was . . . climactic. I can handle all of this, so don't worry about me. I'm going to drop you off at home, then I'm going to drive to the hospital to see Amy."

"Oh, honey, I don't think that's a good idea," Agnes said.

"Mom, I have to go. I have to tell her it's okay, that I understand. I'll probably never know or understand how she could hate me that much, but if I don't go, I'll be just like her. I don't want to be like Amy Hollister Chambers. I'm doing it as much for myself as I'm doing it for Amy. I love you both more than you will ever know."

Agnes wrung her hands. Lola reached for those hands and held them tightly. She smiled.

Back at the house, Cady changed her clothes

and was ready to leave within the hour.

"Wait a minute, Cady, someone's at the gate. I think it's your friends. There are three cars."

Cady's heart took on an extra beat. "Mom, I forgot to tell you, Boomer invited us to dinner this evening. Something must have happened." She ran to the door and then outside.

They didn't have to tell her; she could see it in their faces.

Cady ran to her friends, tears streaming down her face. Boomer reached for her and held her close as she sobbed.

The Big Three that now numbered four watched the young people from the kitchen window. "They don't need us anymore, they have each other, and that's the way it should be. Something good did come of this after all, and for that I will always be grateful," Lola said. "Anthony, make some coffee and bring it to the sunroom."

Epilogue

They stood high on the hill and watched. They stood there because they weren't invited to attend Amy Hollister Chambers's interment.

"I wish I could hear what the minister is saying," Andy muttered.

"He's saying all the right words. He's saying she was a wonderful wife and mother and that she loved humanity, that kind of thing," Pete said.

"When they leave we can go down and place our flowers on the grave," Jill said. "We can all say our good-byes then."

Cady looked around. It was unseasonably hot for late May. Overhead, she could hear birds chirping their morning song. Maybe they were singing for Amy. She hoped so. She wondered if she would ever come here again after today. Would she ever visit her half brother's grave? Would she feel the need to come here and talk to the woman she'd once thought of as her friend?

Boomer inched closer as his hand sought for and held hers. She looked up at him and smiled. Her three childhood friends all looked so nice, she thought. So grown-up, so manly. So full of grief.

"It shouldn't end like this," Cady said with a catch in her voice.

"Maybe it was the only way it could end," Andy said, his voice breaking. He looked over at Boomer. His shoulders straightened imperceptibly.

"It looks like half the town turned out to say good-bye to Amy. I think she would like knowing that," Pete said. "One of my clients told me this morning that Arnie is moving his business to Squirrel Hill. I drove by the house on the way here, and there's a For Sale sign on the lawn of their house. I personally don't think people should make such important decisions when they're grieving. It's just been a few days since Amy passed away."

"I imagine that's the right course of action for Arnie," Boomer said.

"It's over, people are leaving," Andy said, relief ringing in his voice. "My parents don't look like they're overcome with grief. I don't think I'm ever going to speak to them again."

"Andy, don't go there," Jill said.

"You're right. I don't think we should go down there until everyone is gone, especially Arnie. I don't want a confrontation today of all days. He can't stop me from coming here, can he, Boomer?"

"No, he can't. You can come anytime you want, and as often as you want."

"Jill comes here all the time. That's how she met Cady. Now we can come together."

"I think we can go down now," Pete said. "The last car is going through the gate."

They walked hand in hand the way they had when they were little.

"What . . . what should we do, Jill? You've done this before, we haven't," Boomer said.

"You lay your flower on the casket, then you say a prayer. You take a moment to reflect and relive a pleasant memory. You can shed a tear. There really aren't any rules."

There were no dry eyes as the little procession made their way past Amy's bronze casket.

Cady took a deep breath when they made their way to their respective cars.

"Listen, I don't know if you're going to think I'm off the wall or not, but I had this idea," Pete said. "I think we should all go to the pond and have a picnic. I'd like us to go there and play like we did when we were kids. I had my housekeeper pack us a picnic. We can ride the zip line and do all those things we did back then. Then we can lay it all to rest. I don't know why, but I think Amy might like to know we're doing it. Our final good-bye. Am I nuts, or does it all make sense to you guys?"

"Hell, no. I say we go for it," Boomer said.

"Good idea, Pete," Cady said.

"Super, super idea. I wish I had thought of it," Andy said.

"Let's do it. I've heard so much about how

much fun you guys had when you were kids, I want to be part of it," Jill said.

"Wait, there's more," Pete said. "I went to Wal-Mart when it opened this morning and bought five bikes, the same kind we had when we were kids. I dropped them in the bushes before I came out here. We need the bikes to tear around in."

"Let's go," Boomer said.

Thirty minutes later, Cady said, "How many tickets are we going to get for this?"

"A fistful." Boomer grinned.

"It'll be worth it." Pete shed his jacket and rolled up the sleeves of his white shirt. He yanked at his tie and tossed it into the bushes. Boomer and Andy did the same thing.

Cady and Jill kicked off their heels, then their suit jackets.

Pete pulled the bikes out of the bushes. "We can drop them off at the YMCA later, and they'll find some kids to give them to," he said. "Pink for you, Cady, lavender for Jill. Boomer gets the blue one, Andy gets the green, and I get the red one. Last one to the bottom goes first on the zip line. Remember the bump at the bottom, then you do the wheelie. On the count of three we go."

They were children again as they lined up their bikes, their heads low over the handlebars, waiting for Pete's count of three.

"One, two, three!"

They whooped and hollered, whistled and

screamed as they careened down the embankment, popping their wheelies, then skidding to a stop in a half circle. They were breathless as they waited for Pete to announce the winner and the loser.

"I came in first!" Pete chortled. "Jill came in last. She takes the zip first. Last one up the tree is a monkey's uncle. Out to the branch, then jump to the ground, on your bike, and up to the Judas tree. On the count of three!"

Breathless, they lined up again, perspiration dripping down their faces. Cady hiked her skirt up as far as it would go, so did Jill.

"Three!"

They were like a bunch of agile monkeys as they shinnied up the tree, then leaped to the ground and pedaled to the top of the embankment and over to the Judas tree. Boomer took it hands down while Pete came in last.

Exhausted, their chests heaving, wide grins on their faces, they fell to the ground beneath the Judas tree, which, at last in full bloom, no longer seemed spooky, but only protective of this place of their childhood.

"I think we're too old for this," Andy gasped.

"Speak for yourself," Boomer groaned.

"How are we going to feel in the morning?" Jill panted.

"Like a bunch of fools." Pete laughed. The others joined him.

"Okay, it's time to pick the game," Cady said. "I pick Robin Hood."

"G.I. Joe," Andy said.

"Cops and robbers," Boomer said.

In the end they settled for Robin Hood.

Hours and hours later, when they were finally exhausted, Pete announced it was time to do the zip line. They lined up and skimmed down the line as if they'd been doing it every day of their lives.

When Boomer, who was the last to go down, hit the bottom, they all held out their hands, smacking one another and laughing until they fell to the ground.

"Time to eat. Remember how peanut butter and crackers and Kool-Aid were our treats back then?" Pete said. They all nodded. "Well, take a look at this!"

"Annie packed everything in those thermal containers, so it's all still warm. We even have a tablecloth. Dig in, gang."

When the fried chicken, the spare ribs, and the salads were nothing but crumbs, Pete broke open two bottles of wine. He poured generously. "We need to make two toasts today. If it's okay with all of you, I'd like to do it." The others nodded.

"The first one is to Amy and for all the good times." They clinked their glasses together and drank, their eyes misty.

"The second one is to . . ." The others waited, holding their breath, wondering what the toast would be.

"The second one is to" — he looked at each

one of them deliberately — "to good friends."

"Hear, hear," they said in unison as they polished off the remaining wine in their glasses.

When both bottles were empty, their trash picked up, it was dusk. Andy called a halt. "I want to thank all of you. I couldn't have gotten through today without each and every one of you." He choked up when he looked upward. "Bye, Amy."

They all waved, and shouted, "Bye, Amy," as they wheeled their bikes to the top of the embankment.

Cady wiped her eyes on the sleeve of her blouse. She reached for Boomer's hand and squeezed it. "This was wonderful, but I think the best is yet to come. What's your feeling?"

"Exactly the same as yours. What do you say to some lick-off chocolate paint?"

"Best offer I've had all day, Chief."

"Stick with me, kid, I've got a million more."

"I hope that's a promise."

"It is, Cady, it is."

About the Author

Fern Michaels is the *New York Times* best-selling author of *No Place Like Home*, *Kentucky Sunrise*, *Kentucky Heat*, *Kentucky Rich*, *Plain Jane*, and many other novels. She began writing in 1972, and to date more than sixty-four million copies of her books are in print. Michaels lives in South Carolina. Visit her on the Web at www.fernmichaels.com.